ID0989393

Only Great Changes

ALSO BY MEREDITH SUE WILLIS

A Space Apart

Higher Ground

Personal Fiction Writing:
A Handbook for Teachers, Students, and Writers

Only Great Changes

A NOVEL BY

Meredith Sue Willis

CHARLES SCRIBNER'S SONS
NEW YORK

F
WIL

W679 o

Copyright © 1985 Meredith Sue Willis

Library of Congress Cataloging in Publication Data

Willis, Meredith Sue.
   Only great changes.

   I. Title.
PS3573.I4565505   1985   813'.54   84–14170
ISBN 0–684–18240–8

*This book published simultaneously in the
United States of America and in Canada—
Copyright under the Berne Convention.*

*All rights reserved. No part of this book
may be reproduced in any form without the
permission of Charles Scribner's Sons.*

1 3 5 7 9 11 13 15 17 19   F/C   20 18 16 14 12 10 8 6 4 2

Printed in the United States of America.

This book is dedicated to
The Writing Group:
Carol, Eva, Ingrid,
Kate, Suzanne, Sybil, and Vera

Our two soules therefore, which are one,
Though I must goe, endure not yet
A breach, but an expansion,
Like gold to ayery thinnesse beate.

If they be two, they are two so
As stiffe twin compasses are two,
Thy soule the fixt foot, makes no show
To move, but doth, if the'other doe.

—JOHN DONNE

From "A Valediction Forbidding Mourning"

Only Great Changes

One

Before I joined VISTA, I spent a year in college. That year is in my memory black and white like the photographs in the college catalogues I used to pore over. I scrutinized every square inch of those books: pictures of lawns decorated with pretty co-eds, requirements for majors I had no interest in, activities of sororities and fraternities I didn't intend to join. I was searching for a sign, for the exact quality of life at each college—for the life I would have if I went there. At the time it never occurred to me that I would ever drop out, and Franklin State was the least interesting of all the colleges to me. It had the thinnest catalogue and the fewest photographs, but that didn't matter because I knew the campus very well. I had been there for conferences, for high school journalism day, and for my parents' reunion, because they both received teaching degrees from there. I hated to give up any one of the colleges. I felt this terrifying richness of potentiality before me—all the possible lives I might have, each one governed by the college I chose. So I kept Franklin State in my active pile, continued to examine its photgraphs for the thing I wanted, the sudden throbbing or flash that would take my breath away and make me say, That's it, that's the one. This is what my life will be. But I was quite certain the thing was not at Franklin State, until the night the man came to speak to our youth group at church.

It was a Sunday evening in March with a black, driving

rain coming down over the mountains, but a good turnout because a lot of us were in the final throes of choosing a college, and this speaker was at least connected to a college. He was an assistant to the chaplain, although it wasn't clear whether or not he was a preacher himself. His name was Dave Rivers, and he was short and had a beard.

Our group met in the basement lounge, a sort of island of donated couches and easy chairs in the middle of an expanse of vinyl tile and painted cinderblock. It was an uneasy place, always like sitting in a spotlight on a stage, and that night I positioned myself in the shadows, on a folding chair behind the couch. I was keeping my distance, wondering if the speaker would notice me, or if he would pass his eyes over me as just another teenage girl with shiny hair and no obvious birth defects. At first, though, he didn't look at any of us. In fact, he broke every rule of public speaking my mother had ever drummed into me. He stood in front of us saying nothing for a long time, shifting his weight from foot to foot, clearing his throat, getting out a handkerchief and cleaning his glasses. There was an embarrassment among us, a shifting in our seats. I was glad I wasn't in the front row. I could raise an eyebrow, stare at the lack of coordination between his plaid flannel shirt and plaid sports jacket. He was wearing boots too, yellow leather lace-ups—clodhoppers! I had never seen a man wear a sports jacket with workboots, and it was those boots combined with the ginger-brown beard that gave me pause, made me think he might be worth listening to.

He finally finished cleaning his glasses and cleared his throat one last time, wiped his nose with the handkerchief he'd been using on the glasses, put it away and the glasses on. And then his eyes came at me. Magnified by the lenses, appearing perfectly round and rimmed with flamelike lashes, they seemed to be the source of the sudden flow of words, low and urgent. A speech about the Inner City, which I assumed for a while was symbolic like the Beautiful City of Zion. I'd heard that sort of thing from preachers all my life. But no, Dave Rivers was talking about New York City, Washington,

D.C., Pittsburgh. Urban centers and ghettoes. Heroin in the bloodstream of America and apathy like a sleeping sickness. "The City," he said, "is a challenge to the Church that it can no longer sit on its ass." We all glanced at the youth leader when he said that, but the leader managed to retain his bland smile and occasional nod. Maybe he had not let himself hear it. "And let me tell you," said Dave Rivers, "let me tell you that you can waste yourselves on the uncommitted life just as surely as you can on a needleful of dope."

This, I thought, is the first Man. This is the first Man I've ever known.

He wanted us to give some serious consideration to how we were going to spend our lives. "I know you are serious people," he said. "I don't know your favorite musical groups or what you do in your free time, but that's not my business. My business is simply to tell you this: your future will be bitter— your personal future and the future of mankind—if your generation doesn't meet the challenge of the City." He told us about a program at Franklin State that would include semesters working in the Inner City, learning how the new man is being created out of the old. "You have a right to an education," he said. "An education that transforms you so that you can transform society."

And then he sat down. Or rather, he made a sort of sideways dip at the nearest folding chair and straddled it backwards, rested his chin on his crossed arms, and gazed intently at us. Our youth leader tried to start some applause, but Dave Rivers brushed it away as if the sound were hairs blowing over his face. "No," he said, "I'm not making a speech. I want to talk. I want dialogue."

I did not raise my hand with a question. I felt a spaciousness inside me that his words had created; all the concerns of my present life seemed shriveled to little tags of black ash, and even those puffed away. I wanted the others to shut up too, I wanted *him* to fill the space in me that he'd made. Everything was gone, even my desire to be noticed. I kept thinking vaguely that this was it, what I'd been looking for between the lines in the catalogues, in the corners of the pictures. This wind come to sweep me out of my family and my town, out onto this great rising flood tide of action and ideas. I thought it was college, I said to myself, and all along it was the City.

When the questions ended, there were refreshments, and everyone crowded around Dave Rivers with their waxed cups of ginger ale and paper napkins full of cookies. Whenever someone left the circle around him, I pressed nearer, taking my time, taking in the shape of his sentences, the timbre of his words.

"You were awful quiet tonight, Blair Ellen," said our leader. "I usually depend on you to keep the discussion going." And I stared at him as if I didn't understand, not having time for polite chatter. Not having time for anyone but Dave Rivers.

The custodian had begun turning off the lights around the periphery, making our little circle like a flying carpet, humming through the darkness. I had moved very close to Dave Rivers now, close enough to see the powdered sugar on his beard. I wanted to take the napkin from his fist, carry it to the trash basket for him. After a while he stuffed it into a pocket of his jacket. I was amazed by the lack of attention to details. I wanted to be like him. I wanted never again to spend twenty minutes in front of a mirror recombing my hair, checking to see if my bangs were straight, examining my smile to make sure it didn't expose the crooked incisor on the right side.

Just as I gained his side, one of the last people still around him, I had a moment of being overwhelmed by unworthiness, by having nothing to say, and I started to back away.

The hand that had stuffed the napkin in the pocket clamped me above the elbow. I gasped. People in our part of the world didn't touch strangers; the heat of his hand burned through my blouse and I started to shake. He let me go at once, but of course I stayed near because I had been singled out. He turned to me. "I frightened you."

The first two things I ever said to Dave Rivers were, in

order, a lie, and an intimate truth. "Oh no, I wasn't frightened," I said. And then, "You know, it's funny, usually I'm the biggest talker in this group, but tonight—what you were saying—it seemed too important for me to make bright remarks just to impress you."

The group leader was coming with Dave's raincoat.

"Listen," he said to me. "Are you a senior this year? Why don't you come down to Franklin State in the fall? We need people like you."

It had always been an ideal in my family and my church to receive a Call. They used to preach those texts all the time: Jesus tells the Galileans to leave their nets and become fishers of men. Jesus says let the dead bury the dead. My mother jumps up from the dinner table because her neighbor's car is broken and the baby may have swallowed a straight pin. When I was little I used to squeeze my eyes closed and listen for a Call for me, but of course they don't come when you expect them. With a Call, you have to be ready to go anyplace, anytime. Even to the small college your parents attended, in the same range of hills as your own home town.

In mid-September there was a cook-out at the home of the Franklin State College chaplain, Reverend Paul McTeague. He called himself and his wife Martha the foster parents of three generations of Christian students. Martha seemed too young for such an honor, but you could believe it of Reverend McTeague, who was a sort of modern-dress Santa Claus with his wavy white hair and high color in the cheeks, his trademark red ties. He wandered among the students in his yard with his hands clasped loosely behind his back, pausing to smile and nod to each of us before meandering on. Martha was the one who had organized the party, of course. She had the two grills going and a fire in the brick barbecue. She was brown-haired and slight, and had a high sheering giggle that reminded me of my mother and aunt. She looked enough like them to have been another sister too. Franklin State was turning out to be altogether too homey for me: Reverend McTeague and Martha and their borders of mums and the smell of seared fat and charcoal smoke. As if there were a conspiracy to make my first weeks of college calm, clean, and excruciatingly safe.

It was already dusk, and dampness was falling out of the lindens that crowded the lot between the McTeagues' and the Christian Association building. I was sitting on a bench pressed deep into the hedges. It was getting chilly, and the twigs were scratching the back of my neck, but I didn't move because I was hiding, partly from my roommate, who followed me everywhere, but mostly from Roy Critchfield. I had left them together in hopes they would fall in love and leave me alone. Karen was a decent person; she didn't wash her hair or her glasses very often, but she was a mathematical genius. Roy, though, had no redeeming value that I had been able to discover so far. I had let him talk to me at the first Christian Association social, but I never imagined that he would call me every night, wait for me after classes. I never thought I would be hiding to avoid him. I had this terror that if I let him hang around me too much people would begin to link us in their minds. Roy was awkward to look at, but, far worse, he was evangelical and always asking me about the state of my soul. At least, he had quizzed me that first night. Since then he seemed to have become entirely wrapped up in his own crisis. He grew up in the mountains where his boyhood congregation split over the donation of a piano to the church, and Roy's family went with the non-instrumental group. They would sing, but not play. The human body is an acceptable medium for God's praise, Roy told me, but anything else is Of This World. Out of meanness, and because it didn't matter anyhow because Roy couldn't tell when anyone was making fun of him, I said, "Do you dance in your church? I mean, that's the human body, isn't it?"

And Roy was so hopeless that he explained the difference to me. "Oh no, Blair Ellen," he said. "Dancing is worse than a piano."

His other sin was calling me by my whole name. I was

metamorphosing myself into Blair, dropping the Ellen as unnecessarily elaborate and countrified. I had instructed my mother to address my letters to Blair Morgan, and I introduced myself to everyone as Blair. Only Roy Critchfield had discovered the rest of it, called me by the old name. Only Roy seemed to cut straight through to something pitiful and absurd at the heart of me, a part of me that wore its pants too high and cut its hair with clippers over the ears. Just like Roy.

They found me, of course, Roy and Karen. It wasn't as if there was any real hiding place in that backyard full of people. They came across the lawn directly at me, two tall people who carried their heads forward loosely like camels. They sat down one on either side of me; and Roy continued what he had been saying twenty minutes earlier when I went in the house to the bathroom and started hiding from them. It seemed that boys were smuggling beer into Roy's dorm at night, and he had a dilemma about reporting the infraction of the rules.

I said, "Roy, why did you ever come to a state school in the first place? Why didn't you just go to Bob Jones University and not have to worry about boys drinking beer in the dorm."

"Girls are doing it too," said Karen. "I know some girl who has a bottle of whiskey under her bed."

That sounded like someone I'd like to get to know. There was a lack of challenge in my life at college so far. Even my professors were not atheists, or even Jewish.

Roy said, "If I report them, I'll lose any chance of having an influence."

"That's for sure," I said. "Mind your own business, Roy. Nobody likes a tattletale."

"There's something else," said Roy.

Oh no, I thought, and started looking out across the rest of the party. Martha McTeague in a red apron flipping hamburger patties. Reverend McTeague smiling down on Judy Fletcher and her large boyfriend. I wished I was with Judy;

she had a withered leg, was one of the last victims of polio before the vaccines, and she had worked on a lot of Dave Rivers' projects.

"I've broken a vow," said Roy. For a moment I hoped it would be something sexual. "I've stopped carrying my Bible. I vowed on my sixteenth birthday that I'd never be without it. I guess I've been slipping for a long time—for a while I carried a small one I could put out of sight in my pocket, and then I went down to a little testament, but lately, since I've been here, I've stopped carrying it altogether."

"Roy," I said, "you've got Holy Bible written all over you."

Karen said, "Why don't you start carrying it again? Put a reminder on the mirror. I put notes on my mirror or in my books when I have something I don't want to forget."

"It's too late." Roy was as heavy as dinosaur bones. I was looking for a place to go, something I had to do. "Once you've started down a path," said Roy, "once you've started, you can't turn back. Besides, it's not that I forget. Every morning I look at the Bible sitting on my desk, and I walk away from it. I just walk away."

There *was* something I had to do. Something I'd been putting off too long. Reverend McTeague extended his paper plate to Martha. I'm going to ask them, I thought. I am going to go ask. I jumped up, leaving Roy in the middle of his crisis.

"Hello, honey," said Martha, handing me a plate.

"Hello, Blair," said Reverend McTeague.

"Onions?" said Martha. "Relish?"

"Listen, I've been meaning to ask you." He was standing behind her, wide and splendid like Old Glory on television before a baseball game. And Martha was the pitcher with sharp ridges of sinews in her forearms. "I've been meaning to ask if Dave Rivers still works here."

"No," said Martha.

"Of course he does," said Reverend McTeague.

"Then where is he?" said Martha.

"He's due back any day now."

"Any day! Any month you mean. School has been in session three weeks, Paul, and he hasn't shown up."

Reverend McTeague winked at me. "Soon. He'll be here soon. Do you know Dave?"

"He spoke at my church last year and described some projects I was interested in."

"Oh yes, when Dave gets back, things always start rolling. He has the coffee house and all the discussion groups. The students always come out for his discussion groups. He does the volunteers. He had a new volunteer project in the works at Sunrise Farm—"

Roy was approaching. I leaned closer to Reverend McTeague. "Sunrise Farm?"

"Home for the elderly," said Martha, serving Roy. "When they put me out there I'll make them be honest and call it Sun*set* Farm."

"Some lovely, needy people out there," said Reverend McTeague. "We were thinking of letter writing, holiday parties, that sort of thing."

"I'll tell you one thing," said Martha. "If I wanted to do some volunteer work, I surely wouldn't wait for Dave Rivers to set it up for me. I'd get it started myself. He was supposed to be here before school started. He's not three weeks late, he's five weeks late. So far."

"He's doing important work, Martha."

Her mouth snapped shut, and she dropped Roy's burger onto his bun from too high and he lurched to keep his plate flat. Martha apologized, insisted on squirting Roy's ketchup for him. I agreed with Reverend McTeague about Dave, of course. I was sure that whatever Dave was doing was the important thing. Martha was like a mother, wanting everything done by the book. I wondered, though, if perhaps Dave would find what he was doing so important that he wouldn't come back. I couldn't quite imagine him writing letters for old people with arthritis. That was the sort of thing my mother did. That was no New Man, no Inner City. That was just Doing Good.

"Maybe Blair would like to go out to Sunrise and see about putting the project together," said Reverend McTeague.

My heart speeded up a little. I saw myself having meetings, making phone calls. Being very busy with this thing when Dave came back. I said, "I do have a little experience with hospitals and nursing homes. I mean, it was just high school stuff, but we used to organize parties. That kind of thing."

He gave me a big smile, and Martha gave me a dollop of potato salad. I felt better already. Recognition of something. They thought I could handle this. Action had always cleared things up for me. My hamburger was juicy, not like the ones in the cafeteria.

Roy said, "Reverend McTeague, there's something I'd like to discuss with you." Reverend McTeague looked alarmed, as if he had hoped to get through the evening without any personal problems. "I've broken a vow," said Roy.

I let my eyes wander to where Judy Fletcher's boyfriend was leading a hearty laugh around the barbecue pit. That group looked the way college students were supposed to: madras bermuda shorts, knee socks, cable knit sweaters. Once I had my volunteer project going I figured that I could begin mixing with those people more. They would know me as Blair Morgan, the freshman who ran the Sunrise Farm project.

Martha's eyes were scanning too, checking on who needed a refill, probably. Her face described a half circle, then stopped, retraced part of its arc, stopped again. Her lips flattened in a wry smile. I looked where she looked, toward the narrow walk between the house and the clapboards of the Christian Association building. Someone was standing there in the shadows. A man in hiking shorts and boots, watching us. I could not quite make out his face, but he had a beard, and light reflected on glasses. I knew it was Dave Rivers. I knew from Martha's recognition and from the way he stood apart observing. I knew by the way my breath tightened in my chest.

Reverend McTeague said to Roy, "Now, son, surely you don't interpret me to say the Bible isn't true?"

"Do you believe that it's true and every word is true? Do you believe that? Do you believe you can open the Book and find the answer to any question you ask? Do you believe in 'Ask and ye shall receive'?"

Ask and ye shall receive: a shudder went through my shoulderblades. Ask and ye *shall* receive. I had finally gotten up courage to ask for Dave Rivers, quite boldly, with a certain amount of faith, and Brother, here he was. It was as if God, or something, had spoken to me—not in a church voice, in a big raw bellow: You want Dave Rivers? It said. Did I hear someone ask for Dave Rivers? Well here he is, he's all yours. You Asked For It. Martha McTeague saw him too, and she grimaced. Reverend McTeague only saw old shiny-faced witnessing Roy. Karen actually yawned; she would be wanting to go back to the dorm soon so she could get up early and study.

I drew back, concealing myself between Roy and Karen, to see and not be seen, like Dave Rivers who at last moved into the light, slowly, as if he were making an experiment to see just how long it would take for someone to recognize him. As Jesus had walked with the disciples on the road to Emmaus, and they had not realized until hours later who was with them.

But the group around the fire noticed: Judy Fletcher called his name, and her boyfriend sprang out and clapped him on the back. The others gathered round.

"There," said Reverend McTeague, leaving Roy in mid-sentence. "There, Martha, do you see?"

"I see," she said.

The party reorganized itself; we had a center now, we weren't divided into charmed circles and outcasts. Everyone was charmed, gathered near Dave. Faces had more character, the conversation was livelier.

"Who's he?" said Karen.

"Dave Rivers. The assistant chaplain. Everybody's been waiting for him."

Roy said, "Is he a preacher? I may have something to ask him."

The McTeagues sat Dave Rivers at the picnic table between them. Reverend McTeague poured him iced tea while Martha prepared his hamburger without asking what he wanted on it: relish, ketchup, and a thick slice of onion she cut especially for him. Dave didn't seem to notice any of this. He ate what they gave him, accepted refills as well, but he didn't seem to care how the food was provided. He accepted it as his due, as something that did not engage the higher levels of his consciousness. I would have spent half my energy thanking them and complimenting the food, but he plunged into the talking with his mouth full.

"How was Chicago?" asked someone, and I was stunned because it appeared to be no secret. They had all known where he was. There had been postcards, letters, phone calls. I should have asked him sooner, I thought, unable to shake the feeling that I had created this, that Dave Rivers had come for me.

"Chicago is the place where it's happening," said Dave. "There is this man Alinsky out there who is making it happen."

I had never heard of Alinsky. I looked around at their faces, trying to figure out if this was a household name I should recognize. I tried to listen closely; this was the real beginning of what I had come to learn, but I kept drifting, noticing the baked bean sauce on the stiff hairs under his lower lip, wondering what it would be like to have people gather around you like this, attending silently to your needs, to your every word.

Karen said she wanted to go home, she had classes tomorrow. "Go ahead," I whispered. "Get Roy to go with you. I want to hear him."

I redoubled my concentration. I am hungry, I thought, for what he is saying. I am not like Roy who only listens for a chance to get in his own business.

Dave Rivers was saying, "Saul Alinsky is this little roundish gray man, someone you'd expect to see behind a counter selling vegetables. He looks so ordinary, so incredibly ordinary. I guess in a way he is—he's a genius of the ordinary, the obvious. He's a genius at getting people to do things for themselves."

I tried to get it by memorizing: a genius of the obvious. A genius at organizing people.

"But his secret," said Dave, "the thing that trips up all us preachers and do-gooders, is not to try and convince anyone of anything. He doesn't have a secret agenda. His secret is that he doesn't preach at all, but listens. He starts from the felt needs of the people and gets them to choose their own issues."

Roy broke in. "What if those people want to do the wrong thing? What if they are leading you down the broad path to ruin?"

I was humiliated when several people, including Judy Fletcher, glanced at me when Roy spoke. I said, "Well, Roy, he's not talking about personal morality, he's talking about political action."

The flaming eyes of Dave Rivers diverted to me. "I think," he said gently, "I think in this age that political action may be the same thing as personal morality."

I memorized that too. That one that was said directly to me: Political action is personal morality.

Judy Fletcher said, "Still, Dave, he's got a point. What if the people want to break a window or burn a bus? What do you do then?"

Dave said, "We're not talking about the same things. You're talking about good copy, what gets in the papers and on television. I'm talking about essential justice. The most basic rights in the world: decent housing, medical care. Schools. That's all. The simplest, most just, most righteous needs in the world. But listen, hey, the people aren't waiting for us. They can use our help, but they can do it without us too." He suddenly grinned, pink lips and round teeth. "I'm making it sound so serious," he said. "It's wonderful, it's exciting. It's Christ-in-History, if you will. I just want us to be part of it."

Christ-in-History, I thought.

But Roy was not charmed. Roy had lowered his head; his eyes, which were deep-set and suspicious at best, had begun to glitter. He said, "Well, what I want to know is nothing new either. It's the oldest thing in the world. I want to know what you do when you find yourself taking the first step down the Broad Path. When you find yourself too weak to be the only one anymore doing right."

Dave had accepted a coffee now from Martha's hand, two sugars and no milk. He said very quietly, as if he'd finished his public speaking for the night, "Then maybe you should rethink what's right. Maybe what's right for you is what's down the broad path. Maybe you should just say, Hey let's give this one a try and see where it leads us, and stride on down."

Roy's head jerked back as if he'd taken a blow on the chin. That'll get him, I thought.

Things were breaking up, people leaving. Karen wanted to go, but Reverend McTeague was telling him my name. "Blair Morgan," he said, "has not been sitting around idly waiting for you, Dave. She's all for going out to Sunrise and getting that program set up."

"Good," said Dave. "Can you go out with me on Saturday morning? Give me a call at the C.A. on Friday and we'll set up a time."

My nodding turned into a sort of reeling dizziness. I let Karen pull me away. But it didn't matter now, because it had happened. It was really beginning. I was working with Dave Rivers.

Roy was reeling too, from the blow from Dave Rivers. "What did he mean, stride on down? What does he mean, take the Broad Path?" I'd never seen Roy's face angry before. Usually it was balled up in self-importance and self-pity. "He doesn't mean what he says. He can't."

I said, "I think he means some things are not as earth-shaking as you think they are, Roy. I think he's saying there have been good men who drank beer."

Karen said, "Well he's not going to convince me that college isn't important. You have to go to college, don't you? That's where you learn, isn't it? Where else do you learn? You don't learn in the slums like he says. I mean, I feel sorry for them, but what's that got to do with getting an education?"

Roy said, "I think he must be a Communist. They always talk about The People."

"He's an assistant chaplain," said Karen. "He can't be a communist, can he?"

I went up the steps to the dorm hoping Dave Rivers *was* a communist. Well, maybe not a real communist, that was stupid of Roy—no one was actually a communist anymore—but something radical. Something shocking as well as right.

Two

There have been times when I made fun of myself as I was when I first met Dave Rivers. I mock the callowness, the uncritical embracing of every opinion and attitude that Dave so much as hinted at. I even condescend to my taste in art then. I used to keep a print of Andrew Wyeth's painting *Christina's World* on my wall. That picture moved me enormously—I would sit on the bed and stare at it as if it held all the answers to all the questions I had ever asked: the crippled girl in the foreground, the wide swath of cut grass beyond her, the stark unpainted farm in the distance. There was loneliness and splendor in the golden atmosphere of that picture, and when I saw the original painting at the Wyeth retrospective in New York in 1976, I said to myself, He has an uncanny way of painting space, but I chuckled at myself for ever adopting it as a private symbol. Would I really have identified with that woman if I had seen the other paintings of her—the stringy hair, the paunch belly? But I think now that I probably would have. I wanted to embrace everything then. I was hungry at a feast and I was stuffing myself with everything I could reach, and it seemed to me that Dave Rivers had the most platters.

Still, I was able to see that other people took him less seriously. Judy Fletcher often disagreed with him. My roommate Karen preferred calculus to his discussion groups. Roy attacked every point he made, but Roy is a bad example. He was as obsessed with Dave as I was, but Roy's method was to struggle and be overcome time after time. We two were always the last ones by Dave's side: Roy gasping on the canvas, me leaning forward greedily to snap up one last idea, impression, fact. The others all got tired much sooner. Dave usually saw this; he was no monomaniac. He was a skilled speaker sensitive to his audience's moods. He would suddenly collapse his mouth into a big pink smile and say, "Hey, let's finish this some other time. I know what you're thinking—Dave Rivers is full of it again! Let's go have coffee."

On Saturday morning I dressed in a pleated skirt and cultured pearls and went to his apartment. He had given me the address over the phone and told me that if I would come at 8:30 he would give me breakfast, and then we'd drive out to Sunrise Farm. He didn't seem to recall the regulation stating that no female student should visit any apartment off campus at any time. I was thrilled to break the rule, of course, even though he would most likely never realize I had done it because it was so unimportant to him. I walked down the steps from the dorm, set like a citadel above the quadrangle, crossed the walk between Old Main and the library, and strolled off campus as if I were making a mere shopping expedition into town.

I passed the McTeagues' and the C.A. and a few fraternity houses, and then paused at the intersection with the side street where Dave lived. I looked down the hill into Franklin, a town in the same style as my home town: a single shopping street dominated by turn-of-the-century brick buildings, a bank with granite pillars, overhead phone and electric wires, and a river running yellow through the middle of morning. The light from behind me enriched the brick and the far hillsides that had just begun to turn orange and gold; I was struck with an unexpected wave of nostalgia, as if I were never to see my home again. Was this, then, the moment when I would at last *give* myself to something?

I could still phone him and say I had decided to forgo the adventure, that I'd decided to go back to my home town or some town like it—to hunker down, and embrace myself, and live without any challenges that exploded in my lungs like air on a subzero morning.

But then I saw his Volkswagen parked halfway down the block and was drawn by its homely individuality. No one else had a car like it: green with one brown fender, and a titillating, blasphemous bumpersticker, *Jesus Saves Green Stamps Too*. The house he lived in was run-down and covered with a zigzag of fire escapes. The halls were dark, the linoleum on the stairs worn through to the wood. His apartment, on the second floor, had two doors, and between the doors a garbage can, a mop, and a slicker on a hook. I knocked but got no response. Was it the wrong day? Was I early? I knocked harder, and then tried the other door, loud as I could, to drown out my nervousness.

A voice groaned, "Wrong door!" and there was some thumping and thudding. I went back to the other door, knocked again, to show I'd done as I'd been told. This time it said, "All right all right, I'm coming."

Dave with no shirt, his pants on and zipped but his belt undone. Without glasses his forehead appeared very high, and his eyes rolled around, far away. So much brown hair on his chest and belly. Not one of your slim teenage bellies, either, but a man's round one with a central wave of hair down his midline and curls between his nipples.

He said, "I'll be with you as soon as I find my glasses. The other door doesn't open. There's a bureau shoved in front of it."

"I knocked here first," I said. Then, "I woke you, didn't I? Maybe I should come back later?"

From the other room he called, "I slept through my alarm clock."

The room where he'd left me was living room and kitchen both: it had an easy chair and a formica dinette piled with books. Books on the refrigerator too, though not on the half-sized stove or in the enormous sink with exposed plumbing.

He came back with a shirt on, the belt buckled and the

18

wild look gone now that he had his glasses on. He had not, however, bothered to comb his hair. He said, "Let's go out. I'll buy you some breakfast."

"Oh, I don't need anything," I said.

He seized a lumberjack shirt off the back of a chair and stared coldly into my face. "I can't stand pussyfooting around. Did you eat breakfast?" I shrank back. "Of course you didn't. I told you I'd provide breakfast, so I will." I was stunned by his truculence. No one in my family had ever spoken to me in that tone of voice. Then he added, more gently, "I didn't get to sleep till 3 A.M. I won't be really functional till I grease the machine." But my feelings were hurt, and I was afraid of setting off his snappishness, so I didn't say anything going down the stairs and getting into the Volkswagen. I didn't do anything wrong, I reminded myself; I only did what he said!

The gearshift had no knob. It was wrapped with electrical tape. He muttered something about getting it fixed. "It turns my hand black and sticky," he said, and then, when the engine was on, looked at me again. "I was too sharp with you."

"Maybe we should do this another time if you're too tired."

"I did speak sharply. I'm fine. You just have to get used to me. I do this all the time, only I don't usually have to do it in front of somebody so early in the morning." He grinned, the same as the other night, a sort of shocking pink with baby-round teeth in the middle of all that beard. "Forgive me?"

I loved the Volkswagen. The apartment had been dry and bookish, but the Volks was sun-warmed with foody odors: old sandwiches, mostly—meats and cheese. There was a pizza box in the back seat, too, also coke cans, crumpled paper bags, and something that looked like wads of jockey shorts. The engine had no muffler.

"Got to get a new muffler," he said. And then, as we started down the hill away from town, "There's a place I go down by the river when I really want my breakfast heavy."

I said, "Do you usually stay up so late?"

"Insomnia. I've had it most of my life."

I waited respectfully to hear more, but we were already at the bottom of the hill, at Water Street, where you could see some shaky-looking old houses with store fronts. He didn't exactly park, but ended his turn onto Water Street in the far lane and stopped fairly near the curb, facing traffic.

I said, "I read the worst thing to do with insomnia is to try and fight it. You should do something, you know, like read a book or whatever until you're ready to sleep."

He said, "Where did you get that—*Reader's Digest?*"

The restaurant was tiny and old, with no customers but us. Dave led me to the farthest rear of the three booths. An old man wearing a paper hat and a cloth wrapped around his middle came as far as the end of the counter. Dave called out that he wanted the works—fried eggs, fried potatoes, toast, and lots of coffee.

"Her too?" said the man.

I said, "Do you have doughnuts?"

"Joe's got everything," said Dave. "Doughnuts and coffee, Joe." I didn't really drink coffee, but a preference for tea was not the sort of thing I wanted to call attention to with Dave. It would seem completely unimportant to him. Besides, drinking coffee was something I wanted to learn to do.

Dave pushed his glasses up on his head and rubbed his eyes. "Tell me more about what *Reader's Digest* has to say about insomnia."

"It wasn't *Reader's Digest.* I think it was *Newsweek.*"

"Oh, *Newsweek.*"

"It was a stupid article. I don't know anything about it—I've always been a good sleeper. I sleep eight hours every night, it doesn't matter if I've got a lot of studying or whatever, at midnight I just go up to sleep."

"Would you like to hear about real insomnia?" I nodded of course, folded my hands in my lap. He said, "Real insomnia is when you lie in bed, and bit by bit, as if someone were turning a thumbscrew, your nerves extend. They stretch, all along your arms, along your neck and spine. Your nerves get longer and longer and more taut. Your eyes stretch too, so that the lids don't fit anymore and you begin to stare. The staring is the main thing. You see in the dark. No matter how dark it is, you can see. Everything is like you, taut and flat, with no volume, and you think it will always be that way. On the wall you maybe see something, a tiny black spot, like a spider, like an infinitesimal chip of sleep. You try to concentrate on it, to make it bigger, so you can crawl inside and sleep. You try so hard that you convince yourself it is growing, that sleep is coming. You stare so hard your eyeballs burn, but you can't quite hold it, the dark spot shrinks, the spider crawls off to one side, goes up the wall, over the ceiling. You watch for it to hold still so you can try to make it grow again."

So many words. His face became huge to me, like a sunset, hairy with flares, and vast spaces all around him. My body felt as if it were rising to meet him, as if I might go flying right into that vast dark space he was creating, and it left me with my hands cold, a clenching in my shoulder muscles, between my legs. I think I was holding my breath when breakfast came, the bubbles of shiny egg, the mounds of reddish potatoes. Stacks of toast, melted butter. My doughnuts brown and oily with wrinkles around the centers like the insides of elbows.

It was almost a relief to have the old man's lined face, his accent I didn't recognize. "Thank you very much," I said.

He jabbed a forefinger at my plate. "Tell me if you like."

I took a big bite. "Oh, very good! Chewy."

"Homemade," said Joe, watching still, so I had another bite. In a different mood I probably would actually have liked the doughnuts, but my stomach was running in surges of excitement or nausea, and I had to keep swallowing to hold down the two clumps of doughnut.

Dave shoveled in potatoes, broke into the yolks of his eggs. "Joe's breakfasts are the best kept secret in town."

"Lunch too," said Joe. "I fry in the pan, none of that french fry basket stuff."

21

He finally left, and I could put down the doughnut. I drank coffee, and was gratified by the bitterness. Dave soaked his toast in yolk, drank half his cup of coffee in one gulp while simultaneously bringing a load of potatoes to his mouth. I was awed by how completely he gave himself over to eating, ignoring manners. It was as if he knew eating as thoroughly as he knew insomnia. Sheaths of egg yolk hardened on some of the coarse beard hairs under his lip. His hands moved over the table, feeling for more food. I could not quite imagine those hands touching me, or the mouth surrounded by beard, but I had a feeling that would come too, like learning to drink coffee.

He said, "Anyhow, the end of my story about the insomnia is that I had a close friend who killed himself. He jumped off the roof of a building in New York City. This guy had many problems, many, many problems. He'd tried suicide before, the first time when he was only fourteen or fifteen, so I'm not saying the insomnia caused it, but he did have the worst insomnia of anyone I ever knew. Something pushed him over; too many nights without rest staring at whatever was in front of him." He belched. "Don't you want the doughnuts?" I shook my head and he started eating them, waving to Joe for more coffee.

I could feel the bitterness burning my stomach now, and my forehead was folded up, waiting to hear the rest, to hear if Dave had ever tried to commit suicide, too. To hear what this meant to me—this dark world of sleeplessness and despair and excess and not caring if there was egg on your beard. But Dave seemed to have finished. He went on to something else, chatted some more with Joe, and when Joe was gone, started talking about Sunrise Farm: who I would meet out there, how to approach them. Talked invitingly, as if he looked forward to having me with him but I was thinking how hopelessly far behind I was. I don't know anything, I thought. I don't know about despair or insomnia or even what country Joe is from. I've never known anyone to do anything like commit suicide. To make up for my lacks, I nodded and nodded and tried to memorize every word Dave said.

I asked everybody I met to take a turn going out to Sunrise Farm, Karen and Roy and the people in the Christian Association, but sorority girls too. And I spoke about the project at local churches and at the high school. I had the use of a desk and phone at the C.A., and my name was on the bulletin board so people could leave messages for me. By second semester I had two shifts of volunteers for Saturdays, and I drove them out in Dave Rivers' Volkswagen. The best part was when he taught me how to use the four gears and coax the car into an uneasy start in cold weather. My project was the only one that got use of his car, and he also suggested me for the Steering Committee, so I finally got my chance to sit around drinking coffee and laughing with Judy Fletcher and her friends. A couple of times people on the Steering Committee saved a place for me beside him, but that made me uneasy. I was the only one who got to use his car, and I knew where he hid the key to his apartment, but none of it seemed to add up to anything. It wasn't that I wanted to *go with* Dave—even the phrase sounded infantile coupled with his name. I imagined rather a relationship like the one in the metaphysical poem, where the couple become the legs of a compass, always connected, no matter how far one of them roams. Where there is always a film of gold between them, beat to airy thinness, invisible, but real.

A real connection. While between Dave and me there seemed to be only business. There were no more private breakfasts or driving lessons or revelations of insomnia. Often when I returned the car keys he wasn't home, and when he was, he would barely look up from his book to take them. The excitement of going illicitly but for a good cause to his apartment didn't die out, but it often left me with a sensation of discomfort, even humiliation, as if I were pretending a claim to him I didn't deserve. Judy Fletcher might reserve seats, and the girl across the hall might tease me about my predilection for preachers, but I was beginning to think something was wrong. My first year of college was dry. No one was kissing me.

I watched other people and compared. Teale, for example, the girl across the hall, was my social reference. She was pretty much a sure thing to pledge Kappa, generally considered the top sorority at Franklin State. I didn't like the way Teale sneered at my roommate Karen, but I was flattered by the attention she paid me. I secretly hoped she would introduce me to some new people—boyfriends were what I had in mind. I had a fantasy of a passionate fraternity man I would have to fend off because our values didn't harmonize. Teale hinted to me that there were sororities eyeing me favorably. I professed, and I believe I meant, that I had no interest in pledging, but at the same time I very much enjoyed sitting around Teale's room and talking about it.

One cold Saturday black clouds blew in even earlier than usual, and I had just dropped the Volkswagen at Dave's. He was having one of his cryptic moods, reading Bonhoeffer's *Ethics*, murmuring that there was something important he had to announce to us at the coffeehouse that evening, so would I please be there.

Why don't you take me to the movies instead, I thought rebelliously, stomped out, and went and sat in Teale's room while she got ready for Saturday night.

I lay on my stomach on her bed, overlooking the nook at the foot of the bed where she sat on a pillow and propped her sleek legs on the bureau. She was wearing her Saturday night special Lauren Bacall gold robe with shoulder pads, and resting a cafeteria saucer on her belly for an ashtray.

"Obviously it isn't that I despise sisterhood!" I shouted over the hum of her hairdrier and her roommate's. "It's the idea of cutting people out. That's what the sororities are really for, to cut people. All the people in sororities and fraternities want to be in the right clump. They're like little trout fry at the fish hatchery, all lined up facing where the water comes in!"

She was staring at me, but not paying attention to the business about the fish. "The C.A. is the same thing," she said. "You all run around doing things together."

"It's not the same, because anyone can join the C.A."

She squinted and leaned closer to my face. "Why don't you ever wear make-up?"

"I do. I put on lipstick every morning."

"I'm going to make you up," she said. "I want to do a little experiment."

"No white lipstick," I said.

She made a face and unfastened herself from the hairdrier. Her roommate had been reading a tattered copy of the *Iliad* for a semester already. She tossed it across the room now, and it missed the desk, losing its cover falling to the floor. She shrugged and propped her head on her hand to watch the making-up.

I said, "Make me look like a Kappa, Teale." That was one of our ongoing arguments—whether or not Kappa had a type. Teale maintained that each Kappa was unique, but since she agreed with me that all the other sororities did have types, you would think she would eventually have seen the implication. I had a feeling that I could have convinced her if there hadn't been something hypocritical in my own arguments. The truth was that I would have liked to be chosen, and then to reject them.

She made me sit in her chair and brushed my hair straight back with long, strong strokes. I felt the air moving across my forehead with a little charge of pleasure. Teale had slim arms and wrists, but her strokes were so powerful that it seemed to take all the muscles of my neck to brace against the pull.

"More," I said. "Don't stop." But she was getting on to the main business now, slipping a pink headband over my hair to get the bangs off my face. Then she went to work with her fingertips, spreading Covergirl liquid over my cheeks. I smelled the chalky make-up, and the sweet and sour of her hair conditioner and her acrid, smoky breath. Felt the pressure of her hand on my cheekbone as she pencilled my brows.

"Look," she said to her roommate, "Blair's got beautiful brows. You better never pluck your eyebrows, Blair."

Eyelash curler now, and eyeliner and mascara. This was the serious part. She breathed only when she pulled back for a look. As she worked, she made grunts so soft that they were not so much sounds as tiny touches. Her skin was the same color as her hair and eyes; she had been to Florida over semester break. I wanted that tan and honey to spill over me and make me into Teale.

"Don't look yet," she said. "I've got to rat your hair a little." She finally examined me from a distance, then turned my face firmly out to the roommate. "Look," she said. "What do you see?"

Solemnly the roommate nodded. "My God. Tri Delt. Tri Delt all the way."

I jumped for the mirror. Tri Delts dated athletes and student body presidents. I suppose if I'd *had* to join a sorority it would have been a more well-rounded one like Kappa, but there was no question that Tri Delts went out with Phi Delts, and the Tri Delts were always cheerleaders and homecoming queens and anything else that required blondness and wide smiles. I didn't have the blondness, but everything else I saw in the mirror was right. The light make-up had flattened my face to a disc, a setting for the eyes blackly outlined, heavily lashed. Had the hair been pale, it would have been the mask of Beauty. Everyone's ideal Girl. I wondered if Dave would recognize me in it. I decided to go this way to the meeting at the coffeehouse.

Teale stood in the doorway and screamed, "Hey you all! Come and see!" And portable hairdriers, paperback textbooks, robes, jeans, and slips came running. "Is that a Tri Delt or is that a Tri Delt?"

All of them trying to decide if I looked more like the homecoming queen or the head cheerleader. I put a hand on my hip, made a fashion model runway turn, made them laugh. Teale demanded the loan of a Villager outfit in my size. Pink, she said. It had to be pink. "No," I said, "I'll spill pea soup on it—" But they brought it anyhow, pleated skirt, sweater, even the dyed-to-match knee socks. I let them do it. I might even, had it been earlier in the day, have let them bleach my hair. I was in the mood for a change.

We were going to go to dinner, and I was wondering if I should wait for Karen, when Karen herself came thundering down the hall, books clutched to her bosom, hair flopping against her cheeks like cocker spaniel ears. She didn't see the Tri Delt enamel over my face, and I had a moment of disappointment, but then realized that something big had happened to Karen. She dumped the books on her bed and let them lie instead of setting them neatly on their proper shelves. I followed her into our room, and Teale waited in the doorway. Karen's breathing made her shoulders rise and fall, and her eyes widened with each gasp.

"I have to get dressed," she said, unfastening her skirt and letting it fall around her ankles. "I have a date." Another deep, shuddering breath. "I was working in the library," she said, "and I saw this boy from my calculus class sitting over there with some other boys. He sits in front of me because of the alphabet, but he never said a word to me before. I never even thought he noticed me. He's a sophomore or junior. He's in Sigma Chi." I glanced at Teale, who lifted an eyebrow. "After a while he got up and left, and so did the other boys, but then one of them came back and sat down beside me and said there was a phone call for me on the pay phone. I couldn't believe it, but it was him, and he asked me to meet him for a date, tonight, at Sigma Chi house. And oh Blair I didn't even ask him what kind of a date. If I should dress up or what."

Teale's mouth was closed firmly, her jaw fixed. Giving me no help, no help to Karen.

I said, "Well, call him back and ask."

Karen shook her head. "I can't believe how stupid I was. I don't even know his name. I'll have to wear my blue dress, I suppose. It's probably what I'd wear anyhow, one way or the other." It was her church dress she meant, jewel neck, princess cut. I hoped the date wasn't for a real fraternity party.

Teale said, "Did you know the guy who came over and said there was a phone call?"

She emerged through the neck of the dress. "He's some freshman. I've seen him around." She put on her good black pumps, started moving her things to the matching pocketbook. "I've never been so scared in my life."

"You'll have fun. Won't she, Teale?" Teale shrugged. I said, "But Karen, I don't think you should wear white gloves. They don't go with Sigma Chi somehow."

She laid them back on her chest of drawers and stood stiffly in front of us. "I can't think of one thing to say to him. Can you give me a subject to talk about?"

"How about your professor? Professors are always good to talk about."

Karen nodded, big-eyed, color in her cheeks, the rest of her face almost transparent. She had a nudging look without her glasses, as if she had to feel her way with her face. Something about her was embarrassing: she revealed how much she wanted something. Wanted love. I was half-angry at her: I had thought she was dedicated, wanted nothing in her life but math.

She started down the hall at a near run, calling back, "I don't think I could take this every week."

Teale and I didn't try to keep up with her. We went toward the dining hall in silence until Karen was out of sight. Then I said, "I hope she at least gets dinner."

"She won't," said Teale.

"Do you think it's a party? Why didn't you say so? She shouldn't have dressed like that for a party at Sigma Chi."

"There's no party at Sigma Chi tonight. And no dinner either." Teale was moving along beside me with strides longer than mine, more graceful than mine. Her hair not brushed out and teased yet, but gathered back like a bouquet of dark honey loops. She sounded a little tired of me, as if I were being willfully obtuse. "Don't you get it? It's a joke, a pledge prank."

Teale's body seemed to stretch out of shape, to bend and loom over me out of the shadows. "I don't believe it. You're prejudiced. You just don't believe a Sigma Chi would ask out Karen."

"Think about it, Blair. She doesn't even know the guy's voice. She doesn't know who called her."

"She must have heard him talk in class."

"The pledges have to do things like that to get points for initiation. Sometimes they talk professors into letting them into courses without prerequisites, or they put up signs on the water tower—"

"I don't believe they would do that to Karen. It would be cruel."

"They dig up rose bushes from the dean's garden—"

"But she's not a rose bush!"

"Who's not a rose bush?" said Teale's roommate. We had just caught up to the line outside the dining hall.

Teale told the whole thing, coolly, her mouth twisted a little to one side with cultivated, gun-moll cynicism. The others clicked their tongues or made disgusted faces or laughed. But no one did anything. *I* didn't do anything.

Why am I still here? I thought. Why haven't I gone to do something? Why hadn't I seen what Teale saw, and why hadn't Teale done anything to stop it? Would I have fallen for the trick, if I had been the one they picked to try it on? All of us, that mass of girls, twisted and distorted, body merged into body, arm grafted to shoulder, knees attached backwards, hair poured and puddled, committing a sin of doing nothing to save Karen.

The dinner line started to move, and Teale gave me a glance. "Well, I might be wrong," she said, and went back to talking to the others, about something else. I ate half a grilled cheese sandwich, and then walked out without saying good-bye to any of them, feeling betrayal on all sides. Betrayed by Teale, after all my admiring of her, that she could be so hard. By Karen's stupidity too: that she should be my roommate. That I should be as stupid as Karen and as much in the wrong as Teale, and at the same time not even brave enough to tell Teale what I thought.

I caught a glimpse of my face in the mirror at the top of the stairs, and was going to go and wash, but the phone rang. Someone picked it up, spoke briefly, stuck her head out of the booth. "Oh Blair, there you are. Phone call, but don't get excited; it's only a girl."

On the telephone a whisper with a strangely varying pitch. "Blair?" it said. "Blair?"

"Karen? Where are you? What happened?"

"I waited almost an hour, Blair, and he didn't come."

"Where are you? Why are you whispering?"

"Because I'm in their phone booth."

"Oh Karen, don't stay there. Get out, come right home."

"I can't leave. I was in the living room waiting for him, and I waited and waited and he still didn't come, and then all these other boys started walking by. They walked by one at a time and looked at me. There was nobody here but me, and all these boys just coming by one by one and after a while the same ones started coming past again—"

"Tell me about it later. Just leave. He's not coming, Karen, it's a joke; it was a nasty trick."

"But I can't leave because they started taking their clothes off. One came by in his underwear and then another one came by in *his* underwear, and then I realized they were all going to come out in their underwear and I ran in here—"

"Just get out and come home."

I could hear her shuddering breaths again. "Will you come and get me?"

I closed my eyes; I didn't want to go, I felt humiliated for our whole sex, but it was a chance to redeem myself. They were walking past Karen in their jockey shorts, with their hairy thighs. I checked myself once more in the mirror— the clothes, the Tri Delt mask. The hair was still full and smooth. I wanted to give them as little as possible to laugh at.

I went, without a coat, into the raw evening, not running

so I wouldn't sweat on my make-up or make the hair come unteased. I saw two boys I knew and walked the other way to avoid them. Would they expose themselves to get pledge points? The Sigma Chis wouldn't hurt her physically, of course, I thought. They wouldn't really *do* anything to her physically.

But I began to doubt even that as I came up to their house, half hidden behind two dark fir trees, with a steep pitched roof and leaded glass windows. Something Black Forest and fascist about it. Two aluminum beer kegs in the yard. I didn't knock, but dragged the heavy door open, expecting Doberman dogs, and imagining how I would grab for their throats if they attacked me.

There was a staircase to my left, and ahead, a baronial living room with exposed beams and a fireplace. To my right, a little cloak room and a cubicle, with the door open and a light inside: the phone booth. As if someone had hastily left. I could smell dinner somewhere, rich and meaty, and I heard the bass of a distant stereo.

From behind me someone said, "Oh Lord, not another one."

I leaped for the staircase, an instinctive choice of the high ground. With the balustrade between me and him, I turned to look. He was big enough to be a football player, but a little too soft, holding a pewter beer stein.

"I can't believe it," he said. "Listen, it was a pledge prank, he's not coming, whoever it was who got you over here. Go home now."

The terror that had pricked me onto the stairs turned to fury. "Oh don't think I fell for your despicable trick," I said. I really shouted, to get the tearful tremble out of my voice. I wanted the voice to go at him like a horizontal pile driver. "My friend called me from here in the middle of a nervous breakdown, and I came to help her. What did you do with my friend?"

"The tall skinny one?" he said. "I sent her home. We don't have permission for women in the house tonight." A couple more with beer mugs came in. They formed a half-circle of bulky sweaters and square chins. "Listen," he said. "Do you get it? It was a pledge prank, a dirty trick, and I want to apologize on behalf of Sigma Chi house. Okay?"

My fingers itched for their throats, warbling around their Adam's apples as they sipped beer. "It is *not* okay. It was unbelievably cruel. My friend is from a small town and she doesn't know any better than to believe what people say. She had no inkling that anyone in a million years would do a putrid thing like this, and as far as I'm concerned, you and your disgusting little brothers seduced her."

"Hey," said one of them. "She's talking dirty."

Their faces all tipped to one side, listening to me with great interest, and I realized that my speech was probably as entertaining to them as Karen and the underwear parade. I said, "If I had a gun, I would shoot your faces off."

I scared myself so much when I said it that I plunged for the door, feeling I had gone too far. I seized the wrought iron handle and couldn't budge it. The one who had made the apology said, "That door sticks, let me." A nubby woolen arm edged me aside, and opened it, one-handed. "Wait," he said. "Your friend left something," and I had to wait for him to retrieve a royal blue scarf with pale yellow butterflies transmogrifying into yellow roses or some such optimistic idiocy. I snatched it away, lunged out the door.

I look crazy to them, I thought, pounding my feet into the pavement. Making speeches to Sigma Chis. As if they spoke English. Their leader or whatever he was—had he been genuinely sorry? Halfway across the quadrangle I had a fantasy that he would call me up, attracted to a more humane way of life, and ask to get to know me. To be instructed. I would, I realized sadly, be afraid to see him. Be afraid of another trick.

When I got back to the room, Karen's side had been made neat; the books she dropped on the bed were back on the shelf, the clothes hung up, the desk clear of everything but her pencil cup. She came in a few minutes after me with her hair wet, wrapped in a towel. She didn't have her glasses on, and she smiled.

I was immediately furious at her. "What happened? Why didn't you wait for me?"

"I'm sorry," she said. "This guy came and told me I couldn't sit in the phone booth because they weren't open to women tonight."

"Don't say you're sorry! I don't mean you should have stayed there. Don't apologize. Did you apologize to him too?"

"He was very polite. I'm sorry you had to go all the way over there. I thought I'd meet you on the way back."

She took down the wet towel, let it sit a moment in her lap, then folded it square by square into a small, soggy packet and got her bobby pins out of the drawer. I watched her closely; I thought her hands were shaking but I couldn't be sure. I gave her the scarf, and she folded it too into a tiny cube.

She began to make enormous pin curls. "As soon as I knew you were coming, Blair, I felt better. You were a real friend. I was a fool to go over there."

"That's for sure. But I should have figured it out too."

I was sure her hands were shaking, and the curls she was making were much too large. She was already almost done, three enormous curls on each side of her head. She said, "You never would have gone. You would have had more sense. The whole thing is my fault for being so dumb."

"But *you* didn't do it, *they* did."

She pursed her lips and shook her head, just a little shake. "Dumb, dumb, dumb," she murmured, and unfolded the scarf, wrapped it around her head. She put away her pins, got down her calculus book and opened it in the dead center of her desk, pressing the spine with all her weight.

I said, "Well, you can't leave that towel knotted up that way. It'll never dry. I'll hang it up for you."

"You really are a friend, Blair," she said, already sitting down, lowering her face to the book.

I found myself with no words to reach Karen. I wasn't finished talking about it, but it was over for her. And nothing I could say would make an impact on her, anymore than it had on the Sigma Chis.

* * *

The official name of the C.A.'s coffeehouse was the Coal Bin, because of its function in the days before gas heat. We had performances there on Friday and Saturday nights: poetry readers and guitar pickers, sometimes even a barber shop quartet or a jug band. On nights when there was no entertainment, you could drink coffee or hot cider at the ten little tables with their checkered cloths and candle-spilled Mateus bottles. Dave Rivers had organized the place, but Martha McTeague ran it. She baked the tea breads and bar cookies and presided from a broom closet with a coffee machine and a hot plate and change in a cigar box. On particularly busy evenings, some of us would wait tables, but other times it was all Martha, Martha by herself.

I looked for Dave in the main room first, even though I knew it was rare for him to show up before time to introduce the talent. No one was there except Roy Critchfield, all alone in the corner, leaning his head back against the main refuse pipe, apparently napping. Roy had become increasingly silent as the year wore on; he barely passed three of his first semester courses, and he was carrying incompletes in the other two. I never heard him mention this term's classes, and in fact you could find him at any hour of the day sitting in the student union, with no books. On Friday and Saturday he sat here. He had let his hair grow too, in equal lengths down the whole back of his head and now over his neck and ears and forehead, like a creeping moss, or the pelt of a lethargically transforming werewolf. Even though his eyes were closed, I backed away quickly; he wasn't so much a pest anymore as a mood-depressant.

So I went to Martha, thinking that I might tell her what had happened to Karen. I knew that other students used her as a confidante, although something in me wasn't comfortable with her; maybe she was too much like a sister of my mother's. This evening she was wearing her beatnik outfit, black trousers and turtleneck, hoop earrings. Something in me disapproved. This isn't Greenwich Village, I thought, it's the Christian Association Coal Bin at Franklin State College, for heavensakes.

"Martha, have you seen Dave?"

She was just cutting into one of her endless pans of brownies. How can you pretend to be a mother and a beatnik both, I thought. Glancing at me sideways, she said she hadn't seen him.

I knew I wasn't being polite, but I was full of impatience. I was ashamed of my abruptness, but, I told myself, I didn't care. I didn't have time for politeness. This Thing had happened to Karen, but to me as well. I wanted it to change my life, and I didn't want to get slowed down by pausing to be polite to Martha. I had a cry in my mind that was already beginning to lose its raw power, to get smooth from too many rehearsals: *Dave!* I would shout. *I found out something about human nature tonight! I found out how brutal and cruel human beings can be!* I wanted to say that, and then have him explain it to me and make me wise, tough-minded, and safe.

Martha said, "Everyone wants Dave tonight."

"He called a special meeting."

"Ah, another Dave project. Well, I expect he's hiding out in his office. Whenever he gets tired of one project, like he's tired of the Coal Bin, he just disappears."

I felt, as a result of my experience that night, that I could be more daring. "Sometimes I don't think you like him."

"Oh, I like Dave. I like Dave very much, but I know him better than you do."

For half an instant I wondered about her: she didn't really look old; I always made her older in my mind to match Reverend McTeague, but she wasn't old, except her mouth, tonight, which was tight with some pain. Understanding Martha, though, was not what I wanted that night.

Dave's office was in the other half of the basement, but you had to go all the way upstairs and down another staircase to get there. He could have had any of the offices on the main floor with windows and views of trees, but he had chosen this extreme rear of the basement, behind the boiler room, piled with ancient boxes of water-damaged hymnals that no one ever used or went to the trouble of throwing away. I never understood if he chose his office out of self-effacement or out of a desire for privacy. If he had wanted to be alone, though, you'd think he would have closed the door, but it was always open, the only light at that end of the hall.

I hurried through the darkness, knocked on the green metal flank of a file cabinet, and stepped inside. He was in his reclining chair, shoved between the desk and the towering boxes of old hymnals. He raised two fingers of his left hand to bid me hold my peace until he had finished reading something. He held me as still as the obsolete mimeograph machine on his desk, taking up space, covered with dust. His fingers gradually relaxed, drifted down to his lips, to his beard.

Something was making my body burn: was it humiliation? Or envy, that he considered his reading so important that he would make a visitor—me—stand and wait? *I* dropped everything when someone came to see me. *I* carefully chose poems and pictures for the walls of my room so people would think I was an interesting person. Dave didn't have to type out William Blake's "The Poison Apple" for his bulletin board. Dave was already interesting and important, and I couldn't imagine disturbing him until he was ready for me.

He closed the book and laid it on the corner of the desk. "Hello, Blair," he said. "Sorry to make you wait, but I've been working on that chapter of Bonhoeffer all day."

"I interrupted it twice."

"No, you haven't interrupted me." He might *lie*, I thought, with a sudden understanding. He might lie about something important, but he would never be a hypocrite about something small—he would never say you didn't interrupt him if you did. The only thing was, I wished I had interrupted him. Wished vehemently that I was important enough to disturb him, to have an impact on him.

I was aware of myself as an object in Dave's office, myself in the pink borrowed sweater, the pleats flat over my stomach, the knee socks. Of my body as a smooth thing under the clothes. I was aware of the comfortable little valley he made in the chair, his fullish waist, the wrinkles and folds of his khaki workpants. He was relaxed, like my father, just finished reading.

"You look so pretty tonight," he said.

I started to cry: I felt pretty, all of a sudden, thanks to him, but also he reminded me of how I used to sit on my father's lap and be so contented. I felt, too, this wanting in my abdomen that seemed horribly inappropriate after what had happened at Sigma Chi.

"What is it?" he said, not alarmed by the tears, as if he even liked them. He patted the arm of the chair, then patted my back after I sat down.

It all began to come blubbering out of me.

"Oh Lord," said Dave. "She didn't figure it out?"

"Finally," I said. "But it was too late."

"Is she all right?"

"She's back in the dorm studying math. I don't know if that's all right, but it's what she always does. I went over there and made an absolute fool of myself. I made a speech to this bunch of idiots about what monsters they are, and they thought it was more fun than a barrel of monkeys. And I just got madder and madder. I was hopping around like Rumpelstiltskin. I thought I was going to pound myself into the ground." Dave gave me his handkerchief, and I wiped off tears, but didn't know if I should blow my nose. "I felt like such a fool. I mean, they were so *entertained*."

His pat on my shoulders had turned to a gentle rub. "What's the matter with your face? You look bruised."

For a moment I was frightened, thinking I had been damaged, mysteriously marked by the Sigs, but then I realized it was mascara. "Make-up," I said, and started to cry again. He took the handkerchief away from me and wiped the black off.

"You'd better blow your nose," he said. Then, "Let me look and see if we got everything off." He pushed his glasses back on his head and smoothed my hair over my ears with both his hands, touched the corners of my eyes with his thumbs.

I thought: We're about to kiss. We *are* going to kiss. To

make absolutely certain, I said, "You treat me like a little girl."

"Do you think so? I don't think I do. You're always one of the people I think of when I have something new I want to talk about. When I want to bounce ideas off someone."

The patting and smoothing stopped, but his hands were still on me. He knew it was coming too. I said, "I don't think you take me seriously. I suppose it's because you're older—"

"I'm not so old."

"I can never figure out if you're in my generation or the McTeagues'."

"Yours," he said, very quickly. "Definitely yours."

He let one hand fall to my shoulder, and with his other folded his glasses and laid them on top of Bonhoeffer. I could feel it so close then, a heady energy that slid me onto his lap, and he was suddenly under me and all around me and I was against his chest, against his mouth, which was soft in the center surrounded by the rasping beard. His hands clasping my back and unclasping repeatedly, as if he were kneading, making me spread and rise. Such a keening of my body that I started to cry again, and he kissed my tears and said, "Hey, hey," and kissed my cheeks and my eyelids and my eyebrows and the corners of my eyes. "Hey," he said, "why now?"

"Because I wanted this so long, and I thought you never even saw me."

He made a sound, a cry, not very loud, and pressed his face in my neck. It seemed that every time he moved even slightly, there was a new part of me made alive—as if I had not had an earlobe before. "Not see you!" he whispered. "My Lord!" More parts of me, his hands on my chest, kneading that too. A clear thought ran through me: I will do it with him, one day soon. He is the one I will do it with. And I was so glad to have that settled in my mind. He didn't undo my blouse or reach under my skirt, but he touched every part of me through the clothes as we kissed, and I kept thinking how glad I was, how glad.

"Why did we wait so long?"

38

He laughed. "Why indeed? No, the truth is, I worry. I don't want to take you—where you aren't ready to go—"

"You mean sex?"

Laughed again. I liked it that I caused these short exclamation points of laughter. "Actually, I was thinking of Norfolk, Virginia."

I had to sit back at that, comfortably arranged in his lap, our four hands continuing to embrace, resting in my lap.

"It's what I wanted to talk to people about tonight. I'm forming a group to go down there and work in the inner city. We'd go as Vistas, Volunteers in Service to America. It's part of the Office of Economic Opportunity. They assign the Vista volunteers to communities that have existing agencies of same kind, and the Vistas go down and work through the agencies—but on their own projects. So we'd have a base, but be free to look around for ourselves and see what needs doing, and do it."

My first thought was: I won't have to live at home and lifeguard at the swimming pool this summer. I'll be with Dave, instead, not waiting for real life, but in the middle of it. I tried to keep the elation out of my voice. "Why there?"

"It could be anywhere. They have an organization, a Community Action Project called TAPS, or Tidewater Against Poverty Services. Everything's an acronym. It could be Chicago or Pittsburgh or New York. It's the same core of powerless people at the center of the cities."

He made chopping gestures in the air, and I lay against him again, listening to his voice reverberate inside his chest. I thought it was the happiest moment of my life. To have my body warmly nested in another body, to have his voice going on and on, explaining just to me. This was not, I realized with a dawning pleasure, his presentation voice that was careful not to overwhelm, that took into account the reactions of the listeners. He was talking as if to himself, making no concessions. Assuming I understood.

It wouldn't be easy to swing it, he said. He still had to convince the people in Washington that he had the credentials to train us, that we would be prepared for the kind of work we would find there. We would have a study group, read certain books, *The Secular City*, of course, *The Autobiography of Malcolm X*. Documents of the transformation of society.

Every so often I asked a question, more to keep the moment going than anything else: Where would we live? Who pays for it? Who else would be going? We'd get living allowances from Washington, he told me. We'd live in apartments in the neighborhood where we were working. With the people. That part was essential. Using whatever facilities the agency had, but strictly on our own. He wanted up to ten of us from the Christian Association to go. He wanted to have a real impact.

I didn't ask how long we'd be there. I had a feeling, from the seriousness in his voice, that we wouldn't be hurrying back for college in the fall. Oh yes, I thought. Of course. You couldn't just talk, you had to do. You had to commit.

In the distance I heard brisk footsteps, a knock, someone calling Dave, and then there was Martha standing in the cleared space in the middle of the room where I had stood a little while ago. I did not spring up from Dave's lap; I felt a sense of persecution. My whole life I had been stealing kisses and getting interrupted. I intended to stay put.

Martha made a noise, a nervous giggle, but it had the shocking, antisocial quality of passing gas. Then she covered her eyes with both hands, and said, "I didn't see a thing."

Dave dumped me out of his lap. I got my feet under me before I hit the ground. Martha ran.

"Dammit!" said Dave.

"Hey," I said, realizing that he was heading down the hall after her. I followed him to the door. He came back, but only to get his glasses. "Sorry, Blair, but I can't let her go off like this."

"Oh sure," I said, "but we weren't doing anything—is there some kind of rule?" I had never thought about that, that Dave might not be allowed to fraternize with me.

He paused, looking after her, her black shoulders pumping, her elbows stuck out at chicken-wing angles. The footsteps didn't fade at all but were amplified, precise and explosive by the narrow hall. He said, "There's no rule. But she and Paul— I do have to talk to her. Explain."

"About us?"

For a moment his eyes were troubled, and then he gave me a full-face smile and opened his arms. I ran for a hug, for a wet-mouthed kiss, and then he ran after her.

Three

I finished my last exam with an enthusiastic rhetorical flourish. In my essay question I had outlined almost the same ideas I covered in the term paper, and that sociology paper used much the same material as the one for religion class. Both papers came out of our Wednesday night discussion groups, and I even footnoted a personal interview with Dave Rivers about the community organizing methods of Saul Alinsky and The Woodlawn Organization. This is a time for Change, I wrote. We should be learning directly about the lives of the Dispossessed, not collecting statistics and reading scholarly journals. It is an age for action, for the overturning of hierarchies and making America a dream that can at last belong to all Americans.

When I turned in the paper, the sociology professor said, "I've been looking forward to reading what my class firebrand had to say," and I couldn't have been more pleased. A firebrand sounded like exactly what I wanted to be, and it didn't bother me at all that the ideas for the papers weren't original; I had embraced them so fervently that they were mine. I got A's on both those papers, too, and I think I deserved them, if only because the professors must have found it easier to read about a theory passionately held, even though it roundly damned book readers and researchers and was neither sociology nor religion, but polemic for social change.

It was a good time for me when I was writing those papers. I had, for the moment, everything in my life integrated and unified: my studies, my beliefs, my plans for the future, even my love life. When I came out of that last exam, I was ready for the next part, so inspired by my own writing that when I burst into daylight I was shocked that Dave wasn't waiting for me. The sky was high and blue with enormous cumulus clouds running before the spring wind. The buildings were tacked up around me like staggered ranks of rocket ships, and my body was humming too, ready for take-off. But some connection had failed to be made, some circuit was incomplete. I had no arms to run into.

I went up to my room, showered and packed some books, waiting for the taut spring inside me to relax. I put on jeans and my new short-sleeved lavender sweatshirt. Even though my parents didn't expect me yet, Dave and I planned to drive over there, maybe tonight. I told him I wanted him to explain the Vista project to my parents. I knew he would do that very well, but it was actually something else I wanted, a message to them that would be quite clear without his saying a word. I would emerge from the unkempt Volkswagen wearing this lavender sweatshirt, and perhaps a beaded headband, followed by Dave, full beard, shorts, and leather sandals, maybe. Everything perfectly obvious to my parents without a word being said. As obvious as when, during my junior year in high school, my friend Bunny Hoover overturned her whole life—told off school, her mother, me—by getting into a car on Christmas Eve with a sailor she didn't know all that well and driving out of our lives. I used to lie awake sometimes, sexually aroused, imagining *her* moment: the cold smell of vinyl and gasoline, the sailor's aftershave lotion. A pull on a flaming bottle of whiskey, then the motor, the chattering teeth, the plunge into darkness and the unknown.

I went down the hall to the phone and tried Dave, but got no answer. I hadn't seen him in a week. He had said, Sure he was ready to drive me over the mountain after my last exam, but in the back of my mind I kept thinking that maybe we'd stay here a while. Mother and Daddy didn't expect me for a couple of days. Maybe we would just stay here and be really together, Dave and I, in a way we had not yet been. Maybe this was my moment for *that* adventure. He didn't know about my plan, of course. He only knew he had agreed to drive me home today. Unless he'd forgotten. He wouldn't forget a promise, would he?

Restless, looking for a way to make him appear, I walked over to his apartment. The Volkswagen wasn't there, but I went up anyway. When there was no answer to my knock, I reached into the mateless rubber boot for the key, and let myself in. Everything was familiar, books and a plate with toast crumbs on the table, a coffee pot with grounds in the sink. Everything stale, squeezed of life. Without him here, all I could see was slovenliness: the unmade bed, a crunch of grit underfoot, a drape wedged between the couch and wall to keep it clear of the window.

I shoved a casement open, letting in a sharp flow of breeze, but the apartment was still dead without him. I had nothing of his. If he never came back, there would be no evidence of his having been in my life. All the girls I knew had something concrete: Teale was pinned; her roommate had had a pregnancy scare; even Karen had a boyfriend who called with stunning regularity every Wednesday night to make dates for Friday and Saturday. It was silly to think of Dave pinning anyone or making dates, but I did want something concrete. The kisses and embraces in his office, in the Volkswagen, weren't enough. He never kissed me in this apartment, and he never brought me to this bed.

I continued my circuit of his rooms, pausing at the book shelf in the bedroom where there was a pile of books, the ones Dave called the good Germans: Bonhoeffer, Barth, the Neibuhr brothers, Bultmann. I can't read this stuff, I thought. Maybe someday, after the action. When I'm old. Under the books was a stack of old magazines, with one particularly fat magazine at the bottom that caught my attention. I pulled it out a few inches and saw a naked elbow, a navel. It was a *Playboy*. I was shocked. For Dave to have a

Playboy magazine! And all the way at the bottom of a pile too, under his theology books. It was an old issue, so maybe he wasn't hiding it. Maybe it had even been left here by the last tenant. But even if he hadn't bought it himself, I was sure he had read it; he read everything, he said. Not just the cereal boxes, but the address of the manufacturer on the toothpaste tube and the packing numbers of factory checkers.

I had never read one myself. I had seen the covers, of course, even picked one out of a rack once to flip through, but then put it back quickly, for fear someone would see me and think—what? Would they think I liked women? Or that I was trespassing? I opened it on the shelf now, and read a paragraph here and there of the articles, but the main thing was the breasts. There was no question about it, if you were going to look at *Playboy*, you were going to look at breasts. So I looked at the breasts. I had my papers written, my tests taken, my plans made. I wanted all of life's experiences.

I stared for a long time at one particular picture, not the most naked of the girls, not the huge centerfold who assaulted me with her pink and peachiness, but a smaller picture, barely a quarter page. A girl wearing tight jeans, unzipped just enough to show her belly button. She had her gut sucked in like a cavern, and her tee shirt was rolled up to show the bottom of her breasts. It didn't expose the nipple—in fact, it revealed far less flesh than many evening dresses—but there was something about showing off that part that you never see in clothes—the underside—that seemed to me about the most titillating thing I'd ever seen.

I went to Dave's mirror, overhung with dirty shirts and even a tie. I pushed those things aside, unhooked my bra, and rolled up the lavender sweatshirt. There were red pressure marks where the bra had been, but by maneuvering into the shadows, I could hide those, and make my stomach look fairly cavernous too, if I held my breath. If I leaned forward at just the right angle, I made almost exactly the same line as the girl in the magazine: breast bulge, ribcage sharp, barest swell of belly. I had done this before, looked at my body in a mirror, but I had never compared myself directly with a sex model.

It pleased me to think that I had at least part of the equipment. As long as I held my breath and stayed in the shadows, I could approximate the Girl, the one who sells cars and liquor and suntan oil. Not that I hadn't suspected it: I could remember when I was a lifeguard at the pool I would soak up sun for hours, and then, at a certain point, the heat would seem to reverse directions, to be coming out of me. Sometimes during my break the older boys would gather around to talk to me. I didn't do anything, but I could feel how they were drawn by this lazy heat I exuded.

I put my clothes back on and replaced the magazine. I wondered if I drew Dave to me. I thought I must, but it wasn't so clear. He was not here today, for example. I lay on his bed for a while, trying to make him arrive. What I would like would be for him to fade in through the wall, and sink down on top of me. For it simply to happen because I drew him to me. But, if necessary, I would say it straight out: Dave, I don't want to be a virgin anymore. I closed my eyes, and tried to send my heat into his bed. When I heard the door downstairs, and feet on the stairs, I knew they would stop at this door.

"Dave?" I called, running into the other room, but my voice was met by another voice saying, "Dave?"

It was Roy Critchfield. I'd drawn the wrong fly.

He looked at me sideways as he came in, and made a wide path around me to the window where he stationed himself facing out. I said, "Dave's not here. I was looking for him too."

He had had clippers run up the back of his neck, but he had kept long, fluffy sideburns. His eyebrows lowered over his deepset eyes, and he looked like a daguerreotype cowboy, at once uncomfortable and threatening. Maybe yearning for a hat.

I sat down at the table. "Did you have any exams this afternoon? I finished this morning—my last one."

He said, voice muffled, "I'm not taking exams. I would flunk anyway. I didn't even find out when they were."

I had known he was having trouble, but I didn't realize it had gone so far. "What will you do?"

He shrugged, then turned on me suddenly. "What are you doing here?"

"I told you. The same as you, looking for Dave."

"You know what I mean. You shouldn't be here. It isn't right."

"No, I don't know what you mean," I said, although I was beginning to. I thought that in some inchoate way Roy had smelled out my purposes. I pitched my voice deeper than usual, and said, "Well, Roy, to tell you the truth, I've had the key to his apartment for several months now."

Hollows appeared in his cheeks, something like bruises under his eyes. I was amazed by my effect on him.

He said, "I never thought you were . . . that kind of girl."

I wasn't really being fraudulent, I thought. I really would be that kind of girl soon. I was only claiming the status a little ahead of time.

"I've done nothing to be ashamed of, Roy. I would be ashamed if I had hurt someone, or if I hadn't done something that needed doing—" I was seeing rich imaginary examples around me. "If I hadn't written letters for an elderly woman who couldn't see, or if I'd turned my back on a friend. But love is a good thing, Roy. The human body is a good thing!"

I gave him a chance to quote the Bible, but when he held his silence, I went on. "I don't believe that even Jesus meant for people to save themselves that way—he meant for us to connect." I was feeling warm toward Roy. He was a good person, in his own way. *I* was a good person, earthy and loving, just the way I'd always wanted to be. I reached over and touched the back of one of his hanging, big-knuckled hands. "Don't you see, Roy?"

He grabbed at the molding around the window and pressed his forehead into it, making a terrible face, showing his teeth. "What about *me?*" he said. "What's wrong with me? Why can't there be something good in me?" He hit the wall with the flat of his hand, and rebounded from it, dancing in pain, to the middle of the room, shaking the hurt hand. "I should break something!" he yelled. "It doesn't matter anyhow, does it? I should break a window!" He made two leaps, one to his right, one to his left, like a large child pretending to be a galloping elephant, and then, with tears beginning to well up, he shouted, "I should break *you!*"

After he ran away, I stared out the open door after him, and slowly, slowly, it came to me that Roy's fury had not been moral outrage, but jealousy. Well my goodness, I said to myself. What do you know? I tried to arrange my thoughts in sensitive sympathy, but I couldn't help being pleased to know I'd been admired all these months. That I'd had an existence in Roy's mind that I didn't even know about.

There was no Volkswagen in front of McTeagues' house, but I did hear voices in the back, so I went around the path Dave had taken out to the cookout that night in September, infinitely far in the past now, a time when I wasn't sure that Dave would ever have a part in my life.

I peered through Martha's sunporch, crowded with trays of seedlings. I could hear organ music now, and realized that the voices I had heard were electronic. I had a familiar sensation, half-nostalgic and half-anxious, of knocking on neighbors' back doors for my mother: Mrs. Moore! Mrs. Wright! It's me, Blair Ellen Morgan. My mother sent me to get the Sunday School books . . . the tomatoes . . . the donation for the United Fund . . .

Martha was wearing a little checked head scarf that matched her shirt. "Blair," she said. "Come in. What can I get you? Ice tea? Coke? Diet-rite, if you can stand the awful stuff? Just let me get this meat loaf under control."

"I'm fine, I don't need anything, thanks."

She insisted that I sit down on a stool painted high-gloss blue. Her kitchen was all blue and bright yellow. The rest of the house was formal, modern Colonial with cherrywood, but her kitchen had flower designs stenciled all over the cabinets, and geraniums in the windows. She turned off the television with an elbow because bits of chopped meat clung to her hands.

"Was that a soap opera, Martha?"

"You caught me." She made a silly face, but I thought she didn't mind being caught. She seemed to have a freedom I didn't. She could get caught doing something a little silly, she could say things that weren't earth-shattering. I wondered if everyone got that freedom as they became older. "Those stories," she said, hands competently kneading bread crumbs and egg into the ground meats, the rich red chuck, the paler veal and pork. "They've been a lifelong vice of mine. Even before television I always listened on the radio. Actually, I think I liked the radio ones better. I don't mind skipping them when I have something to do—I go weeks without watching them—but then, one day, I'll be back in the kitchen working on something, and on they go. I miss 'Helen Trent' from the radio, though. She was the one who proves life begins at thirty-eight, or something like that."

She asked me to bring over the onion and green peppers. They were on a board, already finely chopped, and I held it over her bowl while she swept the pieces into the meat and eggs and bread crumbs. Again I had a sensation of being younger, in the past, in the kitchen with my mother.

I said, "When I was sick once in high school I started watching them. I was lonely because I was home by myself, and they were like having company."

"Watch out. They're addictive. The plot, of course, but there's something else too. There's something about them that's like a woman's life. They go on and on, with ups and downs of course, but there's this continuation of the same stuff: love affairs and people stabbing each other in the back and lovers who can't quite get together, and then it starts over again with the love affairs and people stabbing each other in the back. The same characters come back. And a woman always has dinner to plan, and the dishes to wash up afterwards, even if she has a dishwasher, even if it's a picnic. Do you see what I mean? I'm not sure I do."

"My life's not like that."

"Oh, it isn't such a bad life." As she washed her hands, she turned her eyes on me, and I noticed for the first time that she had stunningly beautiful eyes. They set me off balance, though, because I couldn't locate their beauty; they weren't enormous-and-blue beautiful or flashing-dark-with-long-lashes beautiful. I wasn't even sure of their color.

She looked away immediately, as if she didn't focus her eyes on people very long for fear of frightening them. "Still," she said, "I hope your life won't be like that if you don't want it to be."

It was the serving that I hated, I realized, as she began to bustle around getting tea ready for me. The endless doing for others. She baked brownies and took care of the Coal Bin and listened to people's problems, and everyone walked all over her. Dave walked all over her. "We'll let Martha take care of that," he would say if something was called for involving cooking or organizing a clean-up detail. "Who wants to help Martha with that?"

"I intend to make an impact," I said. "I know that sounds *young*, but I mean it. I don't want to do busy-work. I want to do the same kinds of things that Dave Rivers does." I cringed; I hadn't meant to say his name yet.

She didn't laugh or purse her lips. "I'm sure you will. You strike me as a doer." She had a little plate of mint leaves preserved in sugar and a pitcher of sugar syrup. "Here is real busy-work," she said. "I am a past master of make-work and busy-work: boiled syrup to dissolve easily in the tea. Sugared mint leaves! I know you don't approve of this kind of nonsense." She made a face over herself. "I don't do it as much as I used to. Dave did that for me, you know. He gave me some real work to do—or, at least, a better outlet for my busy-work." We carried tea, mint leaves, sugar syrup, and sliced lemons to the little breakfast table, glass on wicker, wicker chairs with blue and yellow pillows.

She said, "I know it's been a long time, but I never apologized to you for that night in Dave's office. I acted very badly."

I hadn't expected her ever to mention it. "Oh—it's okay. It was, you know, months ago."

"I always meant to apologize. I was so embarrassed. Sometimes I make a fool of myself and I don't even have a good reason." She smiled. She seemed so calm, as if the whole thing that evening had been a piece of silliness on her part. "You and Dave," she said. "You're working on something serious? None of my business, of course. But you came over here looking for him, didn't you?"

"Oh, sort of. He's supposed to be taking me home to explain to my parents about the project this summer. To, you know, reassure them."

"He'll do that very well."

"But I haven't seen him for a week. I really hadn't missed him till today because I've been so wrapped up in exams." I hoped she picked that up: that I didn't spend all my time thinking about Dave Rivers.

"He went to Washington."

"I'm sure that's what happened. I just wish I knew for sure—when he was coming back."

"When he gets here," she said. "That's how you'll know when he's coming back. You know Dave by now, don't you? He goes and forgets to tell anybody if he decides to stay longer or go somewhere else."

I was surprised by what came out of my mouth. "You've known him a long time. Has he had a lot of girlfriends?"

She blinked several times, as if she were clearing something out of her eyes. "I suppose. I'm not an expert on how many girlfriends he's had." She hesitated. "Does it matter to you? I had the impression you wanted a modern relationship with none of that baggage of jealousy."

I hadn't thought of it that way, but it struck me as just what I did want. "That's true. But there's all this stuff I don't know about him. Things I don't ask him, for some reason. Like, I don't know anything about his family."

She gave a little laugh. "You don't want to bother him with questions about his family. I'll tell you what I know. It isn't much. His father died years ago, and he has a mother, over in Buckhannon, a very sweet little woman, older. He was a late child. She thought she was past the age, and getting a tumor. So he was almost a miracle. He's a wonderful man, too, Blair. A million talents and an immense fund of goodness. He's so kind, really, he is. He lives to help people, but he also—hurts them. In passing. Not because he ever intends to, but he falls into things and makes promises he can't quite keep. When he realizes he's hurt you, he'll beat his chest and chastise himself to the point where you ask him to forgive *you*."

For a moment I saw danger around me, obscurely. Then Martha said, "But that's all I'm going to tell you about Dave Rivers. Just keep your eyes open, and don't get hurt if you can help it. Do you want some more tea?"

I didn't. We got up, we cleared the table. She saw me out. On the sunporch she gave me a kiss, dry lips on my cheeks, her hands pressing my shoulders. "Have a great summer, though. Tell me all about it when you get back. At least down there you two won't have me barging in on you."

I decided to try his apartment one last time, and found him returned, at his ease, feet up on the table, finger-combing his beard and reading *Barchester Towers*. Something clicked in my head; we were supposed to be reading documents of social change, and here he was with a nineteenth-century novel.

He closed the book over his thumb and gave me a big smile. "Blair Morgan!" he said, as if he had completely forgotten my existence and was genuinely glad to be reminded of it. "How about a cup of coffee?"

"No thanks. I just had iced tea with Martha."

He got up and ran water in a saucepan, and put it on the burner. "How are the McTeagues?" He stared at the pan of water, seemed to be struggling to remember what came next, and finally got out a giant-sized jar of Nescafé. Then he stared at the water again.

I said, "You don't have a cup yet. Or a spoon."

"Oh yes." He took down two plastic mugs, one with lurid pink and yellow stripes, the other crowded with enormous flowers of indefinable species.

"None for me," I said, and Dave nodded and put coffee into both mugs.

"I've been to Washington," he said, "and I've been to Virginia, and I've seen the neighborhood where they've assigned us. It's called South Jenkin. Run-down housing, high unemployment, and welfare rolls. The whole thing. I've met the people at the agency and, most important, I've met some of the community leaders down there—some good people, although I wouldn't say any of them is exactly a King—"

I couldn't stop looking at the coffee mugs. I did *not* want coffee, and why didn't he tell me where he was going before he went? I tried hard to get hold of myself, tried to follow what he was saying, but I kept getting stuck: what did he mean King? Why did he want them to have a King? A picture came into my mind of a religious sect, a crown and a feather cape, the resurgent kingdom of Africa or something. Then I realized he meant Martin Luther King, and wondered if I were some kind of a racist to have had that association. And all the time into the incredibly ugly plastic mugs he was pouring not-quite boiling water that sloshed brown particles up on the sides.

Dave extended the one with flowers to me. "I don't have milk, but there's sugar on the stove." It was in an unsealed five-pound bag sitting in a field of spilled crystals.

I was standing in the middle of the room, and I did not want the mug of coffee, and there wasn't room to put it down on the book-covered desk even if I took it. I said, "I told you I didn't want coffee. You never listen to me."

I think I meant to knock it out of his hand and across the room, but I half-stifled the blow, and ended by clubbing his wrist ineffectually. It was enough to spill most of the coffee on his hand, though, and he dropped the cup, which splashed and bounced brittlely on the floor. I ran for the door, thrown back into childhood badness, fleeing great dark-winged birds of adults, but I stopped myself.

"I'll clean it up," I said. "I'm sorry. Are you all right?"

Carefully, carefully Dave put the full mug on top of *Barchester Towers* and retrieved the other one from the floor. His cheeks looked pale, all his pleasure at seeing me gone. He held the empty mug in both hands.

"Where's a rag?" I said. "A paper towel? I want to clean it up."

"Don't worry about the spill, tell me what's the matter."

Of course he would say don't worry about the spill. Don't sweat the small stuff. "I want a rag," I said doggedly. "I want to clean it up." I wished for a long German name and a mind that abstracted and balanced, with priorities in order. I wanted to be black and oppressed, and to know who the enemy was, and go sit-in at his lunch counter. I wanted to be anyone but me, who got stuck over and over on words and cups, and didn't even give Dave pleasure to see. He would leave me alone to my tantrums while he became a Vista.

"Let it dry itself," he said, "and tell me what's bothering you."

I began to cry, and that was the signal for Dave to sit down, invite me to his lap, shush me while I repeated through sobs that I wanted to clean up the mess, and he repeated that I should forget the mess and tell him what was bothering me.

"You never told me where you were going," I said, "or when you were coming back."

"You had exams," he said. "I thought you were giving all your attention to the exams. I thought you wanted me to stay away."

"I did, but I wanted to know where you were. And you said you'd take me home tonight, and I thought you forgot."

He said, "I'm here. Trust me a little, Blair."

He hugged me, jiggled me the way you give a little child a ride on your knee, kissed the tears on my check. Outside, a cloud passed over the sun, causing a momentary gray-whitening of the light, followed by a flowering of bright yellow again. His kisses and chest were warm; the wind came in cool at my back.

I said, "Martha McTeague warned me about you. She said you hurt people, and don't even mean to."

He said, "Down at the project, Blair, we'll be together all the time, no place else to go because that's the place, the work is there. We'll become part of that neighborhood, sink in up to our necks." He kissed me again with more excitement, a tremor in his thighs. "There'll be a chance for a genuine impact down there, Blair, the real thing." I moved till I was astraddle him, thinking, yes, it was going to be like this all the time down there—kisses not separate from talking, and hands on the face, mouth on the mouth, everything at once.

After a while he grunted and shifted his weight. I said, "Is your leg going to sleep?"

He laughed; a dampness had come over him, on his forehead, on his cheeks. He had his glasses off. "No," he said, "my leg's fine, but I think we'd better take a break."

"I don't want a break."

He pushed me back a little. "Just a short break."

I knew what it was, of course, his excitement. I could feel it, and I thought it was exciting too, but I had no idea if it was something that would last thirty seconds or half an hour. I had an instinct, though, that you should use it at once. I said, "Don't take a break for me, because I'm ready to stop being a virgin."

"You don't mean that."

"Yes, I'm tired of always stopping, and I'm tired of being ignorant. School's over; we're going away. I want to do it now."

"Today? Before we go see your parents?"

I hadn't thought about that, but since he'd said it, I realized that I did want to go back to them not a virgin. I said, "I was thinking I didn't have to go home for a couple more days."

55

He put his glasses back on. "I don't know. It's a big responsibility for me, you know, to be your first."

I kept my face calm, just short of smiling. "You see, I do trust you."

"And I suppose you trust me not to get you pregnant?"

"I figured you kept something around . . ."

He twisted his mouth. "Yes, I always keep at least a gross of prophylactics handy. You seem to have this all figured out."

The clear light, the wind, the relaxation of my body after crying: I was fixed again on the thing I wanted. With growing euphoria I realized that I had never before wanted anything this clearly, this precisely. I wanted to enter my next decade as an adult, with knowledge. Bad enough that I got stuck in anger, in ugly coffee mugs, that I cried every time I turned around. I could even understand why Dave would be uncertain about it. I was asking a big favor.

He said, "It probably won't be a lot of fun for you the first time."

I let my firm purpose shine out of my face. Martha McTeague be damned! Anyone who counseled me to save myself be damned! I wanted to know myself, not save myself.

The bedroom was airy now, white and yellow light coming through the windows. "Can't people see in?" I said. He pulled the drape free of the couch, let it fall over one window and then pulled a bedspread off the floor and hung it over the curtain rod of the other window. The room remained white, but the outlines were softened, and the drape and bedspread moved in the breeze. He pulled back the bedclothes and began doing things at the bureau, taking off things: watch, glasses, belt. Without turning, he said, "Are you changing your mind?"

"Of course not!" Something had changed with the new room, with the broad plane of the bed between us. But not my intention.

"You aren't undressing."

"Yes I am."

He sat on the bed with his pants unzipped while he took off shirt, shoes, and socks.

56

"You won't forget the birth control?"

"I thought you trusted me."

"I'm just reminding you."

He got up to drop his pants now, wriggled out of his undershorts, and stood squinting at me, apparently comfortable in his nakedness. He was a tan color all over, no fishbelly bathing suit stenciled on him. His body hair almost the same color as his skin. No wonder he's so comfortable, I thought. No shocking pink bull's-eye in the middle of *his* breasts, no unexpectedly black hair or white, flaccid belly like mine even when my arms and legs were wiry and brown. He would never suck in his stomach and posture in front of a mirror trying to imitate, for a brief moment anyhow, a magazine sex model.

He lay down on his side and propped his head in one hand. I looked below his navel for the first time. His penis was curled to one side, taking its ease, a dark pink, the only part of him not tan or golden. The rest of him leonine—a smallish compact lion, with something barbarian about his body, one of those European barbarians who outraged Rome. There was something terribly unfair about Dave, the intellectual who could think and talk so well, having a handsome body, too. Perfect in its appointments, except maybe for the flushed penis, but seeing it that way was no doubt a sign of neurosis on my part. It was probably as beautiful as the rest of him.

He opened his arms to me, and I stripped quickly, left my clothes where they fell. I fell into bed, pulled close to him to hide my whiteness and floppy breasts. I pressed my face into his neck at the collarbone, and was relieved and comforted by the odor of his hair and skin, the solidity of him under my palms, against my breast. I adjusted my position, felt the sliding of flesh against smooth chest hair. I was at that moment as close, skin to skin, as I'd been to any human being since birth, and I felt like crying again, but this time I didn't, because Dave was beginning to do things in a purposeful way. I would have asked if we could just lie this way a while, but I wanted the business attended to; another time I would enjoy the skin.

Dave leaned over me, kissed my eyelids. Each touch was

like a little irritation. Perhaps there was too much skin exposed. I was used to sexual excitement with my clothes on, a certain indefiniteness about what was stimulating what. This was unmistakable: his fingers manipulating my right nipple, now his lips on the left one. He was taking too long to examine each part of me, to run a finger around my belly button, stroke my flank, press the fatty part under my pubic hair, press this, rub that, manipulate that. It was like a minor operation, a dentist's check-up. I was afraid he would take too long, that we would run out of time; Roy would show up, or Martha.

"You're lying awfully still, Blair," he said.

I was supposed to be doing something too, of course. I had been waiting for him to do the work, but if I just lay like a bump on a log, he probably wouldn't even be capable. I closed my eyes and moved my hips up and down. We began to build up some heat, and a fine slick of sweat covered both of us, made the moving easier until I was enjoying it, at least the carnival motion of it, like riding in the open bed of a pick-up truck or a raft on a lake when the motorboat wake hits. His breathing became faster, and there was a certain speeding up of his movements, and then he broke away, told me to wait, and I lay there, keeping my eyes closed—another time I would watch him do it—and then he was back with me, on me, and I tried to keep the roiling going, this excitement so unlike the excitement when we were making out with our clothes on, and I became aware that where there had been the small rough points of pressure of his fingertips, there was now this larger, duller pressure.

So this is it! I thought, with the joy of reaching the top of the hill, of knowing you are going to make it. He's doing it now, I thought. He's sticking it in me, or rather, he's trying to stick it in me. His sweat was all over me now, and he grunted, my lion turned piggish, rooting at me. He wasn't asking any gentle questions or making soothing suggestions; the dull pushing was coming in, with effort, with the sweat of effort, but it was coming in. It was nothing like pain, but the thickness was a surprise, something at once soft and very wide. I had a moment of wondering if there were some problem, if I were too small, but Dave was pressing harder and breathing even faster, and suddenly arching away from me, a gasp, then relaxing heavily on me.

My eyes popped wide open and I found myself staring at the chandelier on the ceiling, fake gilt with bare bulbs in three sockets. The electrical wire woven through the chain fuzzy with ancient dust. I wondered what came next. Dave seemed to be asleep, and I was having a little trouble breathing with his weight on me. My left breast was stretched and flattened, but I didn't want to disturb him prematurely; I had no idea how much time he needed to recover.

It had been, after all, once the preliminaries were finished, less sharp an experience than I expected. I had thought more would be revealed, that a stylus would trace my inner outlines. That the probe would not be so dull-weighted and fleshy. I watched the yellow-gray shadows play on the ceiling; in the corner a smidgeon of sunlight had slipped in. On balance, though, I thought, it had been a good experience. A normal experience. Not a big thing. Sex is really no big thing, I thought cockily to myself. Not such a hell of a big thing at all. A swaggering girl strode back and forth in my head, and a giggle rolled along at her heels. What the hell. Big deal.

Dave groaned. "Are you okay?"

"A little mashed."

He rolled off at once. He had to blink to keep his eyes open, and I could see that he really wanted to sleep, but was bestirring himself. "I mean, was it okay for you?"

"Oh fine, everything is fine. But, I mean, nothing hurt. Are you sure you got all the way in?"

He rolled onto his back; I was on my elbow now, looking down at him. He was really wiped out, circles under his eyes. He said, "It doesn't have to hurt, as far as I know. You're young and in good health, and you've always been active."

"Will I bleed?"

"I don't know, Blair."

"Would I be bleeding by now if I were going to?"

"I don't know. I never did this for the first time with someone. The way I hear it, some do and some don't."

I had an urge to get moving. A lot of energy flowing in me. I wanted to walk across campus as not-a-virgin. "I think I'll go back to the dorm," I said. "In case something happens."

"I'll drive you over."

"No, no, stay here. I feel like walking."

He was trying to figure out what I really wanted, but his eyes kept trying to cross lazily and go back to sleep.

"Really," I said. "I want to be alone for a while. I'll come back later. I don't think we should go to my house tonight anyhow."

His eyes closed. "Come back later, then. We'll go down to Joe's and get something to eat."

I stuffed some kleenex in my underpants just in case. I felt I had been stretched, marked by him. I hurried out to the street where branches full of leaves shifted and did half-rotations overhead.

I remember how I walked across campus, waiting for signs of the transformation that this new knowledge would give me. Colors were intense; each sound caused a little explosion in my head and chest. And yet I felt anchored, and the objects around me as well. Buildings seemed unlikely to shoot off into space. I could feel the leather soles of my shoes make contact with the concrete sidewalk, and my thighs rubbed together and I heard the scratch of denim on denim. There was the slight soreness of newly used muscles, and I thought everything I would ever learn would be like this, a training of muscles, an intensification of the senses. I would be a woman planted in the earth, powerful and wise, a dedicated Community Organizer.

I lived at Dave's apartment for three days. I moved out of the dormitory gradually, taking a suitcase, a box of books each time. I told the girl on receptionist duty that I had already signed out officially, but had to go back for a couple of things I'd forgotten. The receptionist grunted; she was studying for exams. Karen hardly paid any more attention than the receptionist. I told her I was staying at the Mc-Teagues', making final preparations for the Vista Project. It amazed me how easy it was to lie, and how all the rules—the curfews, the no-apartment visits—all those regulations that had caused my heart to pound, adrenaline to shoot through me, all those rules were suddenly blown to nothing, revealed as ephemeral. They melted away as the school year ended. It was like a vision to me. I said to Dave: "All the rules, all the stuff they told me, it's nothing, isn't it? It's all humbug, like the Wizard of Oz. All the sex and go-to-bed-early rules? They don't mean a thing."

Dave said, "Petty restrictions don't help us live; that's true."

I was amazed. I went to the five-and-dime store. I sat at the counter and ordered an ice cream soda. I called my mother from a pay phone and told her a friend would drive me home in a couple of days. I didn't even have to lie to her. I thought I was the freest person who had ever lived.

I slept a lot too. I guess I needed to catch up on sleep after all the late nights and exams and papers, but mostly it was a kind of half-excited, half-lethargic sensuality that came over me. It felt good to lie in Dave's bed with the spring light and spring breezes coming in the casement windows. He was usually in the other room, reading, making another round of instant coffee.

I thought it was incredibly mature of us, to go about our business without having to be together every minute. We ate a lot. One day we had breakfast at Joe's, and then I spent two hours at different grocery stores buying things for a picnic lunch, and we had the picnic at a farm Dave knew, and then late in the evening we went to Shoney's for supper. I had some books about black consciousness Dave had given me to read for the summer, but I kept falling asleep when I opened them. I took walks around town in this strange state of freedom. It seemed that for the moment there was simply nothing more to learn from books or talking.

I had an experiment I did to see the effect of my body on Dave. I would go quietly into the room where he was reading, and stand there, against the wall, saying nothing, to see if my body drew him. He would be at the dinette table, so engrossed in his reading that he left one hand in his beard and forgot to stroke it. My experiment was to see how long it took for him to notice me. To see if my body would reach him across the room. If nothing happened at that distance, I took two steps forward and stood in the middle of the room. Not once did I have to touch him. A couple of times I had to move as many as six steps forward, but usually it worked from much farther. His hand would begin to stroke his beard, or slide up and scratch his head, or he would cough, stir around in his seat, finally look up, staring at me with his eyes blank till I walked within touching distance, and then he would smile and press his face against my ribs, pull me onto his lap, cup my breasts in his hands. "Beautiful, beautiful," he would say, and "So soft," as if it surprised him anew each time.

I could feel the shape of my body then, its undulating line, and at the same time I could feel the hot sheen that came over his body. In bed too I watched him. His intense pleasure, the complete change from being sunk in the book to this hungry gobbling and grasping. I was almost not inside my own body at those times, almost more in his body, or outside both our bodies, watching his reactions and my swells and curves.

We went to bed so often that he told me I would have to be careful not to catch a bladder infection, the honeymooners' disease. I spent a lot of time going to the bathroom after that, waiting for the burning sensation, but it didn't come, only the continued sense of new muscles being activated. There were questions I wanted to ask Dave. What did he know about bladder infections, and what had been the exact moment that he first noticed me in a sexual way? I wanted to know what was going on in his head when he said,

Beautiful, Beautiful and So soft. I wanted to know if he thought what was between us had a long future, and would we be able to live together like this when we got to our Vista assignment? How, I wondered, lying on the bed again, looking at the light playing on the ceiling, did he rate me as a thinker?

But our bodies did most of the talking. The flow of intellectual conversation I had imagined seemed dry by comparison. I was surprised by the silence, but also by how often I found myself sitting in his lap, kissing on the bed.

He drove me over the mountain to my house. During dinner he talked with my parents so calmly and responsibly about the Vista project as a learning opportunity that they had to repress their fears and be reasonable in return. Everything he said was reassuring: he told them that the organization down there, Tidewater Against Poverty Services, had clean, secure apartments for the female Vistas, and one administrator, a woman, whose full-time job was to oversee the Vistas. My mother was relieved; she hadn't asked about that, but Dave had known what to tell her. Then she asked timidly what exactly would we be doing down there? Dave spoke of helping little children learn reading readiness, and taking homebound people to clinics. In some places, he told them, Vistas had even set up clinics, and schools too. It depended on what the community needed. Everything he said was just right: he was attentive to their mood, to what relaxed them and what made them nervous. He completely snowed them, in our old phrase of that time, buried them in a lovely white drift of personality. Reassured them at any rate beyond the point where they could object. We put a premium on reasonableness in my family. Whenever I could rally myself to clear arguments and no shrillness, I got my way. In this case my parents never had a chance. Didn't they want me to help people? To have a learning experience? To grasp this splendid opportunity to be with a person like Dave?

Four

Dave, Roy Critchfield, and I drove south on a day that began with fog and anxiety as I waited at the window of my parents' house. Why was Dave, after all his careful work of reassuring my parents, casting doubts on his status as a responsible adult by being late? They suspected some small measure of his importance to me, too, because I had talked about him more than I meant to. They began to ask questions. Was he an ordained minister? I wasn't sure. How old was he? I didn't even know that. "He and I don't pay much attention to details," I said.

"Profession?" said my father. "You consider someone's profession a detail?"

I didn't think they would really try to stop me from going, but I did believe they could if they chose to, and I was frantic to get away from their realm, back into Dave's, where I had felt free, or at least new.

Daddy meandered over to stand by the window with me. He made a joke about Big Haul, where Roy's family lived, and how the road up there was probably washed out. He liked to joke about Roy; he had never met him, and he had never been to Big Haul, but he thought the Gilmer County community up above a coal mine was just about the most amusing thing he had heard of in years. He was trying to cheer me up, I knew, but he only irritated me with the jokes and the neverending puh-puh of his pipe. My mother seemed to be making an effort to irritate me too. She ran up with oranges and asked if Dave and Roy liked fruit, and then slipped in a question, and didn't wait for the answer. Oh by the way, she asked, weren't there any other girls going on the project besides me?

The Volkswagen finally nosed its way out of the fog and puttered down the driveway. With no roof rack. Dave had specifically said he was buying a roof rack for the trip. Roy got out first, wearing a thick, reddish vest, and slapping a ten-gallon cowboy hat on his head. Dave had a hat too, a little squashed Civil War cap. I didn't look at my parents as Dave and Roy crossed the yard, came in, shook hands. At close range Roy's vest appeared to be made of matted dog hair or maybe orangutan fur.

My parents gave Dave the benefit of the doubt; in spite of his hat he was still Dave, speaking in full sentences, making eye contact. But Roy's eyes were hidden under the brim of the cowboy hat he did not remove. My father couldn't control himself. "Well, Critchfield," he said, "where did you get that vest?"

Roy scowled. "Out of a trunk."

"Up on Big Haul?" said my father. "I guess a fellow could find just about anything in a trunk up on Big Haul."

My mother waved her hands in embarrassment and cried, "Oh, don't leave yet, I have lunch for you! Don't leave yet!" I hoisted two suitcases and started out. Dave brought the rest of my things. I said, "I thought you were getting a roof rack."

He stroked his beard and looked over the packing situation, didn't seem to have any idea he had failed me. "We sure could use one, couldn't we? Well, Roy volunteered to sit in the back and be a sort of book end." He beckoned Roy away from the standoff with my father: "Roy, you might as well come and get yourself packed."

We had to slide the front seats to their farthest forward position to fit him in. I knew I should offer to sit in the back, but I was determined to be with Dave. I was part of a couple now, and couples sit in the front seat together.

The couple I was leaving behind tried to touch me with

kisses, but I only wanted to get away. I was no longer with Mother and Daddy, nor yet with Dave. My parents scraped dry and brittle against my cheeks, but Dave seemed too soft, even overripe. If I could only pull free of this clinging, I thought. If I could only get out of this fog. I believe my discomfort that morning came from being in transition—neither on dry land, nor in the water. I used to belong *here* and I wanted to belong *there*, and I had not yet completed the move.

I turned my face out the car window and closed my eyes even as I waved goodbye. Closed my eyes against my parents' raised, reaching arms, against the familiar elm and maple trees on our street, against my town, against our river and our hills just emerging from the fog. I didn't open my eyes until I felt the big curve and knew we were on the highway. I would see stark industry: the chemical plant with its mountain of slag, the glass factory where the river was milky green. Good, I thought fiercely: ugly river, ugly factories. No more parents looking hurt and full of old ways of doing things, old rules.

But, somewhere on Route 50, as the sun burned away the last of the fog, and the farm hills rose full and in color, my anger went away. It simply withdrew—seemed to dissipate with the mist. For a long while, though, I kept to myself, around a secretly growing excitement; we were on the way—my parents hadn't stopped me. We were climbing the Alleghenies, hills high enough for plaques to tell their names and altitudes, across the little pie slice of Maryland that cuts into West Virginia and forms our Eastern Panhandle. We drove through Franklin, where I saw the clocktower at the college, then headed east, through Aurora, Terra Alta, Keyser, Romney. Saw Saddleback Mountain where Abraham Lincoln's mother was born. Well-being flooded me, and affection for my traveling companions: Roy with his eyes closed and his big knees splayed apart; Dave coaxing the Volkswagen up the steep grades.

I said softly, "Why were you so late this morning?"

I was talking to Dave, but Roy answered, as if he had been

waiting for an opportunity to speak. "My folks tried to stop me from going."

I had seen Roy's parents once, at school. They were skinny, taut people with deep-set, suspicious eyes, who had walked behind Roy's elbows, peering out and squinting, the man in a blue suit with no tie, the woman in tan gloves and an old fashioned coat with large cuffed sleeves. Roy said, "They don't want me to go down there because they think the whole thing is a communist conspiracy to infect me with Negro venereal disease."

I looked back to see if he was joking. He still had his eyes closed, but his mouth had a bitter twist. There had been something dangerous-looking about his parents, I thought, as if they were weasels or some other small animal you wouldn't want to put your hand too near. I said, "You used to think Dave was a communist."

"I used to believe everything they did. Everything their evil-minded preacher thought up; we all fell for it hook line and sinker."

I wondered if he remembered telling me, not so many days ago, that he didn't think I was That Kind of a Girl. "Why did you go to Franklin State in the first place, when you knew it was a state college with fraternities and drinking and everything else?"

Roy winced. "I was going to witness and save people. What an idiot."

"Not an idiot," said Dave. "You've had a hard year. You've wrenched yourself away from one whole life."

"My whole life was wrong."

"Not wrong, just narrow."

"Wrong and fanatic. That's what I was. That's what my parents are. Does God care if you play baseball? Baseball!" He finally opened his eyes, and they looked as if the light caused him pain. "They convinced me not to play baseball! I was a pretty good pitcher in high school, but the preacher decided that team spirit is idolatrous, and I ended up on my knees in church, saying how I'd been seduced into sin by a baseball! I was going to preach to the teams at college. God doesn't want to stop people from playing baseball, does he?"

Dave's mouth made a little wrinkle at the side. Was it a suppressed smile? I was trying to read from his face how best to help Roy. Dave said, "I guess team sports *do* have an idolatrous side. Your preacher had a point there."

Roy almost shouted, "But God doesn't care if a boy plays baseball, does he? Does he? God doesn't give one good hoot about sports or drinking or sex. God doesn't give a damn and neither do I."

I was frightened; I myself hadn't been thinking about God much at all. I had changed a lot in the last year too, but I hadn't had a crisis like Roy. For me it had been more like dropping excess baggage. A little handbag here, a steamer trunk there. Just letting go of things and never waiting to hear them hit bottom.

Very softly, as if he were afraid of jarring something precariously balanced over an edge, Dave said, "I think we might do well to call a moratorium on talking about God for a while. I think it confuses us, and we tend to get God mixed up with—oh, a lot of things . . . parents, feeling bored in church . . . restrictions that hold us back from things we think we want. I think we might do well to just let it rest for a while . . . wait for the new thing to happen . . . wait for God's new name."

"All right," said Roy. "I'm willing. I'll try anything. You two try things, don't you? You do whatever you want, don't you?"

So he did remember the day in Dave's apartment. "We want to be open to experience," I said. "Right, Dave?"

Dave inclined his head toward me. I felt in tune again. As if, after that strange period of eating and sleeping together so intimately, words had begun to flow between us again. When we got there, to Vista, it would all come together: the bodies, the politics, and God's new name too.

Roy said, "I think I'll have a beer with lunch."

We circled Washington and headed south, and the unearthly flatness of the superhighway and the heavy dampness of the air intensified with each mile. I already missed the mountains and began to feel that we had somewhere along the way slipped through a hole in rotten ice and were now swimming forward slowly, under the thick gray plate, away from our air source, our escape. I would not be depressed, though. I refused. I reached over and squeezed Dave's hand, to make sure of him, and he squeezed back, but too quickly, as if answering my squeeze were another responsibility to be taken care of promptly and efficiently.

He was right, of course, to put personal relationships second for the moment. We had other things to think about. We had to be ready. In a few hours we would be Volunteers in Service to America—Vistas in South Jenkin, our own neighborhood. We would be living with black people in a ghetto, trying to fight the racism in society and—as Dave had pointed out many times—the racism within ourselves. I decided to work on the racism within myself for the rest of the trip. I would not, I promised myself, ever notice skin color or accent, and I would always extend my hand before the other person did. I would stop using the word black to mean bad or evil and, above all, I would not be surprised if the people down there acted differently from what I was used to.

It was five o'clock when we stopped in a shopping center on the outskirts of the city to call the agency. Roy and I leaned on the hood of the Volkswagen watching Dave in the phone booth. He opened his left hand repeatedly as he explained something to the agency person on the other end, but mostly he listened and made notes on a lunch bag. The sun came in at a low angle, and a yellowed sheet of newspaper turned end over end in the hot wind, slapping against the bell-bottom pants of a sailor. There were sailors all over this shopping center; we'd seen the road signs for the big navy base. My skin was sticky, and I felt as if lines had been incised in my face by the wind coming in the car window. I had a yearning for my nightgown and toothbrush and a cool, dim cubicle where I could curl up and sleep for a long time.

Dave stepped out of the booth, examining the scrap of paper. "Well," he said, "the office was closing, but Eleanor-

Byrd Williams, the Vista coordinator, waited to hear from us."

"Like Lady Bird Johnson?" said Roy.

"No, like the rich and famous Byrds of Virginia. She's distantly related, and she keeps the Byrd in her name even when she changes husbands. She just married the chairman of the poverty agency's local board."

I said, "She sounds like Zsa Zsa Gabor."

"Wrong accent. But seriously, she's very concerned and hardworking. She apologized up and down because she can't meet us tonight, but she made all kinds of arrangements. We're going straight to South Jenkin to have dinner at Frank Landell's house. Frank is the Baptist preacher I told you about, I met him last time down. Very good, very solid man. I've got the directions to his place, and he has the keys to where we're staying."

"But we're going to South Jenkin? We'll be in South Jenkin tonight?"

"South Jenkin for dinner."

I didn't mind the grit and dampness anymore; I was cooled by anticipation. This was the beginning. We were having dinner with black people. They would be watching our behavior. We drove past buildings: granite, limestone, neon. Over a bridge, crossing a broad river, or was it a bay? There were warehouses, gantry cranes for shipbuilding, tugboats. In the distance larger ships, charcoal gray and steel: curves of harbor, straight edges of skyline, wake of boats. And then we were on the other side, and I saw children playing in the middle of a side street. "Is this it, Dave? Is this South Jenkin?"

"As I understand it, everything on the righthand side of William and Mary Road is South Jenkin. On the lefthand side is white people. William and Mary Road is the dividing line. No one white lives in South Jenkin except the odd Vista volunteer."

"And I bet the people on the other side think the Vistas are odd," said Roy.

William and Mary Road curved slowly, broadly; it had few

stores, a White Castle drive-in, a supermarket called Dollar Bill's, both on the white side. The apartments all looked too nice to me: oblong brick boxes set on end, three stories high, each apartment with a big balcony or porch.

Then Dave made a right, off the main thoroughfare. There were a few one-family houses with ample porches here, but hard by these were shanties with their doors open for ventilation, and you could see all the way through, out the back. There were whole houses unoccupied too, with plywood over the windows, and planks ripped off the outer walls. We saw an empty lot full of trash, and next to it a neatly kept house with a planter made from a tire and painted with red and white stripes.

"Satisfied?" said Dave, touching my knee. I jumped. It was almost as if I'd forgotten I had a body, as if I had been all eyes, taking in, gathering pictures.

In the middle of all these wooden houses rose a powerful stone structure: Landell's church. His house was around the corner on the same lot, a cream-colored frame house, neat with brown trim. Sitting on the porch steps was a man with a little boy on his lap. When he saw us, he set the child aside and rose to meet us, smiling. He was thickly built, young, probably Dave's age, with beautiful satiny skin that smoothed the line of his large, athlete's forearms. His neck was large, too; everything about him was oversized—the thigh muscles pressing against his pants, his large, high buttocks, the breadth of his gestures. Arms open, he came toward us, seeming to encompass the house, the street, the horizon. "Welcome to South Jenkin," he said. "Welcome to South Jenkin and welcome to our home."

Dave was in front of me, so I had plenty of time to get my hand ready to shake, but somehow Frank Landell extended his first—an enormous, square hand that made me ashamed of my little, damp, hot one.

Landell's wife Yvetta came out too. She seemed reserved compared with him, even shy. She was younger than he was, with stiff wings of black hair held back by a pink band, wearing a sleeveless sweater and slacks, also pink. She was at once round and long—face, arms, torso, hips. She only said, "How do you do?" to us, but she took the little boy and gave Landell a look.

"Yes," he said, apparently speaking for her. We were to get the tour while she finished a few things in the kitchen. "It should really be her tour," said Landell. "She redid the house. She keeps the garden. She makes me the happiest man in the world." She shook her head and went inside.

I found myself believing him, that he was the happiest man in the world. That his wife Yvetta made him that way. I was so glad that they were beautiful. They had an island of greenery here, a vegetable garden connecting the church and the parsonage. Hollyhocks and a little grape arbor. Landell boomed, laughed, declaimed, but his energy relaxed us. We asked a question here, made a comment there, but nothing was demanded. This had been a farm once, he told us. All of South Jenkin had been farms once, and then little summer plantations for well-to-do city people. Some fine houses still here, others lost forever, choked out by cheap slum housing or ruined by neglect of absentee landlords. I saw Dave's eyes light up over that, but we were already in the church, and we had to admire the large sanctuary, the colored glass, the tiled basement, and stainless steel kitchen. Ready for fellowship suppers, wedding receptions. Once, years before, at home, I had seen my minister giving a tour of our church to some out-of-town people, and he had made the visitors rub the drapes between their fingers, and had knelt down to measure the depth of the carpet pile by his knuckles. I had been shocked then to see a minister take pleasure in things, but it seemed right in Frank Landell; everything seemed right about him and his little kingdom here. We smelled the lemon oil on the pews, the growing things in the garden, and dinner cooking in the house.

Back on the porch Dave began to direct the conversation. He leaned forward, elbows on knees, rubbing his beard with both thumbs, asking questions. The absentee landlords first.

Landell raised his arms and cradled his head, smiled and answered everything genially, with thoughtful care. Meanwhile Roy drifted over to the swing at the far end of the porch, and half reclined on it.

What about Chuck Williams, Eleanor-Byrd's husband, Dave wanted to know. How involved was he in TAPS? Chuck Williams' family, Landell told us, was not an old aristocratic family like the Byrds of Virginia, but they had plenty of money: they owned the Dollar Bill grocery chain that was so prominent in the Tidewater area. The old man, Dollar Bill himself, along with Chuck's older brother Bill Junior, pretty much ran the business. Chuck seemed to have a lot of time for TAPS, worked hard, got himself elected chairman of the community board.

Dave wanted to know if Chuck had political aspirations, and Landell opened his big hands on that one, just smiled and shrugged. Dave switched to city government. What was the mayor's stance on the poverty program and the money coming in from Washington? Who was a real reformer here? Who wanted to make sure the money didn't cause waves? Who were the leaders of the black community?

I stayed alert as long as the conversation was on Chuck Williams, who was at least someone I would probably meet, but when Dave started off into all those politicians and municipal government issues, I began to feel a suction around me, the air being pulled away. I wanted to yell, Can't we wait till tomorrow? Do we have to do this now? Roy had actually gone to sleep, while Dave's voice probed on, staccato, urgent. Frank Landell's answers were slow and sonorous, more detailed as Dave's questions became more subtle. I felt my familiar panic—that I would never be able to keep up with him. That we were in wide, smooth water and the others were swimming far ahead of me. I was being left behind.

I said I would go in and lend Yvetta a hand. I said it quietly, and no one seemed to hear.

I followed the smells and sounds of cooking through the house to the kitchen, where she had a skillet on the burner and a platter of already-fried chicken on the table. She ducked her head when I came in, as if she wanted to hide her smile. I had never seen anyone quite her color. I hadn't meant to notice color, but her skin was such a wonderful bright cinnamon, with no variation in tone, not a pale patch or a dark spot. I didn't understand how anyone with skin like that could be shy.

Frank Junior, in his highchair eating chicken meat with the skin and bones pulled off, tossed a piece on the floor, and she made a scolding noise at him.

"You have a beautiful home," I said. I had plenty of words, even if she didn't. But they were my mother's words, all those sentences of compliment and apology I had heard her pour out over the years. "I feel terrible the way they just dropped us in on you, like this—"

"Oh no!" Yvetta stopped smiling. "We *love* company. We *never* get enough company."

"Well, at least let me give a hand—I could do something."

"Just sit down and visit," she said, and I did, promptly. Because although she was shy and I wasn't, particularly, she seemed to be the kind of person who knew what she wanted and expected people to do it. Little Frank too. He leaned over his highchair tray and offered me a piece of chicken with such confidence that I ate it without thinking, and a second piece too. "Frank Junior," she said. "Stop putting your greasy fingers in the lady's mouth."

"Oh, I don't mind," I said, but Little Frank did as he was told, and Yvetta dropped a dollop of Crisco into the skillet and dredged more chicken parts. There was a silence, so I resumed my praising of the house and garden and church and Little Frank and Big Frank, but never said the exact thing on my mind, which was that I had never seen any three human beings as beautiful as they were—perhaps she most of all, with everything flowing down and over, wide-hipped but with a long body and legs, everything balanced, everything graceful.

She put the last pieces of chicken on to fry, and sat down opposite me with her evenly colored, small-wristed arms on the table. I stopped in the middle of whichever compliment I was making because she was ready to speak now. "Listen," she said. "Do you go to college?"

"I just finished my freshman year."

"Is it hard?"

"Compared to high school? Well, it's different. You know. You get bigger assignments, but you have longer to do them. It's more work, but it's more interesting too."

She ducked down over a smile again, all the way to the floor this time to pick up one of Little Frank's scraps. Very softly she said, "I'm going in the fall."

"To college?"

"Virginia State. I always wanted a college education, only I got married so soon. My mama is going to take Frank Junior in the days, and Frank, he says I can have the car. I been accepted, I'm all signed up. I'm taking a liberal arts course to start, but I may go for a teacher."

Awe filled me. I was predisposed to be awed by the Landells, I guess, but this seemed genuinely amazing, that this beautiful young woman, probably about my age, maybe even younger, was doing everything. She was married and the mother of Little Frank, and she could remodel a house, keep a garden, fry chicken for dozens, on no notice at all, and go to college besides. She was going to be a teacher. She could do everything in life all at once, and I envied her. Me, I had no idea what I was doing; I couldn't even listen to important information for more than five minutes.

Landell came in. "There you are! We wondered if we'd lost you."

"I came in to help out, but she won't let me."

Frank leaned over the highchair tray and kissed the baby's forehead. "Yvetta has her own way of doing things."

Little Frank said, "Up, Daddy!" and Landell scooped the child out of the highchair, straight up into the air, as high as his arms could reach. The baby spread out his arms and legs, flying, with his bib dangling and a look of blissful freedom in his face.

I wanted to be the child of Frank and Yvetta Landell. I wanted to eat bits of chicken they tore off the bone for me, and to fly near the ceiling on my daddy's powerful arms. "You people," I said, "you have the Garden of Eden here."

Landell threw back his head in a huge laugh over that one, but Yvetta screwed up her mouth. "In South Jenkin?" she said. "In South Jenkin?"

"We do," he said. "We do, Yvetta. We have Eden in South Jenkin." He brought the baby down, undid its bib. "Yvetta grew up over here, just three blocks from this house. She's the local pure product, and sometimes she thinks she's had enough of it."

"I have." She checked a pot of greens. "It's not a good place to raise up children. I saw how it was."

"Yes," said Landell. "She saw things. She saw one of her own family go to the bad."

"Go real bad," said Yvetta gently, beginning to set the table. Somehow it made me stronger to know this about her. I took the napkins out of her hand and laid them around.

Landell said, "You see, we agree on everything, Yvetta and I, except about South Jenkin."

Yvetta shrugged. "Frank grew up on a farm. In North Carolina."

I was on his side. It was clear from our studies, and Dave had pointed out repeatedly: you have to live *among* people to help them. But at the same time Yvetta knew things. She was the real native here. Frank was a country boy, like my own father. Even this difference between them, though, had a beauty in my eyes: it had a vividness, clearly delineated boundaries.

We had to wake Roy for dinner, and Dave finally eased up on his questions. We talked about our favorite childhood meals, and how people fix greens in Tidewater and North Carolina and West Virginia. We talked about college and the mountains and the lowlands. I forget most of what we talked about, but not the way it felt full in our mouths, or the taste of the sweet potato pie or the blue color of evening out back of Landells' house.

Later, when Roy's eyes were looking swollen with weariness again, we insisted on finding our apartments alone, and Frank gave us keys and elaborate instructions for traversing the two blocks to where I would be staying. 236 Eastover turned out to be one of the good old frame houses with stained glass over the door. When we stopped in front of it, I said, "I wanted to see your apartment."

"Well," said Dave, "if you really want to. It would save time overall if we dropped you now—"

"Oh never mind, I don't care." What I had really wanted was to drop Roy and have a half hour alone with Dave. "It's just that, well, look at this place. It's a *nice* house. I know you got a slum. He said you did. I don't know why everyone is always protecting female people. They act like girls are going to melt in the rain." I could hear grumbling in my voice and I didn't like it, but I didn't like the way Dave was nodding and murmuring gently to me either.

"It isn't so important, where we live, Blair. It really isn't."

"You always said it was before. It's one thing for Yvetta Landell to live in a nice remodeled house, she's one of the people anyhow. But I want to live in a slum, like you and Roy!"

My words hung in the air, embarrassing and stupid. I want to live in a slum indeed! No one wanted to live in a slum. Except that I really did. I wanted to test myself, toughen up, see what it felt like. But what I really wanted was to live in a slum with Dave.

Roy stayed in the car while we took my bags into the female-Vista apartment. There was one bare light bulb down at the end of the hall, but no sign of my roommate. We turned a switch and stepped into an entirely red living room: rosy shades on the lamps, red paint on the floor, red pillows for seating. Dave gave a little laugh, as if he were surprised by the place, and put his arms around me. I could smell his sweat like a plume of anxiety rising from his flesh. A hard day for him too, all the driving and making inquiries. But I did not at that time in my life have any patience for what was happening inside him. I wanted him not anxious. I wanted him to arrange things better.

I said into his chest, "I don't know why we can't at least live in the same building."

He pulled back, looked down at me. "We have to be very careful about that. We can't have the people rejecting us outright because they don't like the way we live."

Yes, yes, yes. He was right. I had known all along that we wouldn't be given a room together, but I felt deserted just the same. I felt as deserted as I had when I was four years old, and my mother decided it was time to stop lying in bed with me till I fell asleep. I had been silently furious then, knowing she was just a wall away, forbidden to me, reserved to my father. Of course I wanted to be a big girl, then and now, too. I wanted to live in a way that would facilitate our work and not offend people. But I didn't want to be left behind in this room with the red glow and pillows. I didn't even know where I would sleep. I said, "Why can't we *do* something tomorrow instead of spending the whole day filling out forms and getting fingerprinted or whatever they have planned for us?"

"We'll live through it. We'll be bored, and we'll live through it, and then we'll get to work."

Another laugh, a little kiss, and then I was standing completely alone in the middle of the red room. After a few minutes my breath began to come heavily; I felt crowded by the fat pillows and long fringes of a magenta lampshade that stirred in a breeze I didn't feel.

I had to find the bathroom, anyhow, so I started down the hall. I stopped short when the shadows between me and the light bulb materialized into a man's form, long-limbed as a spider.

I took a step backwards.

"Hey!" said a voice from the long limbs. "Whoa! Don't

run—don't panic. I'm domesticated, you know? I'm Spencer."
It was a wry voice, joking, but the silhouette was still strung
across the hall. He was thin and tall, and so dark that there
seemed to be no surface to his body, only a deepening of the
shadows. I'm not frightened because he's black, I thought.
I'm frightened because it's a man and there aren't supposed
to be any men here. But what if I am frightened because he's
black?

And then there was a woman, a white woman wearing
something loose like a slip or nightgown. "I *did* hear someone out here," she said. "You're one of the new Vistas,
aren't you? Why didn't they *tell* us you were coming tonight? I can't believe it. Sometimes Eleanor-Byrd is such
an asshole."

They were in a room having sex together, I thought. Dave
and I were bringing in the bags, and they were having sex.
These other Vistas, the old Vistas. Shelley and Spencer were
their names.

She kept talking, and he talked at the same time. They had
a noisy quality; they filled the hall now, turned on more
lights. Everything was suddenly in place and visible. Shelley
had an enormous mass of reddish brown hair. Spencer was
slim, with large eyes and neat goatee beard. Too bad he
missed a ride home, he said, and then, in a deep drugstore
cowboy voice, said he thought he'd better mosey on over
there and meet his new partners. At the door he swooped
down and seized my hand, kissed my fingers, tickling me with
the tiny stiff curls of beard, and said he was enchanted to
make my acquaintance.

"Don't mind Spencer," said Shelley. "He was just embarrassed."

"He didn't seem embarrassed."

"The way to tell with Spencer is when he does more than
three different accents in less than five minutes, then you
know he's under stress. Are you hungry? How about something to drink? Milk? Soda? Beer?" *She* didn't seem embarrassed. She padded into the kitchen barefoot, so much hair

exploding in all directions like an overgrowth of asparagus grass. "God, it's hot already, isn't it? It's like a steambath and it isn't even July yet." The kitchen was painted aqua, and had a fish-net suspended from the ceiling. She got out a carton of milk and poured a glass for herself. "We waited for you for hours, you know."

"We had dinner with Reverend Landell and Yvetta."

"Of course! She would do that and never tell us. Good old Eleanor-Byrd and Chuckie. They don't approve of me and Spencer; they don't like us working with teenagers. They think we should only work with church ladies and little children. So what did you think of the Landells?"

She actually stopped talking, leaned an elbow on the countertop, waited for me to say something. There was antique eyelet work across her bodice.

"Oh, they were real nice," I said, immediately sorry for the insipid word.

"Did you hear about Yvetta's cousin? She grew up in the same house with this gangster who got sent away for life or something right before we came to South Jenkin. All the teenagers used to follow this guy. Literally follow him. He would walk down the street and they would trail along behind. Spencer and I have been trying to fill the vacuum, with a recreation center or something constructive, only TAPS hasn't been very supportive. Frank Landell hasn't been much better— Well, he did let us use his church a couple of times. But we're having a dance next week, it's our big coup—we get to use the TAPS Neighborhood Center for a dance for the teenagers."

I offered to help, trying not to sound overeager, and we carried my bags to my room, an odd space at the end of the house, as wide as the whole apartment but so narrow in the other dimension that the two cots had to sit end to end under the windows. I didn't care; it was my room, I could undress, I could put my things in the bureau.

Shelley stuck her head back in. "I forgot to warn you. I'm hell-on-wheels in the morning. If I don't speak to you, or if I growl something obscene, just ignore me till I pour down some coffee.''

When she was gone again, and I was finally alone in my long skinny room, I took off my dress and undid my bra, got out my alarm clock and lay down for a moment while I set it. I didn't know anything else till the alarm went off, still in my hands, and the room was white with morning light.

Five

      In the morning, in my new room, I looked out the window at a backyard, overgrown with weeds, that ended thirty feet back at a gnarled apple tree and high plank fence. I thought I could see a dog moving back and forth behind the fence. Somewhere in that same direction was the TAPS Neighborhood Center. I showered, dressed, taped *Christina's World* on the wall, and then went out on the porch to wait for Dave and Roy. Up to the left, in the direction of Landell's church, some children were pushing a tricycle back and forth, their high voices blending into the clean morning air. I was thinking of going over and introducing myself, or whatever you do to get to know children, when a dark Chrysler came around the corner, and a thin, bouffant-haired white woman rolled down the window and shouted, "Hey, there, Blair Morgan!" She half climbed out the window, gushing a welcome over me, pressing me into the back seat where she had already arranged Dave and Roy. It was Eleanor-Byrd Williams, and her husband Chuck driving. Chuck was lean too, with small eyes half-hidden in smile wrinkles, wearing a light-colored suit. He didn't say much, but then no one was saying much except Eleanor. She explained at length how she and Chuck just thought they might as well take us into town, since they were driving in anyhow, and she felt so guilty that they hadn't been able to get out of their engagement last night.

      I looked to Dave to see how he was taking this woman. He

had set his lips in a small, noncommittal smile. Roy, sitting on the other side of Dave, was scowling, but at least he hadn't worn the Abominable Snowman vest or the ten-gallon hat. There was going to be no chance for private time with Dave; no time for Dave to reassure me about getting through this morning.

"It's nice of you to come down to TAPS with us, Chuck," said Dave.

Chuck took his time speaking. "Well, I need to check in at TAPS every now and then, and the groceries pretty much sell themselves these days."

At every word Chuck said, Eleanor-Byrd leaned forward slightly closer to him. When he made his little joke about the grocery business, she tossed her hair and chin and laughed up and down the scale.

Dave said, "Now let me see if I'm getting this straight. TAPS has an executive director who makes the day-to-day decisions?"

Eleanor-Byrd answered, "Yes, that's Delbert Jackson. You'll meet him today. He's a fine Negro gentleman."

"Ah," said Dave. "Then the executive director is black, and the chairman of the community board—Chuck—is white."

"We're real integrated," said Eleanor. "You'll see."

"And you, Eleanor, you make the Vistas assignments?"

"I'm your little mother hen," she said. "I try to make sure everything goes smoothly."

I said, "But we choose our own projects, don't we? I always heard we chose our projects."

She said, "Oh yes, you wait and see. Shelley has the cutest little Girl Scout troop, and Spencer has a club for teenagers. They do some real nice things you all can step right into."

I scowled, wanting Dave to set her straight, that we wouldn't be stepping into other people's projects, and most especially would not be playing Girl Scouts, but he ignored me completely and went ahead with gathering facts. He wanted more on the racial balance of TAPS and the racial make-up of the neighborhoods. Also, the number of families on welfare in South Jenkin. He was all glasses and ears now, his voice regular and flat, the passion squeezed out. Furrowing his brow as he tried to penetrate the facts. Meanwhile, I thought, leaning far back in the deep cushions of Chuck Williams' Chrysler, sealed in air-conditioned coolness, South Jenkin had slipped away from us. I kept telling myself that I was an idiot: what did I want from Dave? He was a man, he wasn't a teenager to slobber on my neck and hold my hand under the table while we filled out forms. I tried to concentrate on the work at hand, the way he did, to save the personal stuff for later.

But it wasn't only Dave who ignored me, it was that everyone at TAPS did too. When we were introduced to the secretaries, and later to the Executive Director, the eyes met Dave's. The remarks were aimed at Dave. Roy and I were appendages, supernumeraries, and it infuriated me more by the minute. This time I couldn't even tell myself I'd get a good night's sleep and everything would look fine in the morning. This time it was *already* the morning, with the whole day ahead and Dave as friendly and impersonal as a car salesman and Roy as stiff as a cigar-store Indian. When the forms were finally done, Chuck Williams insisted he could put off going to work a little longer and drive us back for a tour of South Jenkin. His gleaming rich man's car annoyed me, and Eleanor's accent and enthusiasm.

"What about drugs," Dave asked as we drove across the bridge again, under a dull sky too high for rain. "What about gangs?"

Eleanor-Byrd said she didn't think there were many drugs —not that heroin, anyhow. And how they used to have a gang in South Jenkin, but it got pretty well broken up a couple of years back. I had the bad-tempered satisfaction of being the only one of us who knew that the gang leader had been Yvetta Landell's cousin, but my pleasure didn't last. We were coming back into South Jenkin still sealed in the Chrysler. I concentrated on seeing everything, burning impressions into my brain with as much intensity as Dave when he took in information.

I saw two little girls in identical print sundresses bouncing up and down on a mattress spring in an empty lot. As we cruised by, they stopped jumping and stuck mirror image thumbs into their mouths, sucked till we were past, then resumed bouncing.

I saw a man with broad shoulders and a heavy jaw, whose hair was a strange orange color and his eyes light hazel. As we paused for a stop sign, he came toward us waving a pint bottle of wine.

I saw an elderly woman with both arms wrapped around a bag of groceries, moving slowly at a bowlegged pace, her legs buckling at each step. I couldn't believe the others kept on talking, drove by her; I wanted to give her my seat in this car, carry her groceries for her.

On Edgecomb Avenue, at the intersection with Eastover, I recognized my house. "Wait!" I said. "Stop the car! Stop the car, please!"

Chuck coasted past the intersection but stopped. They all looked at me. "I want to run in my apartment," I said. "I can meet you at the Neighborhood Center. It's right up the street, isn't it?"

Eleanor-Byrd looked concerned. "Why, we'll wait for you, honey."

"No, no, please. I'll be right over. I want to stretch my legs."

"Well," said Eleanor, "it's directly opposite the school, you can see the school from here. I don't guess you can go too wrong."

I had the car door open, could feel the damp air out there with smells I wasn't used to yet. "I'll be right over," I said. "I'll catch up." I gave her an enormous smile, thinking that I probably knew as much about hypocrisy and sweetness as she did.

"Well," she said, shaking a finger at me. "Ten minutes now!"

I shook a finger back. "Maybe fifteen!"

"Otherwise we'll send out a search party!"

I smiled and waved, and caught a look from Dave, his forehead knotting up a little, the barest beginning of the look that meant he had been disturbed at last, and was going to give me his attention.

But I gave him the smile too and called, "See you soon!" as they drove away.

When they were gone, I walked past my house and up the street. I had vaguely in mind to look for the old woman with the groceries and bent legs, but first I walked to where the children had been this morning. The tricycle was still in front of a green house with green rattan blinds down over the porch, many slats broken, not much grass in the yard. Toy buckets, a plastic pistol with the silver paint flecking off, a length of heavy-duty, cloth-insulated electrical cord. And then, as if she'd been left there like the bucket and the cord, a very tiny girl. It seemed amazing that such a little person could walk at all, but she was coming toward me, unsteady but unhesitating, tiny braids in her hair, underpants too large, tee shirt too small. I squatted down, feeling my bad temper ooze away. "Hello," I said as she stopped just out of my reach. "Where's your family?" I wasn't sure what my responsibility was in this case. Should I look for adults? Might a baby follow you, the way a puppy would? I said, "Is that your house? Is your mother in there?" Her little pointed eyebrows rose sharply and she began a smile that took a long time to spread across her face. Out of the corner of my eye I saw more children running around the side of the house. "Little Bit!" cried a beautiful, dark, bony girl with earrings. "Little Bit, you ran off!" She scooped the baby girl up in her arms, although she was only seven or eight herself and was weighed down with earrings, silver and brass bangles on her arms, and a woman's gold bedroom mules on her feet. "You shouldn't bother the lady, Little Bit."

"She's not bothering me," I said. "I was just wondering who was watching her."

There were two boys too, and one had dark, circumflex eyebrows like Little Bit's, long, heavy eyelashes and a husky, torchsinger's voice. He said, "Are you another Vista?"

"What makes you think I'm a Vista?"

He laid the lashes down on his cheeks and smiled. "Oh, you look like a Vista. Very nice. You know."

"Well, you're right. I am a Vista. My name's Blair."

He offered his hand. "Pleased to meet you. I'm Charlie Conyers. That's Jewel."

The girl named Jewel, still hugging Little Bit, said, "We got Vistas in our same house as me and my mama. We got two more last night."

"Then I bet you live on Old Fellows Street."

The other boy had a bullet-shaped head that seemed too heavy for his body. He sneered. "Old Fellows Street stink. Old Fellows Street got toilet breath."

Jewel smiled at me, put down the baby, and threw a vicious sidelong kick at him.

Charlie sighed dramatically. "Those two, Jewel and Hooky, they go together. Jewel is my cousin, and Hooky, he lives at my house, but he ain't my brother."

Hooky picked up the electrical cord and started lashing at garbage cans. "Vistas don't *never* do what they say. They *say* they taking us to the beach. They *say* they taking us swimming."

"Swimming *and* the beach?" I said. "Is that one thing or two?"

Charlie opened his hands. "Hooky don't believe nothing. If Shelley and Spencer say they taking us on a trip, we just got to be patient, right?"

"I'm sure they'll do it if they say so." But just the same, I vowed to myself that if Shelley and Spencer didn't do it, I would.

Jewel said, "Spencer already took me lots of places."

"That," said Hooky, "is because Spencer slips it in your mama. He slip it in easy, and it come out greasy!"

This time she seized a chunk of crumbling sidewalk cement and in one smooth motion hurled it at Hooky. It caught him in the shoulder and he whirled around, shouting, "And your mama *likes* it!" Without pausing, he sprang at the drainpipe of the house and began to lash at it, flushing into sight a boy with no shirt.

"Who's that?" I said.

"Just a Duberry," said Charlie. "Name of Gilbert."

Hooky lashed again, barely missing Gilbert. "Get outa here, Duberry." The Duberry was taller than Hooky, but there was something pinched about him, a gray cast to his bare skin, something clotted about his hair. He didn't seem frightened of Hooky, but he went, and Hooky gave a lackadaisical lash in Jewel's direction. She said he had better not come near her, or say another word about her mother. Charlie sighed to me, as if he hoped I would understand these quarrelsome children.

"I'll tell you what," I said. "I have to go over to the Neighborhood Center and I'll look for Shelley and Spencer and see what I can find out about that swimming trip."

"No hurry," said Charlie. "We real patient. Whenever you say."

Jewel said, "Neighborhood Center is *that* way."

"I'm going the long way so I can look around."

They walked me as far as the corner, Charlie and Jewel chatting politely, Little Bit holding my hand, and then when they stopped, they all waved goodbye. Charlie shouted, "I 'spect my mama will invite you to dinner after church, she always invites the Vistas!"

"My mama too!" shouted Jewel.

I was touched by the politeness and thanked them, took a left up a decidedly less pleasant street, but I could see the heavy traffic on William and Mary Road ahead and wasn't frightened. Eastover—*our* block, the Conyers kids' and mine —was a family street. Poor but honest. This street, in stark contrast, was underpopulated and barren. The near side had some houses, but mostly empty lots. The far side appeared to have been bulldozed to rubble except for one large apartment building with all its windows gone.

Out of the desolation appeared Gilbert Duberry. He had, I knew, intercepted me by cutting between the houses, but I was disconcerted by the suddenness with which he appeared and planted himself in my way.

"Hello," I said. "You're Gilbert Duberry." I tried to feel affection for him as I had for the others, even the foul-mouthed, bullet-headed Hooky, but something about Gilbert repelled me. Feature by feature he should have been a pretty boy: shapely lips, long lashes. But this ashy scumble over his skin made him somehow vague and ghostly, and I didn't believe it would ever wash off. He made a single, jerky, beckoning motion and said, "Come to my house."

"Wait a minute— Why do you want me to come to your house?"

But he was already moving, looking back over his shoulder at me. "Sign for the welfare," he said.

"I'm not from the welfare department, I'm a Vista."

He was picking up speed, almost running, head bent forward with determination. His house filled me with panic: half the windows were covered with plywood, and great sections of siding had been torn off.

"Gilbert! I don't know anything about welfare—"

He straight-armed his way into the house, and I was left standing on the bottom step, on the verge of running away, but telling myself this was a call for help. Hadn't I wanted to help someone? I didn't have much time to think about it, though. He burst out again, followed by a woman with big gobbets of uncombed hair. An ashy-faced girl gripped her skirt.

"Mrs. Duberry? I'm terribly sorry—I think your son made a mistake. I'm not from the welfare department. I'm just a Vista volunteer—"

"I'll show you inside," she said.

I followed her because I had decided to help them, and

because her eyes were so dull, and the little girl had the same gray cast to her skin that Gilbert did.

The front room was too dark, but when I hesitated for a moment, Gilbert's hard cool fingertips pinched my wrist and I could feel the force of his body herding me through the darkness. I thought I saw something stir among the furniture shapes. I fixed my attention on the room ahead that had a window. It also had three television sets—an old cabinet model with a little blue portable on top of it, and another, heavier portable on a crate.

"Televisions don't work," said Mrs. Duberry. "Besides that, they turned off the electric."

"I can ask at the Neighborhood Center about your electricity. There must be some law that they can't just turn it off."

She raised one hand palm outward at me. "What I need's a mergency food note for the welfare."

"I don't work for the welfare—"

"We ain't got nothing to eat. Come in the kitchen, you can see."

"It's not that I don't believe you— I just don't know if I can do it—" Gilbert was pressing at me again, his fingers on my wrist. "Really, I believe you," I said.

The walls of the kitchen had rectangular areas of bare plaster where cabinets and the stove had been ripped out; capped gas pipes stood naked next to the sink. Gilbert's mother opened the refrigerator, which was empty except for a can of Sterno and a box of Carnation dry milk that she turned upside down to show it was empty. A few crystals fell into the hair of the little girl. I noticed for the first time a baby in the kitchen, too, on the floor. A silent baby wearing a long garment that seemed to be tangled in its legs, so that when it tried to crawl only its arms moved a little. But it didn't cry, and no one paid any attention to it.

"I got to get some food for these children," the mother said, letting the box of Carnation dangle at her side.

My first thought was to wonder what they would have

done if I hadn't happened along. Was Gilbert's job every day to snare a social worker? But how often did one walk by? Had I appeared in the nick of time, or was this a permanent situation? I had a feeling that there were never supplies of food in this kitchen.

I must have been quiet too long, because Mrs. Duberry said, "Alls you have to do is make a note for the mergency. On any old kind of paper."

Well, I thought, if you can't be made a fool of on your first day in Vista, when can you? "I'll tell you what I'll do, Mrs. Duberry. I don't know about this emergency business, but I will take Gilbert to the store and buy a few groceries to hold you for now."

"Fresh milk," she said without any hesitation. "The baby won't take powdered. And a little Nescafé. The baby takes his milk better with Nescafé." She gave me another look, estimating. "Bacon and eggs would be real nice too."

"And cans of vegetables," I said sternly. If I was being played for a fool by the Duberrys I intended to leave them with cans of spinach and peas on their shelves.

The half-demolished street looked wide open and ripe with possibility after that house. "Where do we go for groceries, Gilbert?"

He jogged a little ahead of me and called back something I couldn't quite make out. At the intersection of William and Mary Road with its two wide lanes in either direction, he turned left. The store was there, a tiny box set among tree-size ailanthus weeds and hulks of discarded stoves and washing machines. The store windows were blocked with faded posters: Del Monte pineapple, Winston Cigarettes. Gilbert was already inside, leaning deep into an ice cream freezer that sat in the center of the store.

Like gunshot a voice said, "Out of my store, Duberry!"

I felt a rush of righteousness. Bad enough that I was suspicious of the Duberrys. I had a right because I was also helping them, but I intended to stand up for Gilbert against whoever this storekeeper was, with his guttural accent with the heavy consonants. I laid a hand in Gilbert's hair, and he immediately sank against my side, pressed against me as if he'd like to stay there a long time. I said, "He's with me."

"Ah, so I got more social workers." The storekeeper was pale white and bald, and his soft shoulders turned in; all his parts clumped close to his body.

I said, "We also need a dozen eggs and a quart of milk and a loaf of bread."

"That's good, you should feed your Duberrys. You should feed your Duberrys every day."

"Bacon," I said.

Gilbert leaped toward the cooler. "We don't want no green bacon," he said.

The storeman smiled. "So why don't you use those sharp eyes for something good, Duberry? For school maybe?" He put back the rejected bacon and took one from the front.

I said, "Are you putting it back? Are you going to sell it to someone else?"

He winked at me. "I take it out later; I poison the mice."

His whole store smelled of dead animals, I thought, poisoned mice, green bacon. I said, "Coffee too, and some canned things."

"Yes, green beans? Corn? Saltines? Such a pretty young girl, you should spend money on yourself. Buy nice things, yes?"

"That's all."

He pointed. "Three ice creams."

Gilbert was just finishing a Brown Cow and he had taken out two popsicles I hadn't noticed. "Put the popsicles back, Gilbert."

"For my sister," he said. "And the baby." He clutched them against his bare chest and stepped backward. The storekeeper was smiling. High entertainment in the middle of his boring day. Another soft-hearted white girl being conned by the Duberrys.

"You want more people with nothing in the house to eat? I'll make you a list. I know all of them."

He actually started ticking off names, right finger to left palm, but I didn't hear because I saw the digits tattooed on the hairless inside of his forearm: the dark-inked six-digit number. I was particularly caught by the whirling crosshatch of the number 4 seen upside down. The words Gilbert had yelled when I wanted to know where we were going came to me clearly now: he had said Jewstore. He called this miserable little claustrophobic box the Jewstore. Well, how am I supposed to know, I thought. How are you supposed to know who to be sympathetic to if the victims are all obnoxious?

"Come back soon," said the storekeeper. "One thing I got is poor people."

I sent Gilbert home and watched the ridges of his spine as he trotted away. "Gilbert!" I shouted, and his back winced. He half-turned, but kept moving. "What do you say when someone gives you a bag of groceries, Gilbert?" He backpedaled with anxious little steps. "Say 'thank you,' Gilbert," I told him.

He nodded and started running before I could say anything else.

He cares about his family, I thought. He's hurrying so I don't change my mind, so Hooky doesn't show up and knock over his groceries. To my relief I didn't feel like a fool. I was glad on my first day of Vista I'd fed some hungry people. I would come back and talk to the storekeeper some day. It isn't going to be cut-and-dried, I thought. It isn't going to be simple. I could see Dave's face as I told him: the curtailed nod, the fingers at the beard as he gave me and my insight full attention. What are you supposed to think when the victims exploit one another, Dave?

The Williamses' Chrysler was parked in front of a white bungalow with geraniums on the porch and a small sign that said "Neighborhood Center: Tidewater Against Poverty Services, Inc." My new friends from Eastover Street, Charlie and Hooky, were sitting on the steps. They jumped up when they saw me and Charlie's circumflex eyebrows sprang three inches nearer his hairline. "There she go!" he bellowed, and pointed. "There go Miss Blair!"

Hooky grinned. "You in *trouble!*" he said. "You in some trouble!"

I was about to make a joke about how grownups don't get in trouble, but judging by the uproar at the door, I was wrong. Eleanor-Byrd came out first, a full-skirted flowerprint dress swirling around her, hands reaching for me. "Are you all right, Blair, honey? Are you all *right?*"

I saw that everyone was here to witness this: Chuck Williams propped against a porch support; Dave, who did not spring to my defense but stayed back with Roy. Even Shelley and Spencer were here, both wearing sunglasses that reflected light like mirrors and made them look very cool and detached.

I said. "I'm sorry I was later than I said."

Eleanor-Byrd grabbed both my hands and looked in my face. "Honey, we were worried sick about you! We had everybody out looking for you, driving up and down the streets—"

Charlie Conyers said, "Spencer interviewed us if we seen you, and we said we sure had but we didn't know where you went off to."

I disengaged my hands, took a step back to where I could see them all at once—the kids on the steps, Dave on the porch. I said, "Nothing happened. I decided to walk over here the long way, and I met these kids and a boy who took me to his house because they didn't have any food and I bought them a few groceries. That's all that happened."

"Duberrys," said Shelley. "I bet it was the Duberrys."

"Had to be the Duberrys," said Spencer. "What do you think, Chuck?"

Chuck looked startled, as if he hadn't expected to be called on. "Help the people help themselves, as the folks up in Washington like to say."

"There was nothing in their refrigerator but a can of Sterno and an empty box of Carnation dry milk. And it's just as well there wasn't anything else, because the electricity is turned off."

"You went *in* the house?" said Eleanor-Byrd. "You went *inside?* Oh honey!"

"Well come on, Eleanor," said Shelley. "She can't look through walls, can she? What do you expect?"

Eleanor didn't call Shelley honey, I noticed. "It's one thing for you to take chances, Shelley. You know your way around."

"Right, I'm from New York City so I must know my way around."

"That's not what I mean. I mean you've been here a while, and you know something about what's dangerous and what's not. Blair didn't even get her orientation yet." I noticed that Eleanor-Byrd had less of a drawl when she was angry.

"Hey," said Chuck. "Why don't we get inside and finish off that orientation so we can get on home, Eleanor?"

That's a short work day, I thought, as everyone began to head inside the Neighborhood Center. Eleanor leaned toward me and whispered, "Now don't think badly of me, Blair, but I'm the official mother hen for you young people. I have nightmares about you girls living down here in these apartments. I *know* you were doing something good, Blair. I know you're going to be a good, brave Vista." She looked like she wanted me to walk in with her, but I stayed back till she had gone because Dave was waiting for me.

I said, "I was doing what I thought you'd do in the same situation."

He grinned and squeezed my elbow. "Did you now? Did you really? I don't think so. I think you were doing what Blair Morgan would do," and I could tell he liked what I had done. I felt it through his fingers, through the bones of my elbow.

Shelley and Spencer had seen the squeeze too, but I was glad. I wanted everyone to know about me and Dave.

Dave kept his grin going, looking into their eyes, or rather into his own reflection in their mirrored sunglasses. "I was hoping we could get together soon," he said. "Just the South Jenkin Vistas. Find out what's up."

"Sounds good," said Spencer.

"I was going to invite everybody for lasagne anyhow," said Shelley.

"Hey," said Dave. "That sounds just great!" He was alert again, out in the world, taking charge.

Now we are really beginning, I thought. I had done something, on my own, and Dave thought it was the right thing.

Six

The problem was that I had expectations. During the three days in Franklin when I stayed at Dave's apartment, I had begun to anticipate what our life would be like together in Vista. I had imagined a calm, silent cocoon, a safe haven of love, where I would sit on Dave's lap, or lie in his bed or merely stand in the room with him and feel the silence vibrate between us. This would be the center of our lives, and from this center we would go forth every day, Dave and I, into the world. We would work hard. We would organize people and fight oppression, and in the evening we would have a couple of hours of passionate conversation with the other Vistas about our work before retiring to our sustaining center.

But instead of having this center with Dave, I was being plunged into a bath of new people. The person I would see first in the morning and last at night would be Shelley, who, like Teale at college, was exotic to me, and attractive, and sometimes repellent. I loved to hear her talk, but was troubled that she didn't talk much about goals and our mission. Mostly she talked about people: the Williamses, the Landells, even Spencer.

She talked now as she sliced cheese for the lasagne, and I iced a cake under the loops of fish net on the kitchen ceiling. She talked as she went down the hall to her room, so I followed and watched her strip out of her dungaree skirt and embroidered blouse. She kept talking as she stood unembarrassed in front of me in flowered bikini underpants and nylon bra. Her stomach was muscular, but her hips flared out into wide thighs, a sheath of softness over strength. She put on a slithery green dress and flat green slippers with string ties around the ankle.

"You're dressing up," I said. "Should I get dressed up?"

"I just feel like a party every once in a while. You know."

Actually I didn't know; I dressed according to what I thought was required for the occasion.

She said, leading me back down the hall, "I asked Frank and Yvetta Landell to come over tonight, but Frank has some kind of meeting at church, and Yvetta won't come without him. She wouldn't come anyhow if she knew the boys might come over. Frank is okay, but she is just a twenty-year-old 'bushwah collard lady.' I'm quoting Spencer; I'd never call her that myself, but Spencer knows all about the black bourgeoisie. He's from a pretty classy family himself. You have to hear him take off on the Cotillion, which is when these black high school girls do the debutante thing. Spencer does *wonderful* imitations. You've got to get him to do his Baptist preacher sometime."

When I heard the Volkswagen pull up outside, I started feeling vaguely guilty, as if I'd been listening to something I shouldn't. Then the house filled with them: Spencer, long and elegant, tan clothes, leather sandals. Beside him Dave looked stocky, solid as a rock, but slightly old-fashioned in his plaid shirt and workpants. Roy followed them, carrying a gallon jug of red wine on each thumb.

"I've got the lasagne in," said Shelley. "We can eat in fifteen or twenty minutes."

"Smells great," said Dave. "Terrific of you to fix dinner for us. Just great."

Shelley didn't seem to smile very much. "It's only lasagne. And I like to cook."

"She can cook, and she's gorgeous too," said Spencer. "Looking *real* good."

To my surprise, after the way she had praised him, she

ignored his compliment and said to Dave, "Has Spencer started pestering you yet? He's in heaven, you know, now that he's got someone to drive him around in a car. He likes his gang to see him in a car."

Spencer didn't seem surprised to be rebuffed. "No offense, but a Volkswagen isn't exactly my idea of the ideal car." He pulled a piece of lettuce out of the salad and ate it. "Besides, Shell, you know me. I want a pink Cadillac with white side-walls."

"Now he's going to make fun of himself. Spencer'll do anything for a laugh. He'd sell his mother for a laugh."

He shook his head. "Starting in on my mother!" I couldn't decide how to take them. Was this an entertainment staged for us, or were they like this all the time?

"I want to drink some wine," said Roy. His voice sounded deep and far away, and there was something new in his eyes. I glanced at Dave for a reaction, but he was turning his face politely from Spencer to Shelley and back again. Shelley put out some glasses, and Roy knocked back wine like medicine. Dave took a glass too, but didn't drink right away. He said, "Why did you join Vista, Spencer?"

" 'Cause I hate the way I look in a uniform. And if I did get into a uniform, I hate even more the idea of blood messing it up." Dave smiled, and Spencer went on. "Seriously, though, I wanted to do something with teenagers. I always felt like I could communicate with them."

"He communicates by standing on the street corner with them all day, drinking beer out of brown bags," said Shelley. "When they get old enough, they graduate to brown-bagging wine."

"What a mean mouth," said Spencer. "Shelley has truly a mean mouth."

"In my family," said Shelley, "you're either a political activist or an accountant. Every generation. I had a grand-father who was a boy in Russia, and he used to hide under a basket when the Cossacks rode by. He was the one who got out and came over here."

99

Spencer said, "The accountant side of her family makes money so the activists don't have to work for a living."

"It's true. I hate to say it."

I decided I admired the way they talked to each other. I admired the smooth way her arms worked, blending garlic butter below the rolled-up sleeves of her good green dress. And I admired Spencer's exposed long toes, with nails pinker than his skin and a crook at the knuckle so they didn't lie flat but rested in a slight cup, making a gesture, eloquent like hands. Shelley and Spencer splashed color wherever they were: deep green, shades of tan, pink, and the russet of her hair. They weren't professionally amiable like Dave, or scowling because they weren't comfortable, like Roy. Shelley and Spencer, I thought, said what was on their minds, directly. I didn't know why they sniped at one another, but at least they weren't hypocritically holding back.

I had a reason for being a Vista too, but I didn't tell it. When I was seven or eight, at church they had given us a beautiful set of paper dolls of missionaries in the Congo. I loved the lithe natives and the little thatched house, and I had wanted to grow up and do good in some of the exciting, far reaches of the earth. But I didn't say anything about it, for fear of sounding racist or stupid, or something far worse that I was too ignorant even to know about.

We ate in the kitchen, crowded elbow to elbow around the big pan of lasagne, the wooden bowl of salad, the jug of wine. Shelley served food and Roy poured wine. I figured it was as good a time as any to start drinking, so every few bites, with my mouth full, I would sip a little wine. All I could taste, though, was garlic.

Roy didn't alternate anything with his wine. He drank glass after glass, and when he caught me watching him once, he said in a low voice, twisting his lips to one side as if he hated the taste, and with that strange dark opacity in his eyes, "Blair Ellen, if I get drunk, will you pray for me?"

"You better not get drunk."

He brought an index finger to his lips and mimed an elaborate shush. "I forgot," he whispered. "We aren't supposed to mention *Him* anymore. I shouldn't have said anything about *praying*."

"Please go easy, okay?"

"Not a word," he said. "Not a word about *Him*."

I looked to Dave again, but Dave was drawing out Shelley and Spencer. I knew his technique by now, the same one he had used on my parents: the receptive smile and nod, the peals of laughter as if he wanted to hold back but their wit was just too much for him.

Spencer performed the cast of TAPS for us. He did imitations of Executive Director Delbert Jackson and Eleanor-Byrd and Chuck Williams and most of the secretaries and neighborhood workers out in the Neighborhood Centers.

Shelley said, "Delbert's the executive director, but Eleanor and Chuck really run TAPS. They're the ones who wrote off the teenagers of South Jenkin."

Dave's smile faded. Why did they do that, he wanted to know. What were the Williamses really interested in?

"The Williamses," said Spencer, "are interested in power. You know? Power for the Williamses."

"Politics?" said Dave. "Is he running for something?"

"Chickenshit," said Shelley. "Running chickenshit scared is what they're doing."

Spencer said, "This dance we're having next week is the first time they've ever let us near a TAPS facility. We have movie parties and beach parties, and one party once at Frank Landell's church, and parties in this apartment, and TAPS does nothing, doesn't lift a finger, to help us. Finally, after months—I'm telling you *months*—of negotiations, they are letting us in their precious Neighborhood Center."

"It's going to be a terrific dance," said Shelley. "Coca-Cola Bottling Company is giving us free soda—"

"We're renting big amplifiers—"

"Alvetta White is up in arms," said Shelley. "She's the Neighborhood Worker. You met her—trim looking black lady who dresses like every day was Sunday? Well, her main concern is the *building* and the reputation of dear old TAPS. She's one of the people who worship whoever's the top man. Right, Spencer? She just *gushes* over *Mr.* Delbert Jackson and *Mr.* Chuck Williams. She's practically demanding an affadavit from us that her precious TAPS building won't get scuffed floors from the dancing or cigarette butts in her ivy plants."

I piped in. "We want to help, don't we, Dave?"

"Of course. Absolutely. You tell us what needs doing and we'll do it. But I was curious, aside from the teenagers, what kind of community organizing is TAPS doing in South Jenkin? What's happening at the Neighborhood Center, for example?"

"Nothing," said Shelley. "Alvetta White sits in the Center and makes cafe curtains for her house on the sewing machine that was supposed to be for classes for neighborhood people. Spencer and I have been working to get a recreation center for the teens." She made a face. "And oh yes, I have a Girl Scout troop. Would you believe it? There's a camp for them, this summer. We take trips. I don't know. We have a good time."

Dave leaned forward, scratching his fork through the sauce on his plate. "What is the really *big* issue with the people here? The thing that would galvanize the whole community? The one thing that people already have on their minds, whether they've articulated it or not? I mean something that, if you asked every man, woman, and child in South Jenkin to make a list, might not appear as everyone's Number One, but would be up there in the top three or four for all of them."

Spencer said, "Everyone worries about the teenagers. The old ladies are afraid to go out, and the parents are afraid their kids will drop out. This neighborhood needs a center for the kids."

Dave made eye contact with Spencer. "Hey, Spencer, don't get me wrong. I'm not denigrating your work here. My Lord! I couldn't agree with you more that this neighborhood needs a teen center. What I'm saying is that people won't go out on the line demanding it."

102

"Why not?"

"Too narrow. And it has a lightweight sound—recreation. Don't get me wrong, I don't think it *is* lightweight, but it doesn't have the universality of an issue like, say, housing."

Spencer said, "Then work on housing. They need housing."

"I don't know *what* they need. I'm asking. I want to ask them. Maybe it's health care. Every community has its issue. A deadline helps, too. For example, do you know of any plans to raze the neighborhood and put up something the people don't want, a shopping center or a military facility?"

Spencer had tipped his chair way back against the wall. "Man, they would rejoice if some fool decided to put up a shopping center!"

"They tore down a couple of blocks for new housing and then ran out of money," said Shelley. "But that was years ago."

Dave nodded. "I think I'll go down to City Hall and see what I can turn up. We need a big issue."

Spencer said, "I've never been all that ambitious myself. A recreation center for teenagers would satisfy me."

"Hey," said Dave. "Me too. One concrete thing at a time. That's all there ever is in the end." He scooted his chair closer to Spencer, trying to make amends. I hoped Spencer wasn't mad. Since we were here, since we were in this, I wanted us all together. One concrete thing at a time, I thought. The dance first. Spencer didn't look exactly appeased. But he did look as if he might be appeased soon.

They went in the living room and Shelley and I cleaned up. Stacking dishes, she said, "Your old man moves right in, doesn't he?"

"He knows about this stuff. He worked with Saul Alinsky."

"Uh huh," said Shelley.

"Dave isn't being critical. It's just that when he thinks we're all in it together, he isn't quite as careful how he says things." It seemed blasphemous at first, to be making excuses for Dave, but after a moment, pleasantly heady. "When he doesn't trust people, he's extremely polite, he handles them with kid gloves. But when he decides they're on the same side he is, he gets very honest. It's a kind of compliment."

"I notice he's like all the rest of them, though, when the dishes get dirty." She stepped out into the hall, and shouted, "Spencer! I cooked, you wash!"

But it was Dave who came in to do dishes, and I was proud, vindicated in front of Shelley. Dave *was* a sensitive person, she could see. He and I did them together, while Shelley bustled around starting coffee, until some of Spencer's boys arrived.

I would never have called them boys if I had passed them on the street; they all looked full grown to me: tall, with long reaches of arm and exaggerated distances between foot and knee. One of them, though, was shorter, muscled like a man who grew up under several times the force of gravity, a native of Jupiter. They caused a transformation in Spencer. He lost his regular voice and began talking in a half-drawl, half-murmur. All his words seemed to be encased in a long sleeve that unraveled slowly or rapidly, but always at a speed that didn't quite allow me to comprehend. I didn't get any of their names at first, except for the thick one named Bo-ji. Perhaps it was because of the way Spencer said the names, and perhaps I didn't want to. They stood in a row along the wall and in the wooden archway between the hall and the red living room, and Spencer stood with them. He put on tinted sunglasses that made his face look languid and sullen.

Dave, Roy, and I sat on the pillows, in a row, with our knees splayed in front of us. The boys said little, but shifted their bodies every now and then, making the floor creak. I began to distinguish among them a little now: Bo-ji the muscular one, next to him one with eyebrows like my Eastover friend Charlie Conyers. Then a slim boy with better clothes than the others, who laughed frequently and had a lot of cloudy soft hair sticking out from under a cream colored golf cap. His laughing and the other boys' taciturnity made me think they were feeling awkward too, but I wasn't reassured. Where were the girl teenagers? How would I ever be a Vista if I had to work with this crowd of thighs and shoulders? They reminded me—against my will, because I wanted to love the people of South Jenkin—of the Sigma Chi's. They had the same group power, the same way of standing massed together, a shield-wall of chests.

I told myself: These are kids who need help. They need a recreation center. Spencer is working with them, he's just being like this so he can work with them better. But all the time I was feeling a threat from Spencer too.

Shelley was undaunted, though. She started passing out plates of cake, stuck one in the hands of each boy. Some of them thanked her politely. "Spence," she said, "why don't you put on the Ledbelly record?"

Spencer seemed enormously slow to peel himself off the wall, but when he did, he bowed. "Yes, ma'am, Miss Shelley."

"Don't joke around," she said. "You're the one who says they should hear the blues. You're the one who says they don't know anything about their heritage."

Spencer began to grin and danced on his toes like a little boy who has to go potty. "Naw, Miss Shelley, my idea of heritage music is the Supremes. And—ah, James Brown. Ain't you got some nice good James Brown records?"

The boys shuffled and made some noises. Shelley's face went hard. I don't know why she was surprised; it seemed obvious to me there was no use appealing to Spencer in his sunglasses with his boys around. "Asshole clown," she said, and turned on her heel.

"Uh oh," said the well-dressed boy; "Whoa," said Bo-ji. Spencer went back to his other voice, midwestern as a television announcer's, "I think I insulted her."

Dave said, "I think you did," and got himself up off the pillow. He headed straight for Bo-ji and began talking to him. Spencer shrugged, put the record on the hi-fi, and drifted out of the room toward the kitchen. I was left with Roy and his wine glass. I decided I would plunge into a conversation just the way Dave had. I could ask questions too: What are the main problems around South Jenkin as you see them? Do you go to school? Why did you drop out? I actually chose the boy I thought might be a relative of Charlie Conyers. He was standing in the archway, and I panicked at the last moment and veered past him, met myself in the mirror on the hall tree, and was unfavorably impressed by the pale face and tight mouth. I looked scared and unfriendly at the same time, like Roy's pinched little hollow-dwelling parents.

Someone was knocking on the door, and as I went to open it, I promised myself that, whoever it was, I would be genial and welcoming and start a conversation. To my intense relief, it was a woman. She was all dressed in orange, and had a sleek red-brown page boy that didn't quite go with the color of her skin. Bracelets jangled on her arms, and she carried two brown paper bags.

"Hi!" I said. "I'm the new Vista, Blair Morgan. Come on in!"

"Where's Shelley?" she said.

She looked vaguely familiar . . . something in the small chin and sharp bones of the jaw and forehead. Then I noticed the gold bedroom mules she was wearing and said, "Oh, I bet you're the one who lives in the same building with Spencer—and you have a little girl named Jewel."

Her cheeks dimpled like the child's. "Jewel *said* there was a nice new girl-Vista over this way. That child is Vista-crazy. She wants to go to Scouts with Miss Shelley and the beach with Spencer— Speak of the devil," she said, as he came out of the kitchen. "Hey, Spencer."

"Hey, Duchess," said Spencer, in still another voice, this one rich and resonant, a setting for the cheek kiss he gave her.

"I brought the forty-fives," she said. "The other bag's got the you-know-what. Now who all's here?" She pressed on into the living room. She knew Dave and Roy already, and she gave Shelley a kiss. "Good God Almighty," she said. "Shelley told me there was going to be a party, but Spencer's got all his little boyfriends over here!"

Duchess removed the blues record without ceremony and called for a plastic disk to make her records fit the turntable. She put on Diana Ross and the Supremes, who sang "My Mama told me, you just can't hurry love!" and started dancing with Spencer.

Shelley danced too, with the well-dressed boy she called Harold. She danced with abandon, but I thought her steps were too big, and her arms moved too much, at least compared with Duchess and Spencer. They seemed to make an invisible alliance between their two bodies, never wasting energy, never moving outside the boundaries they had set for themselves.

But after a while, Duchess said, "Why don't you all dance?" She had a commanding way about her—put a fist on her hipbone and waved her hand to get the boys in a line, and then created a special back row for me and Roy when I insisted we didn't know the dance. Dave, I saw, had slipped out when the group dance began. Roy wasn't very steady on his feet, but it seemed to amuse him to be dancing. He chuckled as he stumbled a couple of times. I got the general idea pretty quickly; it was two steps this way, two steps that, then clap, turn, start it all over. I tried to keep my movements small, the way Spencer and Duchess had danced, but also because I was afraid of being in the wrong place at the wrong time and bumping against one of the tall bodies blocking me from the rest of the room and its red glow. I kept getting distracted, too, by Roy's slow spins and spirals that had nothing to do with the step. He waved his arms, and sometimes reached with them. I was relieved when the dance dissipated before he lurched into someone. When the line dance was over, Dave reappeared with a beer. I was heading toward him, but Spencer intercepted me and offered me a glass of something clear.

"What is it?"

"White lightning. Duchess's brother makes it."

My hand jerked back involuntarily. "That stuff makes people go blind."

"Your friend from the mountains doesn't seem too worried. Maybe he takes to it naturally."

Duchess was pouring from a mayonnaise jar into Roy's glass, and Roy did something stupid and rubbery with his face that made her laugh. Cans of beer had appeared in the hands of the boys. I said, "Are you going to give that poison stuff to the teenagers too?"

"Don't worry. Duchess isn't very generous with it." He was leaning over me, arm on the wall, taking a slow sip, his eyes hidden behind the sunglasses. "Shall we dance?"

I shook my head. I was sorry I did it so quickly, as if I had decided long ago not to dance with him. I didn't like the stuff he was drinking and I didn't like his teenagers and I didn't think it was right to give them beer. I also didn't intend to look like a flailing ninny trying to dance with him.

"Some other time," he murmured, flattening himself against the wall so I could pass, and I did, in a hurry, to get to Dave.

Dave put his arm around me. That felt much better, but I was still restless. I said, "I hope you aren't getting drunk too." He smiled, didn't speak. I wasn't really joking, though. "Are you watching Roy? He's had some of everything there is to drink. And that moonshine whiskey, it doesn't seem like they should have that in here with those boys." Dave was nodding, but I realized it was in time to the music. I said, "It just seems irresponsible to me."

"Okay. I agree. What do you want to do about it?"

I had imagined vaguely that Dave would take hold of things, stop the music, make a speech. Overturn a few tables and chase out the bad guys. "*I* don't know. *I* don't know what to do."

He said, "Well, I was thinking maybe we should leave."

"Go back to your apartment? What about Roy? What about Shelley and Spencer's party?"

"You decide, Blair. Do you think they're irresponsible, or do you want to make sure their party's a success?"

I was overwhelmed by a feeling of things stuck together that didn't match: Diana Ross's voice, at once little and dominant; the woman, Duchess, with dimples like Jewel's, and yet she carried around illegal whiskey in a paper bag. The boys who said nothing and filled the house with a kind of terrible noise. Dave, the one I trusted to answer my questions, turning them all back on me.

Meanwhile Roy had started dancing with Duchess. Or rather, not really dancing and not really *with* her, but making more of his spins and spirals. Once he gave a mountaineer holler and the boys poked each other and guffawed.

"Can't you stop him?" I said to Dave.

"He's drunk."

"It's *obvious* that he's drunk. But he shouldn't *be* drunk." No one was taking charge. No one was taking care of Roy. The room seemed as red and throbbing as the inside of a swollen heart.

After a while Roy did one of his arm stretches and then extended it wide and tipped his face back as if clouds had parted and shafts of light were falling on him. He was tipping, tipping, toppling backward like a great pine tree.

I shouted, "Dave!"

Roy fell like a tree too, with no leg folding, no elbow bending to break the fall. The only thing that saved him from real injury was that his head struck one of the pillows. The rest of him landed on bare floor with a powerful reverberation. He lay there, face red and slimy with sweat, his mouth still smiling beatifically.

Harold clapped his hands and made a sort of half a dance twirl. "Look at that," he said, laughing and shaking his head. "He fell right over!" The others were laughing too. Bo-ji said, "He just went over backwards," and they all made imitations of his fall with their hands.

I couldn't believe they thought it was funny. I started babbling, "He never drank before in his life. They don't drink in his family—he doesn't know how to drink. He's just drunk, though, and not hurt, isn't he, Dave?"

Roy made a lurch as if to get up, then curled onto one side.

"He'll be all right," said Dave.

"Sure," said Spencer. "He just wants to sleep it off."

"You might as well take him home," said Duchess, planting the fist on her hip again and making a sweeping gesture with her long fingers pointed down. "Nobody can't dance with him all over the floor." She swept the boys out, too, and then the rest of us lifted Roy to his feet and dragged him to the Volkswagen. Three of us in the back seat—Shelley, Duchess, and me—plus Roy draped over our knees like a hairless bearskin. Spencer kept making jokes, and Shelley told him he should sit back here if he thought it was so funny.

Everyone fell silent, though, as we turned up Old Fellows Street. This was my first visit to the Vista apartment there, and the pooled darkness made me thankful I wasn't alone. There were more gaping empty lots than buildings, and one streetlamp for the whole dead-end street. Of its existing, identical buildings—grim, dark blocks against an overcast night sky—only three had any lights on, and those lights seemed weak, the windows small. Duchess said she was looking forward to the day when the Vistas did something really useful and got her a new place to live. When Dave asked her if housing was the main problem around South Jenkin, she said she didn't know about South Jenkin, but *her* main problem was Roy's elbow in her stomach.

Their building was as desolate inside as the street was outside, and I felt a shameful pleasure knowing I would be going home to sleep in our place with its mahogany halltree and red living room. The little girl Jewel met us on the raw wood stairs, and it jarred me to think she was being raised in this place. She seemed skinnier here, whiney and demanding. Had Duchess left her here alone while she went to the party? Duchess started yelling that Jewel was supposed to be in bed, and they disappeared into their apartment, opposite the Vistas'.

You entered the Vista apartment through its kitchen, and passed the bathroom, which was separated from the kitchen by two sheets of plasterboard and an ill-fitting door. There was a longish living room next, and two bedrooms at the far end. They dumped Roy in the room with two cots; Spencer had the single room, where he had a lot of Black Power posters and a bookshelf of paperback books. He saw me in his doorway, so I said, "Do you read *Malcolm X* with your teenagers?"

"Have you read him?"

"Sure," I said, too casually to be honest. I had read the book, but only a month ago, because Dave assigned it.

"How about this?" It was plays by Leroi Jones. I'd never heard of him, but I was glad to borrow the book. I thought Spencer probably didn't talk about his serious ideas to most white people.

I said, "Do you read with those boys that were over at our house tonight?"

"A little. When they're ready. You have to stay where they are."

I was going to express how worried I was that I wouldn't be able to work with those boys, but there was a lot of shifting underway. No one was staying in one room very long. Shelley came out, and Spencer went back in with Dave and Roy.

Shelley said, "This place doesn't have rats, hard to believe as it might seem, but they do have the world's ugliest cats. *Dozens* of cats. A special breed that only lives in houses on Old Fellows Street. Every now and then one of them crawls into the oven to keep warm and then gets baked when they start dinner."

She went to the bathroom, another restless shift. I sat down on a prickly couch with patterns shaved into the plush like a case of cultivated ringworm. Dave came back now and sat down beside me, facing forward. "Listen," he said. "Spencer offered to go back to your place tonight. We can stay here and use his room. He offered to do it, and I offered him the car to drive them back over."

I started to say, Why don't we go back and let them stay here, but guiltily realized we were responsible for Roy. "Okay," I said. "Sure, that's great."

I had thought it was what I wanted, this kind of public avowal of our relationship. Dave had always kept me such a secret at college. But now that it was actually happening, now that he was making it clear to everyone that we slept together —arranging it so we could be together tonight—I felt humiliated. I felt as if we were at a fraternity party and the brothers were splitting up the girls, divvying up the couches and sleeping bags. I hated the plasterboard walls of this place, the splinters in the wooden floor, the gas heater in the corner— everything in the apartment soiled me.

I locked myself in the bathroom with the light out so I wouldn't see any more ugliness, till I heard Shelley and Spencer leave. When I came out, Dave met me in the middle of the living room and pressed my face against his chest. I raised heavy arms to embrace him. What do you want? I asked myself. Don't you even know what you want? Don't you want what you want once you get it? You're with Dave; it doesn't matter where you are, does it? But I was jealous that Spencer and Shelley got to go back to our place. I wanted to be in my funny, narrow room with my poster of *Christina's World*. I didn't want to sleep with Dave on Spencer's bed.

I didn't admit it to myself then—I wouldn't let the thought rise to consciousness—but I was disappointed in Dave. I was disappointed in the roughness of his hands rubbing up and down my arms, and in the prickle of his mouth kissing my mouth. I couldn't bear it that he made sordid little arrangements to have sex with me. That he traded use of his car for use of Spencer's bed. That everyone was treating him just like another one of the group. Even during the heavy nudging of flesh, in Spencer's dark little room strewn with clothes and luminescent posters, I felt hugely separated from him. I had no idea in the world of what he was experiencing. And it never occurred to me to ask until long, long after.

Seven

Tossing against Dave's body in the single bed, I slept badly, waking often in a half-dreaming rage at being trammeled, to find his knee on my thigh or his shoulder wedging me against the wall. Sometime in the morning, though, I began to sleep deeply, finally waking at the cessation of a woman's voice. I opened my eyes and saw, as if she had been the one talking, a poster of a black woman with an enormous natural hairdo and long legs. What little light there was in the room was drawn to an aura of luminescent paint around her, pink and livid yellow.

Dave was gone, hours ahead of me, no doubt. He had said he would go downtown to do some research; *he* already knew his work, had gone off to do it, while I was still sleeping. I found my blouse and skirt on the floor, crossed with crumple marks, creased from sitting. The nicest thing I could imagine was a shower, but what if Spencer was still at our apartment? Should I go, or did I have to stay here? I made the bed, picked up the towel that Dave had laid under us last night, and quietly eased myself out into the living room. The place was gray and silent, with no sign of people, but still I tiptoed to the bathroom. It was damp from someone's bath, and I found a pile of wet towels on the floor and hid ours in the middle. I washed my mouth with water, and sat on the edge only of the spotted toilet seat.

I meant to tiptoe right out, go home, even if Spencer was there. Surely he wouldn't be in my little room. I would get to my room, shower, and put on fresh clothes, and then figure out what I was supposed to do with myself now that I was a Vista. Before going, though, I took a peek in the other bedroom, a tiny look to see if Roy was still there, and he was; sitting bolt upright in his cot with an empty plate on his lap. He was looking straight at me, so I said, "Hi, Roy."

"Good. It's you. I have to tell you something."

I didn't go all the way into the room, but braced myself on the door jamb, wondering if he knew I'd been here all night.

"The reason I have to talk to you," he said. "The reason I have to talk—" He shifted his position slightly, but when he did, he grimaced and waved a hand ineffectually toward his forehead.

"Headache?" I said. "You and I, Roy, we have no business drinking."

He lowered the hand carefully back to his lap. "It's got nothing to do with drinking. I got a message last night. I know we're not using *His* name, so I won't name any names. But He gave me a message."

"I don't think I want to hear it."

"The message was, *Become as one of these.* And when that woman came over here this morning, I knew she was part of it. I was supposed to do it through her."

"What are you talking about, Roy?"

"The message was 'Don't mouth names and hollow prayers, just *Become as one of these.*'"

I opened my mouth to say I didn't know what he was talking about, but I did know. I had seen it last night, the way he opened his arms and turned his face up: he had been getting a Call, a message for him alone, a special mission.

He said, "That woman took a bath over here. She brought me a sandwich, too."

"What woman? Duchess? Why did she take a bath here?"

"It doesn't matter. Her tub's broken. But the thing I had to tell you was, what's between us, it has to be over. Everything's okay, because I can't love you now anyhow."

114

Well for heavensakes, I thought. He's presumptuous even when he's crazy!

"You mustn't take it wrong, that's what I have to tell you. It's because of the message. Otherwise I meant to be faithful."

"Roy, there was nothing to be faithful about. Dave and I—"

He lifted his hand slightly again. "I was going to be faithful to both of you. But this changes everything. I'm going to become one of them."

His eyes were closed, sunken deep, with dark stains under them; I was sure he had a fierce headache, but he was smiling. His face was at once pale with pain and relaxed. He's happy, I thought, Roy's got a purpose again. He'll get drunk every night if he can get Calls.

I said, "It's fine with me if you aren't faithful anymore." His smile widened, but he didn't open his eyes. "Okay," I said. "Goodbye. I'm leaving now." I backed out, then looked in one last time, but he still hadn't moved, so I left.

You had a choice for getting from Old Fellows Street back to Eastover. The logical way was to turn right and make a left at the corner, but I saw a group of men standing around a low building with a sign that said Red Hat Bar and Grill, so I went left to where the street ended abruptly at a field of rubble heaps. I scrambled and lurched over these mounds of brick, dirt, and broken glass, each one representing a torn-down house, I supposed. Dirt accumulated between my foot and the leather of my sandals; I broke into a sweat from the glowering sun. Yet I also had this sense of adventure and a sort of pride in taking the direct route through this abandoned war zone to my house. Once I started to slip, and my hand barely missed a rusty bedspring, but I slid down triumphantly to the sidewalk.

I lost courage, though, in front of my house. I could see children halfway up the block at Conyerses', and I thought I would just go up and say hello to them, and meanwhile give Spencer and Shelley a little longer to get up, or leave, or whatever it was I was afraid of surprising them at. I took my time approaching the green house; there was something in the heat, near noon now, that made slowness seem appropriate. Charlie Conyers didn't run to meet me, either. He stood as I approached and said seriously, "My mama's up here."

"I've been wanting to meet her," I said, thankful for something I should do, not even so much worried about the condition of my clothing in this heat that seemed to slick over everything equally with sweat.

The green reed blinds on the porch blocked most of the light, filtered some, creating a rain forest dimness. Charlie stepped aside, and I could see a woman at the far end of the porch taking up most of a couch tipped to one side with a broken leg. A woman so large that she seemed to be held from running over the edges of the couch only by a tautly zippered green dress whose bodice held in her breast, whose skirt contained her sagging knees. The child, Little Bit, was on her lap, smiling a smile identical with the woman's. I was so intent on approaching that I almost stumbled over Hooky on the floor, putting laces into a pair of black basketball sneakers for a smaller boy.

"Well, well," the woman said. "So this is Blair Morgan. Charlie! Clear off that chair and let Miss Blair sit down." Charlie gave me a kitchen chair with a vinyl seat whose stuffing was coming out. "Now what I want to know," she said, "is why you been visiting everybody up and down Eastover except me." She burst out laughing, either because she was making a joke or because she was amused by my appalled expression.

I said, "But, Mrs. Conyers—"

"Call me Marie, baby." She had short black hair that curled around a small, even pretty face that was full of energy, as if it had a life of its own separate from the enormous body spilling below it. The look she gave me was almost flirtatious, a quick sidelong glance, then a spreading grin. "Little Bit, get off your mama now, you make me so hot. I am so hot in this weather, Blair Morgan." She put down Little Bit, who balanced herself against her mother's knee. "Don't you think it's hot, or you from someplace that makes this seem like nothing?"

"West Virginia. I'm from West Virginia."

"Oh, the mountains. I bet it's nice and cool up in those mountains."

"We get pretty hot weather before the summer's over."

Marie shifted herself and grunted deep down in her throat as if that huge belly thrust out between her and me were a burden, but one so familiar and private that her grunting was somehow private too. She still smiled, though, and lifted her eyebrows higher and higher while I told her all I knew about the weather in West Virginia. Something about her made me want to talk; I wanted to talk so much that I would have talked about anything, but she listened so attentively to my discourse on West Virginia weather that it seemed like the best thing I could have come up with. She made a couple of little murmurs of agreement and exclamations of interest as I expanded on my theme. When I paused, she told me how hot it used to be down in North Carolina when she was a girl, but that it never bothered her the way this Tidewater heat bothered her now. She made a joke about how she didn't used to be so fat when she was a girl, either.

"Do you know what I think we need?" said Marie. "I think we need us something cold to drink."

"Sounds good to me," said Charlie, and I realized that he and Hooky and the other little boy had been listening to us the way I used to listen when the grownups talked, on porches, in cars. Little Bit launched herself from her mother's knee to mine. Just like a real grownup, I picked her up.

Marie reached for a pocketbook that was at one end of the couch. It was the only object on the whole porch not broken or worn or needing laces: shiny black patent leather with a heavy gilt clasp and a thick double handle. I said, "Oh, let me pay," but I had the baby on my lap and was too slow. She unfastened the bag and looked in it for a long while before pulling out a change purse. I had a glimpse of some lacy beige garment folded up in there. She gave Charlie a dollar, and the three boys ran off.

She must have noticed me looking at the bag because she said, "That's my new pocketbook. I wanted something roomy. Big as a suitcase." She laughed suddenly. "You don't want that dirty child on your pink skirt."

"Oh, this old thing," I said. I started to say it was filthy, and I was just going home to change it, but I remembered where I slept last night. "Besides, Little Bit's not dirty." Actually Little Bit, who had begun to play with my buttons, wasn't the cleanest baby I had ever seen. In the parts between her little braids there was something like sand, and her cotton undershirt had food on it.

"Oh yes she is," said Marie. "I know when my children are dirty. They play all day in the dirt one way or the other. You can't make a *lawn* around here. You start out keeping everything so nice and fresh and then one day there's another child and you get behind and all of a sudden you look up and there's a houseful and you just *know* you never going to have things nice again." Another short burst of laughter and the sidelong, flirtatious glance. I was having trouble knowing what she laughed at sometimes. I could sense shades of meaning flitting past me.

I said, "I think I met your oldest son. There were some boys over at our apartment last night."

"Brother? He's not my oldest, he's just my tallest. I have one boy in the Marines, and a girl married. I have seven children."

I tried to count them up, Brother and Charlie and Little Bit. The other little boy and the two older ones. Did Hooky count? Little Bit had stopped playing with the buttons and seemed to be falling asleep with her face between my breasts. I could feel her gradual, inexorable relaxation. One foot, fat above, dangling toes with tiny nails, slid off my knee. I was flushed with a fantasy that this sinking into my flesh of her flesh would be impossible to reverse. That the baby would be grafted onto me, and one day I would give birth to her, and wake up like Marie Conyers in a big run-down green house with seven children.

There were footsteps on the walk, and a slim woman in a white uniform with her hair in a long black flip came up the steps, paused for a moment with a hand on her hip, then strode onto the porch like she owned the place, staring at me.

"Look who's here," said Marie.

The woman pulled up a backless wooden chair and crossed her legs, fumbled for a cigarette.

I was on the verge of introducing myself to her when the little girl Jewel came up the steps too: Jewel lovely again with earrings and bracelets and impeccable blue checked shorts and frilly top. She smiled at me, took the drowsy baby off my lap and started walking around the porch with her in her arms.

To my horror, I realized the woman was Duchess. I hadn't recognized her with the long black hair. I had sat thigh to thigh with this woman in the Volkswagen last night. It was the hair that tricked me. Wigs, I thought. A reddish helmet last night, the black flip today. How was *I* supposed to know she wore wigs? You aren't a racist for not recognizing someone who disguises herself, are you?

To make sure Duchess knew I knew her, I said, "I was over at Old Fellows Street just now, checking on Roy. He was grateful for the sandwich you made him."

She stared at me so long I thought I was wrong and it wasn't Duchess after all. But finally she said, "Ain't he an *unusual* sort of fellow?"

Marie said, "You look like a mean mood today, Duchess."

Duchess shrugged. "They call me on my day off and say they just have to have me for the afternoon shift, and my bathtub's broke and I had to go over there to those Vistas again to take a bath and I'm tired, that's what's the matter with me. I'm beginning to smell like that damn hospital."

The boys came back with the drinks then, and Marie sent Charlie in the house for cups. We sipped orange pop and Pepsi-Cola for a while, and then Charlie said, "Well, whose bathroom do I use this time?"

"What's wrong with *your* bathroom?" said Duchess. "Is your bathroom broke again, too?"

I said, "What do you do when that happens, call your landlord?"

Duchess made a face. "Not me. We both of us have Lejeune for a landlord, so we don't waste our breath."

"Yes, baby," said Marie. "You wouldn't know about him. You renting from TAPS, but Lejeune is something else."

"Something evil is what."

Charlie was nodding, like a very short, elderly gentleman. "One of these days somebody is going to shoot old Lejoon and not miss him like Robert Foley did."

Hooky smiled faintly and picked up a broom that was lying on the floor. Charlie and Hooky both looked at the women as if they were expecting to be stopped, but Marie began to fan herself with a comic book and Duchess kept sipping, staring into space. Deliberately Charlie paced off an area, with Hooky just outside the perimeter.

"Yes," said Charlie, "Robert Foley got tired of old Lejoon one day. Robert Foley was there at the house when Mr. Lejoon came collecting the rent—"

Jewel said, "He don't come around in person *now*, do he, Mama?"

"And ol' Lejoon he come knocking on Miz Foley door saying I know you in there Miz Foley, and I know you in there Robert and if you don't pay the rent money I'm sending you and you mama both to jail!"

Hooky began to grin. He stepped back and lifted the broom to his shoulder—slowly, slowly, giving Charlie plenty of time to finish the story, making it all come together at the right moment. No trace of cynicism in Hooky's face now, only an exquisite enjoyment.

"And Robert Foley!" shouted Charlie, stomping a foot

120

and freezing. "And Robert Foley he said Don't you talk about sending my mama to jail!"

"Naw," murmured Hooky. "Don't talk like that, *fool*."

"And Robert Foley! He gets his great big gun and he shoots right through that door, blow that door to pieces!"

"Pough!" screamed Hooky, giving himself a hard recoil to the shoulder. "Pough! Pough!"

Charlie smote himself in the chest and collapsed, wheezing and thumping. Gently Hooky lowered the gun and ducked his face away in a shy smile.

I clapped. "You guys are real actors."

Marie pretended to frown. "Oh they can play-act all right. They good for play-acting."

Charlie sat up. "Only Lejoon never did die. He got up and run off. Takes more than bullets to kill him!"

"Shh," said Marie. "That's enough now."

"He only winged him," said Hooky. "But Robert Foley went to jail for life."

"For life?" I said.

"No," said Duchess. "Those children don't know. It wasn't life, but it should of been. All them Foleys is crazy. Except the youngest one, Bo-ji. He's all right."

"Go away, you children," said Marie. "You showing off too much. Go next door to the bathroom."

"They can come to our place," I said, but Marie shook her head.

There was a silence, the boys gone, Jewel walking Little Bit down the steps. Duchess drawing in her cheeks as she sucked on the cigarette. Marie had let the comic book come to a rest in her lap. I said, "Could I do something? I mean, in my official capacity as a Vista?"

"I wouldn't bother with Lejeune," said Marie. "He don't listen."

Duchess said, "Me, I just hire me my own plumber, or either I get my brother to fix it."

"You got a good job, too," said Marie, more sharply than I would have guessed. "You can hire your own plumber."

"Let me give Lejeune a call," I said. "It can't hurt."

Marie looked into the distance. "I wouldn't bother with calling Lejeune, but *if* you wanted to do something, *if* you wanted to do something, you could call the health man and tell him the toilet don't flush at Marie Conyers' house on Eastover. Then he come down here on a verification and call up Lejeune and *then* Lejeune going to fix it."

"It'll just break next week," said Duchess. "That cheap plumber Lejeune has."

"Sure," I said. "Of course." And immediately was flushed with suspicion, because of how quickly Marie had the pocketbook glistening on her lap again and found the slip of paper. Why hadn't she called this health man herself when it first happened?

"I have the man's name right here," she said. "And his phone number. From the last time, when Miss Shelley called."

Oh, I thought. Shelley. I was going to be following through where someone else had blazed the trail. All she needed anyhow was a white-sounding phone voice; it didn't matter if it was Shelley or me or Spencer, for that matter. This happened all the time, and she just brought in a Vista to make the phone call every time. Was it the Duberrys all over again? I *did* offer. Sure, said the voice in my mind, she's a lot smarter than the poor Duberrys. She knows how to maneuver her Vistas into offering.

Marie had the paper extended to me, but now she drew it back, puzzled by something she read in my face. "If it's no trouble," she said.

I sprang to my feet: "Of course it's no trouble! My goodness! That's what I'm down here for!"

Duchess said, "She an energetic sort of person."

"Only, if it's all the same to you, I think I will call Mr. Lejeune first, just in case."

"Suit yourself," said Marie. "Take a look at the toilet too. It's really broken."

"Oh I believe you—"

"Charlie!" she shouted.

He popped up on the porch. "Yes ma'am?"

"Take Miss Blair in and let her do a verification on the bathroom."

"I really don't need to see it—"

Duchess was practically falling off her seat, laughing. "That's right, honey, you do a toilet verification."

All right, I thought. I probably should check the broken toilet, if I'm going to be reporting it all over town.

The interior of Marie's house was dim, and I had a glimpse of a front room crowded with cots and couches. Hooky came in behind me, and Charlie led up the stairs. Charlie said, "You want to look in the toilet? *I* don't want to look in no toilet."

"Well, maybe not *in* it." A wide upstairs hall, lighter, with toys and piles of folded clean clothes on chairs and boxes. I put my head in the bathroom and saw that the bowl was wrapped in towels. "It's cracked," I said.

"It's always cracked," said Charlie. "That's not what's wrong."

The water level in the bowl was up to the seat; there were floating islands of gray toilet paper and one enormous, mustard-colored turd. "Let's go call Lejeune," I said, and then, finding just the phrase I wanted: "No one should have to live with this."

The phone was in the center room downstairs, along with all the best furniture: a four-poster bed, an armoire where Charlie was looking for the phone book, an uncomfortable loveseat where I sat, watched intently by Hooky, who, I thought, was anticipating my imminent humiliation.

Charlie could find only half the phone book, but it was the right half. To my surprise, I got through to Mr. Lejeune simply by asking. A young woman answered, and I tried out my most educated, smooth tones: "How do you do? This is Blair Morgan of the Volunteers in Service to America? Could I please speak with Mr. Lejeune?"

There was a click, a little hesitation as someone picked up

the phone and held it an instant before speaking. "Yes?" he said, and you could hear the hurry in the voice, a brisk readiness to say No and get on to other business.

"Mr. Lejeune? I'm calling for Mrs. Marie Conyers, a tenant in a house you own at 317 Eastover Street?"

"I don't have a house over there."

Was he lying? "Mrs. Conyers says she called you two days ago about a plumbing problem—"

"Who are you?"

"My name is Blair Morgan—"

"Listen, Miss, I don't know who you work for, but you got your facts wrong. I don't own anything over there. I wouldn't own a chicken house over there."

My mind started to spread out foolishly, but then my eye fell on his display ad in the phone book. "Well, you do manage it, don't you?" He didn't contradict me, so I was firm again. "The problem is that Mrs. Conyers has a broken toilet and needs a plumber—"

"We're working on it."

"She's been waiting for three days, and really, Mr. Lejeune, it's more than an inconvenience, it's a health hazard."

"Who are you? Who do you work for?" I could hear his voice thickening and coarsening, choking with anger. I imagined I could smell blood. Had he been wounded when Robert Foley shot through the door?

"I'm a Vista volunteer over here in South Jenkin."

"My God. You people. Look, we're working on the plumbing problem. All right? It's being taken care of. And while you're running around putting your nose in other people's business, why don't you tell Mrs. Marie Conyers to treat a piece of property like something besides a tissue to blow your nose on. Tell your friends to stop flushing doll babies down their toilets. That's what it was last time—a goddam doll baby. And you tell Mrs. Conyers to stop sneaking fifteen people to live in a house she rented for six. Why don't you stick your nose in that business? Why don't you goddam

Vistas— Why don't you goddam Vistas—" and he stopped himself. I could hear him breathing, huge in my ear.

I had never felt so alert in my life. I was perfectly calm, waiting for something really racist. I hoped to be told to go back to Russia, to have my sexual reputation impugned. But Lejeune got hold of a silence, and clung to it. I said, "I'm glad you're taking care of the plumbing problem, Mr. Lejeune. When can I tell Mrs. Conyers to expect the plumber?"

"When he damn well gets there," said Lejeune.

I got off the phone grinning. "He cursed and hung up on me."

Charlie jumped from side to side. "Ain't he mean? Ain't he the meanest man you ever talked to?" Hooky started playing Robert Foley again, and shot Charlie, and Charlie fell, but leaped up in time to run ahead of me out onto the porch. "Miss Blair told him! Miss Blair told that Lejoon what to do with hisself!"

"I wouldn't say that," I said, but I was extremely pleased with myself.

More people had accumulated on the porch now. A woman with a flowered scarf had my chair, and Marie yelled at Charlie to get another one from inside, but I said I wasn't finished, I still had to call the health department.

Marie had the scrap of paper ready for me with Shelley's purple ink and decorative capital letters. All the kids came inside with me this time, the little ones, Charlie and Hooky, Jewel, who insisted on sitting beside me and entwining her arm in mine. This time there were no receptionists to impress with my northern accent, north West Virginia, anyhow. Several people made me state my business and then connected me with someone else, and one woman said the man I wanted was out in the field, but she transferred me to a man who turned out to be the one I wanted after all. He had been about to leave, but South Jenkin was more or less on his way.

Back on the porch I sat in the chair Charlie got me with

my knees slightly apart, like the other women. Marie's smile was almost theatrical in its slowness and broadness. "How nice of Miss Blair to do all this for us."

Duchess frowned at me. "I don't see any bathroom fixed yet."

But Marie continued to bathe me in this enormous smile which, exaggerated or not, warmed me all the way through. Duchess said, "We'll see. We'll see if the health man comes, and if he come then do Lejeune come."

There was a sound to my left, a sort of stifled belch or curse, and the woman with the flowered scarf tight around her skull was shaking her head and her strange, loose lips. I thought at first a fly was after her, but she was twitching and jerking on her own. The children stopped what they were doing to watch.

"Oh Lord," said Duchess. "If Veronne Foley is starting up, I'm leaving."

I was stunned: was this woman with a head scarf and loose lips Mrs. Foley the mother of mad Robert who shot Lejeune? The mother of Bo-ji with all the muscles? The family Duchess said should be locked up because they were crazy? I had somehow thought of them as legendary people from out of the distant past rather than as neighbors who came and sat on your porch.

"The devil," said Veronne Foley, tossing the bright ends of her scarf and sucking her lips in and out. "Lor lor, that man's the devil!"

Marie said, slow and mournful, "Yes, that's how we *all* feel, Mrs. Foley. We all with you on that. He sure is the devil." She turned to Duchess.

Duchess shrugged. "Oh yes, he's the devil all right."

Veronne Foley seemed mollified, and subsided to mumbling.

Duchess said, "Let me go now. I got all those old people over there with wet beds. The other girls always say it just now happened, and I know better, but I might as well go and get it over with."

Things quieted down now, with Duchess gone and the kids all playing in the yard. I began to feel my stickiness again, and went home for a shower. After the shower, I lay down for a nap. When I went out again, there was an even bigger crowd up at Marie's.

I saw Dave's Volkswagen and an old Valiant I didn't recognize, and some of the boys from last night on the other side of the street: Bo-ji Foley, and the one I knew now was Brother Conyers, and pretty Harold. There were a lot of women I didn't know in the front yard, and Dave was in conversation with a balding white man in a seersucker suit. I hurried to join them, and Dave touched my arm affectionately but didn't bother to introduce me. I kept wanting to say to the health man that I was the one who had talked to him on the phone, but it seemed immodest to bring it up, and I didn't follow them into the house to call Lejeune either. I sat on the steps feeling left out, until Jewel came up to me and put her arms around my neck. "You look so nice," she said. "You look so pretty."

"I took a shower," I said. She ran her fingers through my hair, messed up my bangs, tried to make braids.

"Look at that," she said. "They slip right out."

After a while Dave and the health man came out, and Dave made a speech: The call was made, Lejeune's plumber was on his way. Several people clapped.

While he had their attention, Dave said, he wanted to announce a meeting. This man from the health department, this very man who had ordered Lejeune to send out the plumber, had kindly agreed to come and speak to the community about how to make the neighborhood a better place to live. People nodded, but no one clapped. Someone standing behind me muttered to her friend, Who was that white man with the beard anyhow?

I heard Marie's voice saying how she appreciated the health man coming out, and what a wonderful idea that meeting was, and she just knew everybody was going to come out and make a big success for the Vistas . . .

Another voice behind me said softly, "Well, what I want to know is how does Marie Conyers get the whole damn city health department and the whole damn War on Poverty fixing her damn toilet, and I sit over here and can't even get damn foodstamps?"

Right, I thought. And what *I* want to know is why I get Marie Conyers' toilet fixed, and Dave Rivers gets to turn it into a tenants' movement.

Eight

When I asked Dave directly what he thought of Shelley and Spencer, he said they were extremely generous people, Shelley doing all that cooking for us, Spencer giving him and Roy the best room at Old Fellows Street. If he had thought they were really serious, though, he would have talked about their work. He avoided speaking critically of people behind their backs.

He would never, for example, have talked about someone the way Shelley talked about Yvetta Landell while we were putting up paper flowers for the dance. Shelley had stayed up the better part of the night making these pale green tissue peonies, armloads and bags of them. She pinned one in her hair and had strings of them over her shoulders. She was mad at Yvetta, she told me, because Yvetta had all but promised to chaperone the dance—had said Probably and Maybe right up until lunchtime today—and then emphatically said No.

I said, "We have plenty of chaperones, don't we?"

"No we don't. You can't have too many people at these dances. But the main thing is, Yvetta's good at it. She knows these kids. And that's why she always backs out. She doesn't like it, because they know she knows them. They give her some kind of weird respect because of her cousin."

"The gangster?"

"Yeah," said Shelley. "You have to feel a little sorry for her, sitting in that house all alone, but she cut herself off; she's one of these people who's always looking for something better. She thought Frank Landell was her ticket out of South Jenkin, but it turns out *he* likes it here. He's a pain sometimes, but he would have let us have the Rec Center at the church, I know he would have. Yvetta stopped him. She doesn't want to have anything to do with the kids who knew her Back When." Shelley climbed a stepladder and started taping flowers along the molding above the wall. I unreeled flowers and passed them up to her.

"Maybe she really meant to chaperone and something happened with the baby," I said.

"Something with the baby. Yeah, right." She reared back dangerously to check the depth of her loops. "I don't suppose you've heard the rumor yet, about who's supposed to be Little Frank's real father?"

"I'm not sure I want to."

"Sure you do. Some people say he's her cousin's baby."

"He looks just like Frank."

"Maybe Frank and her cousin look alike. I don't know . . . it's just gossip. Frank certainly thinks the kid is his. But it does show how people feel about Yvetta, that they would start things like that about her." She got down and moved the ladder. "Oh, Yvetta's okay. She's just mixed up. Like the rest of us."

The rumor seemed to make Shelley, if anything, more affectionate toward Yvetta. But it gave me a feeling of uncleanliness, as if Yvetta had become soiled and perhaps untrustworthy. If she could change this much today, what might she do tomorrow?

I said, "It would make a great *True Story*, wouldn't it? 'I used to be my cousin's gun moll, but now I'm the preacher's wife.' "

"That's good," said Shelley, who never laughed at witticisms but only complimented them. "That's very good."

Driving over to the Neighborhood Center that night I told Dave what Shelley had said. "She told me all these rumors. Yvetta Landell's baby's father is maybe that gangster cousin of hers, and Jewel's father is supposed to be even worse. And

Yvetta only married Frank to get out of South Jenkin."

Dave ignored the scandal completely. "I expect Yvetta's instincts are good," he said. "Get an education, get out, start over."

"You mean you don't think she should stay home and help her people?"

"Did you stay home and help your people?"

"My people didn't need help."

"Didn't they? Some of those hollows, up where Roy is from? It's certainly easier in many ways to go somewhere else; you want to be on the cutting edge, to have some of the excitement of the city."

"I didn't come down here for excitement!"

"No? Well, the point is that you didn't stay around home anymore than Yvetta wants to. I wouldn't say chaperoning a dance is the height of service to the community, anyhow. I expect the Landells will be with us when the big thing happens."

He means his housing meeting, I thought. He doesn't think anything Shelley and Spencer do is worth a hill of beans. *That* made me feel a little soiled too; as if Dave were somehow putting dirty thumbprints on Spencer and Shelley.

Neighborhood House was already hopping as we parked. I had always thought that people were supposed to come late to dances, and this dance didn't officially start for another fifteen minutes, but the place was already packed. There were kids sitting on the porch, and on cars outside, and on the steps of the school across the street. Everywhere, too, the percussive impact of the music from inside. Where did they all come from? And no wonder Mrs. White had hidden her plants, her family portraits, her pens and scissors.

Near the door, though, there were familiar faces: Brother Conyers with his sharp eyebrows, and the muscular Bo-ji Foley.

Dave shook their hands. "Nice turnout," he said, as if the boys were responsible for it. I stood beside them awkwardly, struck by the unfairness: Dave didn't give a very high priority to work with the teenagers, yet he could talk to them easily; while I would have wanted to work with them, if I could just stop being afraid and think of something to say. Out of the corner of my eye I had glimpses of the interior, which appeared to be solid with human bodies that swayed like giant bolognas suspended from the ceiling of a vast butcher shop. They seemed to bounce off one another, to ripple and sway in a chain reaction.

Shelley made her way through them, wearing her smock dress again, with green fish net tights. Emerald green eyeshadow too, and a paper flower on either side of her head. "Thank God you're here!" she said. "Everyone came. We're going to run out of Coke, so I called up the plant manager and he said we could have more if we'd go pick it up right now—"

"Of course," said Dave, mock-saluting. "At your service!"

"Bo-ji, Brother, can you guys go with him and help carry? Okay?"

"I'll go," I said, wanting to avoid the giant bolognas.

"No, I need you to sell drinks. We're charging five cents, just to cover cups." She hustled Dave and the boys out to the Volkswagen, giving addresses and instructions, and came back to me still talking. "Where's Roy? We need him too."

"He's waiting for Duchess to dress—she volunteered to be a chaperone."

Shelley made a face. "Like a cat guarding the mice is a chaperone. But don't get me wrong, we can use her. Did you see how many kids came?"

She was in a state, no doubt about it; flickering and flowering, jerking her head in one direction and then the other. I don't care, I thought. I know she gossips and overdramatizes, but I think she's terrific. The remarks in my head were addressed to Dave, who had left me alone. He had been dispatched by Shelley, it was true, but the result was that I was isolated in this unstable place. Alone behind Mrs. White's desk with a plastic pan of ice, a stack of cups, a cigar box for change, and a bowl of potato chips.

Two girls came for Cokes, and asked if the chips were free. "Oh sure, help yourselves," I said. "Compliments of Dollar Bill Supermarkets. You know the Dollar Bill Supermarkets? One of the owners is on the TAPS board of directors?" They couldn't have cared less, of course. I was just jabbering, but I felt a need in the midst of all this movement and music to make a sound of my own.

After counting my nickels and remaining bottles of Coke, I looked around the room and didn't see swaying bolognas. It was just a crowd of kids dancing. Like high school dances I used to go to, except there were fewer people leaning on the walls. Everyone here seemed to dance. Some girls, including the two who'd asked me about the chips, made a line dance. I found myself liking the way the Neighborhood Center looked tonight; the big room, once the whole downstairs of a private home, had a golden glow. Shelley's paper flowers looked golden on one side, green on the other, and their petals trembled in time to the music. Shelley had a goldn glow too, as she danced with Harold, the handsome boy who wore a cream colored cap. Everyone looked handsome to me. I was struck by a boy in another cream colored cap, but this one had sunglasses and a beard—and I realized I was admiring Spencer.

He saw me, and began to move in my direction, passing through a crowd of girls. I had a thrill of being chosen: that the popular one was shaking off all the others to come to me.

"You're looking good tonight," he said. I hadn't dressed for a party, exactly, but I'd worn my favorite oxford cloth dress, with the throat open, and my sterling silver acorn pendant. He touched it with one finger. "Cute."

"It came off one of those charm bracelets kids used to wear."

"Do you want to dance? Or are you still avoiding me?"

"I have to sell the drinks. Besides, I'm too short to dance with you. We'd look silly. And I can't dance."

"You have plenty of excuses."

"I'll dance with you later when there's somebody else to sell Cokes, okay?" He sat on the edge of my table, and stared at me through those opaque glasses, with a grin on one side only. I thought he knew he was having an effect on me and was getting a kick out of it. So pleased with himself. "You better go meet your girlfriends," I said. "They look like they miss you."

"Yeah, well, I always did have a thing for those young virgins. You know. One of these days I'll up and marry me one."

"A teenager?"

"No, a virgin." He crossed his arms, began to sound like a college man again in spite of the shades and cap. "You'll tell me it's a double standard, and I don't deny it, but I could never marry a girl who wasn't a virgin. It's just this thing I have."

Is this a line, I wondered. Is this a joke? "How about if you were the first one for her, would you marry her then?"

"Nope. I want to marry a virgin."

"That's the most outrageous thing I ever heard."

Spencer smiled all the way across his face; obviously he wanted to be outrageous. But I never found out if he really meant it because he bumped me with his elbow. "Look who's here."

It was Roy, and Duchess, who was wearing what had to be her own natural hair at last; dense and short and almost the same color as her skin. The extreme shortness of the cut revealed tiny tight curls at her temples and nape, and the sharp, fine bones of her face seemed more exposed too. Her ears flashed with gold bangles, the toes of her shoes were gold too, peeping from under a sort of pajama outfit.

"Look at that," said Spencer. "I've been trying to get that woman to show her hair ever since I moved in at Old Fellows Street."

Duchess looked good all right, but Roy loomed over her sullenly, wearing dark glasses and an exotic print overshirt. Spencer said, "Hey, Blair, what do you think of your home-boy's outfit?"

"What's he wearing?"

"A dashiki shirt. From Africa."

"Well, he looks like a fool in it!"

"He wants to be the hillbilly soul brother."

Spencer extended a palm to Roy, and Roy slapped it, taking careful aim, his shoulders tight. I looked away. Big joke, everybody laughing at Roy, especially Spencer. Laughing at me too, no doubt, for believing the story about the virgin wife. Or for not believing it. One way or the other I was a fool too. I was determined to ignore Roy, but I couldn't stop watching him. That full shirt seemed to move with stiff dignity to its own beat that had no relation to Roy's lurching, side-to-side steps. He was trying too hard, of course. He reminded me of embarrassing times in high school. I wished he had stayed in bed. I wished he had stayed up on Big Haul.

A lot of people gathered to watch Roy dance. He waved his arms in the air, and Harold pretended to dodge. Next to Harold, like a negative image of his cream colored cap and shirt, was someone I hadn't seen before, a skinny guy in dark clothes. He glared at Roy, saw me looking, and nudged Harold. They came toward me.

Each of them leaned a hip on my table so they were half facing each other, but directing their attention to me. Harold said, "Vistas getting better looking every shipment in, ain't that right, Snake?"

Seen this near, Snake's dark clothes had a rumpled, rusty look and were threadbare around the cuffs and collar. He seemed too old to be one of Spencer's boys; his face appeared wizened around the mouth and creased around the eyes. I couldn't see any hair at all under his cap. He suddenly widened his eyes so that the irises and pupils were islands in the middle of white eyeball. This guy, I thought, wants to look creepy.

"Hello," I said. "I'm Blair Morgan. I hope you're enjoying the dance. Would you like a Coke? It's only five cents."

Snake said, "I ain't got no five cents. I'm a *poverty* person."

Harold gave one of his long laughs that seemed to run from the top of his head right through the impeccable cream colored shirt and trim tan pants to the toes of his brown wingtip shoes. "Miss Blair, this here is my main man, Snake Eyes. I'm buying him and me Coca-Colas."

When I turned to scoop ice, Harold said, in a silky voice that I was definitely supposed to hear, "She got nice hair, don't she?"

And Snake's scratchier voice, coming from down in his throat: "If you like that limp kind of hair." I turned back to them, itching all over, not knowing if this was teasing because they liked me, or insults. Harold thanked me for the drinks, but Snake stared at his without picking it up. "There's a lot of that limp hair around these days. I don't know where they all coming from."

Harold resettled himself on the desk so that they were no longer symmetrical. He extended a shapely, warm-colored hand. "Hey, you don't mind if I touch it, do you?" A full second elapsed before I realized he meant my hair, and he had already picked out a piece of it, drawn it delicately from my head in a little curtain, let a few strands fall back of their own accord.

I jerked the rest free too, pulled my head out of his reach, and gave him the biggest smile I could muster. "I think I would mind."

Harold left his hand in mid air while he smiled at least as hugely as I did. He said, "Now you ain't going to be one of those girls whistles Dixie are you?"

Snake widened his eyes, showing the strange centrality of his pupils again. "You ain't suppose to be prejudice', Vista," he said, only he pronounced it Vusta.

"Naw, man," said Harold. "These Vistas ain't prejudice', they like us real well. I was just joking about whistling Dixie."

I said, "Snake is a perfect nickname for your friend."

Snake went through a couple of changes of expression, flared his eyes, then slit them way down among the creases. "Snake *Eyes!*" he said. "I ain't no reptile; call me Snake *Eyes*. I don't crawl on my belly. Nobody but my friends call me

Snake 'cause that's short for Snake Eyes and I ain't short."

Harold said, quite seriously, I thought, although I couldn't be sure, "Don't fool with him, Miss."

Just then, to my intense relief, Roy came loping over. Reinforcements. "Roy," I said, "you know Harold."

Harold pumped his hand, and Roy said, "Hey, man."

"Hey, man," said Harold genially.

"And this is Snake Eyes, but don't call him Snake because only his close friends are allowed to call him Snake."

Roy extended a big hand to Snake. "Hey, man."

Snake's hand started out, but just before it touched Roy's, he whipped it aside and whirled himself full circle. "What's that *thing* that damn Vusta's wearing?"

Harold said, "That's a dashiki shirt from Africa, Snake. Spencer told us all about them. Ain't that right, Roy, my man?"

"This ain't no Africa," said Snake. "I ain't no *native* from Africa. What you Vustas doing down here anyhow? We don't need no Vustas down here."

Roy nodded sympathetically. "You're right, man. Hey, I'm with you."

Snake's eyes went widest and whitest of all, and he took a leap backwards. "No, you *ain't*! You ain't nowhere with *me*!" And he went backing and whirling off into the crowd.

I was relieved to have him gone. Harold stopped grinning and went off too, as if he lost his confidence without a backup man. They were just a couple of teenagers, I thought, in spite of the lines in Snake's face. He'd probably had a hard life. The two of them were just goofing off, testing boundaries. Like Roy in that long yellow muu-muu of a shirt. I said, "Roy, take off your sunglasses. I know you can't see a thing in here with them on. And why are you wearing that African shirt?"

"I'm going through changes," said Roy in a voice that I could have sworn was an imitation of Snake's scratchy one.

Dave returned then with Bo-ji and Brother, and Shelley commandeered Roy to carry in more cases of Coke. I had a flurry of business, ran out of potato chips, but kept on selling the nickel Cokes. Some girls came and complained that a boy was looking in the bathroom at them, and Duchess volunteered to patrol the bathroom for a while, but none of that was an Event. All of that was just shifting protoplasm, the dance-amoeba nosing around after energy sources.

The next Event was the arrival of Chuck and Eleanor-Byrd Williams, dressed for a party: Eleanor-Byrd especially in a swishing-full dress, floral-print and ruffled, even the gray streaks in her hair bespeaking not age but the custom of glamour. It was as if two movie stars had materialized among us.

"Oh shit," said Shelley. "The Inquisition."

Spencer shook his head. "Hide your hard drugs and liquor, kiddies, here come Big Missy and Chuckles."

"What are they doing here?" I said. "They weren't supposed to come."

But Spencer had already moved toward them; indeed, everyone had—teenagers, Vistas, all gathered in a respectful horseshoe around the Williamses. Dave had gotten to them before anyone else, and stood now with Chuck, mimicking his stance, arms crossed, rocking slightly heel-to-toe. Eleanor-Byrd waved gaily over Shelley's head at me, so I picked up my box of change and joined the crowd.

"Hello, Blair, honey," said Eleanor-Byrd. "How is my little crusader? I hear you're doing such a fine job!"

The main business was obviously to show them that this was a clean-cut dance, that TAPS Neighborhood House was intact. To make them see how smoothly we operated.

I said, "I'm selling Coke by the barrel—these kids love to cool off with Coke!"

Spencer told Eleanor-Byrd she looked beautiful, and Eleanor said she was going to such a boring old party, she wished she was staying at this one. Spencer asked her to dance. The kids pressed around to see the white lady in the fancy cocktail dress dance, and she turned out to be pretty good; she and Spencer did some neat jitterburg turns, far better than I would manage when my turn with him came.

I whispered to Shelley, "Spencer knows how to handle *her*."

"You bet," said Shelley.

I decided to practice handling Chuck, so I told him that his potato chip donation had been a big hit. He shrugged, and complimented *me* instead. "I hear you've been out helping people get their plumbing repaired. That's real good."

I said, "Well, I hope I do more this summer than get a toilet fixed."

Dave was shedding his smile on me too; it must have been Dave who boasted about what I'd done. He hadn't praised me to my face, but now he was revealing his pride obliquely, and I wanted to return the favor. I said, "But Dave is the one who's going ahead and organizing a meeting about housing problems."

Something changed. It was a little hard to catch with the music blaring and Eleanor-Byrd and Spencer coming back breathless and laughing; but there was a failure in the flow of warmth from Chuck. "So you Vistas are planning on doing some of that community organizing, are you?"

Dave said, so quickly that I knew I had to be careful, "Oh, I wouldn't go that far. This fellow from the Health Department has a film about picking up garbage, making sure you're not breeding mosquitoes in your backyard, that kind of thing."

To show Dave I had picked up his signals, I said, "People really want to fix their neighborhood up."

"I'm sure they do," said Chuck. "We all want to see the neighborhoods fixed up nice."

People were relaxing now; Spencer excused himself to do something, Shelley introduced a couple of the boys to the Williamses, and Harold pumped their hands. No one had much to say, of course, and then Spencer was back and the Williamses were leaving. Everyone suddenly gay in relief. Nothing had gone wrong. The Inquisition was over, the Event slipped into the past.

Shelley said to Spencer, "Where did you rush off to?"

"Some guys were leaning on their car. Actually, these guys

were leaning mostly on their antenna, to see how far they could, you know, bend it before it snapped off?"

"Oh God," said Shelley. "That's all we needed."

Dave shook his head sympathetically. "That would not have been good."

I wanted him to analyze the Event, to explain to me the underlying meaning of the visitation, to demonstrate why he didn't trust Chuck. We were all crowded together, and he put a hand on my elbow, almost secretly, as if he knew what I wanted. We were communicating, I thought, in that way I wanted so badly, that delicate flow of messages without words through the gold to airy thinness beat.

But at that same instant, as Dave touched my elbow on one side, like a short circuit, Spencer touched my other shoulder, sent a sizzle through my body. I jumped.

"*Now* are you ready to dance?" he said. He had even taken off his dark glasses.

"Go ahead," said Dave. "I'll sell Cokes for a while. You like to dance."

I do not, I thought. Don't you know I don't like to dance? Don't you know I want to be with you?

But Dave left me with Spencer, who seemed insubstantial in comparison. And yet, at the same time, he was highly charged and caused an agitation through my body. I danced by moving from foot to foot with conservative, small movements. Spencer didn't make me try anything complicated.

"See?" I shouted when I had relaxed a little. "I'm a terrible dancer!"

He smiled and shook his head. Someone changed records, put on a slow song, and he gathered up my right hand, enfolded it in his left one, placed his right hand at the small of my back. My face came to just above the middle of the buttons on his shirt. I pulled my head back. "And I'm too short for you!"

"Shh," he said. He pulled his long, thick eyelids most of the way down over his eyes. "Just listen to my man Otis Redding. Just feel it."

The trouble was that I did feel it; my lids wanted to sink too, make the room be only Spencer's fingertips lightly on my back telling me when to move and the sound of this voice that raked through me like fingers in thick hair. After a while there were fewer words and more cries: "I've been loving you too long," he sang, and then, "Oh oh oh." Something about being a woman; it was as if I understood now what I hadn't understood before. I kept imagining Spencer's body peeled, layer by layer, of its clothes till only the electric charge was left between us.

We had moved gradually to the far side of the room, where it was less crowded, and out of one of the singer's sharp little cries rose a warm odor, piercing but comforting, with no cloying overtone of sweet lotion. I realized suddenly that it was Spencer I was smelling, and the intimacy of it caused me to jump away. "I think I'd better get back to work," I said. Dave should not have sent me off to dance with him. Dave should be the only one I danced with now.

Spencer's eyes were still more closed than open, and his voice had taken on the deep-scored quality of the singer's. "Don't be one of these girls goes through life saying, Stop stop we better stop."

I tried to make a joke. "I just can't trust a virgin-hunter like you."

"I thought maybe it was your preacher worrying you."

"What about you and Shelley?"

He was taking his shades out of his pocket, putting up the barrier. The energy under control again, back in proper channels. "I was only asking you to dance, baby, not go steady."

I stayed in the corner by myself for a while, humiliated by the abruptness of Spencer's departure. Watching Dave take care of customers. I loved him, didn't I? But if I loved him, why this feeling when I danced with Spencer? Was it something that happened to you every time you got close to a man when you weren't a virgin anymore? Did they smell it in you now, and come on to you? Did all the men have this power to agitate you now?

I don't like dances, I thought, as the tight band of singing finally came to an end. I never did like dances. I'm bad at dances.

Dave was pleased with himself. "I've collected fifty cents already. Ten sales. Not bad for a non-businessman."

I said, "What I want to know is, what do you intend to do about Roy?"

"Roy? He's having a wonderful time."

"You know what I mean. Everyone's laughing at him. He's going too far, galumphing around in that shirt. He's making a fool of himself."

Dave's eyes refocused a little above my head. *I* was going too far, too, I could see. "Let Roy alone," he said. "He's trying for a freedom he never had before."

"Some freedom. He hears voices and does what they tell him." The crowd parted now, enough so that we had a good view of him with his arms waving in the air, his face clouded with concentration. I said, "You pretend like it's nothing, and all the time he's cracking up. You brought him down here and now you say let him be. You're just not taking responsibility—"

I stopped, because Dave's face had begun to color high in the cheeks. He looked directly at me.

"I?" said Dave. "*I* brought him down here? I'm responsible for him? I beg your pardon, but he came down here of his own volition, and you came down here of *your* own volition too."

"I know I did. I'm not worried about me, I'm worried about Roy."

Dave's forehead was turning red as well as his cheeks. I had never seen him red before. I made him angry, I thought. Look what I did. "I'm not responsible," he said. "I'm not responsible for everyone and everything in the world, dammit!"

People weren't supposed to get angry at me. I felt like I

was on a spit of land that was being eaten away by a storm, chunk after chunk falling away around me, and I could feel the ground directly under me beginning to give way too.

Dave said, "You expect me to make everything go right for you, to ease your way, and I want to know when you are going to ease something for me!"

He's right, I thought. I'm selfish. I don't think of him. But he shouldn't yell at me.

I was trying to squeeze out some words that would make the yelling cease and the ground under me stop crumbling, but at that moment Dave's anger and my inarticulate terror were interrupted by another Event.

Snake, of the white-circled pupils and rusty black clothes, had stepped between Roy and Duchess. He started screaming at Roy far louder than Dave had shouted at me.

"What *are* you?" shrieked Snake. "What *are* you? A goddam fuckin' airplane? Are you a airplane?"

Harold was there in the circle around them, and Bo-ji Foley. Duchess with her mouth awry. It had to be a joke, of course, except that Snake took such exceedingly deep breaths, each ending in a shudder, before the next blast of words.

"Don't scare him too bad," said Harold.

"Take it easy, Snake," murmured Bo-ji.

Roy tried to walk around Snake, toward Duchess, but Snake stepped in front of him, whichever way he moved. "I'm goddam fuckin' talkin' to you, airplane pilot!"

Roy smiled stupidly and flapped his arms. Several people laughed.

"That's a motherfuckin' bird, motherfucka! Don't you know a bird from a airplane? Who you think you are—Superman?"

They had stopped the music now, and Dave and I moved closer. I looked for Spencer. Surely he could handle Snake; but when I saw him, he had his sunglasses off and looked like a college student.

Snake did a little footwork in front of Roy. "You think you Superman? You think you can motherfuckin' fly? You think you Superman comin' over here fuckin' with other folks' women?''

Duchess thrust a bony fist deep in the hip of her flowing pajamas. "Whose women, Snake? Whose women you talking about?''

A lot of people were laughing now; maybe it was a routine, the way Spencer sometimes stood up and told a whole string of jokes. Snake pulled his lips back over his teeth. "Show me how you fly, Superman! Show me how you goddam fly!''

Roy held his arms out straight at the sides and moved them, banking. He said, "Brr," gently.

"No," said Dave. "Stop now, Roy."

"Bigger!" screamed Snake. "Fly bigger, looney-bin! God almighty, I hate a looney-bin!''

Harold said, "That's 'cause you more looney than him."

There was a long arc of a gasp from those nearer the center than we were, and a change of focus in the crowd as Snake jumped at Harold. "Who's a looney-bin? Who's a looney-bin?''

Harold raised his hands, warding him off. "Hey, Snake man. Hey, Snake," he said. Snake's back was to us, but his arm extended suddenly and the crowd pulled away; there was a knife in his fist. He feinted, and Harold jumped backwards and his cap fell off, leaving his hair standing out babysoft and full around his face. I finally saw that Harold at least was really a boy.

"Hey, Snake man," he said, twitching a smile, keeping his hands up.

Dave moved past me. Spencer was moving too, but they never got to the center because Snake lunged and Harold sprang back again, and the whole crowd suddenly surrounded Snake. I saw Bo-ji grab him from behind and more people grabbing, and there was a struggle and a cry, and I couldn't see what was happening except that Snake was given space again, and he ran to the door, ran out.

It was Bo-ji Foley they converged on now. He looked up at

the ceiling at the limp paper flowers and smiled sheepishly. He held his left arm out by the elbow for people to see, but didn't look himself. A sheet of blood formed in the middle of the bicep and flowed down his arm, dropped to the floor. Shelley burst through the crowd, running for the kitchen, and Spencer began ushering kids out the door. I asked some to go, too, and they dragged their feet, craned their necks, but went. Shelley brought dishtowels to bind the wound, and the room cleared quickly, down to the Vistas, Duchess, and Brother Conyers, hovering around Bo-ji. Over by the door Harold tried to beat his stepped-on hat back into shape and muttered to himself what he was going to do to Snake when he got hold of him.

"I'm all right," said Bo-ji, smiling at the ceiling.

"Oh shut up, Bo-ji," said Duchess. "You don't know." She wrapped his arm with the cloth, fastened it with a safety pin, and blood leaked through immediately.

"It's all right," said Bo-ji, and this time they all ignored him, making their plans. Duchess and Brother and Harold would go in the Volkswagen to the Emergency Room with him. Dave wanted to take Roy too, just to keep him off the street. There was certainly no room for me in the car, but I couldn't help taking it as a punishment. They could have made Harold stay; he was the one who started the trouble. Or Brother. I could have sat with Duchess, and comforted Bo-ji. I kept watching Dave's face for a sign that I was forgiven, that everything was normal again, but he was quietly businesslike, fully concentrated on getting Bo-ji in the car and the others packed in quickly.

From the porch I watched the Volkswagen drive away. There were still a lot of boys out on the street having practice fights under the streetlamps. The anger was not all gone. Inside, Shelley kicked a box to the middle of the floor and leaped into the air, ripped down a strand of her flowers.

I said, "It was getting late. I don't guess the dance could have lasted much longer anyhow." Shelley and Spencer didn't say anything. "It could have been a lot worse. I mean, it could have happened when Chuck and Eleanor-Byrd were here. And it looks like Bo-ji will be okay."

Shelley stomped viciously on some of her flowers. I said, "I mean, it's not like the dance wasn't a success."

"Oh it was a success all right, wasn't it, Spencer? I mean, what's Friday night in South Jenkin without a knife fight? Right, Spencer?"

Spencer took a swig from a Coke bottle. "Yeah, right," he said. "And Jews are all such *rich* bastards."

Her mouth went sour. "I didn't mean to insult your heritage."

"Yeah, well I meant to insult yours."

She ripped down more flowers, and I followed her, shoving them into the trash boxes and plastic bags. What was the matter with us all? Why was this happening?

The door opened and a man came in, wearing a dark suit and high-gloss shoes. He had dull, straightened hair pushed back and out behind him. Not old, but certainly not one of the teenagers.

"My man Ralph!" said Spencer, sounding delighted.

"Oh God," said Shelley. "That's it for Spencer. Ralph's back in town. You haven't met Ralph yet." Ralph and Spencer were slapping hands, slipping palms, letting their voices sheer up, creating a whirligig of camaraderie. Shelley said, "He drives Spencer around in this mile long black Cadillac, so Spencer is his best friend. Ralph's okay though. He likes to do things for people. He likes to drive us around places, and he buys beer. You know. The Cadillac belongs to his mother. He works for her—she's an undertaker." Then, in a louder voice, "Somebody could help Blair and me with all this clean-up, and I don't mean you, Ralph. You just got here."

Spencer said, "I thought there was a clean-up committee."

She put her hands on her hips. "You chased them all out, goddammit!"

"Damn, I hate the sound of a woman cursing," said Spencer.

Her whole face distorted toward flatness, her twisted

mouth the only gash in the plane. "Spencer, will you stop fucking around with Ralph and help clean this place up?"

Now Spencer's mouth spread across his face as if his head were about to split into a top and bottom half. The two of them, Spencer and Shelley, were as exotic and ugly as wide-jawed gila monsters.

"Let's split, Ralph," said Spencer. "I don't like the atmosphere around here."

And then, as if he had himself split the atmosphere, as if their anger together had caused it to explode, there was a sharp crack, an explosion, or rather an implosion, a shower of glass and jets of cool air, and I thought: But we already had violence tonight.

Ralph thundered across the room, skidded on his slick shoes, but recovered and got to the lights. As he flipped them off, the sharp perimeters of the room disappeared in blue darkness. From the front, just enough light came in to mark forms. After a few seconds, we began walking around; our feet shushed in paper, crunched on glass, as we looked out the broken windows, and saw nothing. Even the kids were gone now.

I said, "Was it a gun?"

"Just rocks," said Ralph.

"Well shit," said Shelley. "Shit, shit, shit!"

Spencer walked from window to window. "He's long gone. He didn't stay around to get looked at."

Shelley took a deep sucking breath. "Oh I hate this shit. I really hate this. Mrs. White's windows, too. How many are broken? What about the plant? She left that one plant out. Did they break the plant, Spencer?"

"Don't worry about the plant."

I said, "It was Snake, wasn't it?"

"Yeah," said Spencer. "Sure."

"Two windows," said Ralph.

"Who else? Does Snake have a lot of friends? Let's pull down the shades so we can put the lights on again."

It wasn't so frightening with the lights on. We found two

broken panes. "They got the plant," said Shelley, picking it up by its root ball. "Well, it's only ivy. You can't kill ivy." She fitted the two halves of the clay pot together temporarily to hold it. Spencer got the broom and began sweeping up. Ralph found a dust pan. I was full of an unexpected exhilaration: the humility of Spencer, working with us again, the sensation of being still alive.

"What do we do now?" I asked.

Shelley said, "I'll buy a new pot. I suppose we can get a glazier in here tomorrow?"

"Alls you need's a little putty and the glass," said Ralph. "It's easy."

"We might be able to do it all so Mrs. White never has to know," said Shelley. "What do you think, Spencer?"

"Possible," said Spencer.

I said, "But don't we have to report it to someone?"

"Well, not the police. I hope you're not thinking of the police," said Shelley. "Nothing worse for rapport with the people than calling in the police, right, Spencer?"

"No point to it," said Ralph. "No reason to call attention."

"I didn't mean the police necessarily."

"Who?" said Spencer. "The Williamses? Frank Landell?"

I let the import of what they were saying sink in. No good to come from telling on ourselves. It had only been crazy Snake, anyhow. "But why did he do it?"

Spencer said, "So we wouldn't forget him."

"But it was awful," said Shelley. "That sound—the glass shattering. It was like the sound of hate."

Spencer put an arm around her, and she hugged him with both arms around his waist. The man Ralph smiled shyly. If Dave had been there, we would have all hugged together.

I said, "Do you know, for a second, before my mind started working right, I thought you two had made it happen by yelling at each other. I thought you exploded the windows."

They laughed. The cleaning-up was pretty much finished, and we all agreed to come back first thing in the morning, even Ralph. He said there was no business tomorrow, anyhow. We would work all day Saturday to make it so Mrs. White wouldn't know anything on Monday. Spencer said we should sit outside for a while, cool out, so we locked up and sat on the steps, just watching the night, making sure the danger had really passed. Spencer sat between me and Shelley; he already had an arm around her, and he put the other one around me. I let myself be gathered up against his side. Ralphie was doing something at his car, the long Cadillac with tall, proud, old-fashioned tail fins. He came back lighting a cigarette.

Shelley said, "Sorry I was a bitch, Spencer."

"Hey me too," he said, and I let my weight press a little closer, feeling that I was the only beloved child of Spencer and Shelley.

Ralph squatted on the sidewalk in front of Shelley and passed her the cigarette. She sucked in, then held it between her thumb and forefinger and leaned over Spencer's knee to look to me. "What about Blair?"

I didn't get it at first.

"She's a big girl," said Spencer, taking the cigarette. He tipped his head back and drew in deeply. I could feel the spread of his ribs as his lungs expanded. I was about to say I didn't know you smoked when I put it all together and realized they were smoking marijuana. Spencer groaned gently and rearranged my position against his side. "Damn this is good," he said. I think it was how simply he said he was enjoying it that allowed me, when he offered, casually to suck in a little puff.

They all watched me, and when I nearly choked, gave me advice about how to make the smoke stay down. Every time I had a turn, though, I released clouds of it into the air, and got belches from swallowing what I did take in. I didn't get high, but I felt a pleasant shifting, and I thought, This is what I really want, to have gone through something together, and now to have peace after action, this listening to the deep dark, this freedom and touching.

We had one more Event that evening, a small one, a person

149

materializing out of the dark. Just when we were most calm and quiet, almost drowsy, we saw her coming: a lurching walk I thought at first was drunken, but then decided was high heels. When she came under the nearest streetlight, we saw it was Mrs. Veronne Foley who had muttered and sucked her lips beside me on Marie Conyers' porch. She still wore a scarf tight over her head, but she had necklaces tonight too, and a sleeveless dress with a low neckline. "Where is my boy?" she said. "What did they do to my boy?"

I kept wondering—as we discussed what to do, and decided that Ralph would drive her over to the hospital—I kept wondering if she had been called from a party, or if you always got dressed up when you had to find out how badly your son had been knifed.

Nine

Dave asked me to go for a walk. Our near-fight at the dance seemed long ago; we had been working hard planning and publicizing the housing meeting, and I thought we had decided, without saying it in so many words, to forget the whole thing. That we had agreed to a respectful, mutual silence. Until he asked me to go for the walk.

"Of course," I said. That was what I wanted, wasn't it? Communication? But I was terrified that the discussion would turn into confused tangles of explanation. That I would end up confessing terrible things: how sometimes I was more comfortable with Shelley than with Dave. That my favorite times were when all of us Vistas and Duchess and Ralph went out for pizza or cooked together at our apartment, and everyone laughed and gossiped and told stories and did routines and even practiced dancing a little but never talked intensely head to head. That anymore, whenever I was alone with Dave I had a sinking, distant feeling, as if there were some amorphous, impassable object between us: an enormous tar baby made of swamp mud that I could neither shove away nor get my hands clean after touching.

But I said, "Oh good, a walk. It seems like we never get a chance to be alone together anymore."

We crossed William and Mary Road, over into the white part of town, where I had never gone before. It had the same three story verandah buildings as South Jenkin, some more run-down than others, with their yards worn to dirt like the bad buildings in South Jenkin. There were children, too, who looked wan to me, white children, as if the paleness of their limbs were a sign of wasting, as if they had once been dark and husky and were now fading away. They made me sad, and I wanted to be back in South Jenkin. I had enough to worry about without thinking about hungry, wounded-eyed white children too.

Dave walked with his head bent forward, thinking. I never knew what went on in his mind, but I did know that after a while he would say to me, Blair, what's troubling you? and I would writhe and fumble for an answer. I walked beside him like a boy being taken to the woodshed to have his hide waled.

"Here it is," said Dave as the street ended in a sort of park with a canal of dark green water before us and some benches and paths along its edge. "You didn't know about the canal, did you?"

"It's really pretty," I said.

"I knew you'd like it. I wanted to surprise you. Eleanor Williams was telling me about it down at the office the other day. That's their church up there. The canal and the church were built at the same time so the canal would serve as a reflecting pool." In the lowering evening distinctions of gray become precise: the stone steeple with its almost identical, but slightly silvered image. "We're lucky to have something this pretty near us in South Jenkin, aren't we?" he said.

"Yes," I said, "but I don't see many people from South Jenkin getting to enjoy it."

Dave, who had been so pleased with himself for making this little gift to me, became serious. You could see it in his eyes: What had been a pretty spot to sit and have conversations suddenly become a crusade. Did I want to spoil it for him? Would I have to confess this too? I had a feeling that everything I touched tonight was going to turn to swamp mud.

We walked along the broad retaining wall a little ways,

then sat on one of the benches. Dave laid his arm behind me. "Still, it *is* nice, isn't it?"

For half a second I thought he might have brought me here just for the surprise, not to find out why I had said the things I had at the dance. It passed through my mind, and I rejected it, decided to plunge in and get it over with. "The trouble is," I said, "nothing's the way I expected it would be. I'm not complaining, but I just thought it would be different. I thought we would be together more. The two of us."

"And yet," said Dave quietly, sending a chill through me as if he knew too much—I had known all along that he knew too much—"it seems you want more time alone."

"I just get peeved when everyone seems to forget I'm here and only talks to you."

"It's almost as if you thought you were in competition with me."

My heart started beating rapidly. I *did* want something of my own, my own project, not to be simply working on Dave's ideas, his errand girl, but I said, "Oh, Dave, I could never compete with you. You're so far ahead of me. I mean, I've never accomplished things the way you have."

There was a silence from him, and I had again the uncanny certainty that I was forcing this conversation. He said, "What makes you think I've accomplished anything?"

I laughed. "Of course you have!"

"If I had accomplished so much I wouldn't need to be down here. I have ideas about what we should do, but I don't know that my ideas are any better than your ideas. And I certainly don't know which ones will work. I'm not God."

"Well, I know you're not God."

"Do you? Sometimes you act like I know everything, or should know everything. Or have a master plan for everything. I'm feeling my way, Blair, just the same as you."

I didn't know if that was supposed to make me feel better or not, but it didn't, not right away, anyhow. I felt better that I wasn't down here by the water getting chewed out, but I kept thinking, over and over, Then why am I with you, if you don't know any more than I do? And of course I didn't really believe that he didn't. Didn't really believe he was telling the truth. Believed he was saying all this to test me, to toughen me.

We sat for a while longer, and I realized that I was feeling better. That we were lovers here on our bench, gazing at the deepening green of the water in evening, at the perfect reflection of Eleanor-Byrd Williams's church. There was satisfaction in knowing that we looked right, that the outer edges of things, at least, were as they should be, and thus perhaps some of what was inside would be contained in the proper shape.

That night Spencer left early and Shelley went to her room. Dave came to my room with me, and we were very tender together, and almost wordless, as we had been those first days when we were together. He left sometime in the middle of the night, but I didn't mind; I slept better, and woke early, feeling brisk and lovable.

The kitchen was bluer than green that morning. I started the water boiling for coffee, knowing how to make it with a filter now. Shelley had taught me. When I first came here, I had acted like a guest in her apartment, letting her serve me coffee, even slice a banana for my cereal. But now I took care of her sometimes. I washed out her mug from last night, set it out with milk, sugar, and jelly. I read a day old newspaper and tried to learn the names of some of those places in Southeast Asia that I could never quite get straight. I liked it that I was awake and making coffee and learning the different cities of Vietnam while Shelley dreamed a few doors away.

I heard her get up after a while, the floor creaking, the shuffling, the toilet flush and one of her morning moans as she came down the hallway. She blinked as if even the muted blue kitchen light were too much for her. "Don't speak," she said. "This is not a human being."

I laid a finger to my lips and sipped coffee with my face turned down to the paper, but watching her all the time. She was wrapped in her seersucker robe unevenly so the neck

154

opening was off center, and her right breast looked likely to spill out. Her hair was uncombed, of course, and she lifted a mass of it off her forehead to see better while she poured her coffee. Everything about her seemed like a lesson to me.

One day, when I was in the house alone, I had gone into her room and looked at her clothes. The thing that amazed me, the astounding thing about her wardrobe, was that she had fewer clothes than I did. There was empty space in her closet: there was the green smock dress and a long white one with a lot of lace, there was the blue jean skirt and there were the embroidered shirts from India and Mexico. I had twice as many things, a half dozen little shirt dresses in different pastel colors, blouses, skirts, everything machine washable and planned to match at least one other thing. But my clothes seemed vague and characterless compared to this handful of objects, each one like a work of art you could lay out in front of you and study for a long time. To my despair, even her underpants had style: each one a different nylon flower-print, while my drawer was stuffed with a three-week supply of white cotton, thick and bland as mashed potatoes.

But I was learning. And Shelley was generous. Here, she had said, I have too many of these blouses. And she had given me an orange Mexican one with red and green embroidery on it. I hadn't worn it yet; I was waiting to get a denim skirt, but in the meantime, I did wear sandals every day now.

She closed her eyes while she drank deeply from her coffee. Then she said, "Good morning. How are you? What's in the news? Where's Dave?"

"He didn't stay," I said, then quickly, while the impulse was on me, "You know him. He doesn't want anyone to see his car over here all night."

"You're too serious," she said. "Both of you. The people don't care if Dave's car is over here. I mean, he's just so— driven."

Of course, I thought. That's why it's difficult. Dave is so driven. And I am too.

"And I'll tell you something else," said Shelley. "Not that

155

it's any of my business, and not that there's any way not to have it in your life. But sex never made anything simpler. Sex always complicates everything."

And I thought, Of course, to that too. "You know, I think you're right. I always thought the other way—I always thought, when I was younger, that everything in my life would simplify once I had sex. But I was wrong."

"Yup," said Shelley. "You can't live with it and you can't live without it. That's sex. That's men."

"You and Spencer too?"

"Are you kidding?" She made a wild wave of her hand that almost knocked over her coffee mug. "Nine-tenths of the time Spencer would rather be with his gang than with me anyhow. Or with old Ralphie. I don't know what they do together, drink beer and take turns giving five. Spencer didn't get enough of a peer group when he was a kid or something. He's terrified of being womanized."

"He told me he intends to marry a virgin."

She made a sour mouth. "That's Spencer all right. That's the kind of childish pronouncement he thinks makes him sound like cock of the walk. And all the time, you know, he's such a baby. He wants the whole world to love him and take care of him. He's a youngest son, baby of his family."

"He's sexy though."

"You better believe it," she said, smiling a little and half closing her eyes. *She* was sexy too, I thought, with her hair in her face and her mouth puffed out a little as if she were reluctant to let loose of that smile.

I said, rapidly, because I'd never said anything like it before to anyone, "I can't seem to relax enough to really enjoy it. I'm always worrying I'll make a mess of things by getting, you know, pregnant."

She pulled her knees up on the chair with her, gathered them close in her arms and looked at me straight on. She had fine thick brows; there was nothing prissy about Shelley's features, lots of space around her eyes, and the eyes dominating the space. "What do you use for birth control?"

"Prophylactics," I said, my mouth going dry around the word.

"Oh well, that's your problem right there. It's so mechanical and messy, and of course you have to depend on him to do it. Someone as organized as you, Blair, you were tailormade for the Pill. You just read the little instruction booklet and you're in business. I've got pills by the gross. I'll give you all you need."

I was stunned. She had pills too. Embroidered blouses and pills. Whatever I needed. "I thought you had to see a doctor first."

"Down here? Are you kidding? I'd never go to a doctor down here, except maybe for a broken leg. You'd get some kind of old Kentucky fried colonel with a string tie. He'd say, 'Oh Honey, Ah don't thank a fine little gal lahk you-all wants to go and have say-ux!' Let me give you some of mine. I've got this cousin who's a pharmacist. I've got relatives in every business there is; I have an uncle who makes hats, my cousin Aaron writes poems. What do you want? Hats, poems?"

"Birth control pills," I said. "I think I'll take the birth control pills."

I wore the orange blouse out that day even though all I had to go with it was a poplin skirt. At least the skirt had a nice fit over my rump. I didn't necessarily want to make an effort to be sexy, but I wasn't sorry that the skirt fit so smoothly.

I had gradually come to like the canvassing. At first Dave, Roy, and I had gone door-to-door together, telling people about the meeting, and asking them to help us out with our survey about housing conditions in South Jenkin. Half the people wouldn't open their doors at all, and the other half seemed to open only long enough for a quick refusal and slam. We had our best success when Dave and Roy weren't visible at all. They apparently reminded people of bill collectors, while I looked like something more benign: a social worker, at worst. For a while we split up, and then Dave said he felt he was more productive doing research, and Roy gradually spent more and more of *his* time repairing Duchess's apartment or babysitting Jewel.

I felt myself taking possession of South Jenkin, block by block. When I walked down the street, women and elderly gentlemen waved at me. Children held my hand. I could gossip with Shelley and Spencer about people Dave hadn't even heard of yet. I still itched when I was stared at by the men on the corner: each part of my body seemed to advance toward them separately—breast, hair, hand, butt, like clothes hung on a line. Almost as bad at first had been the porchfuls of women who would let out peals of laughter as I passed. But I soon learned to walk right up and introduce myself, to pass out flyers and say I hoped to call on them individually very soon.

The porches full of women became easy, and the one- or two-family houses where you could stand on the porch while you knocked, but I never got over my discomfort in the large apartment houses where the poorest people lived. I would go through halls and up staircases with garbage cans and diaper buckets on the landings and the lightbulbs always missing from the fixtures. I heard the scrabble of living things, and hoped it was cats not rats. Food odors seeped out the cracks under the doors, giving some comfort: vegetable greens, frying pig parts. I would knock firmly, hear the hasty quieting of the television, the steps, know I was being looked at if there was a peephole.

Sometimes, in the most unexpected buildings, there would be a woman who invited me in without a smile, not because she was interested in my information but because she wanted a witness to the spotless linoleum on her floor, the dustless plastic over the couch, the ornately framed photographs on the television set of daughters in graduation gowns, sons in Marine uniforms. I didn't know you were coming, said the firmly set chin and unsmiling mouth, but look here how neat my house is. I could never bring myself to ask those ladies if they had roaches, waterbugs, or other vermin.

I could tell I was going to have good luck that day. At the first house I went to, the woman was outside hanging up some wash, and at the second house they had a little girl in Shelley's Scout troop. Everyone promised to come to the meeting.

A little farther, on a street almost at the limits of our neighborhood, where South Jenkin came to an abrupt halt near a field of warehouses and an industrial park, I ran across an isolated piece of an old farm, a Victorian frame house with clematis growing up wires on two sides of the porch, and a heavy-set elderly gentleman wearing overalls. He'd been a farmer all his life, he told me; he didn't walk so well anymore, but he still kept a kitchen garden. I told him all about our meeting, our plans for a housing organization, and he nodded and Yes ma'amed me, always gazing out across the low houses across the street toward the industrial park till I thought he was a sure bet to join our organizing efforts.

But then he took his turn speaking. He didn't know about all that, he said. He thought it was too late in his life to start up joining, but he surely did wish he could learn to read the Bible for himself during this last little stretch of his time on earth.

I, of course, trying to be a good Vista, immediately offered to give him reading lessons. He lowered his eyelids and said out at the sky and the low houses opposite, "I'm so old, I don't think there's but one way I could learn to read and that's if I was to go ahead where I left off in the old 'Blue Back Speller' when I was twelve years old. I do think I could pick up and learn if I had me a 'Blue Back Speller' again."

I wondered if this idea had come to him while I was standing there talking, or if it was something he'd been mulling over for a long time. I wondered if I were to be the answer to a respectfully repeated prayer. I had been recoiling lately from prayers, and especially from Calls, but I would have liked to be the answer to this man's prayer. And even if helping him learn to read was a sort of Call, I was willing to be drawn into that too. It didn't seem to seize me or rip me from the direction I was going. I was getting tired of asking people if they Owned, Rented, or Other, anyhow.

"We'll get you a speller," I said.

"Not one of these books for children, now," he said. "I don't want none of these Mickey Mouses. I would need me a real old Webster's 'Blue Back Speller.' "

"I understand," I said. "I think I'll probably have to go to a secondhand bookstore, but I bet we can find one."

"I would pay whatever it costs," he said. "I take care of myself."

When I got up to go, he shook my hand and blessed me, and apologized for not getting up. It was his rheumatism, he said, and also he didn't see so well anymore. I looked back at him when I was out on the sidewalk again, and waved. His heavy hands stayed where they were, on the thighs of his overalls, in the shade of the clematis vine. I had thought his eyes were of some exotic light color, but now I thought that maybe it had been cataracts. If he wanted the old "Blue Back Speller," I'd get him the old "Blue Back Speller"; he could hold it on his lap and rock. It was as if I were not in the city anymore but in a bright, distant country place where different laws held sway and prayers were answered—irregularly but not infrequently. Where heavenbent elders with cataracts could learn to read.

I didn't think there were any more occupied houses on that street. Hot wind blew through the high grass of two empty lots. The last house before the street ended at the back of a metal-walled warehouse was surely deserted; it was one of the cheap shotgun-style houses where one room opens into the next until you come to the back. A shack, really, half the siding torn off of the bare tarpaper. Plywood over the front windows.

I was going to quit and go home for lunch, but I tightened the little leash of discipline over myself and said, No, that metal toy bucket and shovel are not rusted. Children have been playing here recently. There were no steps to the porch, and the porch itself lacked several boards. I knocked, and heard a faint creak inside, so I knocked again. A shy one, I thought. No peephole in the door, not even glass with a curtain to ease back. The gentle creak continued and I bammed harder: I've got the knack now, I thought; I'm thick-skinned and I bring 'em back alive. "Hello? Could I speak with you for just a minute?"

A bolt slid. She opened a third of the way, a half. Plump, shorter than I was, baby and bottle in one arm, and two small children clinging to her from behind. Pinned-up braids and huge terrified eyes. "My husband," she said. "I ain't supposed to open up to nobody, I'm sorry." But she didn't close the door.

I gave her a huge smile. "I'm so pleased to meet you," I said. "I'm with the Tidewater Against Poverty Services? Perhaps you've heard of it? We're working to fight poverty in South Jenkin?"

"We ain't live here that long."

I had an urge to say, Yes, but you sure are poor. There was something about her tremulous softness that brought out an aggressive part of me. "I'll only take a minute of your time," I told her. "I want to tell you about a meeting. You're invited to a meeting."

"Invited?" she said. That was the right word for her, then. I always said a lot of words fast, searching for the one name or word or phrase that would justify my presence at their door. For some, TAPS did the trick, or an evocation of the President's War on Poverty. For others, it helped to mention Reverend Frank Landell, but this woman broke into deep smile dimples when I told her she was invited.

"Well, I suppose *that's* okay," she said, and now I noticed that her skin was a marvelous coppery color, hairless, spread like satin paint over those rounded cheeks and forearms. "I don't expect I'll be able to come, though," she said. "My husband don't even allow me to go to folks' houses around here. But some of these folks is drinkers. I don't get to church that much either."

Her name was Mrs. Murrell, and even the inside of her

house had a look of having been hastily deserted. I could see three rooms of it from where I stood, newspaper over holes in the wallboard, mattresses with no sheets on all the floors, paper bags of clothing. In the middle room was a galvanized tub with water, and two more children sitting in it.

"Oh," she said, "I was just washing them." We both looked around the room: no chairs, only drab colors, except for that rich-hued flesh of her and her children. All of them in their underwear, or naked. I realized that I had thought Mrs. Murrell herself was wearing a sundress, but it was a cotton slip. Her dimples, which had come so suddenly, now turned to tears. "Look at me, asking you in and no place to even sit down." She didn't sob; she never so much as stopped jiggling the baby, but tears seeped out of her.

I said, "Maybe I should come back another time."

"Don't go away. Don't mind. I'm sorry we not dressed, I was washing the clothes and I thought I better just wash the children too. Once I get started, I wash everything in sight." She giggled and gave me a questioning glance as if she had a thought of grabbing me and my stack of pink flyers and wrestling us into the washtub, too. "Yes," she said, "I just woke up this morning and said I'ma wash everything, and that's what I been doing this morning until—you came!" She beamed at me when she said that; her morning had culminated in my visit.

"Let me tell you why I'm here then." I made my speech rapidly, with a strong sense that what I was saying had nothing to do with her life. The Pill, I thought in the back of my mind. *That* would have an effect on her life. I kept talking and she smiled and smiled, apparently just happy to have an adult in the room with her. When I got to the point where I mentioned Frank Landell being a supporter of our program, she tipped her head forward.

"Is he the preacher of that big, fine, stone-looking church?"

"Yes," I said. "Reverend Landell is a good man. And a wonderful preacher. He's one of our biggest supporters. His wife too."

162

"Has he got children?"

"One little boy."

"Which size of mine?" I pointed out one of her babies, and she started to cry again. "My children, they never hear preaching or singing. They don't know hardly what a church is. I don't know . . . it was better when we used to be out in Princess Anne. It was just country out there. But you never had to be, you know, locking your door. Around here my husband don't let me open the door to nobody—" She laughed and hugged the baby to her with both arms. "I don't know why I opened up to you. You sounded nice, I guess. I never had a white lady before!"

I had this feeling that she would like nothing better than for me to keep talking with her, for an hour, for two hours, five. Whatever it took to get her through all her changes from tears to laughter and back again. I gave her the flyer with the little drawing of a neat apartment house with flower boxes and curtains. I drew it myself, I told her, cutting the mimeograph film with a stylus. She showed her children the picture and told them I had drawn it. She read the whole flyer aloud.

"Tuesday night," she said. "And there'll be a movie. Did you children hear that? There'll be a movie, but for grownups. Will church people be there? I been thinking I would start up going to church."

"Absolutely. Reverend Landell himself will be there. If you come, I'll introduce you to him."

She made me describe several times how to get to Neighborhood House, and when I finally left, she followed me out onto the porch in her slip, with the children still in her arms, clinging to her legs.

"Can I keep the picture?" she shouted after me, waving hard. "Can I keep the picture?"

The two biggest children dashed out into the yard and started playing with the bucket and shovel, and the last thing I saw was Mrs. Murrell calling them all back, making them stand close around her, buds of her flesh.

Birth control pills, I thought. Tonight. Don't forget.

Ten

We Vistas took a somewhat contemptuous view of Mrs. White the TAPS Neighborhood Worker. Sometimes we sat around—Shelley and Spencer and I—and discussed whether or not she counted as a real community person. She certainly met the TAPS criteria: she had been on welfare, she had four daughters and no resources, and the TAPS job had been a lifesaver for her. But while she was devoted to the organization, we thought she worked much harder at keeping the office neat than at finding other people in South Jenkin who needed help. She arrived every morning on the dot of nine—a well-built woman in her mid-thirties, hair straightened, oiled, and rollered to smoothness, dresses crisp and pastel, with matching jackets—and made a thorough survey of the premises of the Neighborhood Center. She had discovered the new panes of glass the Monday morning after the dance moments after walking in, and called Spencer immediately. He and Ralph came back and cleaned the fingerprints off the glass, and rescraped the putty. On the other hand, she never inquired about how the glass and flowerpot came to be broken in the first place.

That was what made the discussion worth the hour and a half we went back and forth about it. "She *is* a real community person, isn't she, Spencer?" I would say.

And Spencer would answer, "She don't do no harm, if you know what I mean." This would cause Shelley to launch an attack on the geraniums on the porch, and the flower borders around the little yard, and the use of the sewing machine for identical sundresses for Mrs. White and her daughters.

Meanwhile, Dave read his paper or compiled notes on the day's research, pointedly staying out of the conversation. It became a guilty pleasure for me to curl up on the pillows of our red living room, drinking coffee or maybe a little wine, feeling slightly demeaned but defiant too, gossiping with Spencer and Shelley.

One of the things Mrs. White didn't approve of was night meetings. She didn't like to leave her girls at home alone, she said. There was no pay for night meetings.

"So don't come," said Shelley.

"It's a TAPS rule for a worker to be here for meetings," said Mrs. White.

"You mean it *is* part of your job?" said Shelley.

"It's dangerous too, walking home late on those streets, a lady alone."

"I'll walk you home," said Spencer.

"Be more danger *that* way," said Mrs. White, but she smiled at the same time, and continued to mutter and complain, and then on the night of our housing meeting came an hour earlier than the rest of us and got out the coffee urn and laid a table with paper plates and pink and yellow napkins.

Everything was ready for the meeting. We had the cookies, we had the cream, we had the film projector set up. We decided on forty chairs in rows of eight. I unfolded them slowly, watching the door for arrivals, because there was nothing else left to do. The only person I was really sure of, was really depending on, was Marie Conyers. She seemed so wholly understanding of what we were trying to do. I stopped by her porch almost every day and told her my adventures, and she always seemed so *interested*, and encouraging. There were a couple of other women like her who seemed to me the kind of rocks you could build a movement on. I only wished some of them would arrive so I could relax and stop feeling vulnerable.

Something about Dave troubled me, too. I decided after a

while it was his seersucker suit, identical to the one the Health Department man had worn the day we got Marie's toilet fixed. It made me uncomfortable that Dave would suddenly start wearing a suit. As if he had decided to look like an official instead of an organizer. He was freshly showered, and he had washed his hair, too, and brushed it back so that too much of his forehead showed. He looked all intense and hopeful. Like me. He and I together, we were the ones being tested. Shelley and Spencer had helped out with the surveys and publicity, but haphazardly, without committing themselves. This meeting tonight, win or lose, was Dave's and mine, and I didn't want to look at him.

The Health Department man arrived, balding, in his seersucker suit. Side by side he and Dave looked like a before-and-after commercial for Hair-Grow. I went over and stood with them, but didn't hear what they were saying because I found myself mezmerized by the clock over the door; it was three minutes before the seven-thirty meeting time.

No one is here yet, I thought. It can't be that absolutely no one is going to come. That all my knocking on doors, pressing flyers into hands, and taping them up on store windows— all the dank halls I had stood in, with my heart pounding, the stencils I had cut, spoiled, recut, the oily ink on my hands from the mimeograph machine, the hours of discussing what to put on the flyer—that all this would result in a movie being shown to a TAPS Neighborhood Worker and three Vista volunteers. Not even Marie was here. Had we missed something important? Wasn't housing a felt need of these people? It seemed obvious enough to me; their plaster was falling off, their porches were missing boards, leaking pipes were wrapped in towels.

Dave's conversation with the health man seemed to get softer and softer. Maybe he knew some rule of organizing that he'd never bothered to tell me. That the first meeting is always a sacrifice, that people only come out for the second one?

Roy and Duchess drifted in, but she didn't count, she was

practically a Vista herself, and Roy was something else altogether, in his own world. No one, no one, I thought. A complete disaster.

Spencer arrived with his friend Ralphie, who was dressed in a conservative dark suit as usual, with his hair freshly marcelled tonight. "Hey, Blair," said Spencer cheerfully. "Where's the Masses?" I looked away, and he added, "Cheer up, it's not so bad."

"Nobody is coming," I said. "It's seven-thirty, and not a single community person is here."

He toned down his smile. "Well," he said, "you gotta consider. Colored People Time, and all that. Let me go see if I can scare up some folks for you."

I was touched that he had picked up on my despair. Dave was completely oblivious, entirely engaged in one of his fact-finding conversations, his arms crossed, nodding along with the health man. Dave! I wanted to scream. What happened? It's past time! We've failed! His eyes roamed the room once, passing over me, then came back. "Blair?" he said, as if he didn't quite recognize me. "Blair? When you get a minute, could you see if there's one more extension cord?"

No one noticed that I stomped to the closet. When I stomped back, we did finally have a real community person, who was no one's lover and on no one's payroll—someone, in fact, I had given a flyer to: Mrs. Veronne Foley, mother of Boji and the jailed Robert Foley, here, with her powerful torso, her high buttocks carried on straight legs that were riding down the backs of a pair of men's loafers. She worked her lips and frowned in the direction of the two seersucker suits. She made a wide circle around them.

I ran to her, and said, "Hello, Mrs. Foley, how are you this evening?"

"Fine. This evening," she said, and walked around me too, drew a chair from the back, and made her own row.

More people were arriving, but this time it turned out to be the Landells, Frank, Yvetta, Little Frank, and Yvetta's grandmother. But they don't count either, I thought, they're

167

the preacher's family. Then Spencer came back with three of his boys, Bo-ji, with his arm still bandaged, Brother Conyers and Harold. Bo-ji ducked his head when he saw his mother, and sat at the end of the back row farthest from her.

Where are the real people? I thought. Where are the others? And again Dave's eyes passed over me as if I were of no particular interest, as if I were merely one of the heads he was counting. I couldn't help having a sense that I was being punished—placed outside the circle of his attention because I had failed to bring the people in. I was the one who was supposed to convince them to come. I was the one who knocked on the doors. Dave would never say anything blameful in so many words, but the weight of my responsibility kept buckling my knees until I took a seat. So many had said they would try to come that I had thought a certain percentage of them surely would. But I saw now that the smile, the nod, the half-promise had meant something else: that they would like to come—if it were a different world, if it were possible—but, of course, I should have understood it was not possible. Not even for Marie. Not even Marie Conyers who, I thought, understood everything I said and the importance of this meeting.

Dave consulted with Frank Landell and then asked everyone to take a seat. It was true, then. We were beginning with no one here. Dave didn't seem disappointed, but it may have been a front or maybe the thing he knew and I didn't. People nodded genially back and forth to one another. There is a secret, I thought, there must be. Something he won't tell me yet. Shelley slipped into the chair in front of me, and Mrs. White was at the other end of my row. So many empty seats. The front row solid with the Landell party, Spencer's boys in the back, but the rest of us were tiny dots in the middle.

Dave thanked us all for coming out. He thanked the health man for coming. The door opened one more time; one more person came in. I didn't remember her. Probably not even one of my contacts, I thought dismally. She looked like genuine community, though, in her brilliant red knit dress with a boat neck, a winter dress, too heavy for midsummer, a soft, chubby woman, copper-colored except for pink cheeks, hair in braids doubled over her crown, panting a little. She waved vigorously and tottered toward me on her high heels. Wafting waves of powder, she took the seat next to me, whispering, "Am I late? Oh, I got so lost, they didn't have the movie yet, did they?"

I thought, My Lord, it's Mrs. Murrell. Of all my contacts, of all the efficient looking women who said they always went to meetings and believed in the good work of TAPS and Vista and the OEO—the one at the bottom of my list of the likely to show up was Mrs. Murrell. But here she was, red and copper, like a kettle on glowing coals, so pleased with herself.

Still out of breath, she leaned to me. "I didn't think my husband was going to let me come, but I told him about *you* coming over to invite me." She settled back then, and I felt like crying. It had to do with her having taken the stupid invitation so personally. That she had come because *I* invited *her*. Well, I thought, I don't care about the others. To heck with Marie Conyers. Mrs. Murrell came. When Frank Landell gave an opening prayer, she whispered to me that she could tell already he was a fine preacher.

The movie was a letdown after all the drama I'd been experiencing inside myself. It was a cartoon with a villain called Ghastly Garbage who was outfitted in black from head to toe: mustache, cloak, shoe-polish hair. The plot line concerned a neighborhood of one-family houses with picket fences where the people from time to time left garbage outside of garbage cans. Or didn't repair broken fences. Ghastly twirled his mustache and chortled, and the whole neighborhood began to darken. Picket fences went from gray to charcoal, houses became first livid yellow then brown.

Shelley turned around and whispered, "I can't believe it. The neighborhood is turning colored. Oh my God!" There was a phantom-of-the-opera chord and the one-family houses were suddenly transformed into a grim silhouette of a city slum. A crooked-nosed rat skulked in the foreground.

After a while, a character called Casper Clean-up, who wore a white coverall, began to go around planting tulips, bagging trash, and emptying water from old tires. Each time he performed one of these civic actions, large, clear words would be superimposed on the screen: Get Rid of Mosquito Breeding Places! Use Rat Poison! Ghastly cursed that he had been foiled again; the heavy silhouette of cityscape receded into the background while the houses got fresh coats of paint and the movie ended with the picket fences and flowers again. Remember, said Casper: Only you can keep up your neighborhood!

"Awful!" murmured Shelley, "awful, awful, awful."

Everyone blinked, and a row behind me, Roy yawned enormously and got a poke in the ribs from Duchess. I glanced back to try and catch Spencer's eye, but he had his shades on, so I looked up at Dave, and this time he did meet my eyes, and he lifted one eyebrow and pursed his lips ever so slightly, but enough that I knew he and I understood one another again.

Dave said to the health man, as if there had been no film at all, "We were hoping you could outline the different responsibilities of the landlord and tenant for us."

The health man talked a while about the importance of keeping the landlord-tenant relationship friendly, and then Dave passed out a mimeographed sheet where we had compiled material from the fire, health, and building codes. It represented weeks of Dave's marching from office to office to find out who had jurisdiction over what, and hours of my error beset stencil typing. Just take a look at it, Dave told us, and then maybe we can ask some specific questions.

There was a silence. The Vistas were waiting for the Community to speak. Finally Mrs. White got up and thanked the health man for coming. Shelley and I rolled our eyes at one another. Mrs. White wanted to skip this discussion part, do a quick wrap-up, and get on to the tea party and then home. Yvetta's grandmother started clapping, and we all joined in.

When Dave asked if anyone had any specific questions—
now that we'd looked at the sheets—Spencer unfolded himself from his teen-age slouch and said, "Yeah, I was wondering about the, you know, symbolism? in your movie? The
bad guys all wearing black clothes, and Mr. Charley Clean-
up—"

"Casper," said the health man, color high in his cheeks.

"Oh, yeah," said Spencer. "Oh yeah, I guess I got that
wrong. Anyhow, this character in the white outfit was the
good guy, and I was wondering if you were getting into something about race there—"

"No, no, of course not!" The health man glanced to Dave
for support, but Dave was making a pencil mark on his list.
"You're wrong. Of course it wasn't meant as a racial slur. It
was only a cartoon—"

Spencer suddenly jabbed the air with a finger. "Man, I
think *you're* wrong. I think the movie says what The Man's
society says, and that's Black stay back and white's all right,
and I say that's peckerwood jimcrow bullshit, man!"

Harold jumped up too. "That's a jimcrow bullshit movie!"

Brother Conyers was up too, but Bo-ji stayed low, probably
hoping his mother wouldn't notice him. Other people began
to frown. Yvetta Landell's grandmother made negative noises.
Frank himself stood up, and Spencer and the boys sat down.

"Now," said Frank. "Dave Rivers, and Blair Morgan, and
Mrs. White and Shelley—" he took his time, naming each
name, and skipped Spencer—"everybody has worked hard to
put this program together tonight. We've learned something
already, and I think what we have to do now is take a good
look at this list and see if we can learn even more."

Mrs. Murrell whispered, "Should I raise my hand? I never
raised my hand before, not even in school."

"Sure," I said. "Go ahead," but Veronne Foley had begun
emitting a string of words first.

I couldn't tell if they were something private pouring out,
or if she meant everyone to hear. She spoke louder on her
second breath, though: thickly, as if she had no teeth or as if

her tongue had cleaved to the roof of her mouth, but you could understand. "I got me a house," she said. "I do fine, me and mine, and my enemies *will* suffer, when the time comes. But we got a house now, and we do fine long as we got a roof. I got a roof, but half the time I ain't got money to put something on the stove."

Mrs. Murrell jumped to her feet before it was entirely clear that Mrs. Foley had finished. "I am so happy to be here!" she cried. "I am so happy my friend Blair Morgan invited me here, and I had a wonderful time!" People beamed at her and at me: Dave, Frank Landell, Shelley. Everyone was proud of me. "I only just come to live around here," said Mrs. Murrell, "and I don't know hardly anyone. But everyone is so nice and friendly and"—her deep dimples appeared—"I see you have a fine pastor, man of God—" Frank Landell smiled broadly, kindly. It seemed that she intended to keep going, to say she hoped to be coming to church soon. "I'm like that lady who spoke; that house I live in ain't much, but it's a house, and my husband works hard. But I do know that half the time what he brings home ain't enough to carry through the week, and I don't know what a person is supposed to do." I thought she was going to cry, but they all said That's right, and Isn't that the truth; she ended up smiling, and sat down.

I whispered that she spoke real well, and she cried a few tears, after all.

Meanwhile Yvetta Landell was saying she knew of a supermarket where things were so much cheaper than around here, and Duchess, without getting up, slumped down as far in her chair as the boys in the back, said, "That's fine for folks with cars."

Frank Landell said, "Maybe we could work something out so people from the church who have cars could take people over there to that supermarket?"

The health man, evidently relieved that he wasn't going to have to answer questions based on the information sheet, said, "You know, it's an interesting fact, but down at the department we have statistics, and it is true, you know, that prices are higher in South Jenkin than in other neighborhoods."

"Is that a fact?" muttered Spencer. "So what else is new."

But there was a silence from the others, an odd look of discovery passed around. "It's not new," said Duchess. "But it sure ain't *right*."

Mrs. White said, "Why, you'd think people could . . . I don't know . . . get it cheap together."

Again the heads turning. "Wouldn't that be nice," said Mrs. Murrell.

Dave's face seemed to spread out taut behind the glasses, all the energy focused for the moment in his eyes. There *is* a way to do that, he told us. There is a thing called a food cooperative—not that it matters what you call it. You could call it a buying club, too. People pool their money and buy groceries at wholesale prices. Meat a third off. Chickens. No middle man.

"Now *that* sounds like something," said Duchess.

"You do that, Vista," said Veronne Foley, pacing back and forth now in front of the coffee pot. "You do that and you be doing something."

The coffee pot burbled once in the silence and clicked as its ready light came on. We talked a little more about how we would like to get food at wholesale prices, how the club would work, and then let the warm smell of coffee draw us out of the meeting, toward the refreshments.

I introduced Mrs. Murrell to Reverend Landell. The health man ate a cookie and gave us the name of his brother-in-law, a butcher. Duchess said she was sending Roy over the first thing in the morning to get the Cheap Meat Club started; she could almost taste the steak now, baked in foil with onions.

"In foil?" said Mrs. White. "Is that right?"

As they began to leave, I found myself running and telling each one goodbye at the door. The Landells were going to drive Mrs. Murrell home. She whispered to me that she had

had the best time of her life. I wouldn't go that far, I thought, but it certainly ended up better than I thought it was going to. Shelley and Spencer went off with Ralph; Mrs. White said she would go on home and let me and Dave close up.

When at last it was just Dave and me, I folded the last of the chairs and he put away the projector. I went up three steps on the staircase to flip off the lights, and as I turned around, Dave was waiting for me. He pinned me against the wall, and buried his face in my chest. "I think we've got it now, Blair. I think we've really got it!"

I put my arms around him. It was nice for once to have someone's face in my chest and my head out in the open. "You aren't disappointed with the turnout? I thought more people would come." He undid a button on my dress and started kissing the skin just above my bra. I said, "I really don't understand Marie Conyers not coming. She *said* she would. I depended on her coming. Even if no one else did!"

"She had a baby," he said into my skin.

"She *what?*"

"She had a baby boy."

"Why didn't I know? Who told you?"

"Brother told me. She just had it this morning."

I couldn't believe it. All the time I had known Marie, sitting on her porch in the green jungle heat, listening for her advice as a representative of the community—listening for wisdom—she had been pregnant, and I never knew. I didn't know whether to be humiliated or awed. I had a sudden picture; she was going to laugh at me when I went to visit. She was going to say, You never knew, did you? You thought it was just fat, and all the time some of it was the baby. "I'm so stupid sometimes I can't believe it," I said.

He was unbuttoning more of my buttons, loosening my bra. He wanted to hold my breasts. In the faint light I could see the sheen of sweat on his forehead and cheeks. Waves of heat were coming from him; his weight pressed me down into the stairs, and we clasped one another and kissed.

174

I said, "But what about all the work we did? The housing information sheet? It's all a waste, isn't it? Aren't you disappointed about that?"

"Why should I be disappointed? Don't you see what happened? They told us what they wanted? They expressed their real need."

"Veronne Foley, and Mrs. Murrell, and Mrs. White did."

All around me Dave's voice came flying like brands of light. "No, no, Blair, they were speaking for everyone. Didn't you hear it?" He leaned back, feverishly stroking my arms, feeling my breasts. I didn't know what to do with my hands. "Nothing was wasted. We'll use it all, but first we start where they need to start. It was a privilege to be there, Blair. Don't you feel it happening?"

Light flickered on his teeth, which were grinning or gritted, I couldn't tell which. He was suddenly quiet under an extreme tension, his back bent like a bow. I began to kiss him, to run my fingers over his face: forehead slippery with sweat, nose large, the sharp hairs of his beard. Only his lips moved when my fingers passed over them. He sucked my fingertips. I ran my hands over the arch of his chest, amazed at the breadth and solidity of it.

I'm doing something for him now, I thought.

He groaned and stirred, began to work his fingers at his belt and zipper. I knew what he wanted, and I let him direct my hands to it. I was shocked by its heat. Not moist this time, but thick, dry, and hot. Like a walking stick, or the handle of a good hardwood tool. I gripped it as if it were one of those, and he began to arch himself again, to lift his loins, this upright strong thing moving in my hands, slipping back and forth loosely under its foreskin.

My eyes were popping in the darkness; I wanted to see it all. But he was pressing my head down toward it. I thought with pride: You see, I do ease you, I am doing something to ease you now.

I kept my grip as I lowered my head, and gave it a quick kiss to show I was willing, but a little indentation at the end of it frightened me. I thought there must be something wrong with him, then remembered it would have to have some kind of a hole. Meanwhile his pressure continuing on the back of my neck, his thighs moving, and warm air rising out of his pants: clean sweat, good health. I put my mouth over it, as over a drinking fountain. I could feel ridges on the sides of it, blood vessels. I was afraid of pressing too hard and doing damage: it seemed strong, and yet I could feel the blood pulsing through the thinnest of membranes, such thin skin. I would have asked him to let me see it in the light, but there was no time, he was grunting harder, moving my head where he wanted it, and I could feel only fullness. I was almost gagging, my face sweating, saliva coating him from my mouth, and in the far distance, from his head, noise like barks, and under me the arched power of thighs and loins, and a sudden miraculous doubling and tripling of saliva which ran out of the corners of my mouth, and then I realized it wasn't saliva, but that he had come, and I pulled away and said, "Oh!"

He groaned and held himself with one hand, turned half on his side, and got out a handkerchief which he passed to me. I spat in it, wiped my mouth, and then, to show I wasn't disgusted, wiped him off, too. While I wiped, he stroked my head.

"You're so good," he said. "You take such good care of me."

Do I? I thought. I guess I really do. I lifted him, wiped on all sides.

"When I look at you," he said, "when I looked at you at the meeting tonight, you're always right there, both feet on the ground. So solid. You give me strength."

I felt dizzy. Was he talking about tonight? About me? When I was ready to run out in despair? When I thought he was looking through me, not at me? But I liked better what he saw: a strong woman, indefatigable, unsinkable.

We washed up, locked the Neighborhood House, and walked the two blocks to my apartment where he had left the Volkswagen. We held hands, and from time to time he would put his arm around me and squeeze hard. "So good," he murmured, almost too grateful. "It's like a miracle," he said.

The phone was ringing as we went in the house, and I ran for it, expecting Shelley's voice asking if we wanted them to bring us back pizza or beer, but instead heard a smaller voice that seemed to come out of the past. "Blair?" it said, and I thought for a second it was my mother, or one of my aunts, but there was some unfamiliar emotion in it, and also a quality of having been drenched, as if the voice were speaking out of a storm of barely contained sobs. "Blair," it said. "Oh Blair, honey, is that you? Finally someone's there. I've been calling and calling. It's Martha McTeague, Blair. I called because—Paul had a heart attack."

"Oh no," I said. "You want to speak to Dave?"

For a moment his eyes seemed to pierce the phone to see her, then he pushed his glasses up on his forehead, and rubbed his eyes. He too said "Oh no," and I was grimly pleased that my reaction had been no more stupid than his. Will it always be like this? I thought. Will people always have heart attacks when you least expect it? "Yes," he said. "Where will you be? I'll leave tonight. Now. It'll be okay, Martha. I'll be right there."

He's like their son, I thought. The son they never had.

He said to me, "It sounds bad. He collapsed going upstairs after dinner. He's in the hospital, getting oxygen. You heard how Martha is."

I said, "Shall I go with you?" I had a picture in my mind of talking to keep him awake, driving through the dark mountains.

"No," he said. "I don't want any time wasted on this food co-op thing. I want you to stay and get on it tomorrow. I don't want to lose the moment."

"How long will you be gone? Oh, that's silly, as long as they need you, I guess." I had the feeling, though, that the woman with the planted feet, the one who inspired Dave, would not have any existence without him to tell her about herself.

I offered to make coffee for him to take with him. He said

he'd go over to Old Fellows Street for his clothes and the thermos. But he was already closing in on himself, and I suddenly remembered perfectly the despair I had felt before the meeting began, when I thought no one was coming, when I thought he was mad at me.

This was cruel, I thought, that Dave should be snatched away just when I was about to become the person he wanted me to be. Just when we were about to embark on this enormous project—the real one, at last—after all our preparation and false starts. Everything snatched away. Guiltily, I tried to make myself feel sorry for poor Reverend McTeague, but I hadn't thought of him and Martha for weeks. They weren't part of this life. I felt instead a choking fury at those people who were somehow willfully doing this: jerking a leash to drag Dave back to them, blowing up that man's sick body like a giant balloon, crowding me painfully all the way down here.

Dave brought the thermos, I gave him the coffee. We kissed goodbye, and then he spun away, back through the fogs, into the mountains, leaving me in the tidal flats.

Eleven

I wanted to have the Buying Club set up by the time Dave got back from visiting Paul and Martha. I wanted to show him that I was his true equal, that I could pull things together out of real life—organize. But everything seemed to move too slowly, and I despaired of doing it all by myself. I waited for people to return phone calls. I knocked on doors again. People weren't home; they didn't return the calls. I couldn't see clearly in my mind what it would actually be like, the thing I was working for.

And I seemed easily deflected from my purpose. On Friday Shelley and Spencer were having a swimming trip to the Navy base pool for the kids. Dave would have helped out if he'd been here, I thought. I'm sure he would. He couldn't think there was anything wrong with leaving off work on the Buying Club for one day. It was a kind of trade anyhow; I would help them, and then Spencer and Shelley would help us.

We left the house at 7:30 a.m. Friday, Shelley in a terrible mood, furious at Spencer. He hadn't come over the night before, and she muttered about him all the way through a thick fog up Edgecomb Avenue.

"Spencer has done nothing on this whole swimming trip except have lunch with Chuck Williams," she said. "He loves to put on the three-piece suit. That's what Spencer really wants, you know, to be a big executive with a nice house and a big car. You watch. When we're forty years old, he'll be

179

some kind of vice president at General Motors, or more likely brown-nosing the president of General Motors." She came to a full stop across from the empty lot. "There! Do you see that?" A bedspring and an old refrigerator with the door hanging off at an angle. "The refrigerator!" she said. "That just tears it. The half-assedness of it. My God. Do you know why he couldn't help me yesterday? He had an important thing going with his teenagers. There was this refrigerator sitting around that some child was going to play in and get suffocated."

"So they came and took the door off?"

"But that's the point! It's not off. Don't you see? The only way to make it safe is to take it all the way off, not partly off. Spencer came up here with Harold and Brother and Bo-ji and they sat around and drank beer out of brown bags so Spencer could feel like a blood and then they undid one hinge and got tired and went home. It's so typical."

We saw Spencer himself at the corner, a lean silhouette in the fog, waiting for us. Shelley started blasting from fifteen paces. "Oh it's Al Capone," she said. "Chicago's first prep school black gangster."

Spencer gave me a big smile. "Hey, Blair. Who's your friend Witch Eyes?"

She said, "Somebody really pissed off, that's who."

"Don't be that way, Shell."

"You get away with too much," she said, but she stopped shouting and let him put his arm around her shoulder.

They were hanging back a little, so I went on ahead. Kids were already gathering on the porch of the Neighborhood Center.

Shelley said, "Check for towels and lunches, will you, Blair?"

Just before I got to the Center, I looked back. They stood close, but not looking at each other, like the couples in high school who used to press together every instant between classes as near as their clothes permitted, huddling like cattle in a rainstorm.

Roy was leaning on a car with his arms crossed. At least he wasn't wearing one of his costumes. Except for the sideburns, he looked just as I'd first known him in college: the faded plaid shirt, high-waisted khaki pants. He made no move to stop Hooky from threatening Gilbert Duberry with a chair leg.

"Hooky!" I said. "Give me that." He sneered, but trailed the chair leg on the ground, and I grabbed it and shoved it under the porch. "Hooky," I said, loudly, so he and Charlie and Jewel and all of the other kids would hear and perhaps think me formidable. "Did you know I used to be a lifeguard?"

Charlie's brows rose. "Did you ever save any lives?"

"Well," I said, "at a pool you generally save lives by making sure no one goes in deep water if they can't swim." They waited for the exciting part. I said, "One time a boy fell down because he was running and cracked his head open on the sidewalk."

"That's disgusting." Jewel made a face. "Did his brains come out?"

"No brains, just a lot of blood. The ambulance came." They immediately started playing lifeguard, arguing over who would drown. Charlie got to be the ambulance.

Landells' station wagon arrived, Yvetta was going on the trip with us. She popped out of the car, all in pink. Station wagon, I thought. Buying club. Frank stood the baby on the hood of the car while Yvetta got her things out of the back. Frank wasn't wearing preacher clothes today, but a knit polo shirt that showed off his muscles. He said to Frank Junior, "We aren't going, son. *We're* staying home today while Mommy goes." He gave me a big smile. "I'm babysitting."

Yvetta had her beach bag, looked eager and excited, as if this day away from home were something special for her. She tucked in Frank Junior's shirt and kissed him, and said she had better get started. The baby pointed after her and looked at Frank, but didn't cry. Frank looked sadder than Frank Junior.

I started talking, trying to get around to the station wagon. He had, after all, offered to drive people to the grocery store, or had he meant he would get people from the church to do it? I said something about how eager we were to start the buying club, but we had this problem with finding a way to transport the food. I paused, giving him a chance to volunteer, but he didn't respond at all, wasn't really paying attention. I readjusted my position slightly and saw Yvetta behind me, talking to children, checking towels and lunches. Frank was following every move she made, only pretending to listen. It gave me the sense of being left out again, of looking at lovers in the fog. A mystery between them, something from which I could only be excluded.

"I'm sorry," he said. "I wasn't listening."

"We need a panel truck or something to carry the groceries in."

Frank gave Frank Junior a jiggle, as if whatever had been making him sad—whether it was Yvetta leaving them alone or something heavier, a deeper disappointment between him and her—as if he had briskly, firmly, put it aside. "Why, we can come up with something from the church. Let that be our contribution."

"Would you really?" He was a splendid man, really, just what I'd always understood that a man was supposed to be: deep-voiced and thick-chested. Taking care of things. The very back of his head, as he turned to give Frank Junior a kiss, a perfect hemisphere under his tight, close hair. There when you needed him, the way he had been at the housing meeting. He would call up tomorrow to say he had a shiny red pick-up truck for us. I wanted him to take care of the truck, and take care of us. Either him, or Chuck Williams, the other man who always seemed to know how to make things happen. The way Dave had seemed to me at first. Men magically unlike the rest of us with our moments of distraction, irrational anger, irresponsibility. We need more grown-ups around, I thought, and I asked Frank if he was going to stay and help us put the kids on the bus, but he said he better not, he was afraid Frank Junior would cry.

Shelley beckoned me to a Vista conference. They were talking about television. Apparently Chuck Williams had got the TV station to send a crew to photograph the kids going swimming. Shelley said, "The thing is, we want to make sure they interview community people—not Vistas. We don't want to look like a lot of carpetbaggers from the North."

I said, "Catch Frank Landell before he goes. He's a good community person."

"Not the Rev," said Spencer. "He's already got his face in everything."

Roy said, "Their news stinks. They love to report how many Vietnamese our troops have killed. And all the time, these people here, they're the same as the Vietnamese. They're dying too."

Shelley said, with more patience than I would have expected, "It's not that you're wrong, Roy, it's that there are wrong times to say things. And this time we want people who watch the six o'clock news to like TAPS and Vista. You see what I mean?"

"There's no use offending people," I said.

Roy lowered his head. "I say if you're not part of the solution, you're part of the problem."

Spencer laughed. "Roy's working on his ideology. He's studying to be a *cadre*."

I was beginning to be irritated. Spencer was setting Roy up again. "What's a cadre?"

Roy said, "The trouble with all of you is you're scared to go the whole distance. Read *The Wretched of the Earth*."

"My books," said Spencer, still grinning, as if he thought it was hilarious that Roy had been in that hole on Old Fellows Street, listening to the rats and cats fight it out, and thinking he was part of an oppressed people. Now I'll have to read *those* books too, I thought, feeling that it was all just too much.

"The trouble with you people," said Roy, "the trouble with you people is that you don't feel the oppressor's boot on your neck."

"And you do?" said Shelley. "Sitting over there letting

Duchess make your meals and iron your shirts while you read? That's oppression? Maybe for Duchess."

Roy's jaw slowly and inexorably extended toward Shelley. "None of you know what it's like to *be* them."

Spencer said, "Well hold on there a minute, Kemo Sabe—"

"Except Spencer. The rest of you haven't been oppressed."

"Spencer has been oppressed? What kind of shit is that? Spencer went to *private* school, man."

"On a scholarship," said Roy.

They were turning ugly. Roy gone lantern-jawed and dense, Shelley beginning to screech again, Spencer amused beyond measure by the rest of us.

But then interruptions came from two directions: first a three-car cavalcade with the lead station wagon carrying the insignia of the television station, and at almost the same time, a not-quite familiar voice behind me, strong and disapproving, holding its own even as everyone surged toward the television car. I hesitated and turned around. It was Yvetta Landell towering over Gilbert Duberry and his sister. When she saw me, Yvetta said, "Look at them. Look at these dirty children. They didn't even bring a towel."

"I think we may have some extras."

She clamped a hand on Gilbert's shoulder, and he sank a little under the weight. "Look at the dirt on that neck. And this little girl thinks she's going swimming at the Navy base in her little dirty dress and underdrawers."

Gilbert wrenched his head around. "Ain't got bathing suits."

My hands were fluttering, wanting to protect the poor Duberrys and at the same time to appease this forceful new Yvetta, miraculously larger, with substance and weight like a real community person.

She said, "I saw that paper Miss Blair and Miss Shelley sent home to your mother, and it said you could swim in a pair of clean shorts, but it didn't say a dress, and it didn't say you could wear the same thing for clothes and swimming and it surely didn't say you could come dirty!" Gilbert's head lowered, and the little girl kept her face up, mouth open, wide hazel irises rolling wherever Yvetta went. "Little savage animals get wet and air dry," said Yvetta. "Little human children have towels and some kind of clothes to swim in!"

"I'll take them to their house," I said. "It's just around the corner."

"I know where they live," she said severely. She turned Gilbert around and grabbed the girl's hand. They trotted to keep up with her. "You're not going to show your dirty selves to the U.S. Navy, you Duberrys," she said. "You don't want all those white people seeing your dirt."

I've been to their house, I thought, resenting Yvetta linking me with the U.S. Navy and other white people. I know how they live. Well, maybe I don't really know—I glanced over at Roy, who had his arms crossed again as if he were on some kind of strike. I haven't *lived* with the Duberrys, but it doesn't mean I don't understand anything.

"How you doing, Blair Morgan?" said Chuck Williams. I hadn't seen him arrive. His pleasant, long face, always just short of a crooked grin: reassurance in the very lean and tan flesh, the tendons in his neck, the sun crinkles around his eyes. He had tossed his suit jacket over his shoulder, and he commented on the heat, taking a leisurely look around.

Meanwhile, the kids had clustered around the TV crew as they set up their equipment, one man strapping a camera onto another. The bus had arrived, too, and the kids who couldn't get close to the camera crew crowded around it.

Chuck said, "You know, I was hoping you and Dave could come over to the church one Sunday evening. We have this discussion group, married couples mostly, educated people, lawyers, in business. But some of the fellows are suspicious of TAPS causing trouble, and I thought you and Dave were just the ones to make a little presentation."

"Dave's away," I said, about to add that he would be back any day now, but Chuck didn't give me a chance to finish.

"Why, we'd be happy to have you by yourself. It's just a little informal thing. A real pleasant group of people. I think you'd enjoy it."

I thought so too. It would be my first chance to *explain*

things to people all on my own terms. It would be like talking to my parents, but without the pain. "I'd love to do it," I said. Then I added, "But Shelley and Spencer have been here a lot longer than I have."

He tipped his head to one side and winked, as if we understood one another. "You'll do just fine," he said. "And a pleasure to look at besides."

I was half flattered, half insulted. Did he think the description of what we were doing in South Jenkin would come easier out of my small mouth than out of Shelley's big one? Out of my pale face than Spencer's dark one? And then I thought, to tell the truth, I didn't care. I wanted the opportunity to stand up in front of people and have a half-hour to explain it all exactly my way.

Hooky pulled up in front of us. "Is that your husband?"

"No, Hooky, that's Mr. Williams from TAPS."

Chuck inclined himself toward Hooky. "Looking forward to seeing the Navy base, son?"

"I ain't going to no Navy. I'm going swimming."

Charlie burst through the crowd. "Hooky! Where's Hooky? Oh, good morning"—a flash of politeness before yelling in Hooky's ear—"Come on, I gotta get us on television!" He grabbed Hooky around the neck. "Excuse us, we gotta go be on television."

Chuck touched my elbow, held on to it. "Let's put you on television too. Why don't you get some of the children and we'll set something up?"

I felt a further rush of desire. A speaking engagement in a couple of weeks, and the chance to represent the Vistas on television to all of Norfolk, Newport News, Portsmouth—the whole Tidewater area. "We were thinking it would be better if the Vistas stayed off-camera," I said. "You should interview someone from the community."

"Not at all," said Chuck, moving me by the elbow. "The spot's about TAPS and the Vista program. Why don't you get those children back?"

I found Charlie and Hooky and called Jewel over. Roy was

watching me like an allegory of Conscience, but I told myself they probably wouldn't use the pictures anyhow. I would just let Chuck Williams take care of everything.

The news reporter came at us, hand forward. "Hi there, pleased to meet you. What we need is some action, not just all these kids milling around. Something with a beginning and an end . . . movement, you know?"

"A race?" I said.

"Against *her*?" Hooky stuck a thumb at Jewel.

Charlie said, "She always be beating him."

"Race is great," said the newsman, and I started clearing the walk to Neighborhood House, setting the race from where we were standing to the porch. The glass eye of the camera beginning to run along the path, to run up and down me. I began to burn with excitement, to feel Chuck Williams watching me, too.

I clapped my hands. "Okay guys, the race is from me to the porch and back."

"That's a short race," said Charlie.

"What for?" said Hooky. "What we racing for?"

Jewel had it right: "To be on television, stupid."

"Right," I said. "That's it. We're racing to be on television. And if you don't want to be on television, Hooky, don't race. We'll get a replacement."

They went off without waiting for my signal, scrambling and pushing, the other children screaming. The quick turn at the porch, and Jewel was ahead, all legs and tight pumping arms. Compared to her flight, the boys looked heavy and earthbound. Hooky scowled as soon as he saw he'd lost, but Charlie formed a blissful smile with his eyes closed, face turned to the camera, and shook Jewel's hand. The cameraman said, "Beautiful, but let's do it again with more space between them, they were too bunched up."

Jewel said, "This time Hooky got to congratulate me too."

"You ain't winning next time."

Charlie said, "If she win, you shake hands, Hooky, you got to."

I said, "Did you hear him? You were too bunched. And you didn't wait for me to say go. Now line up. And don't you dare move till I say go."

I raised my arm, making sure my body was angled to the camera. Hooky muttered, "Jewel got legs like a giraffe," and she punched him hard in the ribs, but made sure it was out of view of the camera.

"All right!" I yelled. "Ready! Set! Go!"

They seemed to run in slow motion this time, Jewel especially more self-conscious, moving her arms awkwardly, the way girls are supposed to run by tradition. But when Charlie began to pull ahead, she strode out to win. Charlie repeated his handshaking with the blissful grin, and Hooky came up with an awful grimace and got Jewel's hand in a bonecrusher, but she didn't kick him until there had been plenty of time for a good shot. Then the cameraman obliged the rest of the kids by panning around the yard and letting them wave and jump up and down, and make horns over one another's heads while they lined up for the bus. Then the newsman interviewed Chuck, and Yvetta came back with a Duberry in either hand. Each Duberry carried a little rag of a towel roll and a bag lunch.

The swimming pool trip was a rousing success, and we got back just in time for Spencer, Shelley, Roy, Jewel, and me to make it to Old Fellows Street for the six o'clock news. Duchess was waiting for us with buckets of Kentucky Fried chicken and beer.

Jewel leaped at her: "Mama mama I almost learned to swim! We jumped and they caught us and I'm going to be on television."

"We don't know for sure," I said. I didn't want Jewel disappointed, or Duchess, who had dressed for a party in a striped halter top and her white beachcomber pants. She'd set the table, too, with her good plastic-lace tablecloth and the buckets of chicken and a two-quart mayonnaise jar of white lightning. Her apartment never looked like it belonged on

Old Fellows Street; she had it furnished with floor-length gold drapes, green and gold living room suite, a wrought iron dinette set. The only old object was the daybed where Jewel slept.

I let Duchess pour me a little glass of the white lightning, and I took the tiniest sip of it: I was different now, not the prig I had been a year ago, even a few weeks ago. I thought the liquor was going to make me cough, but the harshness only lasted a second; then it sent a tingle and glow through my fingertips. To make sure I could still see and walk, I went to her bathroom, and on the way back, stood a while in the bedroom. It, too, was more elaborate and expensive than seemed appropriate for the bowed walls with their nailheads showing. A fat lavender comforter on the bed was half hidden by the crocheted tiers of a doll's skirt. Over the bed, in a bronze frame with its own built-in light, was a color print of Jesus with clouds at his feet and a pulpy red heart hanging down his chest.

Spencer came in behind me. I said, "It seems funny—this big fancy bed and the doll, and then this picture. And all of it on Old Fellows Street."

He leaned against the wall, and some of the bronze light fell on his face. "Yeah, well, everybody got their contradictions," he said. "Take you, for example. You give double messages. Sometimes it's Don't do that, let's not do this, and then sometimes you come right on. You look good in a bathing suit."

I felt it through my body, the glow from the liquor and Spencer's admiration. It had been a physical day, holding the kids, pulling them through the water. Sometimes four or five of them clinging to me at once.

Duchess stuck her head in. "It's almost time," she said.

I said, "Duchess, I didn't know you were a Catholic!"

She nodded and pulled a gold crucifix with red stones at each end of the cross from deep in the cleavage of her halter top. I leaned close and fingered it, keeping my eyes away from Spencer. I felt the warmth from Duchess's forehead and

189

smelled perfume from her open neck. I had always been fascinated by crucifixes anyhow, especially after they told us in my Baptist Sunday School that the Protestant cross didn't have Jesus on it because we believed he was risen. I had been confused for a long time by that, thinking that Catholics didn't believe in Easter. At the same time, I always wanted one of the crosses with the sinewy little doll on it. I rubbed it now with my thumb. Wonderful gold-plated Jesus with slit-shut eyes, knees turned to one side, not quite aligned, the long torso, the tiny golden ribs and horizontal wrinkles in the belly.

Shelley called, "It's almost time for us." What does it mean? I wondered. Does he love her and flirt with me? Am I making it up that he flirts with me?

"And after these messages," said the newsman, "anti-poverty workers give some local children a day of educational fun."

"We saw that man, Mama!" called Jewel. "We saw that man on the street."

"Educational fun?" said Shelley.

They showed a long shot of Neighborhood House with the children lined up in their orderly ranks for boarding the bus, and you could see, on the porch, Mrs. White giving someone a talking-to. "A day of fun at the Navy base," said the voice-over. "A day of planned, supervised activities for the children of South Jenkin." And the next shot, giving me no time to prepare, was a pale oval face, mine, with dark bangs and an expression of ingénue enthusiasm. Then came the kids running: Jewel, Charlie, Hooky, and another closeup of me clapping in delight and hugging them, and finally, a closeup of Jewel's face that seemed to caress her dimples and the light of her smile.

"That's me!" she cried. "I'm on television!"

"Oh Lord!" cried Duchess. "My baby's on television!" Jumpcut to an interview with Chuck Williams, and Duchess said, "Hey, I want to see Jewel."

But it was Chuck we got, his reassuring full sentences, his

genuine Tidewater accent. Saying how this project was a demonstration of business and government and the churches working together to solve our poverty problems.

"I was on television," said Jewel.

I said, "Oh, I looked stupid. I looked about ten years old. We never should have done that race—"

"It was good," said Duchess. "Damn, I wish I called up Marie Conyers. I bet nobody saw it. Jewel was on TV and nobody's going to believe me."

"Jewel looked more mature than I did. What an idiot."

Shelley shrugged. "It was okay. It'll make all the good citizens feel warm inside. We can't ask for much more."

Spencer said, "Chuck Williams wants to make all the citizens feel warm inside. 'Hi theyah folks this is gold ol' Chuckie Williams just saying Ah will not run unless you-all asks me real nice and if Ah do run Ah promise to keep the collard folks real quiet.' "

"What's he running for?"

"Nothing yet."

I felt a twinge of guilt again because Chuck liked me and because I was going to speak at his church. I would make my voice deep for that, I vowed. I would not smile at all. I said, "I'll tell you one thing, you won't catch me going on television again."

"You loved it," said Shelley. "Jewel and Blair both loved being on television." Everyone started laughing, and Jewel and I looked at each other and both admitted that we did love it and wanted to see it five more times. Duchess started phoning people. It turned out that Marie had watched the wrong channel, and Duchess's brother had been taking a nap. But the staff at the hospital had seen it, and someone had said, Hey that's Duchess's child. So Duchess was happy— more than happy: she kept bringing out more beer and trying to fill up the white lightning glasses, and offering to go out for more chicken. She finally settled on the daybed beside Roy. He solemnly put his arm around her, and Jewel curled up on her other side, and Spencer had his arm around

Shelley, and we all recounted stories of the day: Chuck Williams setting up the race, Yvetta Landell and the Duberrys, the kids' reaction to the aircraft carrier we toured. I was having such a nice hazy feeling, wondering from time to time if this might not be drunkenness, but whatever it was, I was sure it was a good thing to be here with these people.

In the distance a phone rang, in Spencer and Roy's apartment, and we had a long, silly discussion about whether or not to answer it, and meanwhile of course it stopped ringing. Almost immediately, though, it rang again, so Spencer went. And then Spencer came back; the phone call was for me. It was Dave. He'd tried our house and when he didn't get anyone, he called here.

I was glad of the distance to the phone, so I could get used to navigating with this haze in the corners of my eyes. It wasn't hard, really, to manage. I missed a lot on the periphery, but the dead center was clear enough. I focused on one object after another in their apartment. The lighting fixture with three bare bulbs, the blunt black plastic of the phone lying on the couch a foot away from its cradle. "Dave?" I said. "Is everything okay?"

"No." His breathing came to me as precisely as the black plastic phone, but it was harder to keep his voice in focus. It kept slipping to the hazy perimeter. "He died. We buried him today."

"He died? Why didn't you call me till now? What happened?"

The explanation was too short. There had been a crisis when not even Martha was at the hospital. He went off suddenly. I waited for more. Dave said the doctors had done all they could.

"Of course," I said. "I know they did." I hoped that was the right thing to say. This is terrible, I thought. He'll stay in West Virginia much longer now.

"I would have called you sooner," said Dave. "I tried a couple of times and you were out. We've been busy with details, the funeral, people coming around. A lot of cake and coffee. You know what it's like."

"How's Martha?"

"She feels terribly guilty because she wasn't with him." I closed my eyes, tried to see faces, but got none. Not Martha's, not poor Reverend McTeague's, not Dave's.

Too much time was passing between our words. I hadn't spoken when it was my turn. He said, "I'm going to have to stay a few days."

"Of course."

"They're going to ask me to stay in the chaplain's office, on a temporary basis."

We had never said how long we were staying. My parents assumed I would be back at Franklin State in the fall, but I had always known our commitment was too large for a mere summer. I said, "But you can't be chaplain."

"Oh no, I can't be the chaplain. Nothing has changed. But I do have to stay around a few days for Martha. Help her with some papers."

There was a strange hollowness encasing the wires that extended from him to me. Something that would remain until he was back, fully, in the flesh, with me. I said, "I miss you."

He missed me too, of course, but he had to go. It occurred to me that he might not be seeing my face anymore than I was seeing his, and that seemed much worse.

"Dave? It's so awful."

"Yes, really bad."

"Give Martha my condolences, okay?"

"Of course."

I sat beside the phone a while, trying to see at least Reverend McTeague's face. That seemed only fair, to recall that nice man who had died. I could get the white hair, as if it were a wig, wavy white hair sitting too lightly on a pink cloth dummy.

Spencer came in, stood by the door in the dimness. "Are you okay? Dave told me the man died, but he wanted to tell you himself." He went to the window and raised the shade. To my surprise, out over the waste field where they never built the new projects, the sun was still visible, hanging low, glazed over with gray fog which had never really lifted. Not a pretty sun, but I was thankful for light. Spencer sat beside me. "Do you want to cry?"

"I can't see any of their faces."

"Hey," said Spencer. "Here, use me." He put an arm around my shoulder and made my cheek rest on his chest. I pulled my legs up on the couch, too, and pressed as much of me as I could against him, as if I were shivering. He was not as bony as he appeared. There was a resilient surface that gave me support. We sat there a long time in the coming evening, dry-eyed, watching the sun tremble in its oily gold.

Twelve

I kept telling myself I should have gone with Dave to West Virginia, but what I really felt was that he should have stayed with me. He had upset the balance by separating us, made it too easy for things to get complicated. But, I thought, why should distance matter? What about the two legs of one compass? What about the golden tissue? And what about Paul McTeague? Why was I worrying about my relationship with Dave—poor Paul lay dead. I could castigate myself at great length in those days, using an interior voice something like my mother's when she was indignant. Soon, though, another part of me would stick out its tongue, and say: I don't care. I don't care about Paul McTeague or old Martha. Don't care much about Dave Rivers either unless he gets back here and *takes care of me*! And then, as that rebellious voice got too loud, the Scolder would come back, scandalized, and say, Blair Ellen Morgan, just listen to yourself!

It may have been the effect of the scolding voice, or it may have been that I was looking for someone to take care of things, but I decided to go to church the next morning. Frank Landell wore a voluminous high-church black robe and spoke from a pulpit. His voice took dominion, and his people answered back, not in ecstasy or even very noisily, but enough to keep me alert, to remind me I was in a strange place. Enough to give me an Experience. Yvetta and several church ladies asked me to dinner, but I didn't go, still feeling some of the rebelliousness, not trusting myself to stay polite through a whole Sunday dinner.

South Jenkin seemed almost empty as I walked home, as if all the people who didn't go to church hadn't bothered to get up. It was going to be another scorcher, as we used to say at home, peering up through this kind of grayed, moisture-laden atmosphere. As I turned the corner onto Eastover, I thought I saw the Volkswagen behind Ralph's Cadillac. I took a few more steps, blinked in the shimmering heat, and the shape was unmistakable. Dave's back! I told myself, wondering why I slowed down instead of running toward him. Why was he back today? He had said he needed several more days to finish up Martha's business. Had he driven all night? Was something else wrong?

As I got to the house, Spencer, Ralph, and Shelley came out with bags and blankets, all three of them looking like vacationers: Shelley with one of her sleeveless smock dresses, Ralph wearing a bright-colored Hawaiian tourist shirt, Spencer elegant in wheat jeans and a pale shirt. He said, "Your boyfriend's back."

"He's sleeping," said Shelley.

"Did he say anything was wrong? He wasn't supposed to come back yet."

"Couldn't stay away from you," said Spencer.

Shelley shook her head. "He's really exhausted though."

I said, "You're going to the beach. All this time down here, and I haven't been to the ocean once."

Shelley said, "We're not going to the ocean, just to the bay. Raunchy old City Beach. Next week we'll go down to Virginia Beach, down in the dunes. Ralph says he knows a place."

"That sounds good," I said. "All of us, okay?"

"The whole crew," said Spencer. "Beach-blanket Vistas."

I sat on the steps after they'd gone, feeling a little sorry for myself, left behind. I imagined the day when we all would go together to the beach. Spencer would make a stream of jokes, and Ralph would laugh at him, and Shelley would compliment him on the best ones. Even Roy would smile for a change, and Dave and I would lie on a blanket in the sun, side by side, and not talk, but just feel each other's presence.

The heat was settling in like an invisible balloon that was swelling and pressing my chest, making it hard to breathe. The Volkswagen sat alone in the street now: green body, one brown fender, the fading bumpersticker that had disconcerted me when I first saw it: "Jesus Saves Green Stamps Too." It had taken me several days to build up courage to ask Dave what it meant. That had been back when everything about him caused terror to run up and down my spine. "What do you think it means?" he had said. And I had answered, Won't you please just tell me, so I can know if it's a joke or something else? Just tell me the truth. "Are you afraid it's something blasphemous?" Dave asked. "I don't mind, you know, if people think it's blasphemous. I hope it makes people mad. Stirred-up people are more likely to do something. The bumpersticker means that Jesus lived a real human life. If he had lived today, he probably would have saved green stamps. That's one thing. It also means there's no limit to what he can do. He could redeem inanimate objects, if he chose to. And also it makes fun of people who take their theology too seriously."

In those days I took every word Dave said as a message tailored to fit my ears. I'm one of those people, I thought, the ones who take religion too seriously. So I practiced his explanations and arguments in my head, over and over, preparing for a time when my mother or someone would demand to know what that bumpersticker meant. But no one ever asked, and I hardly noticed it anymore; it had almost faded beyond reading anyhow. I took the bumpersticker too seriously, I thought. I took Dave's every word too seriously. How could he have had patience with me, sucking in everything he said like gospel truth?

I suddenly had a picture in my mind of iced tea. I would go inside, boil water, get out tea bags, make a bowl of real tea to cool down and pour over cubes. I would drink iced tea and read the funny papers till Dave woke.

But the bedroom door opened almost as soon as I got in

the house. "Blair?" he said. He had pulled on his pants, but no shirt, and no glasses either. He stood there waiting for me in the hall gloom, slow from weariness, the familiar softness of flesh around his waist, the ginger scratchiness of his beard, and he was damp from heat and sleep. As we embraced, though, he began to shiver, and he wanted me to undress, to come to bed with him. I began to tremble too at the foreignness of the moment, at knowing his body so well, and yet something was different, there was some stranger in him. Something in his haste reminded me of a book I had read in my adolescence in which two people who had not seen each other for years ripped off their clothes and plunged into bed. The abandon of it had always thrilled me. This was almost the same, Dave touching and kissing each part of me as it was bared—my shoulder, my foot—and his body hard, as if he'd been ready for me from the instant he was awakened, by some small sound in the house, perhaps my Sunday shoes with their hard soles. We hardly spoke, like the couple in the book, and we had the swiftness of movement, the eagerness to penetrate—but in the novel there had been no stale breath from lack of sleep, and she had not been so dry. The couple in the novel came together like magnetized battleships, striking with an impact that would have been brutal had it not been so mutual, but their explosion had been one of waters released and flooding, and this wetness was all Dave's, wetness of sweat and effort, of him working his way through a desert, his weight enormous to me. We had always done this before with a prophylactic. Before he was even all the way in, he groaned and collapsed against me. His weight made it hard for me to fill my lungs again, and he seemed to be getting heavier and heavier, until I felt a panic that he was sick too, like Paul McTeague, that he would never get up. But then he jerked, as if he'd had a dream of falling.

"Sorry," he murmured, rolling off, but keeping one hand on my arm. "Sorry."

"Oh, it's okay," I said.

I was going to explain that I'd taken care of everything. I

was on birth control pills now, and it didn't matter if he forgot the prophylactics, but before I could tell him, he said, "I know there wasn't much pleasure in it for you."

"That's all right," I said, waiting for him to realize he hadn't done anything about birth control, but his lids were sliding thickly over his eyes. I said, "Tell me why you came back so soon."

The eyes popped open: a look of terror; he had been asleep. "I couldn't do any more for Martha. Short of staying there with her . . . becoming Paul." Each word encased in something thick and translucent. "They wanted me to take the chaplain's job."

"You told me that on the phone. You told me you said no."

He was really drifting now, his eyes closed, but the hand on my arm tight, as if he were afraid to let go, trying to stay awake, to keep me near.

"But Dave . . . Dave? I don't understand why you drove all night."

He half smiled, but he didn't open his eyes or speak. It's okay, I thought, I'll find out when he wakes up. I lay a little longer, then slipped out of his grasp, took my second shower of the day, and made the iced tea. Then I spent the rest of the afternoon as I'd planned, reading. My favorite comic first, "Mary Worth," for its melodramatic awfulness. Dear Mary, who was always a house guest, always making a nest for some troubled young woman until such time as that young woman could be paired off for eternity with Mr. Right, at which point Mrs. Worth would take her perfectly molded white bun off to another house, and another young woman to help. I read the rest of the paper too, including sports and business, and studied a map of Southeast Asia, and thought I finally understood where Vietnam was. I thought of Spencer and Shelley and the beach, and hoped sincerely they were enjoying themselves, and the Landells, and the other people who had invited me. After a while, I made a macaroni and tuna salad for dinner.

It was after five when Dave came out. We embraced, and I felt that everything *was* okay again. "You're cooking," he said.

"It's ready if you want some."

"I want to go over to Old Fellows Street and shower and put some things away, and then I'll come back and eat, and you can brief me on where the Buying Club stands." He let his face sink in my shoulder, mouth heat coming through the thin cloth of my housecoat, his hand moving around to stroke my breast which hung free under the summer robe. Smell of starchy water from the macaroni, a little mayonnaise on my hand. Domestic happiness.

"But Dave," I said. "You never told me why you drove all night. When I saw the Volkswagen, I thought something else awful had happened."

He separated his body from mine, began tucking his shirt in. "Yes, well, to tell you the truth, I got scared. They were putting a lot of pressure on me. In some ways, the easiest thing for me would be to go back."

It chilled me. Easy? How could it be easy? We were committed to this, weren't we? To the Buying Club? To South Jenkin? "But you said you wouldn't, didn't you?"

"Yes, I told you I did." He sounded irritated, but he kissed my cheek, and we talked about how long he would spend over at Old Fellows Street. He might well be irritable, I thought, with so little sleep.

As the Volkswagen puttered away, I cleaned up the kitchen. I put the salad in the refrigerator, the extra iced tea. I was giving the sink a rare wipedown with a soapy sponge when I heard another car stop out front, one that sounded too light for Ralph's Cadillac. There was a door slam, and then the car drove away. I went to the window. A white woman wearing a summer suit was looking at my house. She was such an anomaly here—the whiteness, the train case and patent leather pocketbook—that I didn't realize for several seconds it was Martha McTeague, here at my house with blue flowers on her suit.

My first thought was that I mustn't go to the door and let her see me without a bra on. Then I had a flash of guilt for never having asked to speak to her on the phone. I hadn't sent flowers or even a condolence card. And then, as she knocked, another voice said, If she's bereaved, why is she wearing a suit with flowers on it?

I went to the door holding the soapy sponge in my left hand, keeping it a little ahead of me, ineffectually trying to hide my thinly covered chest. "I was going to write you a card," I said as I opened the door, "but we've been working so hard down here. I'm really sorry."

"Oh Blair," she said. "I'm so thankful you're here." Was she here as some sort of representative of my parents' generation, to check up on me? She said, "I'm not thinking straight. I let that taxi go. I was beginning to feel so foolish going from one place to another. I went to Dave's place, and they said Dave was over here, but then I realized after I'd let the taxi go that his car wasn't. . . ."

"He just left. He was going back over there." She shouldn't be wearing flowers, I thought, and she shouldn't be here. She had said she wouldn't come down here. She didn't belong here. I saw now why he felt they had been putting pressure on him. She was down here to get him to go back and be the chaplain. She should be grieving, not running errands for the personnel department of Franklin State College.

She set her things down on the halltree, complimenting the stained glass, the woodwork. "I talked to the prettiest little girl over there," she said. "She seemed so proud of knowing all the Vistas." She stepped into the living room ahead of me and said, "This room is like being inside a jack-o'-lantern."

I said, "How did you—"

"Get down here? I flew. It isn't easy, either. You have to change planes in Washington, and that little thing that flies out of West Virginia is like barnstorming days."

I remember standing there, feeling vaguely but certainly that she was my enemy. I had always liked her, mostly, more or less. At least felt there were things I could learn from her. But it was clear that she was down here to get Dave. "Would you like some iced tea?" I said.

"I'd love some," she said.

She followed me into the kitchen, as if she didn't dare be alone, still talking. "You must think I'm insane, appearing like this."

I said, "Why did Dave leave so suddenly? Wasn't he supposed to stay longer?"

She stopped smiling in that convulsive, probably involuntary way. "What did he tell you?"

"He said he got scared that he was going to turn into Paul."

"Oh." She sat down. The phone rang, and I went back to the living room.

Dave's voice, tight: "Is she there?"

"Yes."

A moment, his breath. "How did she come?"

"She came in a taxi. She flew."

"Stay there," he said. "I'm coming right over. Don't talk to her."

"Don't talk to her!" But he had hung up. Why not talk to her? I went back to the kitchen where she sat as I'd left her, as if she hadn't so much as blinked. "Did you come to get him because he didn't stay as long as he said he would?"

The chattering had passed; now she was thinking before she spoke. "Yes," she said.

And I was the one who began to chatter, to invite her back into the living room where she'd be more comfortable, although of course there were no real chairs there and she had to sit on one hip on a pillow with her slim, stockinged legs on top of the other folded to the side. They gave us this apartment, I told her, but I envied the male Vistas getting to live in a real slum. I walked around the room. I pointed out Shelley's pride-and-joy, a genuine Victorian lampshade with magenta tassels.

She said, "The little girl over there told me Dave spends most of his time here."

"Well, this is kind of a center, we all meet here."

I had forgotten the size of her eyes, which seemed now about to overspill tears. She *is* grieving, I thought. "This is such a mess, Blair," said Martha.

Something was slipping back and forth in my mind—if I could just get hold of it. I heard the screeching of tires at the corner, brakes at the house, and at once Dave on the porch, at the door. I didn't get to ask her, I thought. I didn't even find out about Paul.

Dave had a derelict, wrinkled look to his clothes, and his hair seemed dark and matted. "Martha," he said, not looking at me at all. "Why did you do this?"

I said, "Do you want some iced tea?"

He snapped at me, "No, I don't want any iced tea!" but then I realized he was snapping at me as if I were a part of her. "What are you doing here?" he asked.

He sat on the pillows directly opposite her, and I was just beside her, so I continued to feel he was addressing both of us at once, in anger. At the same time, some numbness was wearing off me, and the slippery thing beginning to rise as water through porous concrete. I thought: she didn't come down to remind me to write condolence cards or to see if men sleep at my apartment. She didn't come down to offer Dave a job, either.

"I came," she said. "I came because I don't have one iota of self-discipline where you're concerned. I tried hour by hour not to come. I said I wouldn't call for one hour, and when that was up, I tried to get through another hour, but it seemed too long, so I made it half an hour instead, and then fifteen minutes."

She came to get Dave for herself, I thought.

She said, "You did tell me you would stay one week. I always thought you were the disciplined one."

"I should have stayed." He looked at the floor. "I broke my word."

"The little girl at your apartment said you're always over here. You see, I didn't think you and Blair—you told me you and Blair—hadn't gone so far."

There, I thought. I am in it. I had known all along I was,

203

and I felt a pressure around my eyes. I'm in it. Something pressing at my eyes, trying to make me see more.

"None of your business, Martha," he said.

"I was a fool not to know you were lying about that, of course. In this day and age. I fooled myself. Still, if I'd known, I would have thought twice about coming down like this. I think I would have. I don't know. But this makes it so much messier."

It was the night in Dave's office when she caught me on his lap, and covered her eyes. I had thought she was embarrassed or shocked. That she was covering her eyes so she wouldn't see something naughty. "Oh wow," I said, sorry that it had to be those words that bubbled out of my mouth. But I went ahead: "I was so innocent. I never guessed. I wouldn't have guessed in a thousand years. You were adulterers, weren't you?"

Martha laughed and shaded her eyes with her hands.

Dave said, "It's none of your business."

"You tell everybody what their business is!"

Martha was laughing and crying at the same time, and talking now, too. "Dave likes things pigeonholed neatly. He likes to keep things separated. Only it never works out. You've seen what his desk is like. Yes, Blair, dear, there is such a thing as adultery, and sometimes it happens between chaplains' wives and their young assistants."

It seemed to make Dave collapse, to have all this said so openly. He dropped his hands in his lap and lowered his head, as if he were leaving the rest of this to us. Reverend McTeague came back to me now too: a physical, fleshly presence, as if he were in the room with us. The broad blue suit, the red tie and cheeks. An American flag of a man, a secular Santa Claus. A smile with sad eyes. So kind, a pleasure to sit near, a sweet smell like baked goods with sugar glaze.

I said, "But Reverend McTeague was a *nice* man."

Martha started to cry with no laughs. "There never was a nicer man, even though he knew all along, and he never said anything."

"He didn't know," muttered Dave.

"Oh Dave, now you're being the fool. He didn't know how long it had been going on or what stage it was in, but he knew."

"How long?" I said.

"Five years," said Martha, and that took my breath away. Five years ago I was still a child. "Five years ago Thanksgiving," she said. "A year after Dave came to work with us. Thanksgiving Day, to be precise. After dinner, when Paul went to visit his Aunt Mamie."

Dave raised his head. "When you give the details, it sounds so sordid."

Thanksgiving Day, I thought. I felt that my eyes were popping dry, that I would never be able to close them. Dave had done this to me too; he had made me vulnerable to seeing what I hadn't seen before.

"We did try to stop," said Martha. "We swore off time and time again, we really did. But I'm not good at sacrifice. I'm greedy and neurotic."

"Shh," said Dave, but more tenderly, finally looking up.

Five years, I thought. Come Thanksgiving, five years. Long before I had ever seen him.

"I'm neurotic too," I said softly.

Only Martha seemed to notice me. "He was so eager to get back here, and I was fooling myself to pretend he wasn't running back here to you."

He said, "I should have stayed while you needed me."

"I'll continue to need you," she said. "And you need Blair."

Dave stirred, ran his fingers through his beard. "Let me speak to Blair alone."

"Of course. I have to powder my nose."

"I'll show her the bathroom." I hopped up and ran ahead of her. I heard her little heels clicking down the hall behind me. "The bathroom's a mess."

"Oh, it's not so bad." And she grabbed my wrist as I stood aside. "The bathroom's not so bad. The rest of it—I really did fool myself, Blair, I really didn't know."

Dave was pacing the living room, active again. He reached

for me, embraced me, but I held still, wondering why he hadn't seemed to notice me while she was in the room.

"Are you going back with her?"

"I have to take her back, you see how she is. It was a bad mistake on my part to leave her. She needs a lot of support. She's a troubled woman, Blair."

"She doesn't look so troubled to me. She wants you to come back, and she came to get you. She wants you to come back and be chaplain and marry her."

"Not possible. Not in that town."

In some other town then, I thought. A despair was beginning to open up in me. I had an idea that my only chance was to sob deeper and harder than Martha did. But I hadn't lost my husband, wasn't suffering with guilt. I would have chosen Martha too. Compared to her, I was a healthy little wildflower, pretty enough, but of little consequence.

I said, "You're going to go back with her for the five days?"

"Or a week, at most." I tried to get my head back far enough to look at him. He had his glasses on his forehead, eyes closed, a smile on his face the way it had been when he was falling asleep beside me. "You don't think I wouldn't come back to you?" he said.

"I think," I said. "I think—" But I had no real idea. I let him pull my face up to his, mouth to mouth. I could feel the warmth, the beard. But we heard her coming and guiltily stood apart. When she came through the archway I wanted to whisper to Dave, Don't have sex with her, whatever else you do, because she's too old for you and it wasn't right what she did to poor Reverend McTeague! She tried to say something to me, but I turned away, made Dave give me one kiss in front of her. Then they put her train case and pocketbook in the Volkswagen, and he helped her into the front seat. How quickly it started up and puttered away on what sounded like three functioning cylinders, as if the whole thing were a joke. How quickly they were gone.

Five days and he'd be back with me, I thought. A week at most. Nothing is any different than if he hadn't come back at all. But that was nonsense; I had been wounded. I was more naked than I had been before.

I went to my room and was glad to see that the clouds were bringing evening early. I lay in my bed, pulled back the blind to let in any moving air. I could see the deep weeds on our side of the fence, looking strong and sharp-edged, and on the other side, a stack of crates and the apple tree, the ramshackle kennel where the dogs whined and scrambled after something. I lay with my cheek on the window sill and my neck getting stiff. I wished for a more precise pain, or for tears or sleep, but felt only a spreading barrenness, the desertion inside me. I kept seeing Dave and Martha together in the bucket seats of the Volkswagen, riding like an old couple, longtime companions. Reverend McTeague's tricolored ghost rose over them. But I couldn't see myself anywhere.

Thirteen

It was Saturday morning, and we were packing up to go to Virginia Beach when Dave called me again. I lowered myself crosslegged to the mattress, watching Shelley pass the archway with towels and blankets. Spencer started to come in, but saw my face and backed out. They were having trouble too; they had only spoken to each other in sarcastic epithets all morning.

"We're going to the beach," I told Dave.

"I'm glad I caught you before you left. How about the club? How close are you to getting it started?"

"Saturday," I said. "A week from today. It's going very well. Everybody's helping." It was his business to say if he would be here or not. Not my business to ask.

"You have your order blanks out? Do you have a butcher? Meat's the main thing."

Meat? I thought. Meat is the main thing? He hasn't said if he'll come back or not, but he wants to be sure there's meat. "Oh we'll have meat," I said.

"Good, that's great. That's the most important thing."

The most important thing, I thought, is whether or not you're coming. "Listen, they're waiting for me."

He hesitated. "Blair, I know you're angry. I hear it in your voice. You have a right to be angry. But I need a little more time."

For what? I thought. To get up your courage? I felt a

blue light falling on me, a knifeblade forming out of my anger. "So you don't know when you're coming. You don't even know *if* you're coming."

"I said I need a little more time."

The knifeblade seemed to hang between him and me, and it made me silent, for fear it would start cutting.

He said, "I know you're angry, but I have to tell you one more thing about the Buying Club. This could be vital. That friend of Spencer's who has the big Cadillac—there's more room in one of those things than you might think. You could use it to transport the groceries."

"Gee, Dave," I said. "What a good idea." Did he really think we were too stupid to have thought of Ralphie's car?

"I know you have to go, but I just wanted to say—"

I think his last word was Sorry, but pressure had built up in my ears, and I couldn't be sure. It was a pressure that kept me tightly gathered around myself, in a sort of cocoon, as I rode to the beach with the others. Gradually I began to see the world outside: a high-clouded, white sky, fields, and occasional settlements. Nothing seemed to stand out in that landscape. The fields had a yellow look, and I couldn't figure out what the crop was. We would pass a collection of shoebox-shaped houses scattered behind a concrete filling station with an attached grocery store, but I couldn't imagine what the people did out here in all this flatness. Did they cultivate the yellow-leafed plant? Take long bus rides to jobs in Norfolk or Virginia Beach? After a while I realized that I didn't care. The people out here were nothing to me. I didn't have to find out about them; I didn't have any responsibility to understand them. Nor did I care when Duchess scolded Jewel for wrinkling her matching white beachcomber pants, and I didn't care when Roy muttered sullenly at her to leave the child alone. I was glad; I wanted the whole world to be truculent.

We headed south around the outskirts of Virginia Beach, down a road Ralph knew, between dunes and expensive-looking modern houses on one side and salt water marshes on the other. The dunes opened up once and I had a glimpse of water.

I said, "That's the first time I ever saw the ocean."

"You never been to the *ocean* before?" cried Jewel. "You never been to the *ocean*, Blair?"

"I was a deprived kid."

Jewel resettled herself on Duchess's lap and put her legs on me. "It's nice at the ocean," she said, "but you have to be careful of the waves and the underwater tow, it sucks you under." Did I ever see a wave, she asked me. A sea shell? Did I ever see a seaweed?

"Leave Miss Blair alone," said Duchess. "Don't bother folks so much."

"I don't mind," I said, and Duchess gave me one of her sidelong glances. I could never tell if she was flattered that I talked so much with Jewel or if she thought I was an idiot for doing it. We all spoiled Jewel, but today I decided I didn't care about that either; Jewel was the only one of them I liked. They were all too sensitive, too snappish, too self-protective and complicated. Jewel wanted to talk about the ocean, and so did I. I had no interest in Duchess's sidelong looks or Shelley's moodiness or Spencer saying Hey he liked my short shorts. Not interested in Dave calling and stirring things up just to put me off again. Ocean today, I thought. I'm going to the ocean.

On the marsh side we passed an old pick-up truck with rounded, rusty fenders and hood. Next to it, in aluminum lawn chairs, were an elderly man in overalls and a woman with an unbelted pink dress who fanned herself with a piece of cardboard. Between them were crates full of what appeared to be seaweed. A sign leaned on the crates with big, drippy red letters.

"Crabs!" shouted Duchess. "Those people are selling crabs!" We had already passed them, but Duchess slapped Ralph on the shoulder. "Stop this thing, Ralph, we want us some *crabs!*"

"What do you do with them?" Shelley asked as Duchess

shoved Roy out the door with one hand and pulled Jewel with the other.

"You build a fire and cook 'em in the seaweed, steam them, you know. We used to do it all the time when I was a little child."

Spencer looked back over the seat. "You coming, Blair?"

"I'll stay." I wished they would all go, but Ralph stayed too, turning the radio up and leaning his head out the window, opening a beer.

He looked back at me, with his eyelids halfway down. "Hey, you want a beer?"

I didn't like Ralph giving me those looks. It was okay for Spencer, who was in college, the same as I was. But Ralph had this unadulterated invitation, or lust, or admiration, or something that he put into his looks at me. He didn't do it when Dave was around, either. It wasn't that I didn't like Ralph—he certainly provided us with a lot of free transportation—but he wore his hair in that weird straightened style, like the old guys did, and he wasn't educated, and he didn't seem to have anything to do with his life but hang around us and drink beer and laugh at Spencer's jokes. I didn't like it that he thought there was no barrier between us.

I said, "Listen, Ralph, we aren't going to drive much farther on this road, are we? I want to start walking. I'm going up over that dune. You just tell them I went on to the ocean and I'll find you all later, okay?"

"Okey-dokey," said Ralph, gazing at the sky, pouring back beer, tapping his fingers on his knee to the music.

I hoisted my bag, and started up the steepest part of the dune. Panting and sweating, sandals loaded with sand, I scrambled and slid till I got to the summit and looked back. This was the highest I'd been since coming to this flat part of the world. I, who had always loved magisterial heights, living in a flatness all these months. No wonder I got confused so easily. The sound of Ralph's music drifted up to me, thin compared to the ocean. The woman selling crabs was a spot of pink in front of the pick-up truck. A flash of white was

Duchess walking briskly. Beyond them spread flat bronze marsh water with smears of muddy green under the surface.

Then I turned to the ocean. It was not the way they had taught me to crayon it in first grade—not blue with white triangles of sails; it was immensely broad and gunmetal gray, with an imprecise shimmer of light across its surface. Good, I thought. I'm glad the ocean isn't pretty today. This is *my* ocean, and it has no other side.

I ran downhill onto the beach, a wide cove that ended in a gradual hook far off to the right and a nearer hook to the left. Straight ahead was a pier built on enormous wooden pilings. It seemed to have no purpose, merely ran out its fifty yards and then dropped off. I changed my direction so I didn't see that human-manufactured object and let myself pick up speed, half hoping I would fall, really wanting to dive into the ocean, but I reached the flat safely, kicked off my sandals, and stuffed them into my bag, dropped everything and ran on to the fat, swelling ocean. There was a moment of wet bronze sand and pewter swells, then the breakers, and I danced backward, laughing aloud, reinventing the age-old game of Chase me, Ocean, I'll Chase You. I let it boil around my ankles, suck away the sand beneath my heels, till I thought I would go out with the water. Then I ran away from it, and back to it. Details began to come to me: a seagull walking at the edge, half following me, broken shells in many shades of cream and tan and midnight blue. I saw a crab leg and a ribbon of red-green rubbery sea plant. I had no idea how long I had played until I saw Spencer a few yards behind me, dangling my bag at the end of his arm.

"Have you been watching me?"

He nodded solemnly. "Observing."

"I've been getting to know the ocean."

"Is that what you call it?" He raised an eyebrow. Behind him our camp had sprung up: a patchwork of blankets and towels, a tall pale man and a little dark girl playing beach-ball, people dragging driftwood to build a fire. I had no idea of how long I'd been doing this.

Spencer said, "If you're so crazy about the ocean, how come you're the only one left with your clothes on?"

They had all stripped down to their suits. Spencer as naked as bones except for nylon swim trunks and tight black curls in a star on his breast. When he moved my bag to his shoulder, the sharp bunching of muscles out of his leanness startled me. I stripped out of my shorts as I went up the beach with him. "Let's all go in now," I said. "Let's really go in."

They were not in the same time frame as I was: Ralph still sucking beer slowly, Shelley reading, glancing at me over the rim of her sunglasses.

"Come on, Jewel," I said, grabbing her away from Roy.

Duchess, adding pieces of broken crate to a little pile of burning newspaper, said, "Jewel, don't you go in that sandy water without your bathing cap."

"You come too, Duchess," I said.

"Not me. I want this fire just right."

"You shouldn't be cooking for us."

"I'm not cooking for you, I'm doing what I want to do. You go do what you want to do."

Jewel put on her bathing cap, and Shelley shut her book. Roy came, and Spencer, and even Ralph walked down to the edge with us, carrying his can of beer.

This time in the water I discovered the other game, where the ocean swells through you and lifts you off your feet gently but powerfully. We played group games too, passing the beachball, giving Jewel rides. Once I turned away for a few seconds, looking at the shifting and swelling, getting pleasantly dizzy, and saw out of the corner of my eye a movement under water: Spencer's shadow, grabbing my legs, coming up under me, lifting me out into the air.

Half-proud and half-guilty, at once discomfited and thrilled by my thighs spread flat on Spencer's shoulders, I called, "Look, Shelley, get on somebody! Let's have a chicken fight!"

She nodded and tapped Ralph. He squatted down, and she got on him, awkwardly because they were still on land, and they lurched into the water. Shelley's breasts rose and fell unevenly in the stiff floral print bra cups. "Watch out," she said. "I'm in the mood to drown someone."

I said, "Ralph can't fight with a beer in his hand."

"My partner can fight any way he damn well pleases."

Ralph tipped back his can one last time and then threw it back at the shore in a long, strong arc. They looked dangerous to me, his broad chest, Shelley's full and high one, and mostly their hair: Ralph's coming free of its grease and spiking out like a representation of sun rays, Shelley's tumbling freely over her shoulders, in her face. Something frightening in her eyes, too, and I believed she did want to drown me, or, more likely, Spencer.

Spencer said, "Come on, Champ, let's take the fools." He tightened his grip just above my knees, and I let my left hand sink into his dense hair, all the way down to the scalp. He patted my knee. "Ready, Champ?"

"Sure, buddy."

"Well?" said Shelley. "Are you two going to fight or not?"

Spencer said, "Hey, Shelley, man, we don't start till the Champ is ready, see? We want the Champ here at the peak of training and not giggling. Stop giggling, Champ."

Shelley and Ralph plunged at us, at a bad moment too, because a swell was just hitting Spencer, and he almost lost his balance, but Shelley caught my arms and actually helped steady us. We grappled and twisted.

"Hang on," said Spencer, backing away quickly so that Shelley had to lean farther and farther to the side, while I was held firmly in place by his head. She tried to let go, and I gave her a tug, but it wasn't enough to keep them from recovering. Just the same, I felt I knew in my arms now how to win. We circled each other and Jewel was yelling, "Go Shelley, go Blair!" as if we were on a team together, and for a second, as we engaged again, I felt that we were, too, and I loved Shelley best as we twisted and strained together.

She had learned the trick now too and was trying to get me at an angle so she could pull me off sideways, but Spencer's fingers guided me, and he was saying, "Steady, steady," and "We've got 'em now." He seemed to have something in mind, was pushing forward, making Ralph back up, and even though I could feel Shelley's superior arm strength, there was a shakiness underneath, and then a breaker hitting and Ralph, a head shorter than Spencer, was foundering. Shelley went over with a big splash, and we waved our hands in the air. Roy and Jewel clapped.

But Shelley came up and dived for Spencer's legs, and suddenly I was falling too, through an arc of air, and then water, overturning ten times it felt like, sand in my face and the terror that I wouldn't find the air again, and then I was shipwrecked on the sand, with the others, all of us in a row, Jewel and Roy too, a band of sleek sea lions too lazy to pull themselves all the way out of the waves: Spencer's long fingers with their neat tan nails curled in the sand, and Shelley's back with the deep midline, a channel between high rounded muscle.

"What do we play next?" I asked.

"You crazy, woman," said Spencer, into the sand.

Shelley said, "She must be high on drugs."

"She's so high she's floating away," said Spencer. "I better hold her down." He pressed his hand deep into my middle, and I laughed and lay back, at ease among the sea lions.

Lunch should have been a continuation of the contented herd together. Shelley had fried a lot of chicken, and I'd made sandwiches, and now we had Duchess's crabs steamed in seaweed. But the crabs looked to me like giant pink woodticks with their shells burst open. I didn't feel like eating, and instead drank two beers rapidly, and they lay in my stomach in a bubble. Meanwhile, Shelley flirted with Ralph, and Spencer sat beside me. Jewel started whining that she wanted her dessert, and Duchess said she had to eat some food first.

"Take some of that good chicken, Jewel. I know you don't like crab. I don't know how I could have a daughter that don't like crab, but I do. Eat one of these chicken legs."

"We have sandwiches too," I said.

Jewel lifted a slice of bread off one sandwich and let it drop back after she saw the lunch meat inside. She checked another one.

Spencer touched my leg and asked me to pass him the potato salad. He acted as if we were partners now, since the chicken fight, but I wasn't sure I wanted to be. There was something presumptuous about the way he touched my leg in front of Shelley. She, of course, was pouring her decolletage all over Ralph, but the whole thing seemed uncomfortably out of balance to me. I thought that if Dave had been here, none of this would have been going on—this flirting game, or playing at exchanging partners, or Shelley spiting Spencer, or whatever it was. The sky had become more cloudy, and the ocean seemed quieter, as if it were beginning to congeal.

Duchess said, "Jewel! Stop looking in those sandwiches and take some of this chicken!"

Jewel's delicate features knotted around a pout. "I don't like that chicken. It's slimy."

Duchess stabbed the air with a chicken leg in Jewel's direction. "You eat that chicken or you'll be sorry! Miss Shelley worked *hard* frying that chicken!"

Jewel took the leg, and tears began to run down her cheeks.

"Hey, Duchess," said Shelley, "It's okay, really, I'm not insulted."

But Duchess kept staring at Jewel as if Shelley hadn't spoken, and Jewel ignored everything but the chicken leg. She put it to her lips, but didn't eat.

Shelley said, "I'm not very good at frying chicken. It *is* sort of slimy, now that she mentions it."

"Stay out of it," muttered Spencer.

Duchess said, "Stop playing with that chicken and eat it! I am not going to be the mother of a child who don't know enough to eat good food people put in front of her. And acts ignorant and sneers at food like a spoiled child that never was taught manners and never had a mother!"

216

I had the feeling that Duchess was humiliating Jewel because she was mad at the rest of us. Roy was the worst about spoiling Jewel, but Shelley, Spencer, and I too, we all did it.

Jewel rubbed her lips over the chicken skin, which looked more and more gray by the second, hunching herself forward so that her shoulder blades stuck out as if she were some kind of scrawny chicken child herself.

"Eat that chicken," said Duchess.

And then, surprising us—we had thought it was only between Duchess and Jewel—Roy stood up, loured over Duchess, seeming to have the same height advantage over her that she had over Jewel. "Leave her alone," he said. "Don't touch her."

"Don't touch who?" said Duchess. "Who do you think you are telling me not to touch my own child? You have nothing, I mean nothing, to do with her!"

"I'm eating the chicken," said Jewel. "Look, I'm eating it." She filled her mouth rapidly, ripping the bone bare and stuffing her cheeks.

"Who do you think you are?" said Duchess. "Who do you think you are?"

I thought, They wouldn't *hit* each other, but even as I thought it, Roy made the fingers of his left hand stiff and rammed them in Duchess's shoulder. It wasn't a blow exactly, more of a jamming shove, but none of us was expecting it, least of all Duchess, who lost her balance and fell backward over the drink cooler and landed on her butt. Jewel coughed and choked, and spat out the unchewed chicken onto the blanket.

"Oh God," said Shelley.

"Just stay out of it, Shelley," said Spencer, turning away. Ralph went Whew! and turned away too.

Jewel was really crying now, and hugging herself against the breeze that had come up. "Shit," said Duchess, on her feet again, and so mad that Roy was backing off. "Shit," she said, "you long-legged bullshit peckerwood." She kicked his beer over, and it spread on the sand and sank out of sight. "Who's got the goddam napkins?" She saw them herself and thrust one at Jewel's face, squatted with another one to clean up the spat-out chicken.

Roy, meanwhile, was standing in a sort of amazement, looking around. "Sorry," he mumbled. "I get mad when I see kids . . . you know . . . I'm sorry."

"Goddam keep your goddam sorries to yourself and keep your hands to yourself too."

"Sorry," said Roy.

Everyone was looking in some other direction, Jewel crying, and Duchess hopping all over, straightening blankets, scraping paper plates into the garbage bag, grabbing Jewel and retying her swimsuit.

I was suddenly overwhelmed by an intense conviction that I didn't belong here anymore. "I think I'll take a walk," I said, and I picked up a beer and sauntered down the beach.

I looked back once, and they were all still facing away from each other. I don't *need* this stuff bringing me down, I thought. I had been in a good mood. I don't need them screaming at each other, I need to be alone for a while. I'm always with people these days.

It seemed that I walked a long time, but the beer had slowed my time sense and made my eyelids and legs heavy. When I went around the neck of land and couldn't see the blankets anymore, I lay down. The sand crunched and clung to my shoulders and thighs. I looked straight up into the sky, gray blending into gray with no defined boundaries between clouds. After a while the lack of focus turned into a kind of sleep, and I was awakened by a violent itching on my face and jumped into a sitting position, sure there was something alive on me, but it turned out to be raindrops. I rubbed my eyes, looking at the emptiness: the horizon blending sky and ocean in a mist. The most direct way back, I decided, would be to swim, so I waded in, defiantly leaving the beer can where it was, and then, when I was about waist-deep in water, I felt a pressure in my bladder and let that go too: there was a cozy warming of the water between my legs and a thrill along my back from doing something antisocial and free.

This was the good of being alone, I thought: you could piss where you pleased. Litter the beach if you felt like it. I had been crowded too long in small spaces—dorms, apartments, the front seats of Volkswagens. Doing things the way other people wanted me to. I floated easily on the swells, letting the raindrops hit my face, opening my mouth to take them on my tongue. After a while I rolled onto my stomach and took a couple of strokes. I could see the pier now, but no blankets. Maybe they had gone back to the car when it started to rain. I took a couple of scissors-kicks to speed up, but realized I didn't want to be back with them yet, so I rolled back and bobbed where the ocean took me.

We should have all stayed in the water, I thought. We should have played in the water and made Duchess come in, too.

I seemed to be drifting out to sea, so I took a couple of strokes toward shore. I was riding some sort of swell because when it broke, I was lower and nearer, but coming upon the pier sooner than I had expected. I took a couple of strong strokes directly in, and found, when I lifted my head to get my bearings, that I had moved no closer to shore, but was again closer to the pier. I could feel a quiet movement under me, a slippage along and out, and I wondered if perhaps an undertow might not be this powerful sideways drift rather than the sucking vortex I had always imagined. The angle at which I was being drawn along would probably take me beyond the pier, maybe toward the town of Virginia Beach, and maybe out into the open ocean.

I dogpaddled gently to avoid panic. I am a strong swimmer, I told myself: Senior Red Cross Lifesaving, two years as a lifeguard.

At a municipal *pool*, said another voice in me. A pool with walls and a bottom. The incredible smallness of that swimming pool repelled me; it had been a little inside-out room, a box of water, while I was now adrift in a vast river of ocean with no boundaries at all.

I lowered my face into the water and counted off fifteen strokes of my best crawl—three kicks and one breath to each stroke. Then I dogpaddled again, listening to the soft shushing of water on the shore, still thirty yards away from me. There were no big waves, but there was a choppiness, and a mist was falling around me like a curtain, replacing the raindrops, muting sound and sight, closing off the light.

I'll get back one way or the other, I thought.

And at once realized, shrinking tiny inside myself, that it wasn't necessarily true at all. That it was well within the realm of possibility that I would float on into the mist, out of sight of land, seen by no one, carried on this secret strong current far beyond my strength ever to swim back. That I might not get back at all.

I burrowed my face in and swam hard again, another fifteen strokes, then five more with no breathing, and when I came up this time, I was only twenty yards out—close enough that I was not going to miss the pier, but I was coming up on it far too rapidly. There were many more black and gray boulders than I remembered, and the wooden pilings seemed thicker than telephone poles, with water chopping and spraying around them. I was out of time for telling myself that everything would be all right, or on the contrary that I would drown and the world go on with no change. I either had to paddle left and grab a pole, or pass between them out to the gray mist where you couldn't distinguish ocean from sky. It was an easy choice: I flung myself at the nearest pole, rough with splinters, sticky with resin and creosote. A wave lifted me, and I sensed the structure overhead and embraced the pole.

I was at once brutally dropped as from a great height, as if the ocean were furious with me for my choice, and I slid down the wood, clinging and scraping, and then the water came back in a rush, doused me, choked me, tried to rip me from the piling. There was another brief respite . . . time to wonder how long I would be able to cling like this, then more water again, bashing and battering me, each wave seeming more enraged, more determined to spin me off.

Out of the roar and echo I heard my name called fuzzily. I wasn't even relieved at first because of the intensity of my concentration on hanging on, but when I was able to look, and saw Spencer climbing over the boulders, I felt a sort of sob run through me, a wanting to let go and be safe, and I was nearly swept off by the next wave.

Coughing and shaking hair out of my face, I clenched my upper arms and thighs against the splinter-surfaced wood. Spencer was up to his waist now, and after another wave, to his chest.

"It's not so deep!" he shouted.

"For your legs!" I shouted back to show I was game, but my teeth were chattering.

Another wave, and there was only one post between him and me, and still another wave, and he was standing with one hand on the last post, and the other extended across the roiling to me. I couldn't see his face in the shadows, but his hand was enough. I yearned toward it, to be done with treacherous thin water that slid you to nowhere. I wanted that flexible five-pointed brown hand.

"Between waves!" he shouted.

I nodded smartly, proud that I could hang on one more time, even two more times if I had to. I was lifted, dropped, and when I hit the bottom of the trough, aimed to his left and pushed off with all my strength. Just as the wave began to rise again, I found his hand, and we clasped, muscle and bone. I used both hands to get hold of his forearm, his elbow, and he drew me to his chest. I clutched it, making a little speech in my mind: Don't grab his neck, the first rule of lifeguarding is Don't let them near your neck. I fixed my hands firmly on his shoulders, my legs around his waist. I was as proud of my wisdom as if I were the one saving the life.

He stumbled when we got to the boulders, and we dropped to the sand, surrounded by stone and slabs of concrete. Now

I did take hold of his neck, and he wrapped his arms around me, and we lay that way a while, shaking, while the waves broke at our feet, hitting us with spray. But it didn't matter; I had land below me, resilient flesh under my hands.

Spencer's thick, blunt lashes lay on his cheeks, tiny crimped hairs out of line along his sideburns and beard, and droplets on the surface of his hair like little jewels collected in a net. Dear God in Heaven, I kept thinking. Thank you I am alive. And then I was looking at Spencer's earlobe, the tendons in his neck. I had never seen such human beauty. I thought I was witness to something extraordinary. There was a dark smear on his collarbone, and when I touched it, my fingertips came away red.

"Spencer," I said, "you're bleeding."

He opened his eyes. "No, it's you." When we pulled apart there were long trails of blood running down the insides of my arms, my midriff, and the tops of my thighs.

"I'm bleeding all over." It was from the rough wood I had been rasped against. Spencer's face was distressed, so I said quickly, "But look, it's only scratches." He rubbed away some of the blood on my belly, and the red sprang back immediately. He touched it again, and we watched it disappear and well back. This too seemed extraordinary: that my life had been in danger, and now my blood was flowing with life. I could do anything. I dipped a finger in my blood and touched it over Spencer's eyebrow, and then over his other one. "You saved my life," I said, not feeling so much grateful as exalted by my aliveness. He shrugged, as if he too knew that what he had done was beside the point. "The ocean tried to take me," I said, stroking his forehead. I had been marked by the ocean, I thought. I had become a natural phenomenon myself. I kept rubbing my hands over his face, exploring the nearness of skull and cartilage beneath skin. The broad, hard brow, the soft depressions at the temples, the cheekbones, the teeth under muscular lips. "I'm glad it was you," I told him, feeling exceedingly powerful, my life connected naturally with his now.

He opened his eyes wide and I saw that he saw it too, the connection, and that I was like the ocean, breaking over him like the waves, towing him under with me. And I was going to take him in.

He began chafing at my back and arms, and we spent a while warming each other like this, and then worked ourselves out of our bathing suits. When we were naked, I looked at the length and leanness of his body next to the round compactness of mine. The way my paleness almost disappeared in the silvery light on the sand, and his darkness seemed to be one of the shadows of the pilings. There were black streaks of blood across my body, and he pulled his fingers through them, slowly, slowly.

But I wasn't satisfied with slowness. I had too much power in me, so I knotted myself against him, knotted us together— mouths, arms, me around him, and then, so smoothly, him inside me, and we were rolling and rising together. There was cold sand on our backs, and the striking of waves at our feet and a great heat at the center. I went into that center, rose and fell with the undulations of the long black tunnels, the heart of motion, as if I had entered the darkness that powered the ocean. But I could ride this ocean, this motion, this joy. I would have laughed out loud, but I passed beyond delight to a cry, and when I passed beyond that, I was aware that the motion and the tunnel were inside me, and then running out of me, so that I felt the water at our feet again. I was sorry to leave it, I wanted to ride the motion again, I pressed Spencer's chest, pressed my abdomen against him.

"Baby, baby," he said. "We have to rest awhile."

He wrapped his arms double around me and rocked us back and forth, as if he were happy. I was not so much happy as excruciatingly aware of the present—the cold on my back and the warmth where our bodies met. Then, after a while, little by little, I began to imagine the future, to rehearse it, almost. How we would wash ourselves off, wriggle with difficulty back into our wet suits, walk up the beach to find the others, and tell them what happened to me, show them my wounds. But never tell them how the ocean carried me over Spencer and Spencer into me.

This happened once, I thought. This one time it happened because it had to, and it was inevitable and splendid, but just this once.

Fourteen

I woke up sore and troubled by a dream. In the dream, distances and colors and sensation seemed exaggerated, which I attributed to the aches in my arms and legs and a crackling like cellophane over the whole front of my body from the newly formed scabs. The dream was of a place, a river-shaped gorge between cliffs, with great walls extremely distant on either side, and yet I was easily able to see the smallest detail of strong black shadow and striation. The colors—burnt umber, sienna brown, orange—were deeply saturated as if the sun were striking them full horizontal, but there was no visible source of light. I seemed in the dream to be moving in midair along the middle of this channel, equally distant from both walls, which undulated irregularly before me like vast strips of ribbon candy. I was struck by how I could see so far and in such detail, yet could not make out a bottom or a ceiling. Below me was not darkness, either, but a mist of exactly the same magnitude of brightness as the mist above me. My eyes could not pierce this vague brightness, nor could I estimate distances. My vision was exceptionally clear, but I could only see these infinitely long curving walls before and behind me. In my dream I said to myself, This is life-after-death, and I was so appalled by the scale of it that I woke at once, happy with the aches and pains that gave such convincing evidence that I was alive.

The dream has recurred to me, and it always wakes me out of terror to acute joy. I have always been at least provisionally convinced that the dream is true, and I date from that first dreaming of it the loss of belief in a heavenly garden apartment as a reward for being good in this life. After the dream I could never accept the idea that this present is only a preparation for something more important. The dream said to me, This is it, now; this is all you have. These muscles aching, these scratches on the surface of your skin. The wind was coming in almost chilly that morning, and we had sunlight too, after all the grayness and vague mist. I wondered what came next, after that vision. What governed the rules of daily life now?

Shelley was sitting at the table as if she had been there a long time. She hadn't brushed her hair yet; it was matted like a bird's nest on top, and she stared ahead grimly.

If she's found out, I thought, or guessed, I'll not lie. I'll tell her straight out it was a one-time thing with Spencer, a moment when something happened beyond us as individuals. Life forces took over.

I said, "Do you want me to make coffee?"

She shook her head no, and I wondered if she would scream at me if she knew. When Spencer and I came over the dune yesterday, they had all been crowded glumly into the Cadillac. They brightened up, though, when they had my wounds to take care of. Shelley and Duchess mothered me, made me sit between them in the back seat. They dabbed at my cuts with kleenex while I closed my eyes and felt perfectly safe, smelling Duchess's breath tinged with cigarette smoke, and Shelley's suntan lotion, their four hands on me. I had leaned back and my eyes met Spencer's for a moment, and I thought at that moment that I could have everything.

But Shelley might have wakened to a strangely convincing dream like mine, might suddenly know more than she knew when she went to sleep last night. She sat so still, not shifting her weight, with no tremor of energy passing though her shoulders, that I thought she must be holding something in, some new knowledge.

I said, "I guess I'll just have instant. I want to go out and remind some people about their order blanks."

Very quick and sharp, as if she'd been waiting to pounce, she said, "Don't you ever stop working?"

I sat down. I didn't think it was me and Spencer bothering her, but if it was, I wanted to get to it immediately, take it on the chin. "What's the matter with you, Shelley?"

"I'm sick of all this," she said, finally moving, waving a hand around the kitchen. "I've got to get out of here."

"Get out of where? Leave Vista? Before the Buying Club?"

She imitated my surprise. " 'Leave Vista? Before the Buying Club?' I've had just about enough of trying to think up ways to save the poor people of South Jenkin. Maybe it's none of our business anyhow. Maybe we should just buy them some guns and send them to City Hall. Or Washington. I don't know. I have to get back to New York anyhow. I have classes and my uncle's sick."

Guns? I thought. What uncle? I'd never heard of any uncle she liked well enough to go home when he was sick. "What's the matter with your uncle?"

She shrugged. At least she was moving more, turning her face from side to side as if she were trying to get away from something. "Oh, it's not my uncle, I just need a shot of New York. I need to get home. I'm sick of all this Southern shit. And there's another thing—" Her face was away from me, so it was hard to hear. "My period's late."

I was shocked. Not Shelley. She knew too much to get caught. How could someone so smart and wise to the ways of the world get caught? "But what about the Pill?"

"I always said *you* were made for it, not me. I forget to take them. My cycle gets screwed up. That's why I'm not really worried, it's happened before, but I can't stand the suspense."

"Does Spencer know?"

"There's nothing to know. And even if there was, I wouldn't tell him. It's none of his business, what I decide to do with my body."

"What would you do?"

"Get an abortion, of course. At home. I was planning to go back in time for classes to start anyhow."

I hadn't realized she meant to leave so soon. I had a flash of despair: to lose Shelley when I had just got her. And then, an answering flash of calculation: without her, why not Spencer? I said, "Would you know how to find a doctor?"

"Oh sure. I mean, I don't have a phone number in my pocketbook or anything like that, but practically all my cousins have had abortions. We have a gruesomely fecund family. Even my mother, years ago. Not that I'd tell *her*."

"I'd never tell my mother either!"

"Don't get me wrong. She'd help me. She'd pawn her grandmother's diamonds or something equally dramatic to send me on a vacation to Puerto Rico. Especially if she knew the father was—let's just say—not Jewish."

"It's funny," I said. "I always imagined that if I got pregnant, it would be the end of everything. But you have all these cousins who've already done it—"

"Just two."

"And you could even go to your mother if you had to. I would never in a million years go to my mother. I wouldn't have any idea what to do if it happened to me."

Shelley gave her hair a sudden shake out of her eyes. "Sure you would. You'd come to me. You should come up and stay with me in New York anyhow. I've got this cousin I've been wanting to fix you up with."

"You'd have another roommate by then."

"No," she said. "We have this enormous apartment in an awful old run-down building—it was my father's aunt's until she died, and all our family always live there while we go to Columbia or Barnard. We even had one cousin who lived there while he went to Yeshiva University, but he didn't last because he couldn't stand the Chinese spareribs in the refrigerator. Anyhow, the place is enormous, always room for one more. You should come, really. You're a good roommate." She was on her feet again, tightening the belt of her robe.

To live with Shelley. She would clean out my scratches and give me a boyfriend. A real boyfriend, not like Dave. I wasn't sure what he was anymore. I felt a rush of desire for life in a big-city apartment with all those famous universities.

She said, "I guess I'll go out with you." And then, in the doorway, "Listen, don't say anything to Spencer, okay?"

I had for the first time, then, a disquieting sense of wrong-doing. I wondered if it had really been so inevitable, what had happened between me and Spencer. Could I be a phenomenon of nature and a good friend, too? Could you love someone and have a secret from them? Had Martha McTeague loved Reverend McTeague and Dave too? Did Dave love her and me? People do, I thought. I do love Shelley and Spencer both. People get pregnant and go on living. People do bad things and aren't altogether bad.

Later that day I went looking for Spencer, and told him it had been a one-time thing, that I didn't want to betray Shelley anymore.

"Sure, baby," said Spencer, putting his sunglasses on, as if I'd hurt his feelings.

"To keep things simple," I said. "For Shelley's sake and the Buying Club."

"You call it," said Spencer. "You called that one."

For the next five days as we rushed to get the Buying Club under way, I kept asking Shelley, as I passed her on the street or met her at breakfast or on Marie Conyers' porch, Did it come yet? And she made a sour mouth, the humor of which reassured me, because in spite of all my new insights, I couldn't believe that she might be both humorous and pregnant.

But mostly we thought about canvassing and collecting and making last-minute calls to wholesalers. The butcher had first insisted on a $200 sale before he would do business with us, but then he agreed to let us start the first week at $150. Even that many meat sales looked doubtful at first; we were, after all, asking people not only to pay out a nonrefundable two dollars membership fee, but to lay out the price of their groceries in advance, before they had seen a single chicken leg or bunch of greens. Many of them hesitated, too. They would ask us to come back later, when a husband or a daughter was home. We told them how Reverend Frank Landell and his church were behind us on this. The church had even donated a frozen turkey to be chanced off at the first meeting of the Club. During the early part of the week, selling chances went a lot better than selling meat. Still, bit by bit, we were getting our minimum amounts of money. And Mrs. White had finally agreed to let us use the porch of the Neighborhood Center, and we were going to use the Landell's station wagon.

In the late afternoons, instead of going to our house or the Neighborhood Center to tally our forms, we usually met at Marie Conyers'. Her kids were among our most active sellers of tickets for the big turkey raffle, and Shelley always said anyhow that Marie was a person who had her thumb on the pulse of South Jenkin. Shelley and Spencer and I were glad anyhow to be in public, working as a team, not really having to face each other alone. I loved being on Marie's porch with my order blanks spread around me, and Charlie and Hooky and all the other kids bringing in more stubs for the raffle and then racing off again to see who could sell another book first. Veronne Foley was often around too, with raffle tickets, or buying a chicken, then coming back later to buy a dozen oranges, and then back once again for another chicken.

And all the time, Marie sat on her glider, not noticeably less bulky now that the baby was born, still wearing a zip-up dress that held her knees together. She kept her hands at rest in her lap, a small, wise smile on her lips, and her eyes shifted to the side, looking out through the slats at what was happening on Eastover. Every now and again she glanced down at her side, where the new baby slept wrapped in a cotton blanket and Little Bit played with chewed and fresh popsicle sticks. "Don't drip on Miss Blair's papers, Little Bit," she would say. She never touched the papers herself, never offered to help us, and she was also one of the last people to place an order.

Spencer said to her right out, "Now, Marie, four pork chops isn't enough for your whole family. What are you going to do with four little pork chops?"

"I thought they were supposed to be big pork chops," said Marie.

"They are," said Spencer. "And the best you ever ate, too, but how are you going to have dinner with just four of these delicious pork chops? Who gets to eat them?"

"Me and my old man," she said. "That's who gets to eat them, until you get some cheaper prices than that."

"Well, what will you feed the children the day you eat the pork chops? Come on, Marie, if you don't buy any more than that, how can we expect anybody else to? You're a *leader*, Marie."

"I'm a poor old woman with too many children," said Marie. "I ain't no leader," scowling till I thought she was going to thunder and shout, but instead she began to smile at Spencer. "Well, two fryers then. But you better make sure I get big ones." And out of a tiny change purse that she carried deep in the pocket of her dress, she picked dollar bills wadded so tightly that it took a long time to unfold them.

After that she became very proprietary about the Club. Whose long order is that one? How much did Veronne Foley buy *this* time? Shelley said this was Marie's way of taking the pulse of the community. She was glad we finally had a community person involved in this project, but I suspected Marie of being just plain, old-fashioned curious. I got suspicious of her every so often. Was she helping us or using us, or were we using her? I had always expected that people—but especially lowlanders and city people—were out to take you, if not for your money, then for your dignity. Marie might be a splendid, enormous Mother Earth woman, but she had never let me live down not knowing she was going to have a baby. "And all the time," she was fond of saying, "I had that big old pocketbook right beside me with a nightgown and a bed jacket, all ready to go to the hospital, and you never guessed!"

"I bet a lot of people didn't guess," I would say, and she just laughed at me.

Late one afternoon when no one was there but me and Marie and the littlest children, she told me she could have been the South Jenkin Neighborhood Worker instead of Alvetta White, if she had wanted to. Something in me was in the suspicious mood that day. Oh sure, I thought. Right. Marie the big organizer. She feeds the baby and braids Little Bit's hair, and every now and then sends Charlie to the store. That's what Marie does all day. I felt vaguely guilty for thinking of her that way, but just the same I said, "I thought you had to be on welfare to get to be a Neighborhood Worker?"

She said, "Well, I'll tell you. Conyers had just got laid off when they started going around talking to people about TAPS. We was about as close to the welfare right then as I ever want to get."

It occurred to me that I didn't even know what Mr. Conyers did for a living, how he supported all these children in this sprawling green house. Surely I could have asked that, but I wasn't sure, and I didn't ask, and the mysteries remained.

I said, "If you needed the money, why didn't you take the job? Why didn't you become a Neighborhood Worker?"

She smiled down at the sleeping Jimmy. "Oh, I would of had to buy all new dresses. You have to dress nice to work in a office."

"You didn't take the job because of *clothes*?" I thought she wasn't telling the truth. She tucked the blanket around the baby, and said nothing. "But you would have been such a good worker, Marie! You know everyone, and everyone respects you."

"Alvetta White does a fine job."

"Not as good as you would have done. You would have been—you would have been a real community leader."

Something in all this made me angry at her: the mysteries, and the way she wanted to know everything about the project and who was buying what but always deferred to the Vistas when there was a discussion. "You college folks know more about it than a old poverty lady like me," she would say, teasing, but still deferring to us. She should be out on the streets too, I thought. It was her community. She wouldn't be so fat then. She could teach us what South Jenkin really needed if it was going to change.

I said, "Well I'll tell you one thing. If the world was the way it should be, someone as smart as you would be running TAPS. Not Delbert Jackson or Chuck Williams or Eleanor-Byrd."

"The world was the way it should be, we wouldn't need no TAPS neither. Lord Jesus would come and take us all home."

"I mean it," I said. "You have this *wisdom*. You could be something big, someone who makes decisions. A judge. I don't know. You could be anything."

She looked up at me from the baby, and for once her eyes were neither laughing nor feigning anger. Came at me with points, and I looked away first. "Isn't that the strangest thing," she said. "How long I lived and never looked at a pair of blue eyes before."

I shivered. I love your porch, Marie, I thought. You wouldn't make me leave your porch.

She said, more in her usual voice, with the familiar chuckle softening the edges, "Now if I could of been a Vista, that would of been something else. If I could of been a college-student-Vista going around *helping* people get out of poverty. If you all could of got me a job as a Vista."

I was relieved. "You're making fun of me again."

"No, no, I would love to be a Vista. I'd like helping people. Going around here and there meeting different folks." The baby woke and she picked him up, laid him on her knees and jiggled him, and held Little Bit by the back of her tee shirt as she slid off the glider. All this as if to make manifest precisely how big the gap was between her and me. Just how much too much I was asking.

Then she started talking about when the other children were babies, a little pleasant conversation so I could feel that her anger or whatever it had been was over, that it was important to her that I should be comfortable again, because she wanted me here, on her porch, for whatever reason. And I did feel comfortable, and I finished my tallies and collected the next installment of raffle stubs and quarters from Charlie and Hooky. After a while I headed out on the street again too.

The night before the Buying Club, Duchess came in wearing her uniform and carrying a pan of cooked greens and a plate of ham. She said we needed a good homecooked dinner to get us ready for tomorrow—no more of that pizza. She took over the kitchen, moving our papers into the living room, heating the greens, cooking rice, frying the ham and stirring up some pan gravy. We sat around the table, expansive with hope.

"I think it's going to come off," I said. "It's the first time I really believed it, but I do think the Buying Club is going to happen."

"But it's bad luck to say it," said Shelley. "It ought to be like in the theater. You say 'Break a leg' instead of 'Good luck.' "

"Eat some more rice," said Roy, as if we were guests at his table. "That's good luck."

Something appeared to have transpired between him and Duchess; he smiled to himself as he watched her moving around the kitchen. She pretended to ignore him, but refilled his plate when he turned away. Shelley and Spencer weren't fighting either, and I didn't feel jealous. It was as if there were some superior kind of love influencing us all now. It should have been like this Saturday at the beach, I thought; then there wouldn't have been any question of betraying Shelley. But the truth was, at that moment I didn't feel like a betrayer but like a member of a large, somewhat quarrelsome, family where people hurt one another but always forgave.

The phone rang: Mrs. Murrell had sold some turkey raffle tickets at the last minute, and Roy volunteered to go over to pick them up. The rest of us spread out again, on the coffee table, the mattresses, the floor. Jewel and Hooky and Charlie brought over some tickets from Marie's, and then left again. Bo-ji Foley dropped in, ate a plate of ham and greens, and then paced around the living room, stepping heavily over papers.

After a while, he said, "Where's that Roy?"

"Out getting raffle money," said Shelley.

Bo-ji shook his head.

"What's that supposed to mean?"

"Nothing," said Bo-ji.

"Nothing?" said Spencer.

"Naw," said Bo-ji. "I was just wondering."

Spencer shrugged and ran a pile of coins through his fingers. "Man, after what I've learned about wholesaling and meat packing, I'm going to start my own store."

"My grandmother used to have a store," I said, "out in the country." The memory came to me full blown and suddenly, something good in my past that I hadn't thought of in a long time. I told them how I used to love to go there, to stand behind her counter and look at the Day's Work and Red Mule chewing tobacco, the wooden cases of pop, the sacks of meal. She let me sell peppermint balls and Maryjanes to the children, and sometimes I also got to write down what the grownups bought in the credit books.

Spencer and Shelley and Bo-ji listened to me, respectfully, the way people used to listen to each other in my grandmother's store, sitting around on nail kegs waiting for the mail boy to come.

This is so good, I thought. I always want to be here working like this, letting them be my family.

Duchess called from the kitchen, "Somebody get the door!"

I liked to get the door. It was one of my favorite things, to open the door and see who had come next with more orders, more excitement. "Come on in!" I said cheerfully, swinging it open.

It was Roy, but for the first long second I didn't recognize him. There was blood running around his mouth—long, brilliant mustaches trickling off his chin onto his shirt. He made no attempt to stanch the flow. He said, "Hello, Blair, the neighbors weren't feeling very neighborly tonight." His lips twitched in a smile; he was making a joke, so he must not be too badly damaged. He even leaned against the door jamb, with his arms crossed over his chest to emphasize his silly nonchalance. There was a cut in his eyebrow too, and a drop of blood fell, shattering finely on the floor.

"Roy," I said, "are you trying to outdo me, or what?"

There was a scream behind us, and Duchess grabbed Roy's arm and pulled him into the living room, pressing at his face with her dish towel, screaming again.

"I'm okay," he said, trying without much force to push the towel away. "The neighbors just weren't feeling very neighborly." She muffled his face in the towel and pushed him toward the pillows.

"Get out the way!" she shouted, sweeping an hour's worth of sorted papers onto the floor. "Lay him down."

"I'm okay," said Roy, but he let himself be laid down. His legs stretched halfway across the floor, and every time he lifted his head awkwardly to talk, Duchess pressed him back down.

"Get me a washcloth," she said. "Real wet."

Shelley said, "We better get ice for the nosebleed too."

"Who was it?" asked Spencer.

"*I* know," said Duchess. "I know who it was. It was Junior, that worthless trash, he *knows* I finished with him, long done with him."

I said, "Who's Junior?"

Roy nodded. "He wasn't making any secret of it."

"Snake?" said Spencer.

"Snake!" I hadn't thought of him lately, the withered boy's face, the flared eye. The broken glass.

"I knew it," said Duchess. "Damn him. And he had some of his lowlife friends he gets off the garbage heap with him, I bet—" Shelley came back with the washcloth and a plastic bag of ice. She held it over the bridge of Roy's nose while Duchess kept washing off the blood that still trickled out. She muttered on, almost to herself. "He gets these awful scabby-headed trash to go around with him. It could make you sick to look at them. They probably *infected* you with something."

Roy looked less desperate now, although he had been hit around the eye, and the top of his cheek had a raw, corrugated look. "He wasn't after money. He didn't take the raffle money. It's all in my pocket. He said he was out hunting Vistas."

I said, "I don't get it. Will somebody please explain to me? Snake Eyes is Junior?"

Spencer said, "He's an old flame of Duchess's."

Duchess snorted and pointed at the floor. "Junior is a mental case is what. But this time I ain't fooling with him. One of you all is calling the police."

We were squatting around Roy like urban guerrillas behind an overturned car. Like guerrillas, we recoiled at the mention of police. "Hey," said Spencer, "not so fast, Duchess, baby."

"Not the police, Duchess," said Shelley. "You don't want to call the police in on this!"

"*I* ain't calling no police," said Duchess. "One of you all Vistas is calling the police. They pay attention to you."

"No police," said Roy. "The police are yellow running dogs of the capitalist system." But there was something odd about the way he said it, almost gently, with his eyes half closed.

Spencer said, "Look, Duchess, baby, you don't like the police."

"I ain't your baby neither and no I don't like no police,

but this ain't right, Junior acting like he owned the street so decent folks can't walk out at night. Cutting up that poor child Bo-ji, and now Roy. He is trouble and he don't deserve to be walking around free."

"You're angry," said Shelley. "Wait till you've had a chance to think it over."

"I want him *arrested* and put *away* outta my sight!"

I said, "He was just trying to give us some kind of message, wasn't he, Roy?" This was a hunch I had, but something had happened to Roy. Even when he talked about capitalist running dogs he had been smiling in that gentle way.

"It's personal," said Roy. "It's not for the police. It's between me and him. He doesn't like me down here, he thinks it's like slave days—"

"*He* never said nothing about slave days," said Duchess. "He don't *know* enough, that ignorant fool, to talk about slave days." She took hold of Roy's hands and turned the palms up. "Look at that. He's got gravel stuck in his hands!" The heels especially were scratched, with stones and bits of glass embedded in them. Duchess said, "If you fell that hard, I bet you bruised all over."

"It's *alright*," said Roy. "I'm alright. And the thing is, Snake is right."

"Ha!" said Duchess, picking out stones, bits of glass, gathering them in a kleenex on her lap.

"He sees it like white people coming back down and taking what's his—"

"What's *his*?" said Duchess. "What's that suppose to mean?"

"He thinks I came down here and used you—"

"Bo-ji," said Duchess. "Bo-ji, you a young boy. Don't you hang around with these insane Vista people. They have little bitty bits of junk or something up where people suppose to have brains."

"Listen a minute, Duchess," said Roy, firmly overturning his hands so that he was pressing hers under his, against his thigh. "Listen, everybody. Snake Eyes is right. I haven't been acting right. Duchess, I didn't treat you right."

"Well that's for sure."

"No, I'm serious. I was lying there with my face in the drain grate and they were running away, and I knew it then. I knew what it was. I want to marry you."

She snatched back her hands. "Get away!"

"I want to marry you."

Spencer said, "Hey, maybe the rest of us should sort of fade away into the sunset about now—"

"Don't leave me here with this crazy man!"

"I mean it!" said Roy, his voice getting higher and louder. "I want to take up my responsibilities. I want to marry you and adopt Jewel and take care of you."

"You take care of us!" she said, but there was a shininess in her eyes, and her mouth wouldn't quite hold a scowl. My Lord, I thought. She's sentimental. Duchess is like all those other women. She's thinking about a wedding dress. "Him take care of me!" she said. "Nobody's marrying me if I don't want to get married and what would I want with some big hillbilly hanging around me for? What would I want with that? Somebody call me a car service, I got to go to work. Don't you people let that crazy man walk home by himself. You go with him, Spencer, and you too, Bo-ji."

When she had gone, Roy drank a couple of beers and fell asleep on the mattress. We turned off the lights and took Bo-ji into the kitchen to find out what was really going on, but he didn't seem to know much. He had only heard a little sooner than we had that Snake was out to get Roy. Snake and his friends had been going up and down the street all night boasting about what they were going to do.

"I just can't see Snake Eyes and Duchess together," I said. "Half the time he looks like an old bum."

"Maybe he changed," said Shelley. "Maybe he got worse."

"He's no good," said Bo-ji. But, then, the inside of his left bicep was still a broad pink slice, like a moon portion, or a madman's grin.

"It's just because he's jealous, right?" I said. "You don't think he'd come after the rest of us?"

"Of course not," said Shelley. "Duchess only wanted to call

the police so she could get back at him for hurting Roy. What I want to know is, will she marry him? What about it, Spencer?"

"Don't ask me. I don't know what's in her head. Ask Bo-ji." Bo-ji made a sheepish face and looked down. Then Spencer said, "She will, though. She'll marry him."

"I thought you didn't know what was in her head."

"I never said I knew what was in her head. I only said I knew what she'd do." He tapped Bo-ji on the shoulder. "Let's see if we can get the groom home without somebody starting a street rumble."

Shelley and I sat up a long time straightening out the orders one last time. "Spencer knows," she said. "His instincts are good for these things."

"But why would Duchess want to marry Roy? He's three quarters crazy, I swear."

Shelley said, "It means a lot to be, you know, special. To be the one picked out from all the others. That's all this love crap is about anyhow."

The morning of the Buying Club was hot and yellow, and the meat was twenty minutes late. We had the vegetables packed in brown bags and lined up along the wall out of the sun: heads of iceberg lettuce, bundles of greens, plastic bags of carrots, loose oranges, potatoes, and onions. Each bag on its own order blank, waiting for the meat to be added. A large, quiet crowd had come, many more people than had placed orders. They were here for the Event, and to see if the Club would really happen, if the charter members had been seers or dupes. The people who *had* bought, too, kept their distance, as if they were waiting with just the same question. Even Mrs. Murrell, wearing a new yellow dress, only waved a chubby arm at me, staying with her new church friends in the meager shade of a street tree. I could hear the low melodic line of their voices, discussing the heat, the unusual stillness of the air.

Shelley and Spencer had gone with the Landells to the

butcher. Roy was with me, sitting on the bottom step now, letting some kids examine his puffy-sided face. Mrs. White, dressed as if for an afternoon tea party, passed down some folding chairs for people to sit on and picked lettuce leaves off her porch. "I don't know," she said. "This weather. Meat spoils."

"They'll bring it straight here," I said. "They'll be here any minute, and the people will take it straight home. It won't be a problem, Mrs. White, I know it won't."

A Buick pulled up with the preacher from the other Baptist church in South Jenkin. His arrival was a surprise because his church and Frank Landell's were rivals. This preacher was a small man, very dark-skinned, with a car full of women larger than he was. He approached me and said in a fine baritone voice, "And when will the distribution commence?"

"Shortly!" I cried, my voice coming out much louder than I had meant it to. "They're running a couple of minutes late, but we'll get started in no time at all. Right, Roy?" Roy gave me a gloomy look that probably meant he wasn't speaking to purveyors of the opiate of the people, but his stare spooked me a little. And when the preacher didn't look satisfied, I started in talking again, unable to stop myself, explaining at great length about it being the first day, and how much trouble we had had with one thing and the other. I was saved from blurting out all our little secrets only by the station wagon coming around the corner.

I ran to meet them, searching their faces. Was everything okay? Shelley? Spencer? Frank and Yvetta Landell were grinning, and Shelley had a certain wild look of success in her eyes.

"Let's load 'em up!" said Spencer, clapping his hands, and the crowd was suddenly in motion, voices picking up energy, surging toward the station wagon, then quickly forming lines in front of the card tables. The meat in the back of the station wagon was wrapped in pinkish brown paper, pound weights of stew beef, whole chickens. I opened one of the flat boxes of pork chops, and the meat inside was thick and pink with solid white lard at the edges. Now those are pork chops, I thought, wanting to hold one up for Marie Conyers to see. The most beautiful pork chops I'd ever seen. I had a vision of South Jenkin tomorrow covered with a haze of blue barbecue smoke, the sputter of black skillets full of chicken and pork chops, bubbling pots of stew. Spencer loaded our arms. I loved the weight of it, the welcome cool coming through. We were giving something real and solid to the people.

Meanwhile, around this center of animal flesh, Frank Landell had formed a parade; he lifted the frozen turkey over his head like a sacrifice, and Alvetta White followed with a laundry basket full of raffle tickets. Frank asked the other preacher to offer a blessing on this endeavor, and he did, at length. My hands itched at the inaction. I wanted to complete the act, to get the meat into bags, the bags into the hands of the people.

The other preacher's wife drew the number, and when she called it out, there was a scream—not a squeal or a little shriek, but a full scale scream—and there stood Mrs. Murrell with her arms extended stiffly and her head thrown back. "I have *good* luck!" she cried. "Everything is going *right*! Oh Jesus!" People cheered, and she came forward running with her hands clasped across her chest. She broke away from her direct line to Frank Landell and the turkey, and for an instant I was caught up against her soft chest. "You bring me good luck!" she cried, and then ran on to get her turkey. "A change is coming, I *know* change is coming!"

And then, at last, still tingling from the hug, I began to hand the bags over to the people. Some so heavy they needed two arms to lift them. Some people with two bags, and Roy offering to walk them home. The other preacher's wife, at the head of Shelley's line, had the biggest orders of all. She complained that we didn't have plastic bags to double-wrap our meat. Shelley's hair curls were damp in her face, and she shook them away and shouted into the glare, "Great suggestion! We have a great suggestion! Hey everybody! Save plastic bags! We need plastic bags and paper bags. Save your bags and bring them back next week!"

Veronne Foley counted her chops and opened one end of her chicken to inspect it, too. She said, "You gonna make me pay the two dollars every week?"

"Membership is only once a year!" I shouted. "Everybody! Announcement! You only have to pay the two dollar membership fee once a year!"

I was getting a little lightheaded from excitement and heat, or the smell of meat blood, or from having slept badly through dreams of disappearing chickens and disapproving faces, but I kept shouting: "Bring back your bags next week!"

"I brought my own this week," said Marie Conyers, arriving with Hooky and Charlie and a big hemp-handled shopping bag. She had dressed for the occasion in crisp blue and white checks and a pink straw hat with a wide brim.

"Oh Marie," I said, wanting to finish something with her, to say something important that I had failed to say the other day when I was so frightened, but she had the twinkle in her eyes today. I said, "You look so pretty today."

She said, "I got one or two dresses I could leave the house wearing." And then, looking around the crowd with me, "Well, it looks like we organized some club, didn't we?" She loaded her bag in Charlie's arms, telling Hooky he could have the next turn, and strolled over to talk to Yvetta Landell's grandmother. No one was in such a hurry anymore, now that the meat was here. Now that they had their armloads of food for so little money. Now they wanted to talk to us, smile, touch, make sure we wouldn't forget them next week.

Mrs. White called me from the porch. "Blair Morgan, you have a phone call. It's Dave Rivers."

Shelley and Spencer both looked at me.

"I'm okay," I said.

I stood in the relatively dim office by the phone and didn't pick it up. Why? I thought. Why am I not putting it to my ear? The Buying Club is working. There's nothing he can say that will change it. Nothing he can say will change the hundred pounds of meat and the hundred pounds of vegetables, and Mrs. Murrell winning the turkey, and Marie Conyers smiling at me that way.

And yet, the instant I heard his voice say my name, everything did change. I slid instantly into an anger that seemed to have pooled inside me. He has no right, I thought.

"I knew this was the day for the Club, Blair," he said. "And I just wanted to call and wish you well—and wish I could be there."

His voice sounded as if it were being sent to me through a smile. A voice in my head screamed, What do you want? How dare you grin at me? How dare you try to mess it up—you're out of my life. Stay out, do you hear me? Why are you doing this? Who *allows* you to do this to me?

But I was not brought up to raise my voice. I was brought up to turn away anger with a soft answer, only they never explained in the Bible what you were supposed to do when the anger was your own. And what I really wanted to do anyhow was heap burning coals on his head.

"How did it go?" he said.

"It went tremendously, perfectly, beautifully."

"I'd love to be there. I'd love to be part of it."

I meant to keep all the details away from him, the raffle, the other preacher, any of the things that would make it concrete. But while I was holding those things back, the other thing spilled out.

"Listen, Dave," I said, "there's only one thing I want to hear from you, and that is if you are ever coming back or if you have decided to stay there with her." It came out of the anger, but it had a ring of truth. I said, "I don't know how to act till I'm sure one way or the other."

"The freshmen are coming in soon," he said. "I told them I'd stay through orientation. We always give a lot of effort to freshman orientation."

"You weren't at freshman orientation last year. You didn't show up for weeks."

244

But I was retreating. He hadn't answered my question, and I was letting him get away with it; he said the obvious, that Paul McTeague had been there last year, how important it was, what special plans he had made. There was a silhouette in the door, Spencer glancing in at me.

Dave said, "How about you? Are you staying there or coming back?"

"Coming back! To you and Martha?" I moved the phone away from my mouth and gestured to Spencer to come in. I couldn't see his face as he approached because the light was behind him, but I was drawn toward him, away from Dave. I put a hand on Spencer's shoulder and said to Dave, "I wouldn't leave the work here anyhow. This work is important."

"I know it is," said Dave.

"But listen, Dave, be sure and pick out a real pretty freshman girl, in my honor, okay? Teach her everything you know?"

"Blair," he said, reproving, but his voice was miniaturized because I held it away from my ear, and Spencer was putting his long fingers on my waist; under my blouse they touched the skin of my back.

I said, "Martha's very understanding about freshmen. She knows you go through them like a box of kleenex."

"I didn't call to fight. I wanted to wish you luck."

I pushed my belly forward, against Spencer, and he made a sound in his throat, a little laugh: Dave's fault, I thought.

"I didn't want it to end this way," he said. "I wanted to tell you—once we get things started here, I was going to come down to see you, to talk things through."

He sounded like a marvel of transistor power: so tiny.

On tiptoe I kissed Spencer, a kiss that ran through the softness of my belly and with equal power up the bones of my spine. I never felt this with *you,* I thought. Never felt anything nearly like this with you.

The phone was a foot from my ear now. "This is not the right way to end," said the little voice.

For an instant I started to come back from my long waves of sensation to realize that it was not the way I wanted it to end either, that I had asked a question that I had a right to have answered. I almost pulled the phone back to my ear, but Spencer interpreted my movement to be a gesture toward hanging it up, and he took it from me, put it in its cradle.

Spencer said, in teasing, melodramatic tones. "We can't go on meeting this way," and I thought, separating from him, But what can we do instead?

Fifteen

The people in the study group at Chuck and Eleanor-Byrd Williams' church were all just dying to hear about Vista work; at least, that's what Eleanor-Byrd told me. I didn't know if I believed her, but it was a pleasant walk over to the Old Stone Presbyterian Church, a real treat for me, something so much less important than our Buying Club that its very unimportance made it like a vacation. I smiled around at the white faces in the panelled meeting room and thought, rather smugly, of how little they knew of what was going on. And then there was Eleanor-Byrd, talking effusively about how special I was, her top Vista, she said, really cream of the crop. It had been a sort of dreamy Sunday afternoon, Shelley and Spencer drinking wine and smoking some grass, talking about the Club. This was like a dream too, as Eleanor-Byrd told about my first days as a Vista, and how I had taken on the biggest landlord in South Jenkin and gotten some action. Well, I thought, she's exaggerating a little, but it didn't seem to matter very much. "She looks like a co-ed," said Eleanor-Byrd, "but I guarantee that what we have with us tonight is a gadfly and agitator in the finest tradition, Miss Blair Ellen Morgan!"

My goodness, I thought, waiting for the clapping to stop, is that really how I look to Eleanor-Byrd? Did I really have a reputation down at TAPS? Or was Eleanor just making the most of the speaker she and Chuck had brought in? Chuck himself gave me a wink, as if he at least knew what the real score was, but I wasn't sure I understood the meaning of the wink.

I made a good speech, personal and straightforward, starting with how when I was a child I used to want to save the starving people of Calcutta, and how shocked I had been to learn that we had poverty here in our own United States. I gave them my South Jenkin atrocity list: evidence of things I had witnessed with my own eyes. "Just this summer," I said, coming around in front of the lectern, "in South Jenkin less than twenty blocks from where we are sitting at this very moment, I saw a refrigerator with nothing in it but a few grains of powdered milk. I saw children with no babysitter but the television, while their mother travelled two hours each way to a housecleaning job." My mouth itched to say, Probably to clean one of your houses, but I checked the impulse. I talked about landlords who wouldn't give services until city agencies were called in, and impetigo and, yes, malnutrition.

I could feel them listening, especially the women, large-eyed, well-dressed, nodding seriously when I was serious, smiling when I offered something amusing or hopeful. The men's faces more skeptical, but also attentive.

The culmination of my speech was the Buying Club. There *is* hope, I said. There is a lot of hope. The people know what they want if you listen to them. I told about the meeting where people said they needed cheap meat, and we Vistas decided to help them get it wholesale. Felt needs, real social change. As I talked, the connections were made so richly, so obviously, that I found myself loving my audience for being the occasion of the connecting.

I had rehearsed the question-and-answer period with Shelley and Spencer playing stupid and hostile questioners. What actually happened, though, was that no one attacked me; everyone congratulated me or asked for more information. The closest thing I had to a hostile question was one barrel-chested older man who asked if I didn't think there was a lot of welfare cheating going on. I'd brought figures to answer that very question, from *Time* magazine, demonstrating that the vast majority of welfare recipients were elderly, disabled, or under the age of twelve. The next questioner offered to give a barbecue in her backyard for the Girl Scout troop or anyone else I wanted to bring. Someone else congratulated Eleanor-Byrd and Chuck and TAPS for bringing these fine young people down here.

And then, afterwards, they gathered around me, these grown men and women, like campers around a campfire. They paused whenever I spoke to make sure I had absolutely finished what I was going to say. I could interrupt them if I wanted to, but they would not interrupt me. After a while, I lost the thread of what was being said because I was so delighted with the sensation of being the one they gathered around. I wondered if Dave used to drift off like this. I doubted it; he would have been too intent on making his point. Some other time, I thought, I'll really try to convince people. This is the first time this has ever happened to me. I didn't really care if the barrel-chested man disagreed with me. I smiled and smiled as he talked, not hearing a word, delighted with him for being part of my experience.

People eventually began to leave, and since Eleanor-Byrd was staying to clean up, Chuck was to drive me home. I offered to walk, half wanting to be alone, but on the other hand glad to be taken care of. I allowed him to hand me into their midnight blue Chrysler, and I sank into the broad front seat.

"Air-conditioned too," I said, as he adjusted the whoosh of air.

At night you couldn't see his eyes because they were so deep-set and dark, but his mouth had its usual self-deprecating smile, and he tucked his chin down as he talked, making wrinkles in the loose skin under his neck and jowls. He apologized for the barrel-chested man at the meeting, and I said I had enjoyed it, I really had. I had enjoyed everything. He adjusted the climate control again. "You tell me if it gets too cold now. This air conditioning will freeze you to death." He hesitated as if he had something else to say, and I could smell very faintly some aftershave or cologne. "You were a big hit," he said.

"Was I? Some of Eleanor's friends didn't really have to be convinced of much." I was in a mood where I didn't really care if the compliments were honest or just flattery; I liked the way they felt.

"Oh yes, a big hit." I waited for amplification, for a description of just how I was a big hit, but he stopped there, and I was sorry it wasn't Eleanor-Byrd driving me home. *She* wouldn't have let it drop so soon.

We crossed William and Mary Road into South Jenkin. The streets, from which I was separated by thick window glass and the hum of the engine and air conditioner, seemed preternaturally quiet. Some boys were playing dice under a streetlight, and they were shouting, but I only heard distant cries, indistinguishable from car honks or sirens.

"Aren't you afraid, living over here?"

"Oh no, I feel at home now—I like the action on the streets."

"Eleanor worries about you. There was a big debate, you know, down at TAPS, about whether or not to put the Vistas, but especially the girl Vistas, in apartments over here."

"But that's the main thing about Vista, to live with the people you're working with!"

"Eleanor about worried herself sick before you came—with Shelley over here by herself." By herself, I thought. Well, I don't think she was by herself very much. He said, "We're supposed to be getting some more Vistas soon. Eleanor rests easier when she has 3 or 4 girls living together."

I felt something slow and sleepy coming over me. If Shelley went, then I would move into her room and I'd be the senior Vista. I'd show the new girls the way we did things in South Jenkin. We pulled up in front of the house, and there was a moment of silence in the dark that reminded me of high school, when the car stops and the boy is getting up courage to ask for what he wants, the kiss, or whatever. Not that I thought Chuck would ever play games like that, but he didn't get out, and I still had this vague feeling that he wanted something from me. I reached for the door handle. "Well, it was nice of you to drive me home—"

"Wait," and he touched me, his hand on my shoulder, very briefly but emphatically, and I jumped, and hoped he didn't notice. "I wanted to ask you—whose idea was your—store?"

"The Buying Club? I don't know, it was like I said at the meeting, the community people gave us the idea. And we all pulled it together." Reluctantly, I added, "Dave was the one with previous experience at that kind of thing."

"Oh yes, Mr. Rivers, of course. A bright man. It's a shame he couldn't have stayed and worked with us."

I didn't like the way Chuck seemed to want to credit Dave with the Buying Club. "We didn't really need him to have the Buying Club—we put it together without him being here."

Chuck laughed. "I know you don't need anyone to think for you," and he actually gave my knee a quick pat, and was out his door, on the way around to open mine. I wondered what I would do if someone like Chuck made a real pass at me, didn't pat my knee but laid his hand on it and stroked slowly. I had had too many thoughts like that since Dave left. Dave's fault, I thought, for doing something, for sensitizing me to that side of life, and then leaving me with no protection from it.

I went in alone, and the house was completely still and dark. The door to Shelley's room was closed, but there was a light in mine coming from the wall sconce on the far side. I hesitated before going in, and when I did, immediately saw that someone was lying in my bed, mostly in shadows, on his side. It was Spencer, with no shirt on, and his pants standing out from his lean belly as if he'd been starving to death for a long time.

"Spencer!" I whispered, closing the door behind me. "What are you doing in my bedroom?"

His eyes were open, but he was completely still. He had his hands pressed together between his thighs, and his whole body was twisted as if he were under some great pressure.

"Spencer!"

In a hoarse whisper that sounded as if he hadn't used his voice in a while, he said, "I have to ask you."

"What are you doing in my room? Where's Shelley?"

"I have to ask you something." He sat up, keeping his hands stuffed between his thighs and shivering. I had never seen him ungroomed like this, either. His hair had gone into little rolls. He swallowed a couple of times, then slowly pulled his hands from between his legs and held them before him, keeping his eyes on me. "Do you see snakes?"

"What? Snake Eyes?"

"No, snakes. Rattlesnakes. Cobras. Do you see any snakes?"

"Are you on drugs, Spencer?"

He lowered his lids for a second, half smiled, as if I were giving him a hard time, and he had to be patient. "Just tell me what you see. Please."

"I don't see anything. I see your hands."

"They keep changing. My fingers turn into snakes."

I looked again. He held them perfectly stiff so that none of them touched another. His forearms, though, were partially rotated and, under tension, the long veins and bundles of tendons undulated slightly.

I grabbed his hands before I saw anything worse and held them tightly between mine. "No snakes, Spencer. No snakes."

"Are you sure?"

"No snakes. Look for yourself."

He closed his eyes and shook his head, but at the same time wrapped his arms around me and pulled me onto his lap. He didn't use his hands, though.

I said, "Are you on some kind of drug trip?"

He rocked me back and forth. "Just what you saw this afternoon, and we smoked a little more grass. I haven't been on a trip for a long time, not for months. It comes back, though. You see things again, you have flashes. Sometimes when I smoke grass, sometimes for no reason at all, my hands do that."

"But you know it's not real."

His shrug ran through me as well as through him. "I see it happen. I don't mean, it looks like it happens, I mean I see it happening. If I look too long, they'll stay that way."

"But you know better!" He shrugged again, as if he didn't really know better at all. We rocked back and forth a while, then I said, "Spencer, you can't stay in my room."

"I want to stay with you. Shelley's been asleep for hours. I want you to check out my hands for me."

"Not in my room."

I took the pillow and sheets from the second bed and we went into the living room. Spencer kept his head high and his hands away from his sides, fingers still spread wide. I put one sheet on the low mattress, and he lay down and let me tuck the other one over him. I sat on the floor beside him with my arm over his chest, watching how, as my eyes became accustomed to the dark, shapes appeared flattened. All the familiar spatial relationships were distorted: the coffee table appeared to jut upward like a slab of ice crowded by other floes. I didn't move anymore than I had to because this heat too was as dense as ice.

I thought Spencer had gone to sleep, but he said, "Blair? Will you do something else for me?" He sounded so young, looked like a child too, with only his head uncovered. "Will you tell me you love me?"

"I don't know whether I love you or not."

"You don't have to mean it. I just want to hear the words."

The stolid country girl in me hunkered down and objected. I had never said those words to Dave; why should I say them to Spencer? "Will it really help? I'd just be saying it because you asked me."

"Please. Say it."

"All right. I love you."

A sigh came out of him, as if it were the first time he'd breathed all evening. "Thank you," he said, bringing his arms out from under the covers and finally using his hands. He touched my face. "It makes the evil go away, like a fairy tale."

I felt it, too, that I had done the magic, saved him, that he was mine now. Something sweet of gratitude in the lightness of his fingertips on my cheeks. I took off my dress, my underclothes. I slipped with him under the sheet so pale it seemed luminescent. In flashes, as we moved together, I thought of Shelley, that she should be with us, that she would bless us if she knew, that she would stab us to death. Once, when I was on top of him with my back arched, I looked down and thought he had turned into her, and her long hair was spread on the pillow. But when I dropped close again, I touched his beard, his bony clavicle, smelled the sharp sourness of his body and mine, and heard the heat disappearing in a rush of wind. It ended with me shuddering over and over, and I thought that I must love him, or else how could this be so enormous?

In the morning I was awakened by Shelley's wooden clogs walking heavily to the bathroom. I was in my own bed, sweating, with a band of sunlight coming in under the blind and hitting me in the face. I shoved the window up, but the air that came in was sun-heated and breezeless. It was ten-fifteen. I never slept this late, and this was the beginning of a new Buying Club week; we had prices to call for, the order blanks to make and distribute. Then I remembered Spencer, and grabbed my robe, hurried down the hall.

He had gone, leaving the sheets folded neatly, with a note on the pillow: "Dear Women," it said, "Went to the butcher with Ralph. Call you later. Spence." Or maybe he signed it Spencer; I couldn't tell the r's from the final flourishes in his large-looped hand.

Shelley came clunking down the hall, and I turned in panic, making my face bright. This time there was something real between Spencer and me, I had really stolen him. But she should have stayed awake and helped him last night, I

254

thought, it's her fault. "Hi, Shelley. Spencer stayed the night. Look, he left a note, he got Ralph and they're going over to the butcher."

She had her hair twisted in a knot, pulled back tight from her face. She turned her back on me, and I followed her into the kitchen.

"It's going to be brutal hot today," I said. "I should go shower. I can't believe I slept this late."

She poured milk into a little saucepan and put it over a flame. She stared down into it. I thought: she must know. She heard us last night and she's toying with me.

I said, "He'll call after they get the prices."

"Look at this milk." She gave the pan a little shake. "Look how it clings to the sides." Bubbles were forming and riding up on the edges. "I've been throwing up like a dog. Smoked and drank all day yesterday and now I'm throwing up. I hate to throw up."

"Spencer was in pretty bad shape last night too."

"I'm sick of Spencer," she said. "There's dirt in the milk too. Doesn't anyone ever clean pots around here?" She turned off the fire, whirled around with the pot in her hand, one burst of milk hitting the floor. She poured the rest in the sink. I squatted quickly and cleaned up what she'd spilled. The linoleum was filthy too: scuff marks, long sticky splashes, crumbs, and a nasty-looking flattened thing, maybe a smashed raisin. Shelley's legs needed a shave, too. There was a fringe of stubble across her ankle.

When I stood, she was still leaning over the sink with her chin doubled, as if she had lost the bones in her face overnight. I said, "Do you think you're sick from drinking and smoking too much yesterday?"

"No, I don't think that's why I'm sick. I think I'm sick because I'm pregnant, and all the drinking and smoking is going to do is make a monster out of what's inside me."

Relief at what she was saying: Spencer and I safe a little longer. I said, "Are you still going to have an abortion?"

"Damn straight I am. Why else do you think I'm making

so sure it's a monster. Oh shit." She put a hand over her eyes. "I'm going to have to throw up again. I'm going to throw up and go back to bed."

I washed out her milk pan, careful to get out all the specks and chips of enamel. Then I got the sponge and started working on the floor. Even with scrubbing I couldn't get rid of the scuff marks, but I scratched up the raisin with my thumbnail. I was beginning to rinse when the phone rang.

"Hey listen, Blair," said a businesslike Spencer. "We've got a problem. The butcher doesn't want to do business anymore."

"We gave him a bigger order than he asked for."

"He said the volume's still too small. He was just doing us a favor, he said, and now he's decided he can't afford it."

I tried to remember this butcher from the first day we'd talked to him. He had been good-looking, dark, thick-set. He'd seemed too young to me. Maybe the real boss had come back. I remembered how he said we were crazy and laughed. I said, "I don't get it. Is he mad at us? Is he some kind of a racist?"

"I don't know. He seemed embarrassed about the whole thing."

I could hear cars passing in the background. "Well," I said, "then we go to the next butcher on the list. That's all. The other guy said he was willing. We don't have to tell him he's second choice." I was proud of the pluckiness in my voice, proud that I had the information in my folder. I had time to rinse the floor and shower before Spencer and Ralph came to pick me up. With a little luck we could have it all percolating again by the end of the day. Still, it was unnerving that a man who had been a good guy yesterday would suddenly turn against us. It made the world feel less safe to me.

Shelley stayed in bed all day, and again on Tuesday. I went home at lunch time, after a morning of painstaking work on the flyer with this week's prices. She was lying on top of her sheets with all the blinds down except one that flapped and let in a little air and a fluctuating amount of light. She was drinking a large coke and chain-smoking, and had a stack of paperback mystery novels beside her and on top of them a stack of crossword puzzles her mother had cut out of the *New York Times*.

"Can I get you anything?" I said. I wasn't quite sure yet of how carefully to treat her.

"When you go out again you could get some more Coke. If you don't mind. It settles my stomach."

"Are you still throwing up?"

She shrugged. She had one ankle propped up on the other knee. Sometime during the morning she had washed her hair and shaved her legs. The foot hanging in the air looked powerful to me, pale, with big spaces between the toes, a foot that could get a grip in the earth and stand up to things. She said, "I'm all right. Throwing up demoralizes me so badly I'd rather stay in bed than chance it. Maybe you could get me some cigarettes too? Spencer was supposed to bring some over, but he seems to have forgotten. Par for the course."

I nodded eagerly. She was going to be okay, I could tell. A little movie ran in my mind: some months in the future when she was safely back in New York, at school, with all this taken care of, I would call her and tell her how Spencer and I had fallen into a relationship—we hadn't meant to, it had just happened. And she would say, Oh wow. That's great, Blair, you two were made for each other. She would have a new boyfriend, a better one, just right for her, and she would invite us to come and visit her in New York.

She was thinking about men too. "Men are bastards," she said.

Some of them, I thought, and in my rush of warmth for her, said, "Dave isn't coming back, you know."

"I know." She said it so gently that it made me feel sorry for myself. "He's not worth it, Blair. I know you think he's brilliant and terrific and all that, but you're letting him treat you like shit." She waved her pencil in the air. "But who am I to talk, right? I don't even tell Spencer what's happening,

I'm so afraid he'll dump on me. Well, it doesn't matter any-how. My cousin's coming to get me Monday."

"And that's it? You'll leave for good?" She nodded. I felt a rush of sorrow that I wouldn't have her here anymore. "I know you don't have any choice—that's what I hate about being this sex. You don't have any choice. One day you start bleeding. Bang. I hate the way we can get caught if we just make a little mistake."

"I don't hate it," she said. "The women always run my family. I never wanted to be a man. I always pictured myself with a bunch of kids. That's what makes this so rotten."

"You don't think it's like a person, do you?"

She looked away, toward the window. "You tell yourself what you have to," she said.

Down the hall the phone rang. As I hurried to the phone, I thought that I had somehow made a bad decision, picking Spencer over Shelley. But it had never seemed like a choice; it had seemed like what you had to do, to go with the man. The way my mother used to put me to bed and then leave me for Daddy.

The voice on the phone was high and excited.

"Oh, Mrs. White," I said. "This is Blair."

"Blair," she said, a little more normally, but still too shrill. "You have to tell all the Vistas. They can't have the Buying Club anymore. They said so at TAPS. It's in a memo from Mr. Delbert Jackson himself, the executive director."

"What memo? What did it say?"

Shelley appeared in the archway, watching my face. Mrs. White said, "We had a Neighborhood Workers meeting this morning and they passed out the memo. Everybody else got a carbon copy, but I got the original typed one, so I knew it was about us in South Jenkin even before I read it. It said No Neighborhood Workers or Neighborhood Centers or Vista Volunteers or anything to with TAPS is supposed to sell goods especially perishable. I knew this would happen. I knew it. I knew we would get in trouble with the health regulations. I knew we couldn't have all that meat in here."

"There never was any meat in the center, Mrs. White," I said, and made her read me the whole thing word for word, and I wrote it down and passed it to Shelley. "It doesn't say anything about health regulations, Mrs. White. Is that what they said it was at the meeting?"

"They didn't say nothing. They just handed out the memos. All the other ladies didn't have any idea what it was about, and I didn't let on it was happening at my Center."

"We didn't do anything wrong," I said, but meanwhile I was remembering the butcher and having this vague feeling that we must have done something wrong, or else why were we being punished?

"And you all Vistas worked so hard too," said Mrs. White.

"Oh don't think it's over," I said. "They won't stop us that easily." Shelley gave me a firm nod, and I got off the phone tingling with resolve and doubt.

Shelley, Spencer, Roy, and I took a taxi downtown. It was almost worth a crisis just to be united like this, and wearing costumes: Roy in his ten-gallon hat that he hadn't worn since we'd come down; Spencer in a white golf cap and tourist shirt of Ralph's, all scarlet leaves and yellow pineapples. Shelley and I were in identical dungaree skirts, but she had a tailored khaki shirt and her hair was in that tight knot that made her look like someone at a court martial. And she didn't smile, either, when Spencer entertained us at nervous length, flashing his teeth and sunglasses like a tropical con man.

"You see what happened," he told. "It was just like the *Untouchables*. Somebody got to the butcher. It was like when Elliot Ness thinks he's got a witness lined up, and the next day the man says, 'Oh no Mr. Ness, you got it wrong, I never saw nothing that night, nothing at all.' "

We passed out of South Jenkin, past Ralph's mother's funeral parlor, the sailor bars and wharfs, up the ramp and over the bridge span. You could see the city from up there: limestone and granite slabs of government and commerce, warehouses, gantry cranes for shipbuilding, and upriver, hazy, but unmistakable, a navy destroyer. Only if you twisted your neck could you see the low houses of South Jenkin. I was shocked by the smallness of our neighborhood, our Buying Club. How could anyone care? I thought: one Saturday morning out of the history of the world.

"I expect they just didn't understand it, that's all," I said. "Somebody told them we were setting up a store."

"Oh they understand," said Shelley. "Don't think they don't understand. They figure it's a communist conspiracy."

"Naw," said Spencer. "They just want the collard folks keepin' on keepin' quiet, keepin' on keepin' poor."

We got out at the old Bank of the South, took the side door, and started up the stairs to TAPS. The stairwell was broad and bright, but it had ancient dust in the air and worn linoleum with chunks broken out. "I don't like old office buildings," I said. "They remind me of my dentist when I was a kid. There used to be a beauty salon on the same floor, but as far as I was concerned, it was all a front for the dentist."

"TAPS is a front too," said Roy. "A front for the KKK."

The long reception room-typing pool with its suspended egg carton neon lights had no windows. All the windows had been partitioned off into the executive office cubicles to the left: Delbert Jackson's big office, Eleanor-Byrd's smaller one, and the board room. The secretaries stopped working to watch us come in. We always said TAPS should turn in some of the secretaries and get more Vistas, and turn in Delbert Jackson too, except that there wouldn't be any trade-in value on him. We made a lot of jokes criticizing TAPS, and I was never really sure which ones were angry and which ones were affectionate.

Mr. Delbert Jackson, said the secretaries, wasn't in yet today and Eleanor-Byrd was out to lunch. "We'll wait," said Roy, and before the secretaries could object, he made an abrupt left turn into Mr. Delbert's own office, and we marched in after him.

"All right," said Spencer. "Way to go, Roy!"

The air-conditioned cubicle had a subdued opulence: deep pile carpet, mahogany desk with an immaculate broad expanse, a great black leather chair behind it, heavy print drapes. Spencer strode around and opened the drapes, but only briefly, because the windows were filthy, a yellow oiliness smearing the light. The air-conditioner vents had waving tendrils of grime, like inorganic algae waving in a stream. He shook his head and returned us to dimness. "Mr. Delbert should clean up his act," he said. He sat down in the big chair, made jokes about cigars, but there was something in the chilly, thick room that muffled Spencer too, and after a while he got up and moved to one of the seats in front of the desk. I sat on the floor, pressed my back against the panelled wall, and Roy and Shelley leaned on the opposite wall, on either side of a framed portrait of John F. Kennedy.

I said, "This place makes me claustrophobic."

"You can take it," said Shelley, out of her severe, flattened face.

Spencer said, "The Commissar of Morale says you can take it, Blair."

Oh don't start in on each other, I thought, pulling my knees up to my chest, trying to keep warm. We were together now, maybe for the last time, and they shouldn't quarrel.

We were saved by the entrance of Mr. Delbert Jackson himself, bursting in, all bright plaid sports jacket and extended meaty palms, his resonant voice deploring the lack of chairs, shouting to the secretaries to bring more chairs, to bring coffee. They brought the folding chairs, but no one paid any attention to his order for coffee. He didn't seem to notice, though, and cheerfully helped open the chairs, arranging us in front of him just so, and then he expanded with a sigh into his chair behind the desk, a large, heavy man with a splendidly sincere smile. "The South Jenkin Vistas," he said. "To what do I owe this pleasure?"

Spencer was smiling right back at him, consciously or unconsciously knitting his fingers over his stomach just as the executive director did over his. "We had something we wanted to talk to you about, Delbert."

Delbert did not blink or stop smiling at being addressed by his first name, but he did clear his throat and make a little speech. "Let me just say how glad I am whenever I have the opportunity of talking to you young people, because here at TAPS we appreciate your enthusiasm—we value your efforts —with those little children over in South Jenkin. I saw you on television the other night."

Shelley leaned forward and said, "But what about the Buying Club? We heard you don't want us to have the Buying Club anymore."

Delbert nodded. His graying hair was cut close above his ears, with a precise line were short sideburns stopped. The long smooth jowls rolled gently with the nod. "You've done fine work. But, my dear *fine* young people, in the end we're dependent on the good will of our local business community." He opened his hands onto the table, all his cards out. What a shame, but there it was.

Something began to form in my mind, troubling me, but I didn't quite see it yet.

Spencer showed more teeth than I knew he had. "Local business community?"

"After all," smiled Delbert, "TAPS is not in the habit of buying and selling—we couldn't begin to afford the freezers."

"Freezers?" said Shelley. "Who said anything about freezers? You never even found out what we were doing, Mr. Jackson. We got fresh vegetables from the wholesale market and meat from a butcher and we passed it out directly to the people who had given the money for it. That was all. We aren't starting a store. We're just getting some stuff for people at wholesale prices."

"Free enterprise in action, Delbert." said Spencer.

Delbert closed his eyes now. "Health regulations," he murmured. "Tax problems for a non-profit organization."

"Hey," said Spencer. "It's just helping the people help themselves, like the man says."

Roy was glowering under the brim of the hat. He got up and began to walk back and forth between his chair and the picture of JFK.

I could feel the tension screwing up in me too, but I thought I knew now that it was my fault. I was the Judas goat. I said, "What business complained? Who objected?"

"Oh my dear child, the whole business community—"

"They haven't had time. We only started last Saturday. It isn't the whole business community, it's Chuck Williams."

Spencer's eyes on me, and Shelley's. "Right," said Spencer. "That's it, isn't it? He got worried about the Dollar Bill stores. The butcher—do you remember? The first butcher knew Chuck. He probably sells to Dollar Bill."

I said, "It's my fault. I spoke at their church on Sunday night and I just stood up there and talked and talked about the Buying Club and how great it was, and by Monday morning he'd talked to the butcher—"

Delbert said, "I don't think we can accuse Chuck Williams of self-interest in this. Why, he doesn't even have a Dollar Bill store in South Jenkin."

"Yeah, right," said Shelley. "The nearest Dollar Bill is on the other side of William and Mary Road. That's true. And it's true people in South Jenkin don't send their kids across that highway to pick up a carton of milk. That's certainly true."

"I should have kept my mouth shut. I thought Chuck and Eleanor-Byrd were on our side. How stupid can you get."

"Damn," said Spencer. "Damn."

"The people in South Jenkin," said Shelley, "pay corner store prices for their hamburger meat and toilet paper. Do you know how expensive a roll of toilet paper is at a corner store in South Jenkin, Mr. Jackson? And I suppose Chuck must have told you how his Dollar Bill store—since it's *all the way* across William and Mary Road—how they make deliveries on that side of the highway but not on our side."

Roy gave the chair he had been sitting on an emphatic little bump. "Listen. This is all bull. There's no use talking here. Either you're for the people or you're against them, and this chickenshit organization is against them."

"Shut up, Roy," said Shelley.

Roy said, "They're for us or they're against us, and he says they're against us. Okay. All right. I'll go out on my own before I'd work another day for this chickenshit organization."

"Don't be hasty," said Delbert softly, smiling more narrowly but still sincerely, as if he were taking pleasure in this confrontation too.

Roy took hold of the chair with both hands and lifted it several inches off the floor and slammed it down hard. "It's over!" he said. "The bullshit's over." He stomped out the door.

Delbert didn't flinch. I thought maybe he had hoped for Roy to come at him man-to-man. "That young fellow has a lot to learn," he said.

Roy shouted something blurred from the outer office.

"Let's go," said Shelley.

"Yeah, we have to talk over our options," said Spencer.

"What options?" I said.

Delbert rose, went to the door with us. "Yes, dialogue is the best way. My office is always open to you young people."

"What dialogue?" I was saying, wishing to explode like Roy, but letting Shelley and Spencer lead me out. "What options? Roy quits Vista, and TAPS says we have to drop the Buying Club. What kind of options is that? What kind of dialogue?"

The secretaries were looking out the door after Roy, and we heard another blast out in the hall, Roy's deep voice scattered, his footsteps thundering down. At the top of the stairs we could still hear him, and between him and us, on the landing, were Chuck and Eleanor-Byrd Williams. She had a hand to her throat, and Chuck's mouth was sour. He lifted one eyebrow at us.

"I see the whole Free Speech movement is here," he said.

Seeing them gave me a pain behind my breastbone. I had

sat in their car. I had let them pour Southern honey all over my head, down my neck and shoulders. I had fantasized about Chuck squeezing my knee. I said, "I can't believe you did that."

He rotated his head past me, erasing me, wary because Spencer had stopped a few steps above him, and stretched one long leg out, blocking the way up.

"The thing is," said Shelley, "the thing is that you don't really want the people of South Jenkin to get out of poverty. The thing is, you're scared about your financial ass."

"What are you talking about?" said Eleanor-Byrd, her voice about an octave lower than usual. "We just got cussed up one side and down the other by Roy Critchfield, and now Shelley is starting in, and I would like to know exactly what is going on."

I said, "You wouldn't know about the Buying Club at all if it hadn't been for me and my big mouth."

"That's right. I heard about the Buying Club on Sunday night and I must say I was surprised I hadn't heard about it sooner. What about the Buying Club?"

"Do you really not know, Eleanor?"

"Ask Chuck," said Spencer.

All of us looked at Chuck, Eleanor now too. Chuck in his shirt sleeves, jacket tossed over a shoulder. Pleats in his pants, flat stomach, lean arms, stringy neck. A wince passed over his face. "This has obviously got all out of proportion. For once in his life Delbert Jackson acted with alacrity, and I see some toes got stepped on."

Eleanor said, "But *what happened?*"

Under attack, Chuck's voice was thin and tight, his easiness all used up. "Some of the boys objected to the idea of TAPS being in business, that's all. Delbert and I talked it over and decided it was bad timing."

"And TAPS sent out a memo," said Shelley. "No more Buying Club."

Spencer grinned. "The profits-over-people memo, right, Chuck? The keep-the-black-folks-keepin'-poor-memo."

I said, "Eleanor, did you honestly not know about it?"

"Nobody told me about any of this." She was looking at Chuck. "I'm the one in charge of the Vistas and their projects, and no one told me anything."

Chuck shrugged. "Delbert goes memo-mad. It wasn't supposed to go this far."

Shelley said, "You mean we weren't supposed to come down here and make a noise."

Eleanor flashed her eyes at us now. "And maybe you bright young people *should* have talked to me before you came storming down here accusing people and things. And maybe you should have consulted me in the first place before you started a major project like your Buying Club."

"I'm going up," said Chuck. "I have some phone calls to make."

Spencer didn't move his leg. "The rest of the butchers, Chuck? You haven't started in on the greengrocers yet. You have a lot of calls to make if you're going to stop them all from selling to us."

"Get out of my way," said Chuck.

"Hey, sure, man, I'm *real* nonviolent. I'm a regular Martin Luther King, Junior, man. You can Bull Connor me all day long."

Eleanor-Byrd turned to follow Chuck, but hesitated, waited till he was inside. "I mean it," she said. "You kids should have come to me in the first place so we could have presented this thing in an orderly way. The Buying Club and your grievances, too."

"Grievances!" I said. "But Eleanor, it's not a *grievance,* they're trying to stop the most important thing we've done!"

Eleanor pursed her lips, moved them around over her teeth a few times as if she were tasting something unfamiliar. She glanced upstairs. "I surely wish it hadn't come to this. In spite of what you think, it isn't the Dollar Bill Stores he's worried about. He has fought his dad and brother on so many issues over that store . . . you don't know. You don't have any idea! It's the business people he's worried about. He doesn't want them thinking TAPS is some kind of rabble-rousing organization. He cares about TAPS so much." She looked around at us. "Chuck is a good man. He's trying to do good in the best way he knows how. Now I want you Vistas to lay low for a while on this and give me a chance to recoup. Do you think you can manage not to make any speeches for a couple of days? How about for one day? Do you think you can just stay out there and take a little rest and give me a chance to do my job, which is, in case you forgot, to be a buffer and advocate for you?"

Shelley said, "I'm checking out, as you know, Eleanor. So TAPS can't do anything to me. I'm going to make sure that the Buying Club happens on Saturday. Maybe the others should wait for you to straighten things out, but I'll be doing the Buying Club, and you can tell Chuck and Delbert for me."

"Me too!" I said.

"Shh," said Eleanor. "As you say, Shelley, you're leaving. But can you be a little circumspect?"

"It won't be at the Neighborhood Center, if that's what you mean."

Eleanor put her pocketbook firmly to her shoulder. "Well, let's just wait and see. Chuck and I are going away for a couple of weeks too." As she headed upstairs, her full skirt brushed us and perfume hung briefly in the air. She said, "You all just take it a little easy for a while, you hear?"

I remember thinking that if Eleanor had really been on our side she would have left Chuck on the spot, and since she didn't, she was betraying us. I felt it burning in me: how could you live with someone who wronged you? I didn't count sexual unfaithfulness, because that was just bodies. Spencer and I had not betrayed Shelley anyhow; rather, time had played a trick and something inevitable had happened out of sequence. When Shelley was gone, it would be all right.

And simultaneously I did not believe that Shelley would ever leave. I was full of conviction that we would always be as we were at this moment—pledging to be thrown out of Vista before we'd let the Buying Club fail. Absolutely righteous. Shelley would always be my strong comrade, Spencer always flexible and electric, Roy heavy with explosions. I would always stride beside them, suffused with the light of our purpose, keeping up even though my sandal made a sore on my heel.

We took the bus home, and halfway across the bridge saw Roy, so we got off at the next stop and waited for him. The four of us walked through South Jenkin, which was red in the afternoon sun. Roy said he was quitting TAPS and getting a job at Dollar Bill's. He would fight the place from the inside out. Organize, undermine, sabotage. Meanwhile, we went to the Landells'. We had to get a place for the Buying Club first; we had to locate our friends.

Frank wasn't home yet, and Yvetta was just putting the baby to bed. We sat on her screened back porch, overlooking the garden and the big stone church. She made us ham sandwiches because we hadn't eaten all day, and we told her what had happened while she warmed greens in bacon grease for Frank, fried his ham, grated cabbage for his cole slaw. After a while, he came across the garden, and we watched him eat his dinner and ate some more ourselves, and we talked on into the evening. I don't know which of us talked when; we seemed to exhale the words, all of us at once. We breathed in the smell of the greens and bacon, and a powerful sweetness of nightblooming moonflowers that grew around the back door. Somewhere outside boys were yelling exuberant South Jenkin yells that trailed off into the distant hoot of a ship's horn.

There was no moment when a decision was made to have the Club at Frank's church; he assumed it would be. Late as it was, we went to the church and recut my stencil with the new distribution place, and we stayed up late, running it off on the church mimeograph machine. Sometime that evening Yvetta told me she was signing up for a sociology course at Virginia State on Tuesday nights, and did I want to come with her? Sure, I said, hardly knowing why that seemed so right too, but it did; it seemed a part of this wholeness, this feeling that this moment could be made to continue indefinitely. That everything would continue just like this, in complete mutual trust, a single point of time filling and filling, overflowing but never spilling: the future with Spencer that had already begun, the loss of Shelley that would never happen, everything at once. Greedy, we would never sleep.

Sixteen

And then, on Monday morning, Shelley left and time resumed its forward motion. I slept that night with Spencer on Old Fellows Street. I suppose I should have waited to hear that Shelley had survived her operation, but when Spencer asked me to stay with him, it seemed as natural to be with him as it had been to be with Dave, and Shelley was in a different world, far away. In this world, all the people were in balanced pairs: Roy and Duchess, Frank and Yvetta Landell, Spencer and me. Like the drawing in my high school biology book of Mendel's sweet peas: light, dark, mixed, dark and light.

I woke early under the poster giantess, and went into Roy's room, where he never slept anymore, to look out the window. There was already pink light on the buildings beyond the rubble field, and I was excited by a desire to get things accomplished, to finish preparations for the rest of my life. I had to move out of my room into Shelley's and clean the rest of the house for the new Vistas who were coming tomorrow. I was looking forward to their arrival, to letting them know that Spencer and I were a couple, loosely bound but closely tied. That I often slept at his place.

I was so intent on imagining how I would explain that I hardly heard Spencer speak to me. "Are you going?" he said in the thick familiar voice common to all sleepers. "Don't go yet." But I pulled the sheet up over him and stroked his forehead.

"Go back to sleep," I said, as the ones who are awake always tell the sleepers.

I thought he had slipped off again, but just as I moved to the door, with my sandals in my hand, he said louder, quite distinctly, "I wish you'd stay."

"I'll be back," I said.

I had never seen South Jenkin so empty of people and so full of light. I felt that these glowing red and yellow bricks were mine. I had everything again; the balance was restored. What Dave had shaken in me was being rebuilt.

As soon as I got home I began to move my clothes into Shelley's room. She had only taken a few things with her: the magenta fringed lamp, her quilt pieced out of silk satin squares. I wondered if, after all, the apartment had been so much Shelley's as I always thought. I knew she put up the India cotton curtains, but she never claimed to have started the redness. I imagined a long string of Vista women creating this place, and that the new ones would think of it as Blair's place; they would associate me with pillows on the floor in a living room like the inside of a jack-o'-lantern.

I put my spread on the white iron bed and tacked *Christina's World* on the wall opposite the window. I sat on the bed for a long time looking at it. First I took in the feeling it always gave me, the proud solitude of endless land, grass, space, and no person in that world but Christina who was so complete that she didn't need other people. I looked at it longer than I ever had before, lying on my side after a while, and seeing new details in the picture: the gores in Christina's skirt, the skinniness of her arms and the largeness of her elbows. The elbows were disquieting: I had always known that Christina was crippled, but I had in my mind filled in a roundness to her arms, made her slim and lovely instead of withered. I also saw for the first time a black scrap flying in the top third of the picture. I wanted it to be a bird, but it was too low, something on a clothesline, maybe, and it bothered me. Some revulsion at the complexity of the picture went through me, and I almost took it down because I didn't understand it anymore. Instead I closed my eyes and fell asleep, curled on my side like Spencer.

When I woke, I jumped off the bed and started to sweep almost before I was awake. Things I had to do: I was wasting my new life! First the room for the new Vistas, then the living room. I scoured the bathroom, swept the kitchen floor. I was going to scrub it too, but the morning heat was increasing, and I thought, Why, I can go and see Spencer now. I don't have to make up an excuse or call ahead. I can go because we're a couple, and I want to see him.

I tested my new strength and freedom by walking past the Red Hat Bar and Grill on the same side as the crowd of men who always hung out there. One of them murmured something to me as I walked by, and I nodded to him as if he had said something polite, and he might have. He grinned at me, and said a very clear "Good morning, how you doing, Miss?" and I wondered if I had been mistaking the crew in front of the Red Hat all these weeks. They were old men anyhow, I thought. A little bit sorry-looking. Somebody's father.

Spencer's door was unlocked, so I walked in and called, "Spencer? I'm back!"

The living room seemed more disordered than usual—books on the floor, dry cleaning in plastic bags spread over the furniture. White morning light on an open suitcase.

Spencer came out of the bedroom wearing the pants to his gray suit and a dress shirt. His eyes shifted away from me, and he made a charming little smile down into the suitcase where he placed a stack of shirts. "Hey!" he said. "I told you not to leave so early. I was just on my way over to see you."

I sidestepped him and the suitcase into the bedroom where the poster of the giantess was rolled in a corner and the bed was buried under a collection of sweaters in beautiful fall colors: amber, ochre, maroon. I had never seen him in a sweater. I only knew him a little while, I thought, feeling smothered by the sweaters. Never knew him in winter at all.

I pivoted back toward the living room. "You're such a neat

packer." His voice started talking; I could see the teeth flash, the fingers swoop through the air leaving trails like an electric pencil. I said, "Why didn't you tell me you were leaving?"

His right hand stopped in midair, raised like a preacher's. "I always said I was going back to school. I never made a secret of it." It might have been true, but I couldn't remember hearing it. "You don't know what my dad would do to me if I didn't show up for college this year. You don't know my parents."

He said this with a sort of pride; he had these incredible parents, and if I knew them, I would understand. Like Shelley, he had a family out there—a context I knew nothing about. I was a stranger. I had written brutal letters to my parents: Don't visit, don't call. Don't write so often, I told them. You distract me from my work. I had wanted to choose my family, and I had chosen Dave, and then Shelley and Spencer, and now I was disconnected and I would float off into space like an air-filled bladder with no ties to the earth at all.

I was so sorry for myself that tears welled up in my eyes, and I tipped my head back quickly so they wouldn't fall. "You should have made me understand," I said.

A tear rolled out anyhow, and he came to me, put his hands on my face. "Hey, hey, hey. This was always supposed to be light. We weren't supposed to get all knotted up, me or you either." Pulling me against the cool pale shirt with little marbled buttons. I let him press my face in, and when I brought it back, I saw I had left a wet blot.

I said, "Tell me exactly when you're going."

"Three o'clock today. American Airlines. Ralph's picking me up at two. I was going to spend the rest of the time with you."

Now that it was clear, very clear, and my tears blotted, I started walking around the room, stepping over books, a row of shoes. "I still can't believe you waited till the last minute to tell me. I can't believe you didn't give me a chance to prepare myself."

"I don't work that way."

"What way *do* you work?" My feet got tangled in a heap of dry cleaner's plastic, and I kicked free. "What about the Buying Club? What about all the things you never finished, like the teen center, and all the other stuff you were going to do and didn't have time for?" He started rearranging the stack of shirts in the suitcase. I'm being a bitch, I thought. Where did this come from? I'm not a bitch. Spencer went to the bedroom, came back with a hanging bag and his other suits. I don't want to be a bitch, I thought, and I don't want to cry. I said, "It's just that I thought we were going to do all those things together."

He zipped the bag. "Why don't you come with me?"

"Yeah, right, your dad and mother would love that."

"I mean it. Come with me. You came down here to be with your preacher, didn't you?"

"I came down for the work. To be a Vista."

"You wouldn't have come down if it wasn't for him. You wouldn't have come down without him."

"Him and the work. It was all mixed up in my mind. I wanted to be where I was needed."

"I need you," said Spencer, and when I shrugged, he sneered. "You don't know anything about how to love, do you?"

It was true, of course, that I knew nothing about love. Distantly I glimpsed a fiery ghost of a woman I might have been, someone more bold and free, who would pick up and follow Spencer. "What would you do with me in Chicago? I mean, what would happen? Would your mother put me up in your room with you?"

He jabbed his index fingers at the floor. "That's the *wrong* question. The only question is 'Will you come?' and you say no. That's all, that's it. It's real simple."

"You never even thought of asking me till this minute."

"That's more wrong questions."

I watched him stomp in and out of his room a few times. Maybe if I said I would go anywhere with him, then he would be brave enough to defy his father and stay here with me.

And then another voice in me, small, but with an edge that cut through the drama, said, Oh come off it, Blair. He just wants to be so lovable that someone would drop everything for him. That's what Spencer wants.

And for the moment, I had myself again, after all. Spencer was still here, with his skill in packing, and his long slim fingers and pairs of long slim dress shoes.

I said, "Well, I'm not going with you."

"I know it."

I said, "I *have* loved you, you know. I wanted to love you more."

It was what he wanted. He froze with his fingers on the suitcase lid. "You love me?"

I did love him, for that moment, with no qualifications. Did love him and believed that he would write long, passionate letters and would come to see me for Thanksgiving. That after a while I would transfer to a college in Chicago, and join him there. I made a nest of my thoughts, and we sank together on the couch, in the midst of clinging plastic, crunching shirt wrappers, kissing and petting like children who had never slept together.

After a while, he said, "How will you remember me, Blair, years from now? What will you say about me?"

I was surprised. "Why, I'll say you were the most exciting man I ever met." He laughed way down in his throat and kissed my forehead and cheeks. I said, "How will you remember me?"

Voice still entunnelled in the laugh, he said, "I'll remember a woman who stood on her own two feet, and nobody could push her around."

I was stunned with pleasure because I thought Spencer meant it, whether it was true or not. At the very least, he and I each knew what the other wanted to be.

* * *

On the way back from the airport Ralph asked me for a date. There was this great place he knew, he said, where we could go dancing and have a great big steak. A place with class, he told me. When I didn't answer at once, he talked on, letting his words slur into each other gently; I heard drinks, steak, music, have a ball. I stared at the wrinkles that his forehead made as he raised his brows to talk, and at the stiff conked hair, his Hawaiian shirt and sunglasses. I imagined that Spencer had betrayed me, had given Ralph a high sign, a wink: I'm bequeathing her to you, man. Don't do anything I wouldn't do.

We were at the intersection of William and Mary Road and King Street, and I said, "Thanks, Ralph, but, I'm sorry, I can't go out with you. Listen, I have to get out here. I have to go do some work." He offered to drive me wherever I wanted to go, but I already had my thumb on the door catch. I was ready to jump. "Thanks, Ralph, really," I said. "Thank you!" I waved as I went, waved and walked away and looked back again, and all the time Ralph didn't hurry, just sat in his car looking after me. Go away, Ralph, I thought. Why don't you go away. In the end, I turned the corner before he drove off.

This is just as well, I thought. This is the best thing, to plunge into work. Not to think about Spencer, not to think about dates with Ralph. I had to tell the old farming gentleman that I had gone to the bookstore and had them put a search out for his "Blue Back Speller." That was work. That would feel good, too, to sit on his porch with him for a while. Then I could drop in on Mrs. Murrell. She was always glad to see me, as if I were a special treat. Once I got onto their street, I would have a sense of proportion again. After I sat with them a few minutes, I wouldn't panic because Spencer had left me.

I decided to take the short cut through one of the barren areas the city had razed for urban renewal and then never rebuilt. What remained was another four blocks of rubble, trash, ailanthus saplings and one large yellow brick apartment building. All its windows were knocked out, not a pane left, not a slat between panes. It was a particularly depressing, dead building, but today it had movement around it, a crawling in and out the door.

As I got closer I realized it was a clot of men. I did fine this morning, I thought. I'll treat these guys just the same. I pushed on, but I walked in the street, unable to go on the sidewalk with them. I wanted to turn back, I felt so weak, but I kept my face straight ahead, determined to do my work. They stopped talking for an instant as I passed, and then a voice said, "Good God Almighty, it's a damn Vusta," and I thought Oh no, it's Snake Eyes! Of all people, it has to be Snake. If we'd had him arrested when he beat up Roy he wouldn't be here now. Snake Eyes and his friends that no one knew. Older guys, one with wide shoulders and a beer belly, and the other as slight as a small woman. They didn't seem to have a corner of their own, and since they'd roughed up Roy, no one had seen them at all. Snake took a couple of steps in my direction. "Hey, Vusta, ain't you got manners?"

I looked toward him, feigned surprise, as if I'd just noticed them sitting on the crumbling stoop. "Hello, Snake Eyes."

He had a nylon stocking on his head and a black tee shirt, lines in his cheeks, something rundown about his pants, faded fold lines running across them in all the wrong places. He came out into the street and blocked my way. Oh damn, I thought. Oh shit.

"You looking good, Vusta, for one of them stringy-haired people."

I stopped three feet away from him, unable to go forward or turn around, like one of those stupid rolling toys that butts its head and whirrs its motor at an obstacle in its path. I focused my eyes on a dark sweat patch in the center of his tee shirt. They're bored, I told myself. They don't have anything to do with their lives. Even hitting Roy, that was just because they don't have jobs and they're frustrated.

"How come you walk out here in the street?" said Snake. "How come you don't be polite and come over and say hello?"

It seemed imperative to wrench my head up and look him in the eye, but beyond the blank width of his shirt was the yellow building with its gaping eyeholes and the sneering friends waiting, and I was in fact terrified—so terrified that I could not stay another instant, and I turned around and started walking back the way I'd come.

He danced around until he was in front of me again. "Where you going? Nobody hurting you. *I* ain't hurting you." I walked around him this time, and he stopped the playful backward dancing and strode beside me, his voice getting harsher. "Where you *going* in such a hurry? Where you *going*?"

On the next block I could see houses, tricycles, cars, somebody's washing hanging on the porch.

"Nobody's messing with you," he said, and even as he said it, he reached out and lightly touched my shoulder. I veered away and he picked up speed, stayed with me. "Where you hurrying off to, Miss Queen Vusta? How come you walk away?" He fell back a little, and my neck crawled, and I felt the awkwardness of my little fleeing trot, the jiggling in my rear end. He shouted, "Hey Miss Queen Vusta! I *know* you like it big, black, and hot. I *know* that, so why don't you come and get some?"

For an instant I thought he knew, that Spencer had talked to him too, had given me away all over South Jenkin.

"Hey Vusta!" he shouted. "Hey Vusta, I thought we all was trading off, white meat for dark, *you* know. Looney-Bin gets the dark meat and I want me some nice tender young white meat!"

Now I could see my way to safety. I could see a lady carrying a bag of groceries, and one of South Jenkin's rare buses turned the corner. I looked back at him.

"Hey Vusta! Come and get it!" He planted his legs apart and grabbed his crotch.

I was so far away now, so near the bus and the bag of groceries, that I could say. "No thanks, none for me."

He jumped at me, burst out of his stance, with his face

distorted, the whites of his eyes flaring. I started to run as hard as my legs would pump, not looking back, but his voice caught me: "Don't give me that shit! I'll fuck you as crazy as Looney-Bin Peckerwood, don't give me that shit!"

I ran all the way to the corner and on down Edgecomb, until I saw some people I knew staring at me. And I waved at them, but jogged on anyhow, wanting to find a hiding place, somewhere safe. I was afraid I would never be safe again. I'll never be able to take the short cut to Mrs. Murrell's, I thought. I won't be able to walk by the Red Hat Bar and Grill men, either. All I wanted was to get inside. I felt a pressure rising in me. Oh, men are bastards, I thought. They are such bastards.

When I got inside, I made a circuit of the apartment, full of an enormous pressure, checking the locks on all the windows, not even opening one for air. I pulled down the blinds, pressed them into the glass, tucked the curtains, so there would be no chinks where someone might look in. I made another circuit and another, each room swollen with hot air. As I walked, tremors passed down my back and I began to wring my hands, finally stopping in my old room where I sat in front of a mirror. Without light all I could make out were shadow hole eyes and a pale T-shaped forehead and nose.

No one, no one is with me, I thought. Not Dave, Shelley, and Spencer. Marie and Mrs. Murrell and the Landells wouldn't recognize me now. They thought of me as plucky and cheerful, on the move: Have you filled out your order blank? Signed your girl up for Scouts? Your little girl for pre-school class? We're going to fight this thing! We have beef roast this week! That was what they expected. Not this body getting more and more still, like a roast about to go bad, I thought: quiet meat.

After a while, perhaps stimulated by cramped muscles, I began to plan actions. I could still go with Spencer. Get a plane ticket, take a cab to his house. I imagined his mother opening the door. She would be tall and broad-hipped, wearing a suit, formal and eagle-eyed. Two heads above me, and my voice not quite carrying. My pathetic smile not mollifying. I would say, Oh sorry, I think I have the wrong house. I think you do, she would say.

I began to pace again, first around the bedroom, then down the hall and back, wringing my hands. Once I slapped myself in the cheeks. Right one with the right hand, left one with the left.

I have to get out of here, I thought. There was no one I would let see me like this in South Jenkin. There was always my parents' house, but somehow their house seemed the same as this house. I had gone to college, come down here to escape their walls.

And then I stopped pacing. Out of my hand-wringing and hysteria came Dave Rivers' name. Dave wasn't afraid of people when they were distraught. Dave used to hold me when I cried, or hold me and then I would cry. Of course it was Dave. It had always been Dave. He had never meant to end our relationship; I had cut him off in my anger. I was the one who had rent the airy-thin gold tissue, and I had fallen through. In a sudden calm, I thought that Dave was the only one who could look at me with my eyes red, wringing my stupid hands over and over like a bad actress. He would see how much pain.

I called Greyhound and found I could probably catch the next Washington bus which would give me a connection to the one a.m. Cincinnati bus, the one that stopped at all the little towns across the mountains. I would get into Franklin around dawn, and sit on the steps of the house with the Volkswagen in front of it, shivering, my face streaked with tears and fog, until he found me. I would say, I don't know how to live anymore, Dave. I knew how to live when I was my parents' daughter, and I did fine at college because I watched you, and I was okay in Vista without you as long as I had Shelley and Spencer, but I don't know how to live by myself. I imagined that he would press me against his chest, and then take me into the house, and Martha would be there, and she would make a breakfast for me, the two of them together taking care of me forever and ever.

The last part made me uncomfortable. I want Dave, not Martha, I thought, dialing the cab, thinking about how what mattered with Dave was not even the words you said, but the depth of your need. I tried not to plan my packing. I grabbed a handful of underpants, a bra, blouses without noticing their color. But my toothbrush and comb sprang to mind so vividly that I couldn't forget them, and while I was in the bathroom, I took some Tampax in case my period started.

The taxi was early, and that seemed like a good omen, leaving me no extra time to think, but as soon as I sat back in the seat, I felt a glow of travel excitement. I was on the move; things were going to work out.

The driver, well out of youth but still wearing his hair in a greasy, blond rockabilly style, kept glancing at me in the mirror. Finally he said, "Do you *live* over here? I mean, it's none of my business, but do you really live over here?"

I met his eyes in the mirror. "Oh yes," I said. "It's the funniest thing, how people always mistake me for white."

He squealed his tires as we cornered onto William and Mary Road. I couldn't help enjoying his reaction, and I enjoyed the rise over the bridge too, and the lights just coming on: all the slabs of downtown lit up—the Municipal Building, the National Bank, the jail. Maybe I wasn't desperate, after all.

On the other hand, I did break down and cry at the bus station. They had already loaded the Washington bus—the driver stood just inside the station counting his tickets and glancing around for late comers—when the ticket seller told me he couldn't take a personal check. The modern, low-ceilinged station, with its dim plateglass reflections on three sides, fiber glass chairs down the middle, a scattering of wrappers and newsprint on the floor, seemed like a symbol for the rest of my life if I didn't get on that bus.

I started to sob. "I have to get to Washington," I said. "I

have to get to Washington so I can get to West Virginia. I have to get *home*."

The driver by the door looked up; the ticket seller started saying, There there and Okay okay, but I was gasping for breath, crying at last, and didn't realize at first that the okay meant he had changed his mind, he would take the check after all. Anything to get rid of the sobs echoing through his station. I wrote the check hastily, smearing the signature, still crying, and then I started to run, but the bus driver told me to slow down and take it easy. He reached to take my bag, but I pulled it away and he spoke to me very slowly, saying I'd be just fine, he'd get me to Washington. He needn't have tried to calm me down, though; the remaining tears were tears of shame for having made a fool of myself. And at the same time, coming up behind the tears was a satisfied clicking of things into place, a small triumph. I had, after all, accomplished what I wanted. I was on the bus. They probably thought women were fools anyhow. In my mind I started telling Dave about it; I just decompensated, I would say. I just sobbed like a baby in the middle of the downtown bus station. And then, as the bus ached and groaned and began to build momentum, I felt again the seduction of travel, of having nothing to do for a few hours now but dream. I couldn't help smiling in the privacy of my dark travel tunnel.

I had an hour to kill in Washington, so I did slowly all the things I would usually rush through: a trip to the cavernous green ladies' room, where I spent a long time soaping my hands and parting my hair. Then I made my way past the lines forming for New York and Harrisburg to the cafeteria, a broad room with many red-topped tables and two large half-circles of counter space. I sat at the counter nearest the buses and ordered only coffee and a doughnut because I wasn't sure I had enough money for the rest of the trip.

I found myself staring at the pink nylon back of the waitress at the other counter. Her hair was straw colored and teased back over a big clip, a couple of strands loose, and she rested her hips on the counter, and carried her neck forward as if the hair were too heavy. I thought probably she was weary to death. She was smoking while a loud man talked to her. I didn't think she had much patience with him, but she was too tired not to welcome an excuse to lean back for a little while and smoke.

I was just eating and sipping coffee, using her as a place to fix my eyes, when I was struck by the idea that she was familiar—her hair and the long slim back. Not the tiredness and rounded shoulders, but the rest of her suddenly configured itself in my eyes as my old high school friend Bunny Hoover, who had run away from home on Christmas Eve with a sailor, heading for Norfolk. I had, in fact, all the time I had been in Vista, half expected her to turn up, in a store, on the bus, at the beach. I imagined she would have kids by now, like her mother, but I also imagined that she would be free, doing things I had been taught were wrong, having boyfriends, maybe, while the sailor was out to sea. There had always been something about her life that I envied—she always pleased herself, if it was at all possible. Nobody else will if you don't, she said. And she snatched what she could: other people's cigarettes, scarves off the counter of the department store. She didn't think she was so important that it would make any difference to the world if she gave her life to being good and helping others. But if this old back was Bunny, then she had got nothing for all her freedom and adventures but a pink nylon uniform and the graveyard shift at a bus terminal cafeteria. I put a dollar under my coffee cup and backed out, making sure she didn't see me, placing myself on line at the Cincinnati Express gate at an angle that allowed me to watch the cafeteria door.

The bus was safe. This was what I really wanted, to stay on buses with my sweater snuggled up under my chin, the stale air conditioning humming around me, drowsiness overcoming me almost as soon as we hit cruising speed. I was sorry the bus made any stops at all; I was especially sorry I was going to be getting off at Franklin in the chilly dawn. Sometime after Winchester we began the lurching climb up the Allegheny

Front. The shifting of my weight and the grinding gears seemed part of a long dream in which I was explaining things at great length. Look here, I kept saying, look here. But when the explanation finally came out of my mouth, my voice was always so low I couldn't make out what I was saying.

Then we stopped, and the driver put on the lights. "Twenty-five minutes, ladies and gentlemen. This is Mount Storm."

Most of the people rolled over and covered their faces with their jackets, but I worked my way out of the dream, rubbing my face, convinced that somehow I had been trying to explain something stupid, that it wasn't worth the trouble. Fuzzy with dream annoyance, I got out of the bus and was amazed by the blackness of night. There were lights from the restaurant and from a phone booth, and very dim lights in the two looming buses, ours and the one going back the other way, but everything was blunted by fog. Beyond the fog was a powerful, deep, cityless darkness, rich with smells: hay, maybe, dirt certainly, and perhaps animals. Living things in that black air. It seemed too powerful to me, muzzy with sleep as I was. I wished I were traveling somewhere ordinary: to my grandmother's, back to school. I wished to be traveling with my parents, or back with my eighth grade class that stopped and picnicked here for our trip to Washington. What I was doing now seemed somehow sickly beside those.

Inside there were a couple of people eating, and the two bus drivers laughing and drinking coffee together in their identical gray uniforms. The waitress had just brought a bacon sandwich to my driver; she was a skinny woman with one hand on her blue-jeaned hip, and her bleached hair teased high. I was on a counter stool, rotated toward them when I realized that *she* looked like Bunny Hoover, too.

She turned from the drivers, too suddenly for me to duck my face, but it didn't matter—she wasn't Bunny. She had lines in her face much too deep to have been cut by a couple of years of hard living.

As she went back of the counter, I said, "You're not Bunny, are you?" She blinked and chewed at something in her mouth, making her chin wag like an old person. I said, "You remind me of this girl I went to high school with."

From the way she stared, I thought I had offended her, but she was just a person who kept her face still. She gave a snort. "*You* thought *I* was someone you went to school with? Honey, you might of gone to school with my kids, but not with me." And then she started telling me how she had thought of naming one of her girls Bunny, but decided on Kimberly Dawn instead.

Out of the corner of my eye I saw the Washington-bound bus driver getting up, taking hold of his belt, and hoisting his pants. "Well," he said, "gotta get it rolling." All of these people doing their work: driving their buses, drawing coffee out of the urn.

I, too, wanted to be one of the ordinary people working. And I had a sudden craving to be sure that the other waitress wasn't Bunny either. It's important, I thought. I want to look at her again and be sure, and I want to get to work. I've been lonely, I thought, for Dave, and for Spencer. That's how people are when they're left alone.

I said, "You know what, I don't think I want anything to eat after all."

"That's okay, honey," she said. "I always wonder how people can eat pie and coffee and then get back in those buses and ride up and down the mountains."

I followed the Washington driver into the night with its black smell of dirt. My feet scrabbled in the gravel to catch him. "Excuse me," I said, "I'm on the other bus, but I need to go back to Washington now. Do you have room?" His eyes narrowed, and I realized that I mustn't sound crazy with him. I pointed at the misty, glowing phone booth. "I called home, and my grandmother is even sicker. They told me to go on back to college—Franklin State College is where I go—but I don't think it's right. I want to go home and be with my grandmother."

"Sorry to hear about your grandmother," said the driver, and he asked to see my ticket.

I was delighted with the thoroughness of my lie. I could

have elaborated: I imagined Eleanor and Chuck as my parents. I knew the church we went to, where they worked. I had not been getting along with this father lately.

The bus driver pointed out it was going to be a little complicated to get a refund on the unused portion of the ticket, and I said I didn't care, I didn't want the money, and that seemed to alarm him. "Oh, you can get it back, you just have to fill out some forms."

"Please don't leave without me," I said. "I have to tell the other driver—I have to get my bag."

And then I was on a bus again, heading back, thankful that I would not be sitting on Dave Rivers' doorstep at dawn. I thought instead of the real morning I would have, and whether or not I would have time for a shower and a nap before the new Vistas came.

When we got to Washington, I went directly to the counter of the waitress who looked like Bunny. It must have been getting near the end of her shift because she had her pocketbook out and was putting on lipstick. She had little sharp breasts, almost hidden in the pleats of her uniform, and Bunny had had big ones that she always kept up high and obvious. When I looked at her face, I didn't even have to ask, she was so completely not Bunny. I splurged and ordered bacon and eggs. I was going to get back so late that the bank would be open anyhow.

If I had gone to Dave that night, or if I had run off with Spencer, what kind of person would I have become? Would I be more free? More like Bunny Hoover? Or, rather, like what I imagined Bunny Hoover to be, because I think the truth was that even her Christmas Eve elopement was less an act of great freedom than a very specific means to an end, an escape from fights with her mother and taking care of her brothers. Sometimes when my present life looks routine, I imagine I did it, threw myself at Dave or ran off with Spencer. More often, though, I'm glad I went back and finished out the Vista year, chose what I called work over what I called love.

Many other things happened that year, of course: I invited my parents down for the long Columbus Day weekend; and I went to New York for Thanksgiving, where I found Shelley alive, healthy, and full of rage at what our government was doing in Vietnam. I went to West Virginia for Christmas, but didn't see Dave. I saw him one more time, in South Jenkin, for the wedding.

Seventeen

The wedding took place between Christmas and New Year's. I had been expecting something to happen for weeks, but I only heard about it officially when I got back from West Virginia.

After being on the bus for eight hours, I didn't want to go inside; I stood in front of my apartment, looking around, smelling something different in the chilly, damp air. The featureless low ceiling of gray clouds was anchored to earth by long trails of smoke. I held very still, trying to identify the odor. It made me uncomfortable not to identify it. My roommates wouldn't be back for another week, but I had come back early so I wouldn't lose my connection. When my mother had said, Those people can spare you for a few more days, I had been incensed at her callousness and terrified that she was right. I've missed one Buying Club already, I told her, not mentioning that I had called Yvetta Landell and found out that it had gone just fine without me. I was back early out of a desire to make sure I was still the spunky, two-fisted Vista who could walk down the street and be recognized by all the people in South Jenkin. I wanted them to need me, or at least to have a place for me. It's not that I'm so important, I told my mother, it's just that I don't want to lose the continuity.

But the smell threw me off, and there was an unfamiliar low-pitched buzzing in the background too. I pushed it aside and concentrated on the odor. It was not, I realized with relief, completely unknown to me. I had smelled at least a tinge of it sometime before I left. It was an oily, industrial odor, and suddenly I had a picture in my mind: the first really cold morning we had, Veronne Foley had been wearing a man's argyle socks and carrying a gallon glass jug of something yellow. "Winter cold these mornings now," she had said. Kerosene is yellow, I thought. People heat with kerosene here when it gets cold. Duchess had talked about a relative of hers out in Lambert's Point who lost everything in a fire when the kerosene heater tipped over. I felt a rising excitement. The last time I had been at Mrs. Murrell's had been a cold morning too, and she didn't have a kerosene heater, but she did have her gas burners on, and the oven door open for heat. When it gets cold in South Jenkin, I thought, when it gets cold here, the landlords don't give heat! The danger of little home-made stoves, the cost of buying the stuff a gallon at a time. Open blue flames leaping in kitchens. It seemed like months since I'd had one of these moments when things came together. We couldn't allow this. Landlords should provide safe heat! I would go door-to-door again. I'd survey. We'd have a meeting.

I was going to put my bag inside and go straight to Marie Conyers and try out my idea on her when the buzzing sound in the distance gathered itself as if a propeller plane were taking off on Edgecomb Avenue. It became more insistent, then divided into a tremendous clatter of many wheels, dozens of small wheels, and a rolling crowd came around the corner from Edgecomb onto Eastover: a pack of teenagers— Bo-ji and Harold and Brother Conyers. Boys and girls taking over the street, racing on roller skates, bearing down in an intense mass, all tall and wild, leg over leg, pumping hard, giving little shoves to one another with their elbows.

The bizarre thing was that I could not remember having seen anyone skate before that moment in the whole time I had been in South Jenkin. Surely I had seen some mateless old roller skates on a porch or in a hall, but I couldn't remember even one. And now, dozens of them: mostly the old-fashioned metal clamp-on kind, but there were black leather racing skates too, and white lace-ups. Were they all Christmas presents? Something the kids only took out during the Christmas vacation in a ritual I knew nothing about?

Strung out in the rear were the younger kids, among them Charlie and Hooky, who was having trouble keeping his rusty-looking old ones on. Jewel, who had white shoe-skates, detached herself from the crowd and rolled over to the curb. "Blair! I got to tell you!"

"What's going on?" I shouted. "Does this happen every year?"

"I've got to tell you!" she shouted. "I got a new dress! It's lavender." She scrabbled off, gathering momentum until she overtook Charlie.

The mass of skaters reached the intersection and turned, started racing back. The younger kids turned too, and tried to stay ahead of the pack by flailing their arms and screaming, but the big ones bore down on them with a kind of awesome inevitability, and they were lost to sight as the big kids thundered by, took the corner back onto Edgecomb again.

But Jewel and Charlie and Hooky were still alive and straggling. This time Jewel rolled to the curb and took a lurching step up on it, clumped over the half-frozen dirt to the sidewalk where I was. "I got me a rabbit's fur jacket too, and it's in two days and you *know* you're invited!"

"To what?" I said, but I knew.

"To the wedding, Blair! Duchess and Roy getting *married!*"

"I'm going," said Charlie, making a grab at Jewel, but she used me as a pivot, whirled around, and he attached himself too, as if I were the upright post and they the carousel horses.

Hooky came limping up with a skate in one hand and leered as if he had the dirtiest joke of the year. "And they going on a *honeymoon* to New York!"

Jewel reversed directions, slammed into Charlie, knocking him off the carousel into Hooky. "That's a secret! Nobody knows for sure!" Still in motion, leaping back into the street, Charlie stumbling after her, she shouted, "You can come, Blair? Have you got a dress?"

"I wouldn't miss it for the world! And I got a new dress for Christmas!"

Hooky sat on the sidewalk working on his skate.

I said, "So they're going to get married. That's really something."

Hooky shrugged. "I'll take that suitcase in the house. For a quarter."

"No thanks. I can do it."

He hopped on one foot, skate in hand, and grabbed the suitcase with the other hand, frowning fiercely. "I don't want no quarter, I ain't no redcap."

I thanked him. Of course I had a place here, I thought. I had my friend Hooky.

Marie was folding clothes in the room she used as living room and master bedroom. It had probably been meant as a dining room because it was next to the kitchen, but she kept her mahogany armoire there and a four-poster bed where the baby was sleeping and Little Bit lying beside him, thumb in her mouth, eyes wide open. The furniture had belonged to her grandmother, Marie told me once, a grandmother who had gone to college and been a school teacher. That was before the turn of the century, she said with a pride that made me sad because nothing was left of this grandmother's education and aspirations and accumulation except three pieces of Victorian furniture. But there was more, I thought: there was Marie, and maybe something extra for the next generation, for Charley and Little Bit and the baby Jimmy. For the moment, though, the bed was full of babies, the armoire of clothes, and the plush loveseat with Marie and a pile of clean undershirts.

I tried to get her to reveal how she felt about Duchess marrying Roy, but she ignored all my subtle probing, so I finally said, "Do you think they're making a mistake?"

"Marriage never was easy," she said, and her face was

turned down to her folding, so I couldn't even tell whether or not she was smiling.

"I don't mean marriage in general, I mean those two in particular—do you think they're making a *mistake*?" The trouble was that I still wasn't quite asking what I wanted to know. She was smiling, though, and folding slower, so slowly that it irritated me, one tiny sleeve, then another tiny sleeve, then the whole thing folded forward once. It didn't seem worth the effort to me, especially when so much else remained to be done. The enormous basket of unfolded clothes, toys on the floor. Little Bit's hair unbraided. I didn't understand how she organized her days.

She said, "Things are better around here than they used to be. Not that long ago—a man and a woman down here, black and white—" She shook her head, grunted. "Well, maybe they'll go live in New York. Duchess always talking about New York this, New York that. I *know* folks have a better chance up there."

"They're going to New York for their honeymoon."

"He could get a job up there. Maybe they could stay."

The heat began to bother me. She had an oil stove connected to a hundred-gallon tank outside that threw off so much heat I could feel my cheeks reddening. I said, "That's not what worries me, exactly, not the *race* thing."

"That don't worry you," said Marie.

"Well, I mean, it *worries* me, but like you say, it's different than it would have been a few years ago."

"Pray the Lord it is."

"But what I don't understand is why Duchess wants *Roy*."

"Roy's a good man."

"Oh, he's good—"

"It sure beats starting out with a *bad* man."

"He fixes things for her," I said, meaning it as a joke. The last few months, although he still collected his Vista stipend, Roy had been a sort of volunteer handyman around South Jenkin. First he got Duchess's bathtub draining and then he rebuilt Veronne Foley's tumble-down back porch for her.

Pretty soon everyone was calling Roy over and getting him to fix things that the landlords should have.

"Why do anybody want anybody?" said Marie. "But I'll tell you one thing: God must love us or either he'd let us see the future, and then nobody never would get married."

But what, I wondered, did she really think of Roy? Did she think he was a fool? Did she really like him? Did she like me? I said, "One of these days Roy will be gone and I'll be gone, and you'll be relieved to see us go, I bet."

Marie looked me in the face and shook her head. "I don't know why you talk that way. You Vistas our *guests.*"

Is that it? I thought. Is that the answer to my question? "Some guests. We work pretty hard for guests."

"Family type guests," said Marie, smiling as she looked away again.

We had done some things, I thought. Roy and I. We deserved some credit. The Buying Club and the Scouts and my own project, my pre-school playgroup I took on walks, or bus rides, to the canal or the zoo. Between doing odd jobs and buying candy for the kids, Roy had actually set up a teen center. It wasn't what Spencer and Shelley had imagined, but Roy had talked a local man into giving him an old shack rent-free in exchange for repairs. He had done more of the work on it himself than they would have thought correct, but from time to time the boys did show up to work on it too. Roy had thrown a party when it was almost finished, and invited all the teenagers to come and see *Raisin in the Sun* on a used television he had bought, and the party went well, but that night someone broke in and stole the television. I said I would lay money it was Snake Eyes.

"I expect so," said Roy. "He was there."

Duchess said, "Just don't you dare ask me to put my hi-fi in there or my radio or even one, not even one of my records in that place. Why do you act such a fool, Roy?"

And yet, the teen center continued, and there was a Christmas party, and some of the girls came too, and Snake slept over there when he didn't seem to have anywhere to go, and he didn't steal anything on those nights, but then there wasn't anything to steal except beat-up furniture and the books Spencer had left.

After all, I thought, there's a limit to what guests can do.

I wore my new Christmas dress to the wedding. It was real wool, blue, with a tiny mink collar, and my mother had been very excited when we bought it together. "Don't worry about how much it costs," she had said. "You look so pretty in it. Don't even look at the price tag. For once we'll just splurge." I considered leaving the collar off for the wedding, but then I thought, No, the fur collar makes the dress. And Marie is going to be wearing her best clothes.

She was too: an ensemble in closely matched shades of brilliant spring green; a coat—open in spite of the cold—and the shoes, hat, and bag, all matching. She took her time coming down the steps, rolling a little from foot to foot in her high heels, flanked by Charlie and Hooky, silent retainers, in suits —Hooky's perhaps a half size too large, but Charlie's a perfect fit, set off with a sporty hat that had a feather in the band.

I unbuttoned my coat to show off my dress too, and we all stood around admiring each other. Marie said the dress made my eyes look so nice and blue, and I knew that meant she could look into them now, and I knew I had been right to wear the dress and the collar too. When we finally started off, we walked slowly, partly for Marie's feet, and partly out of respect for the occasion, and maybe a little to let the neighbors have a chance to see us.

"I remember my wedding day," said Marie, speaking slowly too, like a quart of honey poured out of a jar. "My wedding was all so pell-mell. The worst thing I regret is my own mother wasn't there. We could of brought her up too. Conyers was making good money those days, and I was working. But we had to be in a hurry, couldn't even get ourselves to a church. Had to get married at City Hall and hop a train to Baltimore. Don't ever go off and get married and not invite your own mother, Blair!"

"I doubt I'll ever get married," I said.

"You'll get married, honey. A nice, natural young woman like you."

She made me feel soft inside, like one of those people who cries at weddings. To harden myself, I said, "I ran into Veronne Foley. She told me they invited her, but she wasn't coming because she doesn't believe in race mixing."

Marie snorted. "Veronne Foley shouldn't of talked like that to you. She don't mean nothing."

"Then why isn't she coming to the wedding?"

"She's coming. She showed me her hat. She just got it into her head Duchess didn't invite her soon enough. Duchess invited *everybody* late. You watch and see." She shook her head, as if to get rid of that bad subject. "Look up now, the sun's coming out." There was a chink in the overhang of clouds, a pale passage of white light that fell on the street and sidewalk twenty yards ahead of us. "Isn't that nice," she said. "It makes everything look so cheerful."

A voice came out of me, as if I hadn't been able to squash away the softness after all. "Happy is the bride that the sun shines on." Marie nodded her head as if she thought that just about summed it up. "That's something my mother always says. Someone told it to her on her wedding day, and she always tells it to whoever gets married."

"That's real nice. You tell it to Duchess; it'll make her feel good."

Ralph's Cadillac coasted up alongside us, reflecting rays of light from its fresh coat of wax. Ralph sat in the front seat, alone in his semi-official capacity. He raised his eyebrow when he saw me, and nodded to let me know he noticed how I looked. In the back, overflowing the wide seat, were Jewel, Roy, and, above all, Duchess in her vast creamy wedding gown. She rolled down her window quickly, and then stared at us as if she had forgotten how to speak: her eyes were huge, her mouth taut and small. The three of them seemed to be all eyes and splendid clothes.

"Look at you," said Marie, giving a grunt for each of them, or perhaps three for Duchess. "Just look at you."

Duchess began to smile a little, even though a line remained incised upright between her eyebrows. She sucked in air suddenly, so violently that hollows appeared above her naked collarbone, and the sweetheart neckline of the dress stood out from her as if she were shrinking inside it.

I was suddenly angry at Roy. He shouldn't be doing this to her, I thought. Something awful always happens when you finally say, Okay I will love you.

"Why you going so early?" asked Marie.

Duchess said, "I want my aunt over in Huntersville that can't go out to see me, and we got to pick up my brother over there."

Jewel was causing a commotion. "Aunt Marie! Miss Blair! Charlie! Can you see my dress?"

"They can see it later, baby," said Duchess, but everything about her seemed a little tentative today, and Jewel was already out of the car, betiered in lavender splendor, standing in front of us, but at an angle so that Hooky and Charlie would get the effect too: white tights, rabbit's fur jacket. The boys looked at each other and in unison took steps backward as if stunned. Jewel jerked her chin up with satisfaction.

"Look at my hair, Blair, do you see my hair?"

Two glossy braids, as thick as a child's wrist, had been worked back from her forehead, and two thinner ones looped up from below, all caught under a mass of tiny purple blossoms.

I said, "That's lilac! Where on earth did you get lilac at this time of year?"

"I don't know. Roy got 'em."

Roy was out of the car too, unfolding his white-suited long legs.

"Well *I*'m not getting out," said Duchess.

"You stay right there. Don't you go wrinkling that dress," said Marie.

Roy bore down on us around the car, as if he were in some kind of hurry, and I was suddenly not angry at him anymore because I saw in his face that he was at least as scared as Duchess. His temples were shadowed and sunken, dark around and under his eyes. "Listen here, Blair Ellen," he said. "Listen here." His face crumpled up, and I reached for it, and he threw out his arms, surrounded me with lotion, dampness in his hair. Still wet around the ears, I thought.

"He's crying again, Mama," said Jewel.

I said, "Oh no, I got lipstick on you. Hold still, Roy, let me wipe it off."

"Listen here, Blair Ellen," he said. He let me use a kleenex on the smear I'd left on his cheek, and on a spot of shaving blood. He said, "I always felt like you were my sister or something. We've been through a lot together."

"That's for sure," I said.

"I want you to stand up with me," he said. "At the wedding."

"I can't do that, Roy," I said.

"I want you to. I want you to stand up on my side like you were my sister."

Duchess said, "You better do what he wants, Blair, I never saw anyone so set on getting his way."

"Well, if you want me to." I am his family, I thought. I'm not like them, but I'm the closest thing he's got right now. "Look, I got lipstick on you again."

"Stop kissing people, Roy," said Duchess. "Get in here and let me fix you, and you too, Jewel."

Jewel grabbed Roy's hand and tugged him backward. He almost fell at the curb. "I can hear," he said. "It's like all the people saying—" he waved at the shafts of white and yellow light playing among the clouds—"They're all saying they love us!"

Marie laughed. "He got the feeling all right! He got that getting-married feeling!"

The Cadillac rolled away, and I said, "Duchess has it too, doesn't she?"

"Sure she does. That's why she got the dress. I just hope it don't wrinkle up on her, though. They don't make those dresses to sit in."

I suddenly wanted it too: the white dress, the voices in the light, one overlapping the other, saying We love you We love you!

Marie began humming under her breath; the boys dropped back and gently bumped into each other, whispering something private. Ahead of us rose the magisterial bell tower of Frank Landell's church. We turned the corner, and there was only one car parked on the block, just at the walkway. It was the green Volkswagen with its rusting rear bumper and metallic brown fender. Marie stopped humming, and Charlie said, "Hey, Blair, I think he's here."

All my equanimity, all my serenity and insightfulness seemed to slip off my shoulders like a cape that had never been fastened properly, and there was a pressure behind my eyeballs. How dare he, I thought. Again. How dare he? I turned to Marie, but she and the boys were spinning away, distant as the pigeons on the bell tower. I ran ahead of them, into the hall which was still dim and empty except for a few lights at the far end, where Yvetta Landell was arranging the serving table.

"Where is he?" I said.

There was sympathy in her face, but she too was far away. "He went over to the house looking for Frank."

I almost ran into Marie as I turned on my heel and burst out. I didn't think there would be any relief until I struck against his chest, like the blow of a fist.

I scanned the lawn and saw the man coming out of Landell's garden: a man the size and shape of Dave Rivers, but wearing a broad, fleshy face I didn't recognize. The intensity of my stare wavered, and he walked on toward me, hesitating, stopping. He had thick, pink lips and too much jaw.

I said, "What did you do to your face?"

He touched his chin. "I cut off my beard."

"I see that! Why? Why on earth did you cut your beard off?"

His forehead gathered into folds of seriousness—that much was familiar, anyhow. "What's the matter, Blair?"

"Nothing's the matter. Won't you ever give me a straight

answer? Why can't you ever just answer a simple question?"

"Let's drive somewhere," he said, opening the car door for me, not politely, but taking charge, almost professional. I was so shocked by my own tantrum that I was glad to be taken in hand. Tears were gathering too, fury grinding into reverse. He started the car, we drove, and his voice whirred on smoother than the engine. "I cut the beard off because the student body at Franklin State seems to get more conservative every year. I didn't want a beard to stand between me and them." He made a U-turn, headed toward the empty blocks. "It isn't such a big thing, is it? A beard?"

I watched the houses slowly pass by. As long as I didn't look at him, only heard his voice, I didn't cry. "It isn't fair," I said. "I've never seen you without a beard, and it's like meeting a complete stranger."

"It's me," he said. "Same person."

Who I never knew, I thought bitterly, glancing at him out of the corner of my eye. At least the beard hadn't hidden a weak chin. He didn't look all that different, seen sideways: the same thick glasses, the short, blunt nose and forehead. Bone and skin jutting under his lips now instead of hair, but the same heavy line. The car smelled the same too, the old lunchbox odor. Years of sandwiches in bags. A faint petroleum odor now too, as if one of the engine's minor ills had begun to seep into the passenger space.

"The engine still sounds awful," I said, and he smiled as I had meant him to. I was still able to cause certain small effects in him then, even if I had never known him.

He pointed down at the gearshift which was covered with a fresh-looking ball of electrical tape. "I *almost* got that fixed, but the dealer didn't have the part the day I was there."

We made another slow loop of a U-turn and stopped in front of the empty apartment building where Snake had threatened me. I was going to ask him to park somewhere else, but he said, "I had an idea for this building once. I went inside one afternoon, walked all over it, imagined making it into a real community center. Not a little TAPS base, but a place that would be open all the time with the whole spectrum of human needs met. It would have been a recreation center and a clinic, and day care, and the Buying Club, of course. I thought maybe a credit union someday. High school equivalency classes. I didn't tell anyone, but I set that for my goal." He made a small, ironic smile that was new to me—perhaps it used to be hidden in the beard.

I said, "You always did think big."

"And look where it got me. Back at Franklin State listening to students who got drunk for the first time, who think they're going to hell for it while you and Roy are down here creating the New City of Man."

"Your students sound about like Roy and me a year ago."

"No," he said, "no, you two aren't like any of the others. You are the only ones who went ahead and left me behind."

I was sure he was condescending. "We never went ahead of you. We got blown down here. You were the wind and we were the fluff, and we got stuck where you left us."

"I'd rather say you were the seeds and I was a big windbag."

He looked me in the face now, and I braced myself, as I always had, for the flaming eyes, but instead he was rolling them, showing too much white, making fun of himself. I didn't remember him making fun of himself so much. To my own surprise, *that* was what made me cry, or at least, that added to the aftermath of anger, to the nearness of the gap-eyed horror of a building, and the familiar odor of the Volkswagen.

I laid my head back on the seat and let the tears flow out the corners of my eyes, over my cheekbones, down my jaws. "What can I do?" he said, and a little later, "I've never known anyone but you to look pretty when they cry."

"That's because I do it all the time," I said, but his words were like strokes over my face and shoulder, and when he actually did touch me, first shoving the gearshift out of the way, I sighed: it was not everything, to have his arms clasped around me and his strangely soft chin against my neck, but it was what I wanted for this moment.

I said, "You're wrong about me and Roy, though. Everything we did was because of you. We've gone on doing it, but it was you who started it. Everything." He stroked my shoulder. I said, "Even Spencer. I went to Spencer for a while, you know."

"I thought you might have."

"And that was because of you. I was so mad at you." Even as I said it, I was faintly uncomfortable: it wasn't only Dave that sent me to Spencer, and I had never really been milkweed fluff being blown around by him, but I said it anyway. "Everything was because of you."

He said, "When Roy invited me down for the wedding, I didn't know if I should come. The main reason I finally did was that I wanted to talk some things through with you."

I felt a flash of my anger coming back, and pulled partly away from him. "Why now? Why didn't we talk things through a long time ago?"

He bowed his head slightly. "We should have."

"You should have before you left South Jenkin."

"I've been at fault, Blair." His face was so serene that I had a feeling I was doing him a favor, that he had come to be punished.

"What you should have done a long time ago is answer my questions."

"Ask them now."

"All right. I will. And don't you dare smile. First I want to know how old are you, and how old is Martha."

"Martha is thirty-eight, and I just turned thirty."

I was stunned. "You're thirty? You're closer to her age than mine?"

He nodded, and again I had the sinking feeling I had when I found out how long they had been adulterers, that sheer numbers weighed against me. "And I want to know exactly when you decided to stay with her. I want to know . . . all those phone calls when you kept saying you would come back to South Jenkin—"

"I meant to come back."

"That's not what I'm asking. I'm asking at which moment you actually knew you were staying with her."

He pulled back a little now, still touching me, though, one hand on my shoulder. Something tightening a little in his face, an effort he was making. He said, "I think what you're asking is, Was I lying to you? Was I taking you lightly? I have never taken you lightly, Blair, absolutely never. What is between us was never a light thing."

A ball of warmth glowed inside me. "You're doing it again," I said. "You're answering the question you think I'm asking instead of the one I am asking." And all the time I was feeling like crying because he understood me so well.

"I can't answer it," he said. "I don't know exactly when I decided to stay with Martha. It was the same as when I met you. I didn't notice it happening until I'd already done it." He shrugged. "That's the best I can say it. I genuinely thought, four months ago, that it was over between me and Martha, and then Paul died, and everything changed."

"And I guess if Paul had died and you and I had been married for fifteen years you still would have gone back to her? *That* is taking me seriously?"

He was irritated—took his hand off my shoulder, moved himself back into driving position. "Don't be stupid."

"I'm not being stupid. I don't understand you."

"I never see what's coming, emotionally. I didn't see what was happening, that I was back in Franklin and settling in. Taking on a little more work for the college, staying a little longer. I didn't see it until it had happened."

It was, in fact, what Martha had told me about him, and I could never believe, because I saw his intelligence as so vast, his mind so capacious, gathering up many threads, making many connections. I said, "I guess you just had your mind on the big things and never paid any attention to the little ones."

I was trying to be ironic, but Dave turned his face to me in that needy way again, that way that looked as hungry to be understood as I was. "That's it," he said. "That's exactly it." He picked up my hand and squeezed it.

I said, "Will you and Martha get married?"

"Maybe. We'd have to leave Franklin. I have a couple of irons in the fire." He leaned closer to me and I saw, for a passing instant, the flames around his eyes again. "Listen to this: I want to go up into the mountains, in the southern part of the state. Not as Vistas. I might even take a church although I think that would be difficult—those people are more fundamentalist than the students at Franklin State, and I'm still waiting for God's new name—"

I said, "You know, I was never even sure if you were an ordained minister."

"Of course I am," he said. "Anyhow, I might go as a social worker. But the main thing is that it would be our own people. It wouldn't be like missionaries coming down to the natives."

"Now you're going to tell me and Roy this whole Vista thing is a mistake, and we should have gone to the mountains."

He laughed. "Come with us, try it out."

"Right, I'll come and live with you and Martha. You can adopt me. I'm thinking about going to New York City to finish college anyhow. Shelley said I could stay with her."

"You want to keep moving on." He lifted the hand he was holding and kissed it.

We stayed that way for a few seconds, my hand under his lips, until I noticed a movement outside and saw a child hurrying along the street in front of the empty apartment building. It was Gilbert Duberry, wearing pants too long and sweater too small, with his clumpy mass of hair even less combed than usual. I waved, and he loped out a few feet to get a look at who was in the car. He waved quickly, as if it weren't a gesture he used often, then cut across the rubble toward home.

"That's Gilbert Duberry," I said, "I don't think we'll ever do anything for the Duberrys, but I'll finish out the year here." Gently he put my hand back on my lap. "We'd better go back, hadn't we? Roy asked me to stand up with him while he gets married."

"He asked me too. He said he wanted both of us beside him."

Still we sat, and after a little longer, Dave said, "Blair,

there was one more thing. I'm sorry for the pain I caused you. I wouldn't have hurt you intentionally for the world."

"That's funny," I said. "And I was wishing I could have hurt you. You're sorry for hurting me, and I wish I could have had enough of an effect to hurt you."

"I'm hard to hurt. I usually take care of that myself."

I realized suddenly that I was glad to see him without the beard. He started the car, and I wondered if he would stay tonight, and if he did, would he stay at my apartment? No, I thought, he should stay at Old Fellows Street but spend the evening at my house. We'd analyze everything. I'd tell him about Snake Eyes and the business with Chuck Williams. We'd discuss my idea for a home heating project. I said, "What about after the wedding, are you staying around?"

"I could. If you wanted me to."

"I'd like you to." We eased across the intersection and could see the Cadillac parked in front of the church, the white expanse of Duchess's dress as she got out. I said, "I'd like you to stay around, but I don't want you slipping back into my life when I'm not paying attention."

"Don't fool yourself, Blair," he said. "I never slipped anywhere with you. You seized me like a duck after a June bug."

I was astonished. Was it true? Had I thought all along I was chosen—when in fact I chose him?

We parked behind Ralph. Roy leaped the low hedge in his white tuxedo and I watched Dave stride to meet him, and how they embraced. Not a bad man, I thought. A good man, and I did choose him. I chose him, he caused me pain, and I'm still living. I would probably choose him again, if I were younger.

I got out and looked around, pleased by the church tower against the clouds which had parted again and begun to let light through. Dave and Roy were patting each other clumsily on the back. Duchess's brother smoothed his hair, Ralph checked his tie in the side mirror. Duchess was spreading out her veil, giving it a shake. She waved her fingers at me.

"Blair, tell me if my dress got wrinkled."

I circled her, and could honestly say the skirt was smooth as satin, rich and pale as cream. The sun hit down suddenly and turned the veil into an aura, caused leaps of brilliance from the rhinestones on her breast. "Duchess, can I say something real corny to you, for good luck?"

"Give me some good luck, baby, please."

I took a deep breath. " 'Happy is the bride that the sun shines on.' That's what my mother always says when people get married."

Her eyes got big and she clutched my wrist with one powerful, cold hand. Her bare, skinny arms were covered with goosebumps below the little puff sleeves.

I said, "Hey you guys, Duchess is freezing to death."

Roy turned at the sound of my voice, not really attending to my meaning. He had his face up in the light again, and he threw out his arms. The men advanced toward us, behind Roy, absorbing sunlight in their faces.

Roy said, "Let's everyone get married!"